HIGH HEELS AND HAYSTACKS

BILLIONAIRES IN BLUE JEANS, BOOK TWO

ERIN NICHOLAS

ISBN: 978-0-9988947-5-1

Editor: Lindsey Faber

Copyeditor: Nanette Sipe

Cover artist: Lindee Robinson, *Lindee Robinson Photography*

Cover designer: Angela Waters

Cover models: Alexis Susalla, Anthony Parker

ABOUT HIGH HEELS AND HAYSTACKS

A boss-employee romance...with a twist

Only three things stand between Ava Carmichael and her twelve billion dollar inheritance:

1. A year of living in Bliss, Kansas.
2. A relationship that lasts six consecutive months.
3. And pie.

Ava has run a multi-billion-dollar company, negotiated with shark investors, and hobnobbed with business royalty, but she's about to be defeated by her inability to turn sugar, flour, and apple pie filling into something edible.

Conveniently, the owner of the diner next door, Parker Blake, is magic in the kitchen. And he technically works for her. So she can make him teach her to bake. And, hey, if everyone assumes they're heating up more than the oven during their time in the kitchen...well, that's called multitasking.

Parker Blake likes his women the way he likes his coffee: not in his diner. But gorgeous, strong-willed, type-A Ava clearly isn't going to stop messing up his kitchen—or his simple, stress-free small town life—until the conditions of her daddy's will are met. So, sure, he'll teach his "boss" to bake.

But once the kitchen door closes, it's pretty clear who's really in charge.

PROLOGUE

From the desk of Rudy Carmichael...

1. Move to Bliss.
   1 year. Live in house together

2. Run pie shop. → profit by year end. $$

3. AVA- kitchen, baking, all products.
   NO business!
   Date a guy from Bliss. Give it
      6 mos. Have fun.
                   No checklists!

4. BRYNN - customers/waitress.
   Time with people, get to know them.
   no kitchen, no business.
            Date a guys from Bliss.

5. CORI -books/accounting. no baking.
   leave customers to B.
   make a commitment. but NO DATING 1 year!
                                    6 mos

1

Parker

PROS:

1. Not my type
2. Tall
3. Hot
4. From Bliss
5. Rudy loved him
6. Can bake (probably)
7. Business owner
8. Pie shop

CONS:

1. Grumpy.

A va looked up as Parker Blake came through the swinging door that separated the front of his diner from the kitchen. She underlined *tall* on her list. He was about six-four and that meant she could wear any of the heels in her wardrobe when with him without a problem. That was definitely in his favor.

He carried a coffeepot to the only other occupied table in the diner. She watched him, noting the way his jeans fit across his ass, then forced herself to note the way he interacted with his customers instead. That was far more important to her plan. She needed Parker, but the fit of his blue jeans had nothing to do with it. Probably.

He leaned in and picked up the plate in front of one of the men at the table.

"Hey! Come on!" the guy called after him as Parker pivoted and headed for the kitchen.

"You don't put ketchup on steak. And you snuck that ketchup in here." Parker didn't even look back.

"It was for my fries!" the man protested. "It must have oozed over onto the steak."

Parker stopped and turned. He stabbed the steak with the fork that was balanced on the plate and held the piece of meat up. "That's a lot of oozing," he said.

The man sighed. "It's just ketchup."

"You don't like how I make steak, eat somewhere else," Parker told him. Then he stomped into the kitchen with the plate.

Ava knew her eyes shouldn't be as wide as they were. She'd seen him take a glass of iced tea away from someone who'd added sugar to it and a plate of nachos away from someone who had dared scrape off the sour cream. But it never failed to amaze her. He not only did this stuff, but he got away with it. She didn't know the customer's name, but she'd seen him in here before and she knew he'd be back. They always came back. "They" being the entire town of Bliss, Kansas and a huge surrounding area.

She looked down at her list and underlined *grumpy* twice.

The problem was, it was the only con she could come up with, and she wasn't entirely sure it was that much of a problem. She needed to date him. She didn't need to *like* him.

But she did like things about him. What you saw was what you got with Parker Blake. He didn't like people lingering in his diner. He grumped about it all the time. He also had very specific views about food. If you ordered the jalapeno burger, you'd better, by God, eat the jalapenos. You didn't eat a steak with ketchup on it, apparently. Potatoes, of some kind, came with everything. No, you couldn't ask to hold them.

It was no secret that he felt that the diner was a very straight-forward setup. He was there to serve food to hungry people in exchange for money. The food he was willing to serve was clearly spelled out on the menu, as was the price for that food. If you ordered a burger and fries, that's what you were going to get. There were no substitutions. There was no "on the side". The menu said burger and fries, so you would get a burger and fries. Period. And after the customer had eaten, he figured they were no longer hungry, and could move on.

Ava had to admit this was something that fascinated her about the guy. It was an odd way to do business. On one hand, it seemed logical to placate the customers and make them happy by giving them what they wanted. Especially if it was something simple like *not* serving them fries or letting them put ketchup on their steak. On the other, his methods saved him a lot of headaches, and it honestly kept the entire interaction simple.

And people here put up with it. Because it was the only restaurant in town. No, she did not consider her pie shop a restaurant. It served pie. And coffee. Period. Which should also be straightforward and simple, now that she thought about it. Yet it seemed to have complicated her life more than any merger or new contract for Carmichael Enterprises ever had.

Parker stayed in business in spite of his clear the-customer-is-not-always-right stance because his food was really good and the diner had been a mainstay in town for over a decade. And because Parker's rules had always been in place. When you walked through the doors, you knew what you were getting.

She was actually envious of that. She was a master negotiator, with a well-deserved reputation as being fair but tough in her business dealings. But she never went into a meeting knowing *exactly* what was going to happen. Everything was a negotiation, and she had to give to take. It was why she took control of everything else in her life as firmly as she could. The company was the core of her family's security so she did what she had to do to keep it going. But the sometimes-winning-sometimes-losing thing caused her to grab onto schedules and lists and plans whenever she could with both hands. She liked control. So, yes, she envied Parker Blake being able to say "this is how it is, take it or leave it" with his business. And succeed.

Ava studied the other pros and cons list in her notebook. There was another guy on her page.

Noah
PROS:

1. Not my type
2. Tall (enough)
3. Hot
4. From Bliss
5. Rudy loved him
6. Business owner

She added *NOT grumpy* to Noah's list. Then she sighed. She still had only seven to
Parker's eight pros. And then there was Noah's one con.
CONS:

1. Brynn.

Ava drew a heart next to her sister's name. Brynn and Noah were close, and Ava didn't know for sure if their relationship was romantic or friends-only, but they had a way of making a girl feel like a third wheel when they were together. Ava didn't get it, but there was a connection there, and it made her feel a little weird about considering dating Noah.

Still, she had to date *someone*. Someone from Bliss, Kansas. For six months. There was twelve and a half billion dollars riding on it.

Well, kind of. Her father's company was worth twelve and a half billion, and her chance to take over the position of CEO depended on her dating someone here for six months. Along with a few other stipulations her father had put in his will. Like living here for a year and running the pie shop next door with her sisters.

Ava colored in the little heart she'd drawn as she thought about her options.

It was crazy. Of course. Who found out he had cancer and decided to use his will to influence his daughters' love lives? But Rudy Carmichael had *never* been a conventional father. And he'd known Ava would do anything to be in charge of Carmichael Enterprises. It was all she'd ever aspired to. It was the only thing she was good at. And it was the only way for her to take care of her mom and sisters. The philanthropist who took care of everyone from abused women to the local libraries, the free spirit who made everyone smile and feel a little lighter, and the genius scientist who was working to rid the world of disease. Ava's job enabled the three of them to make the world a better place without worry about money or security. It was *her* way of making the world a better place. Indirectly.

She'd thought it was a given. She'd already been acting CEO of Carmichael Enterprises for the past five years, ever since her father had decided to move to BFE, Kansas. When she'd found out that her father had passed away, she'd mourned, then taken a deep breath, quelled the butterflies in her stomach, and headed to the meeting with the lawyer. Only to find out that she had hoops to jump through before she could officially etch her name into the glass next to the CEO's office door.

So many hoops.

But the craziest part of all? She understood where her father had been coming from.

Not at first, of course. At first, she'd been confused and pissed off and hurt. She'd worked her ass off for the company. Even her social life had to do with work nine out of ten times. Okay, ten out of ten times. She could make *any* event into a networking opportunity. She'd always dated men who were very much like her father. Men who understood that she did, and always would, put the company first. That she'd be late for dinner more times than not. That she would take phone calls in the middle of conversations. That she would be traveling and gone for days, sometimes even weeks, at a time. She was, first and foremost, married to the company, and she had been dating men that would understand that. And who had important business connections to bring to the relationship.

Had it been romantic? No. Had it been sexy and exciting? No. And she was good with that. She liked predictable. She liked things spelled out ahead of time. She liked knowing what she was getting into and what was expected of her.

"You can't even eat an entire salad?"

She looked up at the sound of Parker's deep voice. And quickly covered her notebook page with her hand. "Um, I'm still working on it."

He lifted a brow and reached for her plate. He turned the plate over and emptied the rest of her salad into a take-out box. She'd been expecting that. Parker didn't like people lingering. The diner was for eating. Not talking on the phone, not reading, not working on your computer. And not making pros and cons lists. You came in, you ate, you paid, and you got out. Everyone knew that was how Parker's diner operated. And you either ate everything on your plate, or you took it home with you. The only thing that wasn't good at the diner was the coffee. And that was on purpose. It was supposed to curtail the lingering. It didn't work, but that was what it was supposed to do.

"Hey, I didn't even smuggle in any contraband condiments," she said. "You can search me."

From where he was standing, he could see her entire right side, and as his gaze tracked over her from head to heels, she felt tingles all along that path.

"I'm not worried. There's nowhere in those little skirts you wear to hide anything."

Ava felt her body warm. She loved her pencil skirts and yes, they were fitted. But she knew that Parker was just trying to fluster her. And she didn't fluster easily. In fact, Parker Blake was the first man in a very long time to get her even close to ruffled. Which should probably go on the con list, come to think of it. But there was one very important pro that should be added as well.

Parker Blake was a great choice for a six-month Bliss boyfriend in spite of the items on the con list, because they'd already spent three months together. Kind of. That meant she'd only have to put in three more to get to her six-month dating quota. Sure, the past three months had involved going back and forth from each other's business kitchens—when she came over to borrow butter and eggs, and he came to her kitchen to bitch about it, for instance. But they'd also had a few game nights with her sisters and his two best friends, Noah and Evan. That might be stretching the "date" definition—especially considering she'd been supposedly dating Evan...but that was a long story—but it was still socializing unlike any she'd had with the men in New York. It had to count. She was *not* starting over on the six-month time frame stipulated in the will if she could help it.

Besides, there was a chemistry between her and Parker. And

that made the idea of spending a few months with him on a "personal" basis, a lot more appealing.

"So what's with the take-out box?" she asked, resisting the urge to cross and uncross her legs under the table. The legs his gaze stayed on for an extra few seconds.

He set the box on the table along with her bill. "It's one o'clock," he told her.

Right. Closing time for the diner. Parker was open for breakfast from six a.m. to nine a.m., closed from nine to eleven, open again for lunch from eleven to one, and then closed again until four when dinner started. The dinner shift was from four to six. And heaven help you if you tried to order eggs after nine or a BLT after four. There was a specific breakfast, lunch, and dinner menu, and Parker was God when it came to deciding what people should be eating for each of those meals. But again, if you came in for lunch, you just knew that waffles were not an option.

"It's actually one eleven," she told him. "And I came in close to closing time because I was hoping to talk to you about something in private."

Something flickered in his expression. Surprise? Curiosity? More likely irritation.

"But I close at one."

He didn't. Yes, the sign on his door said he did, but people were always in the diner until at least one thirty. For all of his grumping and strictness, the one thing he didn't do was throw people out if they were lingering. It was weird. And fascinating. Ava found herself wondering about Parker Blake and his habits far more than she should.

"I'm not the only one still here," she said, looking pointedly at the still occupied other table.

"But you're finished."

Well, her salad was in a box now. But she'd discovered that the diner food was pretty good even left over, so she would, in fact, take it home and eat it later. "Yes, I'm finished *eating*," she said.

He looked at her for a moment, clearly waiting for her to go on.

Ava fought a smile as she added, "I just have a few more things to go over on this...report." *Or list of why you're the perfect man for me,* she thought. *For the next three months,* she thought quickly. *Because of the will,* she added. Even if it was just to herself, she had to be careful about thinking of Parker as anything other than...Parker. The guy who could get her through the stipulations in her father's will and into the CEO's office in New York City. "So it's no problem for me to wait until everyone leaves so we can talk." She fought a smile, knowing he would hate the idea of her just hanging out.

"So the diner closing at one doesn't matter to you?"

"Of course it does. It's the perfect time to talk to you without anyone else around."

"There's a reason I close at one o'clock," he said.

"And what is that?" she asked. She actually really wanted to know. Some of the time between meal shifts he spent in preparation for the next, of course. But he left the building between nine and about ten in the morning and then again between two and three. And, in spite of herself, she was curious about where he went and what he did. She didn't know why she was curious. It really didn't matter to her at all. But he was such a regimented guy, that she assumed his patterns and schedules had a purpose.

She liked that in another person.

There were things about Parker she didn't like, of course. How he was completely rude to her every time she came over here to borrow eggs. How he called her "Boss" in a really sarcastic tone of voice. The way he seemed to think that her being a dismal failure in the kitchen was pretty funny. And the way that whenever he looked at her, he seemed to know more than she wanted him to.

Oh, and the way her face got hot whenever she happened to

catch him bending over in his kitchen. The man had an effect on her libido that she was still unaccustomed to. She dated handsome men, men who knew how to dress and always smelled good. Which made her reaction to a guy who wore blue jeans and T-shirts that were often covered in food of various types, who shaved every third day or so, and who smelled like bacon and pancake syrup very strange. But she couldn't deny that there was something about this man that kicked her pulse up a few beats per minute.

And she liked that he had never once complimented her.

She almost frowned as that thought went through her mind. That sounded strange. But it was true. She was used to compliments from men. Those she dated and those she did business with. But she never fully trusted them. There were reasons for those men to compliment her that went far beyond simple courtesy or even to make her feel good. They all wanted to be on her good side.

Parker didn't care about her good side. And he'd never said anything nice to her.

And she trusted him because of it.

"I have a life outside of this diner," Parker said, in answer to her question about how he spent his time between shifts. "I have things to do."

"Things like what?"

He frowned at her. "Why don't you just tell me what you think we need to discuss?" he asked.

"Fine. We need to talk about your employment at Blissfully Baked." She barely resisted wincing as she said the name of her pie shop. She didn't care what anyone said, it sounded like a place to buy pot.

"You can't fire me, Boss," Parker said. "And you know it."

She did. The employment agreement he'd signed with Rudy said that the only way for Parker to be removed from the Blissfully Baked payroll was for him to quit, die, or go to prison.

He'd been put into place to help with the time in between Rudy's death and the girls getting to Bliss, but the intention was also for him to take the shop over after the girls met their twelve-month obligation and, supposedly, returned to New York.

"Oh, well, I don't want to fire you," she said. In fact, if he did quit, her whole plan would go to hell. "The opposite actually."

"What's that mean?" He looked highly suspicious.

"I want you to step up and actually do the job."

He glanced at the other table, then back to her. "I've got customers. Can't talk about whatever this is right now."

Ava glanced at the other table as well, then back up at Parker. "What are the chances of me taking that weak excuse and leaving you alone, do you suppose?"

He sighed. He did that a lot around her. "Poor."

"Exactly." She slid out of the booth and stood. She smoothed her skirt and stepped around him.

"What are you doing?" he asked. He didn't try to stop her, but he looked wary and curious.

Ava bit back a smile. "Helping."

———

P arker watched Ava approach the table where the Wilsons sat, finishing their lunch, her heels clicking over his tile floor. Those damned shoes made him crazy. And not just the three-inch black ones she wore today. The shoes she wore every damned day. She had heels on no matter what she was doing. And not a single pair was practical in the least for anything anyone did in Bliss, Kansas. Except for drawing attention. And that they did very well.

But he didn't want her to take them off.

Damn, he'd never been a shoe guy before. He was fairly certain he'd never noticed what his dates wore on their feet. But with Ava Carmichael, her heels were as much a part of her as the long blonde hair and the I'm-out-of-your-league attitude.

"Hello," she greeted the Wilsons, giving them a smile. "I'm Ava. I own the pie shop next door."

Parker had no idea what she was up to. "Helping" was pretty vague and definitely made him suspicious. But he didn't move to stop her. He had a feeling he wanted to see this. And she wanted him to step up and do his job at the pie shop next door? Yeah, he was going to hear her out about that too. And not just because there wasn't a chance in hell that she was going to let it go. He was curious about what, exactly, she thought his job over there was.

"Of course. Hello," Cindy Wilson said. "We've been meaning to stop in."

Uh-huh. Not a lot of people in Bliss were stopping over at the pie shop. The girls had hosted a great public event just two weeks ago to introduce themselves, and their pie, to the town. The turnout had been decent. But the Carmichael triplets were new to town and they were redoing the pie shop, and one thing people in Bliss didn't get excited about was change.

"That would be lovely," Ava told her graciously. "Ask for me and I'll give you a discount on your first slice."

"That's very nice," Cindy said, glancing at her husband, Brandon, and their son, Kyle, who was now steak-less.

"I look forward to seeing you," Ava said to them all. "But right now, I need to ask you to leave."

Parker felt his eyebrows rise and he crossed his arms, waiting to see how this would play out.

"I'm...sorry?" Cindy gave her a puzzled look.

"It's after one p.m.," Ava said, looking pointedly at her watch. "The diner closes for the afternoon from one until four. And while Parker has always been very lenient about that rule, I'm going to have to insist it's more closely observed since he's now going to be working for me at the pie shop during those hours."

Parker resisted the urge to laugh at that. Well, that was one way of filling him in on her plan. And making it so he couldn't yell at her right away.

She didn't even glance in his direction.

"Oh. He is?" Cindy asked. She *did* look over at Parker.

"I'm sure you've heard that baking isn't my forte," Ava said with a surprisingly self-deprecating smile. And the Wilsons all smiled with her. Parker rolled his eyes. She could be charming, he'd give her that.

"So, I desperately need help," Ava went on. "And it's going to be his pie shop soon."

Well, that's what Rudy's trust said. But Parker had been wondering what was going to happen with the pie shop now that Ava's sister Cori had fallen in love with Evan and had decided to stay in Bliss. Ava was an utter failure in the kitchen—and he had a number of theories about why—but Cori was magical with an oven. If she wanted to bake pies for a living, she'd be amazing at it.

"So we're going to use his recipes and techniques, we're going to update the menu, and really give it Parker's touch," Ava was explaining.

"Well, then we'll get out of your way." Cindy looked up at Parker. "You're so sweet to let us take our time, but you have work to do."

"Unlike how I usually spend my days," he muttered. He knew Ava was the only one to hear him.

The Wilsons all slid out of the booth, and Kyle headed for the register to pay.

Parker joined him there, not giving Ava the satisfaction of any reaction to her announcement about his new duties next door.

"Didn't know you knew about pie," Kyle said as he tucked his wallet back into his pocket.

"That pie shop has been one surprise after another for everyone," Parker replied, shutting the register drawer.

Kyle nodded. "Looking forward to what you're going to do over there."

"Are you?" Parker was surprised at that.

"Sure. You've never done dessert, but you're a hell of a cook. Guessing your pies will be awesome."

Huh. He was fantastic at pies, as a matter of fact. But no one but his mother knew that.

Ava followed the Wilsons to the door and as it bumped shut she turned the lock, then flipped the sign to CLOSED.

2

"There." She faced Parker. "Now about your job at the pie shop. I'd like your new duties to start today."

"You are..."

Ava lifted an eyebrow.

"Something," he finally finished. Then he turned away from her and shut the coffeepot off and started wiping the counter.

He knew she was waiting for some kind of blow up, or argument, or at least a *what in the hell are you talking about?* And he knew that it would drive her crazy for him *not* to give her any of that.

Ava went back to her table and grabbed her notebook, then boosted herself up on one of the stools at the counter and said, "I'm going to overlook the past three months of paying you for doing nothing. We'll just start from today."

She was definitely *something*. He just didn't have a word for it. He'd never met a woman like Ava Carmichael. Most of the women in and around Bliss were sweet and accommodating and seemed to want him to be happy and in a good mood when he was with them. Ava didn't give one fuck about if he was happy or about his mood. As evidenced by the fact that she continually did things that made him scowl and grumble.

"Or we could say those paychecks covered all the stuff you've been stealing from me for the past three and a half months," he said.

She rolled her eyes. "Borrowing."

"Borrowing?" he repeated. "I haven't seen any payment or replacement of any of those items."

"I'll buy you a dozen eggs and a bag of sugar next trip to the grocery store."

"First, you don't go to the grocery store. Second, that isn't even close to what you owe me."

"Well, it's not like I've been counting every egg."

Okay then. Parker headed for the kitchen and the corkboard he had up on the wall next to the pantry.

She kept talking. "And how do you know I don't go to the grocery store?"

He came back through the door and handed her a piece of paper. "Because Mr. Tomkins noticed that *I* was buying a lot more eggs and butter than usual and he guessed it was for you. He also told me that they teased you when you came in there three times in one day and that he hadn't seen you since."

Ava blew out a breath as she looked at the paper. "They shouldn't do that. It's not good for business to make fun of your customers."

Parker grinned at that. He was sure that Ava was not only *not* used to being teased, but she probably wasn't used to an entire town knowing—and caring about—every move she made. He couldn't deny he enjoyed watching this gorgeous fish out of water. He didn't know why except that it was fun to see a woman who was so confident and put together, and who obviously kicked ass in New York City, rattled a bit by a simple little town that had three stoplights and whose biggest news was the reopening of a pie shop that had four items on its menu.

She looked down at the paper he'd handed her and he watched her eyes widen. It was an itemized list of the food she'd "borrowed" from his kitchen.

He didn't actually care about the butter and eggs. What bugged him about her pilfering was the way she walked into his kitchen at random times and made it impossible to not watch as she bent over to rummage in his fridge. If her shoes made him crazy, her sweet ass in her tight skirts jacked his blood pressure up to dangerous levels.

She looked up again. "Okay, so we'll call the last three months even?"

"Fine." He began gathering the salt and pepper shakers from around the restaurant, knowing that not having his full focus would bug her.

But truthfully, she had every bit of his attention. He refilled salt and pepper shakers by rote anyway, and Ava couldn't be within ten feet of him without his entire system going on high alert.

It was annoying as hell.

"The income at the pie shop is just now inching up," she told him. "After the Parking With Pie event Cori threw, we got the bank loan paid off. But you know that we have to turn a profit by the end of our first twelve months according to Rudy's trust. So, we need a better product. So, I need *you* to make the pies."

"No fucking way." He set the tray of salt and pepper shakers on the counter in front of her.

"The pies have to get better, Parker," she said, not the least bit deterred by his answer. Of course, negotiating and making deals was what she did for a living. "We both know our current process was just a stop gap to get the shop back open."

"You mean the process where you don't actually make the pies?" Parker asked.

"I do make them," Ava protested. "I fill the crusts and bake them."

Which still, somehow, didn't turn out well. She bought the crusts from a lady in the next town and used canned pie filling and they still sucked. It drove Parker crazy, because he knew Ava's approach had not been what Rudy intended when he'd put her in charge of the pies. But the will didn't say *how* she had to make the pies. Just that she had to be the one doing it.

"But that doesn't matter," she said, waving that away. "I have to make a change. People aren't buying the pies." She took a deep breath. "They're not buying *my* pies."

Parker glanced up, hearing something in her tone. She looked chagrined, and for just a second he softened. She was right. The pies offered at the pie shop were the ones Ava made. They had to be. The trust stipulated that her sisters couldn't help her in the kitchen—she had to do it herself. So if the pies weren't good, that was all on Ava. She was failing to make money at something that was her full responsibility. That had probably never happened to her before.

But Parker knew that Rudy had intended for each of the girls to learn something from the jobs he'd given them, so Parker brushed off the softness he'd felt for a moment there.

He started pouring salt from a bigger container into the shakers. "I'm *not* making the pies for you, Boss."

"But people will not only trust you to make good ones, the fact that you've always refused to serve dessert in here will make them curious and bring them in."

She had a point there. "Too bad."

"We need good pie, Parker. You're the best option to make that happen."

"But *you're* supposed to make the pies and you know it." He pointed a finger at her. "Dammit, Ava, if you don't do what you're supposed to do, *I* get stuck as the CFO of Carmichael Enterprises. So you can come over here in your short skirts and high heels and bat those big blue eyes at me all you want—that is *not* going to happen."

Those blue eyes widened and he mentally kicked himself. He didn't need to let on that he'd noticed all of that. He needed to concentrate on making her fulfill all of the requirements needed to keep *him* out of New York City.

As crazy as it was, the will stipulated that if the girls refused, or failed, to meet all of the stipulations for their inheritance, Evan, Parker, and Noah would be named CEO, CFO, and VP of Carmichael Enterprises respectively.

And Parker and his friends wanted *nothing* to do with running a multi-billion-dollar worldwide conglomerate in a huge city fifteen hundred miles away. Hell, he didn't even know what exactly a CFO did. He, Evan and Noah all had the lives they wanted to have right here in their hometown. Parker's father had brought their family to Bliss from Chicago with the sole purpose of finding a simpler, safer, happier way of life. Parker had no intention of changing anything about it. But he knew that Rudy had put that plan B in his trust because he knew it would motivate the guys to make sure the girls did what they were supposed to do.

Ava leaned in, resting her forearms on the counter and linking her fingers. "I've been over the trust with a fine-tooth comb. It says nothing about me making everything from scratch or by myself. Only that I have to be in charge of the product and the kitchen at the pie shop. I can't help Cori and Brynn with the business or PR efforts, and they can't help me with the pies. But it doesn't say that I can't have *any* help."

Parker shook his head. No. She wasn't talking him into this. "Your dad wanted you to learn what it was like to actually *make* the product you sell." He started replacing the lids on the salt shakers.

"Yeah, well, I'm not *selling* much product at all. That's the problem."

"It's because you're half-assing it," Parker told her bluntly. "And having me do it for you is also half-assing it."

She sighed. "You're right."

Parker looked up quickly, surprised by her agreement.

"I have been. But that has to change," she added. "I thought this would be easier. But the shop has to be successful for me to get back to New York and my real job. Which means I have to give one hundred percent."

Yeah, only another eight and a half months of dealing with going hard in the middle of the day when walking into his kitchen to find her raiding his pantry. Only another eight and a half months of smelling her perfume in the air of that pantry for what felt like hours after she'd left. Only another eight and a half months of hearing things crashing against the shared wall between their kitchens and listening to her swearing like a sailor. And finding himself laughing in the middle of flipping burgers. Thank God that was all temporary.

"So start giving one hundred percent." He started on the pepper shakers.

"I am. I'm giving one hundred percent to finding the best way to make this happen," she said. "And that's you."

Parker kept filling the pepper shakers. "Your dad begged me to make him pie. He even offered me a million dollars—which I thought was a joke at the time—to make him pie. And I still wouldn't do it."

He didn't fucking have time, for one thing. And his father had never served dessert, and the diner's menu hadn't changed since they'd opened fifteen years and four months ago. And it wasn't going to change now because a hot, bossy blonde asked Parker to bake for her.

"Well, you know for *sure* that I *do* have a million dollars," Ava said.

Parker looked up. "You're offering me a million dollars to make the pies for you?"

"Something even better," she said.

"What's better?" he asked. "Two million?" He didn't want her money. Money and loans had a way of complicating things, and complications were the *last* thing Parker wanted.

"How about this building—including the pie shop—free and clear?" she asked. The pie shop and diner were actually two parts of one big building that had been a farm supply company long ago. The wall divided it into two separate businesses, the diner about twice the size of the pie shop.

He frowned at her. "Why do you think I'd want that?" But he did kind of want that. He "owned" the diner, but he was actually paying the bank for it, one month at a time. It was fine. It was how a lot of people did business. Maybe most people. Small business loans were no big deal. But there something about the idea of really, truly, fully *owning* the diner that made his heart beat a little harder. His father had given him the business, and Parker took a lot of pride in what he did inside this building. And the idea of it being completely his, from the bricks and drywall to the eggs and whisks, was tempting, he couldn't deny it.

Then he frowned harder. How did Ava know that about him?

She shrugged. "I did some research."

"You researched *me*?" he asked.

"I always get as much information about the people I'm negotiating with as possible before we meet," she said. "Interestingly, my team couldn't dig much up about your business dealings."

He rolled his eyes. "My business dealings are 'what can I get you?', 'here's your burger' and 'that will be eleven eighty-five'."

She nodded. "Exactly. Direct. Simple. You pay your bills on time. You give to charity. You've never done anything even slightly sketchy with your business."

He gave her a look.

"But I have learned some things about you over the past three months," she said.

"Oh?"

"Your entire life revolves around this diner. This town. These people."

Parker gripped the shaker he held tighter. She was right. And ninety-nine percent of the town could have told her that. But there was something about Ava having figured that out about him that felt...different. More personal.

"So," she went on. "I figured the best thing I could offer you was a chance to really, truly *own* this place."

Hearing her say what he'd just been thinking felt strangely intimate.

"And," she added, "since clearly making food for these people is what turns your crank, I figured you'd appreciate having a chance to make even more food for more people."

It turned his crank, huh? Well, he supposed that was one way to put it. But he didn't have the time or energy to make *more* food for more people. He was perfectly happy with things exactly as they were. Exactly as they always had been.

"I could pay off my own loan with the million dollars," he commented. "And buy a boat."

They referred to business deals as getting into bed together. He was pretty sure that getting into bed with Ava, in *any* capacity, would absolutely make his life complicated.

But it would be temporary. She'll be leaving town in eight and a half months.

Still, he had a feeling that a woman like Ava could have an effect that would be felt long after she was gone.

She nodded. "But then you wouldn't have a fifty-fifty partnership with Cori in the pie shop."

Okay...*what*? Parker set the big container of pepper down and braced his hands on the counter. "A partnership with Cori?"

Ava nodded and wet her lips.

Per the trust, Parker was supposed to run the pie shop after the girls left, but Cori was now staying in Bliss because of Evan.

Parker had assumed that she would want the pie shop, and he had no intention of fighting her for it. He'd actually been relieved Evan had hinted that Cori would like to keep the shop open after the triplets' year in Bliss was up. He'd made it sound like Cori would be willing to run it and work for Parker, but Parker had planned to just sign the whole thing over to her. It had been her dad's and, seriously, Parker didn't have the time for another business anyway.

A partnership had never been mentioned.

"Fifty-fifty," Ava confirmed. "Fully backed by Carmichael Enterprises. But it has to stay a pie shop. I don't know if you'd planned to knock the wall between the diner and shop down and expand or something, but if you're interested in the pie shop *as* a pie shop, then it can be half yours. No investment required up front. You just come in and take over next March. Very low risk."

Really, *no* risk if Carmichael Enterprises was behind it. Per Rudy's will, Carmichael Enterprises couldn't be involved with the shop for this first year, but after the twelve months was up the triplets could do whatever they wanted. And this didn't surprise Parker. According to Evan, this was what Ava did—she financially backed everything her mom and sisters did so that they had no worries about money or security. Ava would be able to insure the financial stability of the shop for the rest of Cori's life if needed.

"What if I want to keep it all for myself? No Cori?" Parker asked, just to see what she'd say.

"Then I'll give you ten million for it."

He blinked at her. She was serious. Her sister's happiness was worth ten million. In fact, he was pretty sure she'd go even higher if she had to.

That was a lot of money. That was the kind of money that changed lives. Maybe for the better. Maybe not. But it didn't matter. Parker didn't want a changed life.

"Cori is okay with sharing it?" Parker asked.

"Definitely. She's never run a business before. She *wants* a partner. In case you've missed it, Cori doesn't really like to be alone. She's much better with people. Especially people who can help with the 'boring stuff' like the books and accounts," Ava said.

Parker chuckled. Parker liked Cori a lot. She was fun and sweet and sassy and smart. But she didn't sit still well, and she hated the accounting Rudy was forcing her to do for the pie shop this first year. Yeah, he could be her business partner. He could take care of the books and inventory stuff while she had fun in the kitchen. He couldn't run two kitchens anyway. And if he was ever slightly jealous of her getting to create and concoct over there, he'd never let on.

"Let me think about it," he told Ava.

"Sure. Of course," Ava said with a nod. Then she leaned in again. "But if you're going to take over the pie shop, it makes even more sense for you to be making the pies now. You can make the pies you want *your* pie shop to be known for, and we get things going strong for both you and Cori before I leave."

He rolled his neck, taking a deep breath. This woman never stopped pushing. "What makes you think I have pies I want the pie shop to be known for?" he asked, looking up again.

Ava met his eyes. "Because, for all the bitching you do about people coming in here to eat, you take pride in the food you make. You have very specific ideas about how it should all be done. So, if you're a part of the pie shop, you'll want to make really good pies in a very particular way."

He just looked at her for a long moment. Dammit. She was more observant and insightful than he'd given her credit for.

And suddenly a new thought occurred to him. One that made all of this a lot more appealing. "I just don't know that you'll like me being your boss," he told her.

She lifted a brow. "Uh. Owner," she said, pointing at herself. "Employee." She pointed at him. "Until March."

"Good at pies," he said, pointing at himself. "Not." He pointed at her. "If I'm teaching you to make pie, that means I'm in charge and you have to do what I say."

"*Teaching* me? No, no, I just want to *help* you do it."

"Not what Rudy intended and you know it."

She blew out a breath. She clearly wanted to argue further, but finally she said, "Fine."

Parker nodded and resumed the pepper filling, trying not to look too smug. Could he teach Ava to bake a pie? Hell if he knew. But he could try. And in the process, get his recipes into the pie shop—so what if she somehow knew that would matter to him? —get full ownership of the diner, and ruffle a few more of Ava's feathers. Because, for whatever reason, that was really a hell of a lot of fun.

"But you've got your work cut out for you," she said. "And keep in mind that *all* of the pies will be known as *yours.* You'll want them to be good."

He looked up at her. "Yeah, I caught that," he said. "The Wilsons now think that I'm going to be baking over there. That will be all around town by dinnertime."

She nodded. "Exactly."

"And you're feeling kind of cocky because you think that if you keep messing the pies up, I'll just step in and do it for you to save my reputation," he guessed.

She looked mildly surprised, and he realized he was right in assuming that was her plan. But she shrugged. "You know everyone will be expecting great things from you. You won't want to let them down."

"But they'll also know that Cori and I are partners," he said. "And considering they've been eating my cooking for twelve years and have never tried Cori's, they might just assume that anything bad is hers."

Ava frowned. "Cori's an amazing baker."

"Well, of course *you* would say that. You're her sister."

"But they know *I've* been doing the bad baking so far."

He nodded. "But the town doesn't know all the details of the will. They don't know that you *have* to be the one baking. From what I hear, they assume you're the best of the three of you."

He couldn't help but grin at Ava's little gasp. "I didn't know that. They actually think Cori and Brynn are even worse bakers than I am?"

"Well, what are you going to do? Tell them that your dad sent the *worst* of you into the kitchen to torture the town?" Parker asked. "That would just make *him* look crazy."

She frowned, clearly processing all the ways her family could end up looking bad here. Parker fought his smile.

"So, you really think you can make *me* a good baker?"

He felt a surge of triumph. Ava would do whatever she had to do to protect her family's reputation. He liked that about her. And he was going to unabashedly use it against her. Rudy wanted *her* to learn to make pie. So she was going to learn to make pie. "I can," he said with a solemn nod, trying not to give away how much he was going to enjoy this. "But you'll have to do everything I tell you."

She chewed on her bottom lip, clearly torn between agreeing for her family's sake, and telling him to fuck off. "Fine. You can *teach me* how to bake the pies. For now."

For eight and a half months, he reminded himself. Which could be a very long time. "Fine."

"Oh, and Hank and the guys know you're going to be working at the pie shop too," she told him.

Parker sighed. Hank and his friends, Walter, Ben and Roger, went to the pie shop every morning for coffee after eating breakfast at the diner. They were a font of information and gossip.

"You're okay with the whole town knowing that you've begged me for help?" Parker asked.

She laughed. "Admitting that *I* suck at baking? Yeah. Because I don't care about pies."

Parker nodded. "Exactly."

"What?"

"I think you're really good at anything you do care about."

She seemed surprised by the compliment. "Thank you," she said. "I am, actually, good at the things I really try at."

"Do you even like pie?"

"No."

"It's hard to care about things you don't like."

"But I like Cori."

He acknowledged that with a tip of his head.

"So, let's get started." Ava slid off the stool and started for his kitchen.

"Whoa." He caught her arm, bringing her to a stop.

Her skin was soft and warm under his hand and he realized that he'd never touched her before. He cleared his throat and dropped his hand. "We're not starting today," he said.

She looked up at him. Even in her heels she still had to tip her head slightly, and it occurred to him, as he looked into those big blue eyes, that they hadn't stood this close before. At least not for more than a second as she scooted around him to escape his kitchen with eggs or butter.

"Um, why?" she asked.

Was her voice a little husky?

"I have things to do today," he said. "I wasn't prepared for this. But we can start tomorrow."

"Oh, tomorrow. Right. We need to go fruit picking tomorrow."

He blinked at her. "What?"

"Hank and Walter might have overheard me mention to Cori and Brynn that we're going fruit picking."

"Why are we going fruit picking?"

"I figured you'd insist on getting rid of the canned pie filling for the pies."

"I am going to insist on that," he agreed.

"So we'll need fruit, right?"

"I guess so."

"So fruit picking is a good idea," she said. "We'll go after your breakfast shift tomorrow."

Parker didn't respond right away. Did she really not know that there was no fruit in season right now? And why was he hesitating to tell her? Maybe because she was so damned bossy, even when he'd tried to make it very clear *he* was going to be in charge in the kitchen. It might be fun—good, he meant *good*, as in a good lesson for *her*—to take charge of this and have her show up to pick nonexistent fruit. It might be good for her to realize that she didn't know as much as he did about some of this. Maybe it would make her more likely to listen to him. He almost laughed at that.

"Fine," he finally agreed. "We'll start tomorrow. And I'll give you three days a week."

"I need more than that."

Pushing. Always pushing. "Well, I've got stuff to do. So, three days a week, and you can practice on the other days."

"Why? Will there be a test?" she asked sarcastically.

He narrowed his eyes, studying her face. And made a decision. He nodded. "Yes. I will be testing you."

Of course, that could be taken several ways, and he would, no doubt, be testing her patience. And enjoying it more than he should. And more than he had interacting with any other woman in a long time.

He had a flash of *she's gonna mess things up*. But he quickly reminded himself *temporarily. It's just temporary.*

"Very funny," she said.

"Oh, I'm not joking," he told her. "I'll be the first taste-tester you'll have to get through. If I don't like it, you'll have to try again."

Her eyes flared with irritation and, if he wasn't mistaken, a touch of excitement.

It shouldn't surprise him that being issued a challenge would get her going. Though it was hard to think of a time when Ava wasn't going.

"Fine," she finally said.

Yep, being Ava's boss was going to be a good time.

3

"Ava and I are going fruit picking tomorrow," Parker told Evan and Noah as he refilled their coffee cups. Without being asked. Which was a signal for *something is up*.

He didn't like refilling coffee because he was a grump who didn't like people paying a measly eighty-seven cents for a cup of coffee that, with the free refills, turned into four cups of coffee and caused them to sit around gabbing, taking up a table, and keeping him waiting on them and preventing him from being able to get their cups and table cleaned up.

At least, that was what everyone thought. And yeah, that was part of it. But it was also because it was one of the very tiny ways he could exert some control in this damned diner.

He knew most people would think that was crazy. The diner was his. He owned it. He ran it entirely on his own. He loved this place, he really did. And he loved being able to honor his father by continuing the business that had meant so much to Bill Blake. But the place was still his father's in almost every way. From the menu to the décor to the dishes. Parker had kept everything the same on purpose.

Except for the food. That was all his. He was still serving

burgers and BLTs and pot roast like his father had, but his was even better than his father's had been. And he wasn't about to let people muck it up by adding ketchup where it didn't belong or holding the cheese from things that were so obviously better with it.

"You and *Ava* are going *fruit picking*," Evan repeated.

"Yep." Parker pushed the silver cream pitcher closer to Evan.

Evan looked at Noah. Parker never offered cream with the coffee. They always had to ask. Noah was regarding Parker with narrowed eyes.

"Is that a euphemism?" he finally asked.

Parker let a half smile curl his mouth. "That's what Hank and the boys probably think."

"Well, is it?" Noah asked. "Because there's no fruit to pick this time of year."

Parker couldn't help but let his full smile stretch his lips. "Ava doesn't know that."

"It was Ava's idea to go fruit picking?" Evan asked.

"Yep." Parker poured more coffee—straight black—into Noah's cup as Evan, the one with the sweet tooth, added more sugar to his own.

"Why?" Evan asked.

"Because it's part of her plan," Parker said. The plan that he was going to have a very good time messing up.

He'd never met a person who had as many plans and lists as Ava Carmichael did. It was hot. He couldn't deny it. *He* didn't make lists. He didn't make big, elaborate plans either. But he appreciated it in others.

Actually, that wasn't true. He did make big, elaborate plans. Then he erased them, tore them up, or just ignored them. Because he didn't need a bunch of new ideas in his life. Everything was already going according to, well, plan.

"Parker?" Evan snapped his fingers in front of Parker's nose.

Parker focused on his friends instead of thinking about all of the ways Ava drove him crazy. And how much worse it was likely to get if he didn't take charge from the very start.

"What plan?" Evan's tone indicated it wasn't the first time he'd asked the question.

"Her plan for my pie shop," Parker said. And that was definitely part of what had kept him up thinking last night. She said that she wanted his input, his recipes, his hand in getting the pie shop business going strong, but she was still driving the train. Or so she thought.

"She talked to you about the partnership with Cori?" Evan asked.

Of course Evan would know about the plan for Cori and the pie shop.

But Parker was relieved that it was only *half* of the pie shop now. The pie shop that hadn't even existed six years ago, had never made any money, and had come to be only because Parker had refused to put pie on his own menu for Rudy. The pie shop that Rudy had asked Parker to look after when the older man had realized the cancer was going to win. The pie shop that had sat empty in the days after Rudy became too sick to go in and before Rudy's triplets had come to town. The shop that the girls had brought back to life.

Parker would never admit it, but he liked that. Ava had brought back the noise—the sounds of someone banging around in the pie shop kitchen—and Parker had felt some of his sadness lift just knowing someone was over there using the measuring cups and plates and space that Rudy had filled. Even though Ava was far louder and did a lot more swearing than Rudy ever had.

"Yeah," Parker finally answered Evan. "But Ava wants to be sure it's going strong before she leaves. She wants to actually put in some effort now that it's going to be Cori's too."

"And you're going to help her?" Evan asked.

"Sure. I want the pie shop going strong too," Parker said.

"Why wouldn't I use a brilliant business mind like Ava's to make that happen?"

He lifted a shoulder, trying to keep his posture and expression nonchalant. He wasn't going to let himself get too worked up or excited about this. It was pie. It would be a business in addition to the one he already had that took more time and energy some days than he wanted it to. Cori was a fantastic baker with a lot of creative energy. The kitchen on the other side of his wall could be all Cori's. That made the most sense. He could help and support her, but she could do the work.

And all the new recipes and plans that he *did* have in his head, could just fucking stay there. He only had to survive eight more months with Ava Carmichael in his world and then she'd go back to New York and things in his life would go back to normal. Quiet. Easy. Straightforward. Boring. He wanted boring. He needed it. He'd promised his father he'd appreciate it.

Flat out, Ava was a threat to his simple, even-keeled life.

Sure, the heels, the hair, the don't-fuck-with-me air about her, not to mention the fucking-with-me-could-be-really-fun attitude...all of that was part of it. How could it not be? But it was the ambition and creativity that really drew him. And worried him. A lack of change was one very important ingredient in his lifestyle. He had a routine, patterns, habits that worked, kept him happy and healthy. And when he went to bed at night, he slept peacefully without a million thoughts of bigger and brighter things keeping him awake. And without dreams of bossing a long-legged blonde—wearing nothing but red heels—around in his bedroom.

At least that's how it had been before Ava Carmichael came to Bliss.

"So you're just going to use her brilliant business mind?" Evan said, his tone full of skepticism.

Parker grabbed a tray of clean silverware from the counter behind him and placed it in front of his friends with a stack of paper napkins. If they wanted him to talk, they were going to have to help him work. He had at least another hour of work to do to prep for breakfast tomorrow. And he wanted something to do and focus on besides just thinking and talking about Ava. The familiar, menial tasks like rolling silverware, were exactly what he needed—the things that he appreciated about his work and focused him on how simple and comforting his routines were.

The hours running this place were long. Six a.m. to six p.m. without any of the extra prep and cleanup he put in. But they were also soothingly familiar. It was always the same, and his body, his whole system, was so used to the hours he kept that he didn't think he could ever do anything else.

"I'm going to teach her to make pie," Parker said, rolling a set of silverware and setting it aside without looking.

"*You* are going to teach *Ava* to make pie?" Evan asked, reaching for a napkin and a set of silverware.

"Is making pie a euphemism?" Noah wanted to know, also grabbing a napkin.

That sent Parker's mind spinning again and he had to consciously stop the thoughts that wanted to branch way out into directions they shouldn't. "No," he said firmly. "I'm going to teach her to bake a decent pie. My recipe. So that when people walk in they'll be getting *my* pie instead of that crap she's been doing."

Well, that already screwed up the plan to just let Cori do her thing in the kitchen, Parker realized as he said it out loud. *Fuck.* So much for just focusing on the books. According to Rudy's will and the stipulations in it, Cori couldn't do anything in the kitchen for another eight months and two weeks. The plan was designed to get each girl out of her comfort zone and trying and appreciating other sides of the business. Cori was doing the accounting and books right now rather than being colorful and creative in the kitchen. Ava was creating—or attempting to create—the product rather than working on marketing or increasing the profit margin...clearly her natural talents.

So Parker *was* going to be in the pie shop's kitchen, baking pies. And it was very difficult to ignore the kick of anticipation he felt in his chest thinking about that.

"Okay," Evan said, in his reasonable lawyer tone of voice. "But why are you taking her fruit picking when there's no fruit to pick?"

"Because she said so."

"You're letting her be the boss?" Evan asked.

"She *is* the boss," Parker returned. At least on paper.

The idea of taking Ava out of her boss comfort zone too sent an arrow of anticipation through him. He liked control, but he always had it. He ran the diner—hell, his whole life—however he wanted to. He didn't answer to anyone. He didn't have a partner, in business or personally, so there were no concessions, no compromises, no fights. He didn't even have to substitute baked potatoes for French fries if he didn't want to.

Evan chuckled. "She's going to be pissed when she finds out."

Parker couldn't ignore the jolt of anticipation that gave him too. Fighting with her would do nothing but up his blood pressure. He wasn't going to go there with her. And yet, his stupid pulse raced at the idea of Ava getting riled up and squaring off with him. Even the few times she'd mouthed off to him when he caught her swiping flour from his kitchen had gotten his heart rate thumping.

"Doesn't matter," he said, as if he wasn't remembering how her eyes sparked when she was irritated. "She can't fire me. And she can't piss me off. She needs me." And he liked that far too much.

"I guess that's true," Evan agreed. "And it makes too much sense that you be the one to teach her. So she's kind of stuck."

Parker nodded, rolling three more sets of silverware, weighing his next words.

"But I don't want you two correcting anybody who thinks that fruit picking *is* an euphemism," he said, rolling another spoon, knife, and fork together inside a napkin. Tightly, quickly, perfectly. He wondered how many times his hands had done those exact motions in that exact pattern.

"You want us to let them think you're doing something else with Ava?" Noah asked. His tone was curious, but not surprised.

"Three months of fruit picking and making pies with a guy who's nothing like the guys in New York, who's from Bliss, who she'll slowly get to know as we spend time together..." Parker trailed off, letting those words sink in. "I think that could be good for her."

"You want to be the one dating her," Evan filled in. He also didn't sound shocked.

Why didn't Evan sound shocked? That idea should be a little shocking. Shouldn't it? But Evan was a smart guy. Maybe he'd realized what Parker had.

"It makes sense," Parker said. "She and I have spent time together for the past three months and we'll be spending more time together coming up. It could count." He finally looked up at Evan. "Right?" he asked. He said it firmly, as if he wasn't going to take no for an answer, but he definitely wanted that confirmation from the man who'd actually written Rudy's will.

Evan nodded. "Yeah. I think it could. The trust says simply that she has to spend time with a guy from here, get to know him for reasons other than furthering the Carmichael Enterprises business connections, not see anyone else for six months, have some fun."

Rudy had told them that Ava's social life in New York had always doubled as business meetings. She'd never shied away from mixing business with pleasure, dating men who were business associates or who could help her make connections, and attending events where there were other CEOs, politicians, and powerful people who could strengthen her business ties.

Rudy had wanted more for her. Or maybe less. Less business, less pressure, less stress. More simple fun. And more time just being with people for the sake of being with them, getting to know them...and maybe getting to know herself.

Parker had, over the years, heard many of his older customers wax poetic about life lessons and dole out advice to the younger patrons about living in the moment and figuring out what was truly important in life. But when Rudy had talked about his daughters, Parker had found himself paying closer attention. The regret in Rudy's voice had been palpable, and watching him die had been excruciating. Parker had lost his father when he was only eighteen, but the brain aneurysm had taken Bill Blake in a flash. Watching Rudy get sicker and weaker had been horrible. But it had also given Parker the chance to say all the things he hadn't been able to say to his dad. Things like "thank you" and "I love you too" and "yes, I promise".

It was that last one that made Parker want to use the baking lessons with Ava for more. Rudy didn't want Ava to be like him—consumed by work, all his relationships about Carmichael Enterprises, all his time spent inside glass and steel buildings in suits and ties.

Since Evan had fallen for Cori on the first day he met her, and Noah had appointed himself Brynn's new best friend and her personal matchmaker—to fulfill *her* requirements, which included dating multiple men in Bliss—that left Parker to help Ava.

For better or worse.

The only thing that had really happened exactly according to Rudy's will so far was that Ava was now baking pies in a little shop in Kansas. She still talked to people back in New York daily and still had a wound-tight energy about her, like a spring that was ready to be sprung any moment. And she still wore her skirts and heels.

Parker would be very happy to help her out of those.

No. He shook his head. He couldn't think like that. This was about the pie shop—*his* pie shop—and Rudy's hopes for his girls.

And since Evan was no longer available, and Noah had his hands full, Parker almost *had* to help Ava meet her dating stipulation as well.

"You think you can do that?" Evan asked. "Make sure she works less? Has some fun?"

"I can get it done," Parker told him. "But you guys can't tell Cori and Brynn."

"Can't tell them what?" Noah asked with a frown.

"That all of this constitutes a dating relationship," Parker said, almost wincing at the word *relationship*. He wanted one of those. Or so he told himself. A nice, simple, steady relationship with a nice, simple, steady girl.

Exactly what his father had wanted for him when he'd thrown a dart at a map and moved Parker and his mother from Chicago to the tiny Kansas town. He'd felt the name Bliss was a sign that this would be the perfect place to escape from his high-pressure job in the city and get his son away from the friends who had turned into bad influences as Parker entered high school.

"Why can't Cori and Brynn know?" Noah asked.

"Because I don't want Ava to know."

"You don't want Ava to know you're dating her?" Evan asked.

"Right," Parker said. At his friends' raised eyebrows, he said, "Look, that woman needs to learn to just go with it sometimes. In a normal relationship, you don't sit down at a conference table, say "let's date", and then spell out the terms of the agreement. You just meet someone, spend time together, and get to know one another. You just let it happen. Ava Carmichael never just lets things happen."

"So you're going to *make her* just let things happen," Noah said.

"I'm going to take her fruit picking and teach her to make pies," Parker said. "Whatever else happens isn't going to be labeled, or put in her planner, or overthought, or overanalyzed.

It's just going to happen and be whatever it is. Like a normal relationship between two people."

Evan finally nodded. "Okay. Yeah. That would count. As long as she doesn't decide that she needs to find someone else to meet that six-month requirement with."

The idea of that sent a hot jolt of what could have been jealousy through Parker—if they'd been talking about *any* other woman and man in any other situation. Since it was Ava, it was probably just annoyance. Like how *annoyed* he'd felt when she'd been pretending to date Evan for the very short period before the guy had realized he couldn't stay away from Cori for even three more months. Parker had definitely felt *annoyed* whenever Evan had put his hand on Ava's lower back or made her laugh.

"She won't," Parker said resolutely. He'd be keeping her too busy to fit anyone else in. "As soon as everyone in town believes that she and I are dating, the other guys will stay away." There was that too. It was a small town, and not only was Parker well respected and liked, there was also a strong bro code in place.

"Good point," Evan said. "Though I don't know how you're going to keep this from her when the whole town knows."

At that, Parker laughed. "Ava isn't really out socializing and chitchatting with everyone, you know? I don't think she'll find out. As long as Cori and Brynn don't say anything."

"I think Cori would think it was a good idea. Get that part of the trust taken care of."

"Brynn too," Noah agreed. "Get it over with."

Parker nodded. "Exactly. And it will keep her from breaking some poor sap's heart who might actually fall for her."

Evan gave him a funny look but nodded again. "Yeah, we definitely want to avoid that."

Parker rolled up the last set of silverware and put it with the rest. Neat and organized and stacked exactly the way they had been every night for the past fifteen years. Just the way he liked things.

———

T he next day, the diner was packed. Every chair, booth, and stool was filled. There were even a couple of guys standing off to one side, leaning against the wall, eating their burgers.

And every single person turned to look as Ava stepped through the front door.

Including Parker. And he almost dropped the plate he was holding.

Holy hell.

Her hair, normally stick straight and sleek, was now pulled back into a ponytail. That alone was strangely sexy. But she also had a pair of sunglasses propped casually on top of her head and the bright red rims matched the T-shirt she wore.

A *T-shirt*. He'd never seen her in a T-shirt. She'd worn a hoodie for the game night she and her sisters had hosted at their house about a month ago, but this...well, this shirt was Cori's. It had to be. It was bright red and said, *In my defense, I was left unsupervised* across her breasts in large sparkly silver script letters.

That quote didn't fit Ava at all. But the shirt itself...it fit against her curves a little too well.

And then there were the jeans. He had never seen her in blue jeans before either. He'd wanted to. In his mind, that was going to be a sign that she was trying to fit into small-town life, and that she was going to figure out how to dress for function and comfort rather than the I'll-take-over-your-company-make-a-million-dollars-by-lunch-and-look-hot-as-hell-while-doing-it look she usually had going.

But the jeans hugging Ava's hips, ass, and long legs were making *his* jeans fit a lot *less* comfortably, and the only functions he could come up with here were inappropriate, probably sexist, and involved smudging the lipstick that matched her sunglasses and T-shirt perfectly.

He supposed that she thought she was dressed for fruit picking.

Until he got to her heels.

His eyes finally made it past the slim-fitting denim to her feet. And these shoes, if nothing else, reminded him of exactly who Ava Carmichael was.

The silence in the diner stretched, all eyes on her, until she smiled and focused on him.

"It's twelve fifty-five."

That's all she said, looking straight at Parker, but several people turned back to their plates and started eating faster.

"Boss is here," Mark Johnson commented to Parker.

"She the boss of you everywhere?" Don Arnold asked under the diner noise so that only Parker, Mark, and Brian Watson heard.

"I'd let her tell me what to do," Brian agreed.

"Shut. Up," Parker told them. But it didn't have a lot of force behind it. He'd expected to get crap about Ava being his boss at the pie shop. And lots of waggled eyebrows and innuendo about the time they spent together.

He didn't care that everyone was enjoying the idea of Ava as his boss. Even outside of the diner. He didn't get too worried about what people thought of him in general. The people here knew him. He'd been the same guy for the past fifteen years and he had no plans to change.

So there was no way anyone here actually thought that he was going to get all worked up about Ava. No way they really thought that he was going to suddenly change all of his habits or shirk his responsibilities even for a chance to peel those blue jeans off of her. So what if he was closing for a couple of hours this afternoon. That was *supposed* to be how this worked every day. Working six a.m. to six p.m. every single day in a little town where everything else was open eight to five left little time for chores at his farm, changing the oil in his truck, errands like

45

picking up a new phone charger, or even stopping at the post office.

And frankly, no one needed a burger at three in the afternoon. He supposed some might say that was just his opinion, but truthfully, it was right. He didn't like the whole breakfast-for-dinner idea either. Don't even get him started on brunch. Breakfast, lunch, and dinner were three distinct meals that each had their own special tastes and style. In his diner, breakfast ended at nine o'clock, lunch ended at one, and dinner ended at six, and that was perfectly reasonable. And had been the schedule for twelve years now. Ever since Parker had taken over.

However, he *did* care that their teasing words about how Ava bossed him around did nothing to get *his* mind away from the idea of her telling him exactly what she liked—how hard, how fast, and how long.

"I'm suddenly in the mood for fruit pie," Mark added.

Parker gave him a stern look. "Knock it off."

It was only because he didn't need his mind wandering to the idea of Ava with pie filling spread all over her...

Fuck.

Parker worked on not reacting. And not moving out from behind the counter that was blocking the erection that was suddenly pressing insistently against his fly.

But he was torn between laughing and rolling his eyes as she crossed the diner, the red purse swinging from her arm, her heels clicking on his tile like some kind of fucking countdown clock ticking away. He simply reached behind the counter and started handing out to-go boxes. Which people filled immediately.

This damned town. He'd been trying to get people out of the diner by one p.m. every day for the past twelve years. But the door rarely closed behind the last customer until at least a quarter after. That was one of those things where he tried to exert some control over that didn't really work. The food really was the only thing he was completely in charge of, it seemed. Yet all Ava had to do was strut in here in her kick-ass red heels and mention the time.

Of course, no one was shoveling their fries in because they were scared of her. It was because they all wanted Parker to get lucky. It should probably be disturbing to think that the entire town was this interested in him getting laid. But he was used to these people being in his business—his actual business and his personal business—and this was exactly where he wanted their minds to be right now.

He didn't respond to Ava as she leaned a hip against the counter next to the cash register, watching as people reached for their wallets. As if she was overseeing her subjects.

Amazingly, the door bumped shut behind the last customer at 1:03 p.m.

Ava hadn't even blinked as people told her to have a good time, and that they were happy she was getting Parker out of the diner for a while and to enjoy the fruit picking. If she'd noticed the way they'd said "fruit picking", she didn't show it. She'd smiled, nodded, and said goodbye sweetly to everyone who had spoken to her.

After they were gone, she crossed back to the door, turned the lock and flipped the CLOSED sign around as if it was her diner, her door and her sign.

4

———

"Ready to go?" Ava asked, turning back to him.

Parker lifted an eyebrow. "My dishwasher is full of dirty dishes, my workstation needs cleaned up, and I have some tables to clear off."

She sighed. "I thought we'd agreed on you spending the time between shifts on pie shop business?"

"This shift isn't really over as long as there's cleanup to do," he said mildly.

"I can't believe you do all of this by yourself," she said, looking around.

He did it by himself because he liked it that way. No one loaded the dishwasher the way he wanted it loaded. No one cut the onions the way he wanted them cut. No one garnished the plates the way he liked it. But when things got crazy, he could call his mom and her best friend to come help. They didn't cook, but they helped with waiting on tables and cleanup. They didn't do it the way he did either, but he could tolerate the differences from them.

Right now, though, they were spending a couple months in

Florida with a friend from high school. Partying like it was 1984, according to her last text.

"Thanks," he said with a lift of his shoulder. He was proud of his business. And yeah, he might occasionally wish he could experiment with creole shrimp pasta or even change up the meatloaf recipe, but for the most part, keeping things the same worked. It allowed him to keep running the place on his own, which was more important than having an expanded menu with new dishes. Routine. Habits. Patterns. Those were good things.

Ava looked back at him. "That wasn't really a compliment. It's very inefficient."

Right. "Well, if you want to get out of here faster, how about you pick up some dishes? Or is your manicure too fresh?"

Yeah, it was a dig at her girly-ness. Because it drove him crazy. In a I-don't-want-to-find-all-of-that-hot-but-I-do way. He didn't want to get turned on by the things that screamed *high maintenance*. He didn't consider himself one to notice lipstick, for instance, but he knew every color Ava had worn this week—and if they made him think of things like cotton candy and red wine and Red Delicious apples, well that was just a symptom of being a food guy. Probably.

"My manicure *is* fresh, as a matter of fact," Ava told him, wiggling her fingers that boasted red nails that matched her shirt, shoes, lipstick and purse. "But I can probably handle carrying some plates and cups."

Parker fought the urge to grin at the way she regarded the dirty dishes on the counter in front of her. Like they were something new and puzzling. Something disgusting and new and puzzling. He waved at the diner as a whole. "Start anywhere. I'll be in the kitchen."

As he straightened up in the back, he listened to the clacking of plates and silverware and the tapping of Ava's heels on the tile and the muttered swearing. He let himself grin then. He heard her cussing a lot when they both had only the screen doors to their restaurants open and she was in there "baking". There wasn't a day that went by that something didn't crash or bang over there. Sometimes it was the metal pie pans and the stainless steel bowls she had, but she'd gone through plenty of glass bowls and measuring cups as well.

He could only imagine that she'd stuck her finger in some leftover ketchup or something when he heard, "fucking disgusting", and he assumed she'd tipped over a not-quite-empty glass when he heard, "son of a bitch".

This was the most entertaining cleanup he'd had in a while.

"Speaking of inefficient," she said, coming through the swinging door with a stack of plates held as gingerly as possible in her hands. "Making a bunch of trips like this is going to take forever. Did the entire damned town come in to eat today?"

Miraculously, she had nothing on her clothes. Not a wet spot, not a dab of mustard, nothing. It was like even the food knew better than to mess with Ava Carmichael.

"They did." He pointed to where she could set the dishes down. "But it's your own fault. Half of those people usually eat well before one, but they all came in late and then stalled so they could be around when I had to throw everyone out."

"They didn't think you'd do it?"

"Oh, they were absolutely hoping I would."

"Why don't you ever make them leave on time?" she asked, tipping her head. "You get all grumpy about the food and the way they eat, but you let them sit around well after closing time."

"Because the food is what really matters," he said simply.

He would love it if people respected his business hours, but he also understood that this was how life in Bliss was. People were laid-back here. It was why he loved this town.

Opening and closing times were estimates. It didn't surprise anyone if they walked up to a storefront and found a "Gone Fishing" sign on the door. Literally. If someone *really* needed something from the pharmacy after five, the pharmacist, Bob Larson, could be reached by his wife's cell phone and he'd come down and open up. But if Bob's granddaughter, Abby, had a piano recital at two p.m., then you'd have to wait until it was over, and Bob had eaten cookies and punch, to get your prescription refilled.

It was what Parker, and everyone else, loved about Bliss. They all just worked together to get everyone what they needed. Though it would just be a lot more convenient if they got out right at one.

But no one got to put ketchup on a steak he made. The food was the one thing he had full control over.

Ava was studying him in a way that made him shift his weight. "What?" he finally asked.

"I get it," she said with a lift of her shoulder. "The stuff that's most you is what you get protective of and worked up about. The rest is just...noise."

Parker had to admit her insight surprised him. "Is that why you swear and throw things when you're making pie?" he asked. "Because it's something you're doing directly and it's not turning out?"

She gave him a slow smile, and Parker felt his heart kick against his sternum as it reached her eyes. "Parker, there is something you really need to understand as we work on the pie shop."

"What's that?"

"I don't give a flying fuck about pie."

That caught him enough off guard that he didn't have time to cover his laugh. "Okay, got it. So what's with the swearing? You just don't like having to do something you don't care about?"

He knew that was true. Ava was the type of woman who was simply good at everything she did. Except pie.

She seemed to hesitate for a moment, then she said, "I care about getting it right mostly because it has to be good for my sisters."

"And your sisters are the most you?" he asked, echoing back her words.

"Taking care of them is the most me," she said. Then she gave him a little half smile and turned to head back to the front of the diner.

"Hey," he said, grabbing a big gray plastic bin and handing it to her. "You can get more in a trip with this."

She took it from him. "Did you let the place get so messy because you intended to make me work?"

He lifted a brow. "I can honestly say that having you bus tables in my diner didn't occur to me for a second."

She laughed and Parker found himself standing in one spot, staring at the door she'd gone through for several seconds longer than he should have.

Wow, picking up other people's dirty dishes was really disgusting.

And it took forever.

This was the third day she'd showed up just before one to get started on her baking lessons, and it was the third day the whole thing was taking so long they weren't going to make it fruit picking. Or even to the pie shop kitchen. The first day she'd believed Parker when he said having her help out hadn't even occurred to him, but she could swear yesterday and now today, the place was an even bigger mess. Either Parker had pulled out every dish and utensil he owned, or people in town had gotten wind that she was bussing tables and had decided to be especially messy.

Ava loaded the plastic bin with another stack of dishes and dumped two plastic water glasses on top. She was half kneeling on the booth to reach the far end of the table so she had to scoot back and push herself out of the booth. In retrospect, she should have kept the bin on the table until she was on her feet, rather than dragging it with her, but she didn't realize that until she tried to stand up.

Her left foot slipped on something wet on the floor, her ankle turned and she pitched to the side, the bin of dishes hitting the floor with an ear-shattering crash. "Son of a bitch!"

Parker came storming through the kitchen door a second later. "What the *hell*?" He scowled at the bin of dishes then up at her. "Are you okay? What happened?"

Well, asking if she was hurt was nice, considering she'd just broken at least five plates and a couple of cups. "I slipped on some water and twisted my ankle."

He scowled at her shoes and muttered something that sounded like "death of me." He strode to the bin and lifted it off the floor, setting it on the table. Then he turned to look at her. His eyes tracked over her from head to toe, and Ava felt some of the jumpiness from the other day before skitter over her skin. "Unbelievable," he said, shaking his head.

"What?" She propped her hands on her hips, feeling like she was bracing for...something. She wasn't even sure what.

"You don't have a single drop of anything on you. And every broken dish is still in the bin. How the hell do you do that?"

She looked down at her clothes. Huh, he was right. She shrugged. "I don't know."

"You're like Teflon or something." He stepped to her and before she realized what he was doing, put his hands on her waist and picked her up.

"Parker!"

But before she could even muster a good protest—though her nerve endings had no idea why she'd be protesting his hands on her—he'd deposited her on one of the stools at the counter.

"Wha—" She tried again, but he squatted in front of her and cradled one of her feet in his palm. He slipped her shoe off and dropped it to the floor. His hand continued to hold her foot, the heat of it sending waves of warmth and prickly awareness up her calf to her thigh and then higher.

He looked up at her as he moved his hands to her other foot and slid that shoe off too.

The opposite of what Prince Charming had done to Cinderella with the glass slippers.

Ava wet her lips, watching him, and was startled to see his gaze drop to her mouth. The warm prickles of sensation intensified.

"You're going to kill yourself on these things," he said as her second shoe dropped to the floor.

"I'm—" She swallowed. "Fine. My ankle is fine."

He held her gaze for a moment. Then he nodded and stretched to his feet. "Good." He reached for her, his hands at her waist again, lifting her off the stool and depositing her on the floor. "Watch out that you don't step in anything weird."

Then he grabbed the tub of dishes and headed into the kitchen.

Yeah, Prince Charming's opposite all right.

She didn't love the barefoot-on-a-strange-floor thing, but she wasn't about to act prissy or squeamish about it. She *was* a little prissy at times. Especially compared to Cori and Brynn. Cori was the daring one and would go anywhere and try anything once. Brynn's mind was that of a scientist and she could rationalize anything. Like the fact that it was *irrational* to be scared of things that could be easily caught or killed—bugs, snakes, and rodents. But overall, Ava was just not the barefoot or blue jeans kind of girl. She liked dressing up and she *loved* her shoes.

But she'd already learned that stiletto heels and slick tile floors didn't go well together over in the pie shop. Most days over there she kicked her shoes off and replaced them with flat, satin slippers. Still, if she was leaving the kitchen, she put her heels back on. Because she liked them. They made her happy. They made a statement without her ever having to say a word. Some of them said I'm-in-charge. Some said I'm-feeling-playful. And others expressed things in between those extremes. The colors, the styles, the heights...they all helped with the message. Today's trip to pick fruit—because they *had* to do *something* pie related today—had inspired her to choose red again today. The red theme she had going on. And every time she looked at the red shoes on her feet, they'd made her smile and anticipate the trip.

And that anticipation was all about the shoes and the fruit. And nothing to do with the idea of spending the day with Parker Blake. It was work. A means to an end. A way to make sure the pie shop was everything Cori needed it to be.

If she had to put up with Parker Blake to do it...and pretend she liked him...well, then, she could probably pull that off.

Even if he kept putting his hands on her. And she kind of hoped he did. *Damn.*

Men didn't touch her without permission. Not that he'd done much. He'd touched her waist and her feet. But yeah, that hyper-awareness she seemed to have around him had washed over her just from that. She did *not* like that jumpy feeling. It wasn't a bad feeling exactly. It definitely wasn't creepy, and it hadn't made her push him away, or pull her foot away, and it had kind of made her feel warm and tingly...

And that was the problem. It was unexpected. He made her feel something she hadn't been prepared for. She didn't like unexpected. She wasn't always the smartest person in the room, or the most creative, or the most powerful, or even the richest. But she was *always* the most prepared. She went over what-if scenarios in her head constantly, a habit so engrained now that she did it without thinking and even in the most normal, mundane situations. Situations that didn't really require a plan B or a plan C. *What if Cori doesn't make dinner tonight, what will we do instead? What if Brynn doesn't get the new plates ordered in time? What if I never figure out how to make a fucking pie?*

Okay, that last one wasn't unimportant. But she'd already

figured out her plan for that one. And, incidentally, for the dinner thing and the plate thing. She always had a backup plan, even when she didn't need one.

What if I keep having butterflies in my stomach and itchy feelings when Parker is around? What if he touches me again? What if I started wanting him to touch more of me?

Lost in her thoughts about Parker, Ava carried a huge stack of plates into the kitchen and came face-to-face with the man that was unexpectedly making her *feel things*. She looked at him as he turned.

And realized she'd been stupid not to do the what-if thing prior to this. Because this awareness of him was not, actually, new. She vividly remembered the first time he'd stepped into the pie shop kitchen, all scowls and sarcasm, telling her that she better figure this all out, and calling her *Boss* in that way that made her *really* want to boss him around.

Dammit. She'd ignored it. How? Why? The attraction didn't make sense. There was nothing about him that made her think she should want him. Well, other than the biceps. And the brown eyes. And the scowls.

The scowls? Ava frowned herself. But yeah, the scowls. She was used to guys who smiled. A lot. With lots of teeth and an enthusiastic handshake and lots of words. Lots and lots of words meant to compliment and convince. Words to show off how smart they were and all they had to bring to the table. Her dinner dates had been undistinguishable from her business meetings.

But Parker Blake didn't smile at people to make them feel more at ease. He didn't say things like "I'd like to talk about how we can further both of our agendas". As far as she could tell, he didn't really have an agenda.

And that was all...attractive. And unexpected.

Dammit.

He drove a truck. He lived in Kansas. He made hamburgers for a living.

And he made her aware of body parts that she hadn't given a lot of thought to in a long time.

"Ava?"

He was watching her with both eyebrows up.

"We should really get going," she managed.

He glanced at the clock and nodded. "Yeah, we should." He pulled a rack of clean, steaming hot dishes from one side of the industrial dishwasher and shoved a full rack of dirty dishes into the other side. "Let me load the last of these and then we'll head out."

She nodded. Then looked around. She'd been in this kitchen a number of times, *borrowing* eggs and butter and sugar and vanilla and a number of things she'd never used in her life. She vaguely recalled baking cookies as a kid, but Cori had always been the one who enjoyed that stuff most. Ava had mostly watched...and taste-tested. She smiled thinking about it now. She and her sisters had been close. They still were, mostly. But things had changed when they were about ten. Their father had developed more of an interest in them and their activities and had spent more time with them then, for some reason. But Ava mentally shook her head. She knew why. He'd realized they were his only hope for heirs to his company and fortune, and he'd decided to start molding them.

"You okay?"

Ava looked up to find Parker watching her. She swallowed. "Yeah. Of course. Just...hungry," she said, grasping for an excuse for her distraction.

Something flickered in his eyes, and Ava found her breath lodged in her throat. Hungry could mean so many things...

"That I can actually help you with," he told her.

And he'd enjoy it. She wasn't sure why those words whispered through her mind just then, but she knew it was true. And she wasn't talking about cooking.

Ava cleared her throat. "I'm sure you can."

Yep, still not just talking about food.

"Do you want a burger or something?" he asked.

It was possibly the strangest thing she'd ever felt, but she had the craziest notion that if she said yes to something on the menu, he'd be disappointed. And why that mattered to her at all, she had no idea. But it worked out, because she wasn't a burger girl.

Her eye caught on a bowl of fruit and vegetables on the center island. "Hey." She crossed to the bowl and picked up an avocado. "You don't have anything on your menu that uses avocado."

He leaned back against the edge of the sink. The dishwasher was still whooshing beside him. He crossed his arms. "You sure about that?"

She widened her eyes. "Trust me, if you did, I would have noticed."

"You like avocado?"

"Who, in their right mind, doesn't like avocado?"

"You'd be surprised."

She tossed it up into the air and then caught it again. Then, on a whim, she tossed it to him. He caught it without moving anything more than his one arm and hand.

"Everyone says you're amazing with burgers," she said.

"I am."

"I don't really like burgers."

"Because you've never had mine."

It was *ridiculous* to feel a hot, tickling sensation down her back from that, but there was something in his low, rumbling voice, and the confidence that exuded from him like the steam from the dishwasher, that made her stand a little straighter. "Well, hot shot, you've been making burgers most of your life. What if I told you that I want something amazing made with avocado. And—" She looked back at the bowl. She picked up a bunch of green onions and a lemon. "And these." She held them up.

He just looked at her for a long moment. Then slowly, one side of his mouth curled up. "I don't take orders in my own kitchen," he said. "And this isn't some damned cooking show on TV."

She'd never watched a cooking show on TV. "So you're saying that you can't make something on the fly with these three ingredients?" she asked. "You can only do the same old recipes you always do here?"

"I am not saying that."

"Okay, then. Do it."

He lifted one eyebrow. Then he shook his head and pushed away from the edge of the sink.

It wasn't as if leaning like that had made him *short*, but as he stretched to his full height, Ava found herself mentally measuring where she'd come up to in her favorite heels. Even in the four-inch Louis Vuittons, the top of her head would maybe come to his nose.

She really freaking loved that.

"I'm doing this only because I'm hungry too," he said, crossing to the fridge.

Ava grinned behind his back. Sure he was. He was totally rising to the challenge she'd just issued. But she didn't care why he was making whatever he was about to make. Parker had bought an avocado. He wasn't the type of guy to have a bunch of stuff lying around that he didn't intend to use. And she wanted in on that. He was a really good cook. Really good. She hadn't had his burgers, but she'd had his tomato basil soup, his grilled chicken sandwich, his white chili, his cheesy baked potato soup... he made a lot of soups, come to think of it. And those didn't make it on the menu either. They were just under Soup of the Day. But they were all really good. Really, really good. She never cared about food that much, but she'd dreamed about that tomato basil soup.

Parker rummaged in his fridge for a few seconds, and Ava unapologetically leaned to the right to get a better look at his butt in the blue jeans he wore. The jeans she had on today were only the second she'd ever bought, and she didn't find them particularly comfortable. They were fine, but she was so used to skirts, it felt strange to have something between her legs.

She blushed as those words went through her mind. Which was really stupid.

Just then Parker straightened, his arms full of food, and she was effectively distracted. So, yes, she had a personal chef. An actual person she paid to come in and cook for her. And she went out a lot. No, she didn't make meals. If her cook had the day off, Ava poured cereal, opened yogurt, scooped cottage cheese. And yes, ate soup from the take-out place on the corner. She loved soup. But that was pretty much it.

He carried everything to the center island and set it all down. There was a package of bacon, two hard-boiled eggs, a container of shredded chicken, and an ear of corn.

The hum of the dishwasher and the sound of bacon frying and Parker chopping filled the air as Ava watched. She could admit she was a little mesmerized. She didn't often watch people preparing food for her either. She'd been in the kitchen with Cori a number of times while she made dinner or dessert, but Ava hadn't really paid attention.

Then again, she didn't think that she'd find it hot to see Cori grasping an ear of corn and slicing the kernels from it with long, sure strokes of a butcher knife.

She did when Parker did it. She also found the way he deftly, but gently, scooped the avocado from its skin, and the way he chopped the bacon, a little hot for some reason. And then there was the lemon squeezing.

He mixed it all together in a glass bowl, then dished it out onto two plates, handing her one with a fork without a word. He was that confident that she'd eat it. And like it. But she was actually a little hungry and this was not on his lunch menu, so she was curious. Maybe he knew how to do more than make soup and burgers.

She scooped up a bite that contained avocado, chicken, bacon, and the lemon and olive oil dressing. She was aware that he was watching her as he also took his first bite. She closed her lips around the tines of the fork and...her taste buds lit up. Ava felt her eyes widen as the salty, lemony tang of the dressing mixed with the other flavors. The textures were divine together, the creaminess of the avocado and the crunch of the bacon a perfect complement to one another.

She might have moaned.

When she looked at Parker, he was still simply watching her. He'd even stopped chewing.

"Wow," she managed, without completely *gushing*. "That's delicious."

He swallowed. "One of my favorites."

"You make this a lot?"

He nodded, taking another bite.

"Why isn't this on the menu?"

There was a little crease between his eyebrows for just a flash before he smoothed his expression and said, "This is a burger town."

"A burger town," she repeated. She took another bite, because she couldn't help it, before continuing. "No one can eat burgers every day."

"That's why I have BLTs and Philly cheesesteaks and Reubens and tuna melts on the menu too." He turned toward the sink, scooping the last couple of bites of the chicken avocado salad into his mouth.

She scooped up another big bite too, then said, "Well, then a sandwich town anyway, right?"

"Yeah, I guess so." He rinsed his plate and then pulled the rack of clean dishes from the dishwasher and shoved the last load inside.

"And soup," she added, taking another bite and chewing slowly, savoring it.

"Yeah, soup too," he said flatly.

"And of course, pancakes and eggs and meatloaf and pot roast and steak and—"

"Do you have a point?" he asked, facing her again.

She took the final bite and considered licking the plate. "Just that it's not only a burger town."

"It's a town where people like what they like."

And she realized that frustrated Parker. Making the same things over and over because people didn't want to try new things. She didn't know why she thought that. He gave no indication he had any emotion about it, really. He stood, feet slightly apart, meeting her gaze directly, his hands tucked into the front pockets of his jeans. He looked almost bored.

But that was what got her instincts humming.

Her father hadn't taught her nursery rhymes or how to throw a ball or about the classics of literature. But he'd taught her about reading people—body language, the things they *weren't* saying, their reactions. And she knew this guy cared about food.

He was completely at home in the kitchen. The look on his face when he'd been mixing everything up was exactly how Cori looked when she was baking. Even back when she'd been making cookies as a kid, she'd had an air of delight about her as she turned several simple ingredients into one delicious concoction. And Cori loved to watch people take the first bite of something she'd created. Ava could swear that Cori got more pleasure from that than she did from eating the food herself. And that was saying something.

Ava swiped a finger through the dressing left on her plate. "Well, I don't care about everyone else. If you just make this every other day for *me*, it will all be good." She lifted her finger to her mouth.

He didn't reply immediately, and Ava looked up. And froze. He was watching her lick the dressing from her finger. His eyes were hot, and Ava felt the snaps of awareness along her nerve endings.

"You think I would cook for just you?" he finally asked, his voice low and with a gruff note around the edges.

Ava dropped her hand and shifted her weight. Dammit. She never shifted her weight. That was a body language signal that confirmed discomfort. But dang, having little fireworks going off all over her body *was* uncomfortable. Why did the idea of Parker cooking—doing something he so clearly loved—just for her, set off those fireworks?

"People do things just for me all the time," she said, putting a note of haughtiness into *her* voice. It was true, after all.

"You don't say," he practically drawled.

5

Okay, he needed to not do *that* anymore. It wasn't a deep southern drawl or a Texas drawl. It was more of a hot-alpha-male drawl. And she was really into that. Apparently.

She shrugged. "People like to be on my good side." Which reminded her of a very obvious way Parker was unique.

"And why would I worry about that?" he asked.

Exactly.

"I'm *a lot* easier to get along with when I'm well fed," she said.

That was true. She didn't have a close, lust-filled relationship with food. She didn't even really like sweets. Which made her owning—and *baking* in—a pie shop ironic. She liked chocolate but preferred it in liquid form. Like hot cocoa. Or a martini. But most of the time she just didn't give a lot of thought to food.

"What's your favorite food?" he asked, surprising her.

"Oh, well, probably..." but she trailed off. Huh. She wasn't sure.

"You don't know?"

"I like...a lot of things."

He didn't look like he believed her. And she wasn't sure she believed her. She liked avocados. And chocolate martinis. And...

the rest was kind of just there. She ate it. She had things she *didn't* like. Beets for one. Things with pumpkin spice for another. And octopus. No thank you.

She decided to level with him. "A lot of my eating happens during business meetings, or social outings that are about networking and making nice with business contacts. So I'm usually a lot more focused on the conversation than I am on the food. I can eat almost anything."

She ate. She had learned the hard way that her mental and physical energy suffered if she skipped meals. But other than beets and octopus—which she doubted she'd run into in Bliss anyway—she could handle most other things.

Parker scowled. "You can eat almost anything," he repeated.

He sounded *very* judgey about that.

"Shouldn't a guy who cooks for a living love people who will eat anything?" she asked, truly curious about why he seemed annoyed.

"People who will eat anything don't really care about what they're eating," he said. "They don't—" He broke off.

"They don't what?"

"They don't actually enjoy it. None of it is special. It doesn't matter to them."

Ava thought about that. He was right. None of the food really ever mattered to her. Except maybe this chicken avocado salad. "You want your food to matter to people?" she asked.

He frowned, and she was sure he wasn't going to answer her. But he shocked her by saying, "Have you ever seen the look on a person's face when a plate of their favorite thing in the world is set down in front of them? Have you ever seen someone try something for the first time and fall in love with it? Have you ever seen someone start off upset or angry or tired and then, after they eat, start smiling and take a deep breath and relax?"

Ava knew her eyebrows were nearly in her hairline. But she felt herself nodding. "I've seen ice cream do that to Cori."

And he cracked a smile. Sparkles of fire danced along her limbs in response.

"Exactly. Food can actually mean something to people. And food is what I do. It's the only thing I really know how to do. So yeah, I want *my* food to matter."

Wow. That was...personal. And she was shocked. She couldn't deny it.

"So the burgers matter to the people around here?"

And the shuttered look was back in his eyes, and his mouth set in a straight line. "I wouldn't go that far," he said.

"But—"

A high-pitched beeping hit the air, and Ava lost her train of thought. She looked around, but Parker reached for the watch on his wrist and pushed a button. The beeping stopped.

"An alarm?"

"We should head back from the fruit picking now," he said wryly.

He'd set an alarm on his watch so he'd leave on time to get back to the diner. Forget all the cooking and low, rough drawling and the hot gaze on her mouth—being on time for stuff was sexy.

Then what he'd said sunk in. "So we missed it again?" she asked. *Dammit.*

"We can go tomorrow," he said.

Of course they could. There was nothing saying today had to be the day. The way Hank had said "fruit picking" the other morning made Ava think that perhaps the town thought they were going to be doing something else entirely. Which was fine. The town thinking she and Parker were having nooners played right into one of her goals here.

If he was going to be in her space on a regular basis and act like God's gift to pie lovers—which he would—then she was going to get something extra out of it. Like closer to completing her dating stipulation.

"I guess so," she said. She glanced at her salad plate. She

couldn't quite regret hanging out in his kitchen today though. And she wouldn't pass up lunch from Parker again tomorrow. Maybe people would just start believing the nooners were happening on his kitchen island.

Of course, the health department might frown on that.

Parker let out a long sigh and she looked up. "Come here," he said, starting for his back door.

"Hang on a second." She hurried to the front of the diner and slipped her heels back on to walk outside. The back parking lot was different from walking around in the diner barefoot. Parker's diner was immaculate, honestly. She would eat that chicken salad off the floor of his kitchen probably. Hell, she might eat that chicken salad out of a dumpster.

She joined him a few seconds later and he pushed the screened door open and let her pass in front of him. She started to turn toward his truck that had been parked in the closest spot to the building the first couple of days after Ava and her sisters had taken over the pie shop. Now he parked a spot over, leaving the closest one for Elvira, the 1937 370-D Cadillac their father had left to them. She supposed that was chivalrous. She hadn't really thought about it before that moment, but yeah, that was nice of him.

She took a step in the direction of Parker's big red truck—stupidly pleased that the truck would go with her heels today—but he caught her wrist, stopping her.

The freaking pricks of sensation went tripping up her arm and she had to resist the urge to pull away from him. It wasn't unpleasant exactly, but it was unnerving.

"In here." He tugged her in the direction of the pie shop's back door.

"Uh..." She followed him, struck by how comfortable he was walking in and out of the shop. It made her wonder how much time he'd spent there with her father. She assumed a lot.

Had Rudy ever slipped next door to borrow sugar? Had

Parker given Rudy baking tips? She'd never, not once in her life, seen her father make so much as a bag of microwave popcorn. The idea that he'd baked pies still amazed her. Had Parker come over during his "downtime" from the diner for pie and coffee with the rest of the guys who'd hung out here on a regular basis? She'd gotten to know Hank and Ben and Walter and Roger over the last three months. Brynn handled the "waitressing" duties, as she was supposed to, and Cori joked and teased with them. But Ava found herself drifting to the front of the shop more often when they were there, or even blatantly standing near the swinging door that separated the front of the shop from the kitchen. The men loved to talk about...well, anything really. But they told stories about the town, about Evan, Parker, and Noah— the guys who had seemingly been appointed to oversee the girls' transition to life in Bliss—and everything in between. And they talked about Rudy.

The Rudy Carmichael everyone in this town had known was a very different man from the one who had seen his triplet daughters only every other weekend and who had clearly been more comfortable as Ava's boss than as her father.

The thoughts and memories of her father made it feel like someone was playing ping-pong with her heart in her chest. She went back and forth between emotions. She felt like she could never settle on just one thing—one feeling, one memory, one idea of him. And she felt a little dizzy and bruised if she dwelled on it all for too long. She'd known him as the man she'd most wanted to win over. And she had. Eventually. She knew she had. He'd never said it, but she knew it because he'd finally felt like he could leave the company, leave New York, and find some peace and happiness. He'd found it in a tiny Midwestern town, of all places. And he'd started making pies. But she believed he'd been happy here and that mattered to her. As did the fact that she'd finally proven she could run the company for him while he kicked back in Kansas.

And then he'd made *her* come here.

"There's something you should see," Parker said solemnly, dropping her wrist as he stopped in front of the storage room door.

Ava wasn't sure that was a great lead-in for a guy to use on a woman he didn't know very well. "Oh?"

He reached for the knob, but before he turned it he asked, "You haven't spent much time in here, have you?"

"The storage room? No," Ava said. She wasn't nervous right now. Just curious. And she thought that was an important realization. Considering how jumpy Parker made her feel, it was good to realize and admit that it wasn't about nerves or trust. It was purely physical awareness. She didn't like it, but it wasn't something she was *concerned* about.

He looked over at her, his hand still on the door. "Have you *ever* looked inside this room?"

She narrowed her eyes. "I glanced inside. Once."

"Where do you keep your pie filling and ingredients?" he asked.

She waved toward the cupboard behind her. "There is so much storage space in this kitchen it's ridiculous. Everything's in cupboards."

Apparently, the pie shop had been a dime store and soda fountain years ago. Evan said Rudy had chosen to remodel this building because it was next to Parker's diner—and Parker's refusal to add dessert to his menu was the reason Rudy needed a pie shop in the first place—and because he'd liked the front windows. But he'd had to put a lot of other work into it, like putting up a wall to separate the front from the kitchen, plus adding to the kitchen area. But he'd simply put in appliances, countertops, and cupboards that he'd salvaged from around town. Nothing matched in here, and none of it was restaurant quality. The stove had come from a woman who had remodeled and gotten new appliances. Rudy had bought the fridge from a guy who was cleaning out his late mother's house. He'd gotten the countertop from a contractor who did remodels and had extra. He'd taken the cabinets and cupboards out of a house they were tearing down. And there were a lot of cupboards. Especially considering Rudy had owned and used exactly one set of mixing bowls, three wooden spoons, a couple of spatulas, a set of measuring cups and spoons, and a hand mixer. And pie pans, of course. Definitely not enough to fill the plethora of cupboards and drawers he'd put in.

The whole thing still baffled Ava after spending time in his Madison Avenue office building in Manhattan. Everything there had been high-end, sleekly professional, and incredibly sophisticated.

Here the fridge was yellow and the stove was white. And both had clearly seen better days.

Parker shook his head. "Okay, so you haven't seen this." He pulled the storeroom door open and flipped on the light, stepping inside. He glanced back at her. "Come on."

"Get into the storage closet with a guy I barely know when no one is around to hear me scream? I don't think so." It was weird that she didn't feel like the *barely know* part was completely accurate. She'd met him three months ago, and they didn't spend long periods of quality time together, but she still felt like she knew him. Kind of.

And then Parker did the most awareness-skittering-all-over-her-body thing he could have done. He laughed. A real, full laugh.

She stared at him. And decided she not only *would* get into that storage room with him, she might not want to come back out for a very long time.

"What's so funny?" she asked, propping one hand on her hip.

"I didn't peg you for an exhibitionist," he said, still grinning.

"Excuse me?"

"You *want* people to hear you scream." His voice dropped

lower. "And, darlin', there's only one reason for you to be screaming when I'm around."

Parker Blake was *flirting* with her? He had just called her "darlin'"? And her mind would not stop replaying the words *only one reason for you to be screaming when I'm around.* But she was a single, heterosexual woman with a decent sex drive. It didn't mean anything special that she was responding to that. Probably. She tipped her head. "You mean screaming in frustration, right?"

He just grinned and pointed at the metal shelving unit that occupied the east side of the room. It was filled with glass jars. "Do you know what that is?"

She finally gave up and stepped in next to him. The room— really more of a closet— wasn't very big. And Parker took up a lot of space. She made herself focus on the jars. The labels were handwritten and said, *Apple, Cherry,* and *Peach.*

She frowned, then looked up at Parker. "It looks like pie filling."

"Bingo."

"*This* is pie filling?"

"Rudy's pie filling," Parker told her.

Her head whipped around and she stared at the jars. "He *made* his own pie filling?" Well, of course he had. Obviously you needed pie filling if you were making pie. But he made it and canned it and stored it?

"How do you think people make pies around here when it's not apple or cherry or peach season?" Parker asked.

"Oh." She considered that. Then admitted, "I never thought about it."

"He picked his own. Then canned it."

"Huh." So she didn't need to go pick any fruit. Not that she'd been dying to do that anyway, but it had seemed like a way to spend time with Parker that was both business and social. As far as everyone else knew. "I think canning pie filling is going to be a little beyond me," she said thoughtfully. Hell, she hadn't even mastered the pie-from-scratch-thing yet.

He picked a jar from the shelves then moved toward the door, forcing Ava to either move with him, or stand still and end up plastered against him. Which she considered for a few seconds longer than she should have needed to. She scooted for the door and moved out into the kitchen as he clicked off the light.

"I think canning is going to be a little beyond you too," he said, handing her the jar. "You'll notice the labels all have the fruit as well as a number on them. Each number is a different recipe. You know that he never found the perfect one."

Apparently, according to Evan, Rudy had been trying to recreate a pie that tasted like his grandmother's had when he'd been growing up. He'd never quite gotten there, though he'd tried hundreds of combinations of ingredients. For a second, sadness gripped her chest and she had to pull in a deep breath. She hated doing things she wasn't good at, and she knew Rudy had been the same way. Not being able to recreate that recipe had to have driven him a little crazy.

Not having a recipe here was driving *her* a little crazy. Literally. And metaphorically. She'd followed her father's recipe for business since the first day she'd set foot in his office on Take Your Daughter to Work Day. And it had worked. It had turned out beautifully.

Here in Bliss, he'd never found a specific recipe to follow. And yet, he'd been happier here than ever. But he didn't have anything exact to pass on to her, nothing for her to replicate. Literally. And yes, again, metaphorically.

"What do you want me to do with those jars?" she asked, looking down at the label that was clearly written in her father's handwriting. That also made her chest tighten. She missed him. They hadn't had a perfect relationship, but she'd always felt like she'd known him better than most.

And then she'd met Parker and Evan and Noah. And realized

that maybe she'd known Rudolph Carmichael, CEO, but she hadn't really known Rudy. The man. The friend. These guys had. And she was jealous of that.

"Your homework," Parker said.

She glanced up. "What do you mean?"

"Take five jars, taste them, and compare and contrast. I'll expect you to be able to discuss the similarities and differences tomorrow."

She stared at him. "Seriously?"

"Seriously."

"You want me to make five pies and then just...taste them?"

Parker gave a small eye roll. "Just the filling. Use a spoon. I don't think your diet plan will suffer too much."

She frowned. "I wasn't worried about my diet plan."

"Then what?"

"I just—" She glanced down at the jar again. "I don't know what I'm doing."

There was a short stretch of silence before he said, "Put your phone away, turn off your computer, sit down and breathe. Then open the jars and taste them. Focus on the ways they're the same and the ways they're different. Tune in. Give it your full attention for ten fucking minutes."

She frowned at him and his harsh tone. "Hey."

"Do you deny that you're always doing ten things at once? That you're always working while you eat? That sometimes, two hours after a meal, you have to really think about what you ate to remember it?"

He seemed personally offended by all of that.

But she had to shake her head. "I don't deny any of that." Because he was completely right.

"So, your homework," he repeated the word, almost as if he was relishing it—and the idea of ordering her to do it, "is to shut everything else off and focus on what you're putting in your mouth for a few minutes."

Ava had never realized what a dirty mind she had, but *what you're putting in your mouth* definitely tripped off some not-very-ladylike thoughts. She swallowed and nodded. "Fine."

"Fine." He gave a satisfied nod.

"Are we going fruit picking though?" she asked quickly.

She didn't want to, exactly, but she had a notion that Parker wasn't going to let her get away with just using her dad's pie filling. He was going to want to use his own recipes for one thing. So she needed to know what her dad's filling tasted like before she could know how Parker's was different. And then she had to put Parker's in her mouth too. She hid a naughty smile, shocked by herself and not about to explain why she was grinning to him.

"Ava, I have to tell you something," Parker said, again solemnly.

"What?"

"I can't take you fruit picking."

She frowned. "Why not?"

"There's no fruit in season right now."

She shook her head. "But it's spring. Things grow in the spring, right?" This was the heart of farm country in America. This is where they grew things. That was pretty much all they did here.

"Things are planted in the spring," he agreed. "But these things take time."

He was being completely patronizing. But she had to admit that her assumptions may have been naïve. She'd taken biology in high school. Hell, she could have looked all of this up.

Then her eyes widened. "This is why Hank and the guys were all winking at each other when they talked about us going fruit picking."

Parker nodded and slipped his hands into his front pockets. There was a hint of a smile on his lips. "Pretty much."

Well, *that* certainly worked for the story about her and Parker being more than boss and employee. Ava hid how pleased she was with that. "Huh. Well, I guess I'm going to have some explaining to do."

Parker pulled in a breath, then let it out, seemingly considering something. "Tell you what. We'll pick fruit. When it's in season. Okay?"

"When are apples in season?"

"Fall."

Oh. Her six months of dating would be up in early September.

"But strawberries will be ripe...in June."

That would work. But... "Strawberry pie isn't on our menu."

"It should be."

She thought about that. Cori had been coming up with some specialty pies, but hers were more unique. Things like s'mores pie, and bacon and Nutella pie, and a root beer float pie. Strawberry would be different but not crazy. And it was something they could make sure everyone knew Parker had contributed. The pie shop was going to be his and Cori's together. He needed a chance to put his mark on it too. "Okay."

He gave her a quick nod. "Okay, so it's a...plan."

Had he almost said date?

"Great," she agreed.

"Then I'll see you tomorrow for the first lesson."

"Okay." It definitely felt like her employee was making a lot of decisions all of a sudden. She frowned, but couldn't quite work up the motivation to put him in his place. Maybe because making decisions and telling her what to do when it came to pie *was* his place.

He headed for the door and she suddenly felt like she didn't want him to leave. They'd had a nice time together. Strangely. "I thought you said you were giving the pie shop your time every *other* day?" she said.

"I did say that," he agreed, his hand on the screen door.

"Already making an exception?" she asked, her tone teasing.

"Well, tomorrow isn't about the pie shop," he said.

"Oh." She frowned. "What's it about then?"

He lifted a shoulder. "You." Then he was gone.

The screen door slapped shut behind him, and Ava found herself staring at it for several long seconds.

She wasn't used to being surprised. She wasn't used to a man making her want to take her clothes off simply by grinning and laughing. And she definitely wasn't used to being in the aftermath of a meeting or a negotiation and still feeling off-balance and like she didn't know what the hell was going on.

But that was all exactly how Parker Blake made her feel.

She looked down at the jar in her hand.

And she was going to be taste-testing pie filling tonight. And writing up an essay about it.

Because if Parker thought he was going to challenge her to something like this and *not* end up with a typed essay in a plastic report cover in his hands, he didn't know anything about her.

———

"L et's talk about loopholes."

Evan looked up at Parker with an expression that was part amused and part curious. "I love loopholes," he said, setting his coffee cup down.

Evan was a lawyer, so loopholes—closing and opening them —were part of the job. But it was also personal for him. Cori was only his girlfriend right now because of a loophole in Rudy's will.

And Parker was beginning to think that had been Rudy's intent all along. To make them all really look at what they wanted and then work for it.

"Is it really okay for someone else to be in the kitchen helping Ava? The will doesn't say she can't have any help at all. Just not from her sisters. Right?"

"Right."

"You're *sure*? Because I do *not* want to be a CFO in New York City."

"I'm definitely, completely, absolutely sure," Evan said.

He wanted the pie shop products to improve, and it was a smart move for the business that would be *his* down the road. Even if Cori called dibs on the kitchen overall, he didn't think she'd be opposed to using his recipes. She'd come up with some fantastic specialty pies—s'mores and PB & J for instance—but Ava was still the one faking her way through the classics they were currently serving to customers, like cherry and apple.

"Why? You going to make Ava your sous chef?" Evan asked with a grin.

The idea of being in charge with Ava was way too appealing. Especially now that he'd fed her. Technically, yesterday hadn't been the first time. She'd eaten his food before. But he'd never watched her do it.

It seemed ridiculous that chicken salad could be seductive, but that was *his* chicken salad. His creation and something he made for himself. He didn't make that for anyone else.

And then there had been the way she'd closed her eyes. And the moaning.

Food—making it and eating it—could be a very sensual thing, of course. It could be an intimate thing to feed someone. Food was a basic human need. Right up there with breathing and sex. It was a way to nurture, to comfort, to reward. And yesterday with Ava, it had felt like a bonding experience. The people he typically fed were people he'd known for years, people he cared about, people who appreciated him. Ava wasn't any of those things. And yet feeding her seemed more exciting somehow. He had no idea if she was an adventurous eater, but living in New York City, if she *wasn't* adventurous, or at least eating a huge variety of foods from around the world, that would be a tragedy. He also felt challenged by her. She wasn't overly impressed with him to start with. Or with anything, it seemed. But she'd been impressed with his chicken salad. That was something. He liked the idea that a small-town boy from Kansas might be able to surprise her with nothing but a few herbs, a whisk, and his hands.

And that sounded dirtier than he would have expected.

But it had definitely seemed seductive and intimate when she put things into her mouth that he'd had in his hands. The pleasure she'd gotten from it absolutely had been.

Parker shifted and cleared his throat. "If we're baking, she'd be my pastry chef," he told Evan. "But yeah, kind of."

He didn't cook for the women he dated. He always used the excuse that he cooked all day long and liked when someone else was in charge of the meal. Which wasn't *untrue*. So they went out to eat. But the full truth was, cooking was personal for him. And the idea that he might make something and they wouldn't like it, or would want to add ketchup, made his eye twitch. And he'd definitely never fed a woman in his kitchen at the diner before. He was never spontaneous about food. Or turned on by avocados.

But he didn't shy away from nice restaurants and candlelight. So why was chicken salad and avocados feeling sexier than any other dinner he'd had with a woman?

Because this kitchen means more.

He knew the answer even before the words formed in his mind. His kitchen at the diner was more his than any other place in town. Even his house. Because he'd shared it with his father first. Because this was where he was most *him*. Because here he was fully in charge and did things his way. Because this was where he felt talented and successful and fulfilled.

Which was probably why it had felt like Ava was intruding even more in his personal space when she was sneaking into his kitchen than if she'd showed up at his house and stolen his television. Which was probably why it made him more irritable too. Plus, she'd been stealing his butter. He'd considered buying a cow recently with the number of trips he'd been making to the store to restock.

"There's nothing to prevent that," Evan told him.

Parker blinked at him. There was nothing to prevent Ava from stealing his butter? Or there was nothing to prevent her from getting under his skin and driving him nuts? Yeah, he'd been afraid of that.

"You can definitely help her in the kitchen," Evan said, watching him carefully.

Right. The helping her in the kitchen, thing. *Her* kitchen. Which would absolutely not feel as intimate. He'd hung out with Rudy over there from time to time but he'd never worked over there. And it definitely wasn't *his*. Yet. Nor was it really Ava's. Her heart wasn't over there. So it was just a kitchen. And they were just going to be making pie.

Parker didn't have a bell over the door to the diner like the pie shop now did. But he didn't need it to know that someone had just walked in. And he didn't need to turn around to know that it was Ava. It was as if the energy in the room shifted. Or heightened. Or something.

He glanced over to find her heading straight for him. She was in one of her skirts and another pair of heels. These shoes were black, but her skirt was red. Of course. Ava wore a lot of red. As in, she had something red on every day. Whether it was her blouse or her skirt or her shoes or her accessories, she always had red somewhere. She often wore black. But she also wore navy blue and gray. All of which, apparently, went with red. He sighed, even as his body tightened. He should *not* know that. He should also not like those skirts and shoes. Since when did women's clothing really have such an effect on him? Okay, clothing that wasn't jeans, anyway. He loved a woman in blue jeans. He especially had loved Ava in blue jeans. With her fucking red high heels.

She stopped in front of the counter next to Evan.

"It's only twelve twenty," Parker told her with a frown that had a lot more to do with the sudden tightness behind his fly than it did with her being there early.

"I know." She handed him a booklet. It was bound in a plastic report cover. The spine of which was red. Of course. It also had colored tabs.

"What's this?"

"The results of the pie filling taste-test," she told him. She pointed. "The red tabs are my references and the blue are the photos."

"Photos?"

But she'd slipped behind the counter and was tying on an apron. An apron that she'd brought with her. That was white with tiny red cherries all over it. And a ruffle around the edge.

Ava Carmichael didn't seem like the ruffle type. And yet, she looked absolutely fucking perfect in that apron.

6

P arker rolled his eyes. God, he was a fucking mess. He was all about the food. So that was one thing. But now *aprons* turned him on? And this wasn't some Oedipus thing he had going on where he associated aprons with nurturing from his mother as a child. Patty Blake hadn't so much as baked a cookie her entire life. When they'd lived in Chicago, they'd had a cook and when they'd moved to Bliss, his father had, obviously, been the cook in the family. Patty was great with the customers and loved to pitch in and help with dishes and chopping and clean up and such. But she didn't go near the griddle or the oven. And she made no apologies for it either.

No, he didn't want a wife who would stay home and bake all day or whip up amazing four-course meals. That apron and the tiny cherries that seemed to mock him were all about the woman inside it.

"Are you finished?" Ava asked Al Jenkins, who was sitting at the lunch counter.

"Uh, yeah, I guess," Al said. He was probably distracted by the cherries too as Ava picked up his plate and carried it to the kitchen. And possibly the perfect breasts filling out the top part of that apron.

Parker, on the other hand, was enjoying the view from behind, where the apron's bow tied at the small of her back and where the apron opened as if to frame the gorgeous ass in the red skirt that seemed at odds with the frilly apron. He went ahead and continued to appreciate the view the rest of the way down to the shoes that were in no way practical for any job that required an apron.

"You have an apron?" Parker asked as she came back through the door. He'd never seen her wearing one when she snuck—or stomped—into his kitchen for supplies, or the times when he'd stomped into *her* kitchen to demand to have his butter back.

Of course, that never worked. She'd always used it by the time he went after her, but it still gave him an excuse to see her and spar with her a little.

Parker felt his eyebrows slam together at that though. He did *not* go over there just to see her. He didn't want to see her. He didn't enjoy their tiny arguments over butter.

So why did he keep having them? Why didn't he keep his back kitchen door shut—and locked? Why didn't he hide his butter?

He was going to think about all of that. Later.

"I got it this morning," Ava said, turning to show off the apron. As if he hadn't already checked out every cherry and ruffle.

"Where did you get it?" Parker asked. No place in Bliss sold aprons.

"From the post office."

"You ordered it?"

"My assistant did."

"You have an assistant?"

"Of course I have an assistant," she said, perturbed. "And my assistant has two assistants."

Right. Her assistant in New York. The one that worked for her at Carmichael Enterprises. "She bought you an apron?"

"She ordered it and overnighted it here for me."

In the time it had taken her to ask her assistant for assistance, she could have ordered the damn thing herself. But she'd probably never placed an order for anything in her life. Parker reached behind the counter and pulled out one of the white waist aprons he wore. He held it up.

Ava lifted a brow. "That does not go with my outfit."

He looked at it. "It's white. White goes with everything."

She gave him a pitying look. "Let's just say that mine is a lot cuter."

Cuter. Also not a word he'd typically apply to Ava. Or assume she would use. Ava was a lot of things—sharp, intelligent, bossy, intimidating, gorgeous—but cute was not on the list.

Except when she wore a frilly apron with cherries on it. It was probably a good thing that she *hadn't* worn that apron before, come to think of it. She seemed a lot more...approachable, or something...in it.

"And you needed to look cute?" he asked.

"When the alternative is looking *not* cute, then yes," she said, her gaze running over him from head to toe, clearly insinuating the not-cute thing applied to him.

He moved in closer to her and watched her pupils dilate. "You don't find me *cute*, Boss?"

She wet her bottom lip and looked up from his tennis shoes, past his apron, over his chest and to his eyes. Slowly. "Nope."

He gave her a half grin. "Darn."

"What I do find you is in my way," she told him, stepping past him, and putting an elbow into his side as she did it, nudging him back.

He watched as she refilled a water glass, picked up another plate from the lunch counter, then started on the tables. She picked up dishes, handed out to-go boxes, and chatted with everyone while at the same time making it clear that they all needed to start wrapping lunch up.

He felt...flummoxed.

And he didn't like it.

"You okay there, Parker?" Evan asked, sounding more than a little amused.

"Not really," he muttered.

Evan laughed. "I think it's genetic."

"Me not being okay?"

"All of...that."

Parker glanced over as Evan waved in Ava's general direction. His gaze found Ava again. "But Cori's so bright and bubbly and Ava's...not."

"But they have a way of taking over a room and making it impossible to ignore them."

"I should have asked Brynn out," Parker said, almost under his breath. "I knew it."

Again Evan laughed. "Because she's the sweet, quiet one?"

"Exactly."

"Yeah, well, that doesn't seem to have helped Noah ignore her."

That much was true. And was the reason Parker couldn't ask the introverted scientist out now. She and Noah were...friends. Close friends. He knew for a fact it hadn't gone beyond that. Yet. But there was something about the two of them together that made it seem wrong to even think about taking the middle triplet out to a movie.

But he wanted sweet. And quiet. He wanted someone who would just let him do his thing and she'd do her thing and they'd coexist contentedly, with lots of routine and habits and... He frowned as Ava approached Al at the front counter again. And no *surprises*. He wanted to know the woman he was with was exactly who he thought she was and would do exactly what he thought she would do. At least when they weren't having rocking, blow-his-mind sex. That was the one time when some noise and few surprises would be just fine.

He watched Al grin and Ava laugh, and he shook his head. He definitely wanted sweet, unassuming, not-pushy, and not-bossy. But without any conscious thought, his gaze dropped to Ava's heels and he added *looks like a sex goddess and makes me want to do more than cook on my center kitchen island.*

Ava turned toward him, and Parker wondered if he'd said any of that out loud accidentally. She came to stand in front of him but didn't say a word as she continued to watch him. And reach for him. And into the center pocket of his apron.

His body tensed and he felt like his nerve endings were being touched with the tip of a fireplace poker. It was hot and sharp, almost painful.

The slide of the stack of order receipts from his pocket sent a jolt of awareness from his scalp to the soles of his feet. He honest-to-God had never felt that before. It was...

Then she broke eye contact to look down at the slips of paper she held. And Parker could suddenly think again.

"What the hell are you doing?"

She flipped through the papers, then looked over her shoulder at Al. "Reuben and fries?"

"Yep."

She tucked the other receipts into her pocket and turned on her heel, handing Al his ticket without answering Parker.

"It's not added up," Al told her.

She put a hand on her hip. "How long have you been coming here, Al?"

"As long as the diner's been here."

"And how often do you order a Reuben and fries?" she asked.

"Probably once a week."

"And has the price of anything on this menu changed?" She glanced at Parker. "Ever?"

"No," Al admitted.

"Then get your phone out, put the amount that you usually pay in there, add a twenty-five percent tip, and I'll meet you at the register."

Parker shook himself. What the hell had just happened? "You're covering the register too now?" he asked as she moved past him, a puff of air that smelled surprisingly like apples, floating behind her.

She was taking over his diner.

Of course she was.

"I'm really good at taking money from people," she told him with a smile.

That was almost flirtatious. No. No, no, no. He most definitely did not want apple-scented bossiness taking over and *flirting* with him.

He started to reply, but saw Pam Conner and Tina Lawrence watching from one of the booths with a smile. Ah. Right. He was supposed to be the three-months-left boyfriend. Crap. She was driving him nuts. He didn't know why Ava was flirting with him, but he couldn't shut it down. Not for about eleven weeks, two days and twelve hours, give or take.

"Anything you'd like me to do?" he asked Ava, quietly, with lots of sarcasm but also a smile. That he hoped didn't seem too fake.

"As a matter of fact, you could go in the kitchen and start cleaning up so we can get out of here on time today," she said, also quietly and also with a smile. That looked a little forced.

But she had a point. He did need to get her working on the pies and he couldn't do that here. Well, he could, of course. He had a *kitchen,* after all. And seemingly, a lot of the supplies that Ava needed. But he would not bake with her here. Making her chicken salad was bad enough. He wasn't going to spend even more time with her back there. Feeding her. Showing off new recipes that no one else would appreciate. Watching her lick the spoons...

Parker mentally slapped himself. He was *not* going to cook or bake with Ava Carmichael in the diner's kitchen. Period.

He watched as she bumped the kitchen door open with her hip, shooting him a look that clearly said, "come on already" as she disappeared through it.

"I know that it *seems* like she's working for you here," Evan mused. "But doesn't it kind of feel like she's in charge?"

"Shut up," Parker told him flatly, not looking away from the swinging door.

Evan just laughed. "She also seems very eager to be alone with you."

"She's—" Yeah, she really did. He knew it was because he'd told her she needed to learn to make pie, and he was her means to that end. But this could definitely work in his favor. He looked at his friend. "She is definitely eager to be alone with me." That was true. It might not be for what Evan was insinuating—and what everyone was, hopefully, thinking—but she was definitely going to do whatever she could to make sure she had him to herself.

"What's that about?" Evan asked.

Parker looked around and raised his voice slightly. It wouldn't hurt to have a few people overhear this. And assume what they wanted to about what he said. "We never got to the fruit picking the other day. Or the day after that," he said. "Never made it out of the kitchen."

Evan lifted a brow, but he simply said, "Oh."

Parker was sure Al had heard him and, with any luck, so had Pam and Tina.

"And what's *that* all about?" Evan asked, pointing at the report Parker still held.

He looked down at the bound pages. She'd done a report. With a plastic cover and colored tabs. Damn. That should not be hot. Or funny. But it was both. Or rather, *she* was both. And that was a problem.

"I made her taste-test pie filling."

"Seriously?"

Parker wasn't sure if Evan's surprise came from the idea of anyone *making* Ava do something, or if it was the pie filling part. He nodded. "Seriously."

"And she wrote a report about it?"

"Evidently."

"Wow," Evan said, nodding. "Look at you, being in charge. I didn't realize you had a professor-grad student fantasy."

Parker gave him a look. "I don't."

"But you do have an Ava fantasy. And you made her write a report," Evan pointed out.

"I didn't *make* her write a report," Parker said.

Then belatedly realized he should have protested the first part as well.

"So maybe *she's* the one with the professor-grad student fantasy," Evan mused. Putting that thought firmly into Parker's mind. And imagination. Exactly where he did *not* want it.

"She's just being a smart-ass," Parker said. "But I knew when I gave her the assignment she'd..." He trailed off, realizing that none of that discounted anything about any fantasies. And now he was picturing a big, solid, very sturdy wooden desk. And Ava in glasses.

Crap.

"You knew she'd do a report?" Evan asked.

"No. But I knew she'd do the taste-testing. She likes being challenged." He scratched his jaw and worked on not grimacing. That was all sounding *very* sexual.

"Does she now," Evan said, thoughtfully.

"She loves stuff like this," Parker said, waving the report in his hand.

Plastic report covers and colored tabs were very in character for Ava. Making a mess in the kitchen, less so. He straightened as a realization hit him. Ava didn't like messes. But she made them when trying to make her pies. She made huge messes actually. Usually because she got frustrated and threw things around her kitchen. But it clearly irritated her and made her uncomfortable. But messes were a part of cooking. He loved organization and having everything clean and in its place too. But when he was actually cooking, he let go of that. He lost himself in the scents and textures and colors. He didn't worry about splashes and spills. He cleaned up immediately after cooking, but for the time it took to create, he let it all go, and it was...therapeutic. It was true that Ava seemed immune to getting dirty. Not so much as a crumb touched her skirts, and she never had even a dribble of anything on her shoes. That had to mean that she wasn't really getting into it.

"She's into charts and graphs and shit?" Evan asked with a wince.

Organization and schedules and planning were not Evan's thing. Which made him perfect for the spontaneous and creative Cori. And vice versa. Their house would probably be a mess, but they'd be having a hell of a good time in the midst of all the clutter.

"Definitely," Parker said, feeling a sense of accomplishment at having figured something out about Ava. And a hint of anticipation, if he wasn't mistaken. He could teach her so much more than how to make pies. He could teach her to get a little dirty. And how great that could feel. And he didn't even mean that in a sexual way. At least not entirely. If anyone needed to learn to unwind, it was Ava. And he didn't mean *that* in a sexual way either. At least, not entirely.

"Hell, you two are perfect together then," Evan said.

Like a bucket of cold water had just drenched him, Parker felt shock, then cold, then heat pump through his system as another very important realization about Ava hit him. He shook his head but lowered his voice, as he was aware of the people around him. "No. Fuck no, even."

Ava wasn't the type of woman to just take advice or to learn something new and tuck it away. She was driven. She was incredibly focused. She got shit done. And if he *did* convince her to get a little messy and enjoy baking then...he'd be screwed. She would go all in, one thousand percent, get all caught up. He couldn't have that. *His* messes were therapeutic and pleasurable. Hers would be...messing up *his* world. He could deal with his own stuff. He could handle messes he created and contained. But he couldn't get someone like Ava all fired up and going at it without getting some of her mess on his.

And he didn't mean that sexually either. Probably.

Evan just laughed as if he hadn't just sent a chaotic mix of emotions and thoughts coursing through his friend's system. "I'm just saying, if you show her your inventory system, she'll be all over you."

Yeah. His inventory system was awesome. Ava would love it. So he had to keep that, and all of his other *stuff*, under wraps. She needed to see only the laid-back, grumpy diner owner next door. Who was being put out by having to teach her to bake. Who was taking over the pie shop only because it had been important to Rudy. Who was willing to help her, and the shop, out because it was going to be his someday. Not because it drove him insane the way she was going about everything. And not because he actually liked the idea of being creative over in the pie shop in a way he couldn't be in the diner.

He hid—and tried to resist as much as possible—the organized, dot-every-I, color-coded side of his personality because it went against everything his father had wanted for himself and his family when he'd moved them to Bliss. The drive, the give-everything-one-hundred-and-ten-percent, the always striving for more, for bigger and better, had killed his father.

Bill had moved them to Bliss three years before the aneurysm hit. It had been his hope that Bliss, and its laid-back, simple life-style and relaxed routine, would save his and Parker's life. It had probably given him three years more than he would have had under the stress of his job in Chicago. But the sixteen-hour days, the lack of exercise, the pressure and strain of being in the financial world of Chicago had caught up with him anyway. The doctors had told them that aneurysms sometimes happened for no apparent reason. But in Bill's case, there were definitely contributing factors.

Parker was determined to enjoy the life his father had given him here in Bliss. He was going to breathe deeply of the fresh air, take time to appreciate the people in his life, do the things that made him happy. And resist the urge to knock down walls to expand the size of the diner or add to the menu or open another location. Just because those things occurred to him, didn't mean he had to act on them. His restlessness simply meant that he needed a hobby or something. And yes, he kept binders that had color-coded tabs in them. And yes, he was a stickler about the food. Otherwise, he was laid-back and fucking *relaxed* about things. He let customers linger past closing time, didn't he?

"Yeah, well, I don't want her all over me. Or my business," he told Evan quietly. "I don't want anyone organizing me."

"Or bossing you."

"That too." He took a deep breath. "Well, I'd better get in there," Parker said, a little louder. "If she's working this hard to get me alone, can't make her wait too long."

"I don't know what you're doing exactly," Evan said, clearly confused by Parker's *fuck no* a minute ago and now saying that he'd better get in to Ava. "But this is going to be entertaining."

Parker started for the kitchen. At least he knew what he was doing in there. Mostly.

As his hand hit the swinging door, he heard a clatter, a clicking, and then another clatter.

The first sound was the clatter of metal on metal. The click was high heels on tile. And the second clatter was plate on plate. He'd know those sounds anywhere.

When the door swung open, Ava was putting plates into the dishwasher rack. But he glanced at the stove where he had soup simmering. In a metal pot. There was a spoon resting on the stovetop next to the pot. A spoon that would definitely make a clattering noise against that pot.

"I've got that." He moved in next to her, setting the report he still carried up on the shelf above the dishwasher and reaching for a plate.

She faced him. "I'll finish these. Have you read that?" She gestured toward the report.

He lifted a brow. "You want me to read it now?" He'd known better than to think she'd been joking with the report. Someone else might have put blank pages inside the report cover just to mess with him. But Ava would *enjoy* doing the report. He was sure the report was thorough and perfect too. Not a single typo to be found. And he could only imagine what references she'd used. He was a little curious about the photos though, now that she mentioned it. What the hell had she taken pictures of? "Do you want me to grade it too?"

Her cheeks got a little pink. That intrigued him. Ava didn't blush easily. The only time he'd seen her cheeks red were when they were flushed because she was irritated with him. Maybe she didn't blush because no one teased her. It would take someone with big cojones to tease this woman.

But Parker would like to think that he had big ones.

"No, of course not," she said primly.

Yes, prim fit her much better than cute.

"Because I'll warn you," he told her. "I'm a tough guy to impress."

There was a flicker in her eyes and Parker realized that being graded by someone who would be tough got her going. She liked to be challenged. Or, at least, she was used to it. And to rising to the occasion.

Had Rudy been the one who had been hard to impress? The thought flashed through Parker's mind. Had Ava grown up trying to win her dad's praise? That made some sense. Rudy had been one of the most laid-back, accepting guys Parker had known, but he also knew, directly from Rudy's mouth, that he was a very different guy in Bliss than he'd been in New York. And he'd had regrets about his daughters.

Parker moved in closer and found his eyes dropped to the front of her apron. There was a dab of what looked like some of the cheesy chicken tortilla soup he had on the stove.

So maybe Ava wasn't *completely* immune to spills and messes.

He felt that surge of anticipation again and quickly tamped it down. Sure, getting a little messy would be good for her, but it wasn't his responsibility to make sure she let her hair down.

Rudy's will says she's supposed to have fun. That's the main intention behind the dating stipulation.

Parker really wished he didn't know as much about Rudy's will as he did. Or about Rudy's daughters, come to think of it. Rudy had talked about his girls a lot. And he'd been concerned about how serious Ava was and how hard she worked. He'd hoped a nice guy from Bliss could help her relax a little.

Dammit.

If he was stepping in to help with that requirement, then he had to make sure she was having *some* fun. For Rudy.

This was getting complicated. Of course it was. Relationships were like that. Especially with women like Ava. He needed to take out some sweet, small-town girl.

"Did you at least try the tortilla strips and stuff with it?" he asked, not pretending not to see where she'd spilled. Probably when she'd jumped guiltily when he'd been on his way into the kitchen.

She chewed the inside of her cheek for a moment, clearly trying to decide how to answer. "What stuff?" she finally asked.

He shook his head and turned. He crossed to the fridge and pulled out the garnishes for the soup. Though, he was stupidly not upset about feeding her again. He dished up a bowl of soup, tossed crispy tortilla strips on top—which he'd made from corn tortillas dusted with a special blend of spices—added a dollop of sour cream, sprinkled cheddar cheese and green onions over it and then handed her the bowl. With a napkin.

She rolled her eyes at the napkin but took it anyway before taking a big spoonful of the soup, getting a little bit of all the extras in the spoon as well. Parker approved. But he didn't let it show.

He also didn't let it show how awareness and heat slid through him as she closed her eyes and gave a happy sigh as she swallowed.

Damn, he liked feeding this woman.

"That's my lunch," he said. "Again."

She opened her eyes and took another big bite before saying, "That's why I was sneaking bites of it."

He snorted before he could stop it. "You don't have to sneak around." He wouldn't go so far as to admit that he'd made extra soup today with the thought that she might like some before they started baking. He had no idea what she typically ate for lunch unless she was eating from the diner. She'd had salads and sandwiches and soup from him in the past three months. She usually stopped in and got it to go though. And he was definitely not going to tell her that he added things to her orders that he didn't to everyone else's. Simply because they didn't care. They wouldn't appreciate it. But he'd thought from the beginning that Ava might be someone who would appreciate chipotle mayonnaise and cilantro-lime dressing and basil in her tomato soup.

And he'd been right.

She was in the midst of another bite, but she lifted her eyebrows. "I have to sneak the butter."

"You never *sneak* the butter," he countered. "I hear you every time. You bang the doors and you stomp around here in those heels. There's no way to miss you."

She didn't respond to that. But she did run her finger around the edge of the bowl and lift it to her mouth, sucking the rest of the soup away. Parker swallowed hard. Yeah, there was no way to miss this woman. She wasn't as bubbly as her sister, Cori, but you didn't ignore Ava Carmichael when she walked into a room.

She sighed. "This is amazing."

The jolt of satisfaction was ridiculously strong. "Thanks."

"I have no idea why you don't put this stuff on the menu."

"They like chili and chicken noodle."

"And tomato basil," she said.

Well, tomato anyway. He just gave a single nod. She didn't need to know that he'd added the basil only to hers.

"You really don't think they want to try anything new?"

He lifted a shoulder, feeling the tension creep up his neck. "I've tried new things. It doesn't usually do well."

"They complain?"

"They don't even really try it."

She frowned and opened her mouth, but he cut her off. "I'll finish in here and you can make sure no one's heading out without paying, okay?"

He needed her out of his kitchen. He would prefer to get her out of the diner altogether, but he shared the front of the diner with people all the time. The kitchen was another matter. And he didn't need her in here, changing the energy, talking to him about his frustrations, and getting his wheels turning about new ideas and what-ifs. He could feel it in her—the absolute inability to *not* be creative and driven and to look at everything with a how-could-it-be-*more* in her mind.

The diner was exactly the way his dad had wanted it to be,

and it was giving Parker a very nice life. He had an income, he got to do something he loved every day, he got to help take care of the town that meant the world to him, carry on his father's legacy, and *not* keel over from a heart attack before he was forty. And he had plenty of time to hunt and fish and play poker and watch ball games and all kinds of other relaxing, fun stuff with his friends. It was all good. Fine. Perfect. He didn't need Ava Carmichael in here making him think about other things. About *more*.

7

E van was the last person to leave the diner.

"Be gentle with him," he told Ava with a grin as he slid off of his stool and laid a twenty-dollar bill in her outstretched hand.

"Oh, I'll be very good to him, I promise," Ava said, with a straight face and no hint of sarcasm.

Of all the people in town who needed to at least suspect that she and Parker were doing more than baking, Evan Stone was the most important. He was the lawyer in charge of her father's trust. *He* had to agree that her time with Parker could count toward her dating stipulation at the end of the next three months.

"It will be just him and me," she added. "For the next few hours. Alone. It will be...interesting."

Did that sound mysterious? Or like she was worried? She had no idea. And Evan's grin looked more amused than curious.

"It certainly will."

Did he suspect something? And if so, was it something good?

Of course, Evan was spending a lot of time with her sister— though they couldn't call it dating—and he could come right out and ask Cori if something was going on with Ava and Parker. He knew she and her sisters told each other everything.

So the plan was to go home tonight after spending the next few hours with Parker, and tell her sisters about how funny and sexy he was and what a good time they'd had. Cori and Brynn could start suspecting something first. Then Cori could relate her idea to Evan. And all of their imaginations could take it from there. But she had to be subtle about it for now. Even with Parker. Mostly because...she didn't want him to say no. Sure, he had reasons to go along with it. If she failed to meet the will's stipulations, he'd have to be the Carmichael CFO. But he could easily suggest she date someone else. And, well, she didn't want to. And she didn't really want Parker to suggest it because that would mean he did *not* want to date her, no matter how many good reasons there were to go along with it.

Ava took a deep breath. Okay. For now, she'd be subtle. Not exactly her strong suit.

But saying Parker was funny and sexy was hardly a fabrication. It was more like...an admission.

She locked the front door behind Evan and turned the sign to CLOSED. Glancing around the diner, she untied her apron as she headed for the kitchen. The front was clean and ready to go for the dinner crowd. A huge improvement over the day before.

And she'd worn her heels the whole time. Because she'd taken small loads and watched what she was doing. But her feet hurt. Not that she would ever admit that to Parker, but even at eight hundred dollars and with a wider heel than her shoes yesterday, these pumps were not made for waitressing.

Or maybe it was *her* that wasn't made for waitressing.

She tucked her apron behind the counter—she was going to need it tomorrow after all—and pushed through the door into the kitchen. She really wanted more of that soup, but now that Parker was camped out back here, she was going to have to resist. Or maybe she really could just have another bowl. She wasn't sure why she felt this need to keep from saying things like "I'd like to take a bath in that soup, just so you know".

Why was it hard to compliment Parker or let him know that she had nice thoughts about him? Or at least about his soup?

Because you have no idea what to do with a guy like him.

And that was absolutely it. Parker was unlike any guy she'd ever spent time with before. She hadn't dated a lot in high school. When she had, it had been the sons of men her father knew or guys she met at her elite private school. They had worn suits and ties to school every day. They'd been planning for careers in finance, law, and medicine. They'd been looking for a life partner, even at age sixteen, who had goals and ambitions in line with theirs, who would be able to navigate the social scene of the wealthy in New York, who would always look perfect and say the right thing in every situation.

Nothing had changed as she'd gotten older. Except for the fact that *she* was the one searching for, and essentially interviewing candidates for, the perfect life partner. Who would align with *her* goals and ambitions. She'd taken control of that plan when her boyfriend her senior year had been frustrated that she'd spent the holiday with his family, talking to one of his uncles about his merger with a company in Istanbul. Her attention hadn't been on her boyfriend. And that was the last time she gave any man the impression that her time, attention, energy, and resources were going to be about him before herself. She had more influence, money, and power than most of the men in her social circle who were her age. So she'd taken control and decided that she was going to be the one choosing her dates based on what *she* needed.

Unfortunately, she'd left orgasms off the list.

She'd dated men with great business connections, who had assisted her with networking, who had brainstormed ideas with her, who had understood that they would always be second on her priority list after Carmichael Enterprises. Good-looking men. Men who admired her and wanted to be a part of her world.

But very few of them made her feel jumpy and itchy and like her skin was too tight and too hot when they were around. Like Parker Blake did.

She had sex. She had orgasms. But she'd had to take control of those too a lot of the time.

She didn't think that would be a problem with Parker.

And *that* was not the kind of thing she should be thinking when she was going to be alone with him for the next few hours. Or ever. At all. Parker was the guy she was pretending to date. Without him even knowing it. She needed him for his pie skills and that was it. None of his other skills were of any importance.

But why could she *not* get out of her head the look on his face when he'd seen that she'd spilled soup on her apron? It was as if he'd been...pleased that she'd spilled. And turned on. Which was really crazy. She was hardly the laid-back, burger king of Bliss's type.

Ava frowned.

When was the last time she'd worried about being someone's type? She had twelve and a half billion dollars behind her name. That made her a lot of guys' type.

The fact that she already had a prenup drawn up and just waiting made her sad. And that made her frustrated. Of course she'd have to have a prenup. It was just smart and careful and responsible. All things she'd always taken pride in being.

Romance was fine. Falling in love would be nice. But trust? Twelve billion dollars worth of trust? That was going to be hard to come by.

Frustrated and a little ticked off, she pushed her way into the kitchen. The put-together and completely clean kitchen.

Parker was leaning against the counter on the far side of the room, reading her report.

"Well?" she asked. She'd worked on it for a couple of hours.

She'd actually been surprised to find that there was a difference in the pie fillings. Not just in their taste, but in their consistency and even their color.

"This is...very detail oriented," he said, looking up.

She considered that a compliment. "Thanks."

He gave a short laugh. "I guess I should have expected this."

"A very thorough, perfectly presented report?" she asked. She cast a look at the stove. The soup had been put away. Damn.

"Yes." He closed the report and set it on the counter next to him. He crossed his arms. "Several objective details. Observations. Facts. And not a single typo."

She smiled.

"Which isn't what I was going for."

Her smile dropped and she crossed her arms too. "You said to compare and contrast the fillings." She'd even made a table.

"Yes," he agreed with a nod. "And I should have known you'd take that completely to heart."

"I don't see the problem." Except that he was clearly relishing his role as the instructor and her as the student...who had messed up her assignment.

"You just gave me facts."

"And you wanted me to discuss pie filling philosophically?" she asked.

"Kind of."

"I have no idea how I would do that."

"Which one did you like best?"

She shrugged. "None of them."

"*None* of them?"

"I don't really like sweets."

He looked like he wanted to sigh. "Fine. Apple pie isn't your favorite food. But there had to be one of these fillings that you liked more than the others."

She thought about it. "Not really. They were...pie filling. They tasted like apples. And sugar. And cinnamon. One was a lot thicker than the rest. One was sweeter than the rest. One was darker gold than the rest. But in the end, they were all just pie filling."

Parker did sigh now. "I wanted you to think about how they made you feel. What you liked and didn't like. What appealed to you as the taster. It doesn't matter what the color is. And the thick and sweet part only matters if that's what makes *you* like it or not like it."

Ava was surprised by the earnestness in his voice. He really wanted to know what she'd liked about the pie fillings. She made herself think about it. "Okay, I like the one with more cinnamon more than the others, if I have to pick."

His shoulders actually seemed to relax a little at that. "There we go. Was that the thickest one? Or the sweetest one?"

It was *pie filling*, for fuck's sake. She didn't eat pie. That was one of the many ironies about this whole situation really. She tried to remember how thick the one with the most cinnamon had been. Then she realized that Parker wouldn't know if that was the thickest one or not.

But as she was about to answer, she did remember something. "The thicker one was tarter than the others. Which I did like more than the sweet ones. But not as much as the one with the most cinnamon."

He let out a breath, almost as if he was relieved. Wow. She simply never gave food this much thought.

"Why does this matter?" she couldn't help but ask.

"Because you can't make something that tastes good to someone else if *you* don't think it tastes good. You can't adjust things that don't taste good if you don't know why it doesn't taste good."

"That makes no sense," she said. "I should be able to follow a recipe and have it turn out. That's what a recipe is for. It's the instructions. Sugar tastes like sugar, whether I like it or not."

"Do you taste the food as you make it?" he asked. "Did you taste the pie fillings you were trying to make?"

She widened her eyes. "I. Don't. Like. Pie."

"So that's a no."

"That is a no. But I followed the recipes to the letter. You can't tell me that chefs don't ever make food that they don't personally like."

Parker braced his hands on the counter behind him, the action drawing his shirt more firmly against his chest and shoulders, and for an instant Ava lost her train of thought.

But then he said, "A true chef enjoys food and can appreciate the taste combinations and make adjustments to improve those combinations even if it's not their favorite."

She thought about that. "If that's true, we're in big trouble. I'm just not that into food in general."

He looked at her for a moment. Then he pushed away from the counter and went to the fridge. He started pulling out ingredients.

"What are you doing?" she asked, now more aware of the bunching of all of his muscles under his plain blue T-shirt. His back. His shoulders. The way his body moved. How big his hands were. The way his biceps bulged as he cradled jars and containers in the crook of his arm.

"Proving you wrong."

That brought her back to what he was actually doing with all those muscles. Proving her wrong. Well, that seemed very in character. "You said yesterday that today was about me," she reminded him. She didn't know exactly what he'd meant by that even yesterday, but she was pretty sure that so far this hadn't been about her.

"It is."

"I thought we were making pie."

He set everything on the center island and shook his head. "I didn't say that."

The ingredients he'd set out included Dijon mustard, some kind of meat, a vegetable she couldn't name, and shredded cheese. He was, clearly, cooking. "This is because I said I'm not into food?"

He nodded. He turned on the stove under a skillet and added butter, then began slicing the vegetable.

"You're going to *make* me like food?" she asked.

"I'm going to help you find food you like," he returned.

"You know, it's okay not to like food," she said. "I mean, I eat, obviously. But my relationship with food is more of an as-needed thing than a true-love thing."

He looked up. "Everyone deserves true love."

She had a hard time swallowing for a second. "I, um...it's... better to not be obsessed with food," she finally managed. "It's healthy to only eat when you're hungry."

He set down his knife, braced his hands on the island, and pinned her with a look. "Ava," he said, his voice low and rumbly in a way that made her stomach dance. "If I thought you truly just didn't care about food, that would be one thing. People get pleasure from lots of things. Many times it is food, but there are other things—music, nature, art. The thing is, I don't think you get pleasure from anything. I think you're too busy, too distracted, too focused on perfection to ever lose yourself to something as simple and selfish as pure pleasure."

The difficulty with swallowing happened again. There was really something about how this man said the word *pleasure*. Not to mention his seemingly intent focus on making sure she actually got some of that.

And there was something else. He thought she was *not* selfish? That was a new one. Many people she knew thought that she was enamored with being rich and powerful and yes, all about herself. That Parker thought differently made something that felt like those sharp prickles of sensation he usually caused to trip up and down her arms. But this time it was far more pleasant.

"I enjoy spinning," she finally said, because she had to say *something*.

"Spinning? Like with a spinning wheel?" he asked, looking at her like she was a little crazy.

"No, spinning. On a bike. It's an exercise routine."

"You bike?" He seemed surprised. He gathered the sliced vegetable in his hands and deposited the pieces into the hot pan on the stove. He salted and peppered them and stirred them around in the butter.

"Well, it's a stationary bike," she said, watching him stir and keeping her eyes from wandering to his ass. Even though, with him facing away from her, it was hardly her fault that she noticed it. The cooking thing was kind of nice, if she were into ogling hot guys' asses. There was lots of bending and reaching with the fridge and cupboards.

"Ah," he said. "A stationary bike. In some upscale gym in New York, no doubt."

She didn't answer. Because the answer would have been *yes* and she had a feeling he wouldn't approve.

And why his approval mattered, she had no idea. It was ridiculous to think that she cared about Parker Blake's assessment of her exercise program.

"What do you like about it?" he asked, turning back to the counter. He began slicing the meat.

"What is that?" she asked.

"Mortadella. It's an Italian sausage. Like bologna, but better. This one has pistachios in it."

He didn't ask if she'd had it before—she hadn't, that she knew of. He didn't ask if she wanted it—she wasn't sure. He just continued preparing it, regardless.

"What do you like about the spinning class?" he asked again. He pushed a box of puff pastry sheets toward her. "Here, roll these out."

She looked from the pastry to him. "Isn't this cheating?"

"I could make the pastry," he said, lifting his gaze to hers. "If that's what you're asking. But this will save a little time."

She slid the pastry sheets from the box and unrolled one. Then looked up at him.

He stood watching her as if she'd confused him. Then he turned, opened a drawer, and handed her a rolling pin. "Flour is in the big canister over there." He pointed over her shoulder. "Roll it out thin, to about 14 inches in size."

Okay, she'd watched an online video about rolling out crusts on a floured surface.

"I need to go get my apron." She started for the door, but his voice stopped her after only one step.

"Ava."

She turned back.

"Just...get a little messy."

She glanced at the flour canister, then back to him. Why did she get the impression he wasn't talking about the flour? Or just the flour, anyway? Messy wasn't really in her wheelhouse.

"I—" she started. Her mind flashed back to the look in his eyes when he'd noticed the drop of soup on her apron. She didn't know what it meant, exactly, but she wouldn't mind seeing it again. That was...also outside of her wheelhouse.

This whole damned town and pie shop and *everything* here was outside of her wheelhouse.

And she was pretty sure that was exactly what her father had been going for in insisting she and her sisters come here.

She didn't say anything more, but retrieved the flour canister, sprinkled some on her side of the island, and began rolling the dough out thinner.

They didn't speak for a few minutes as Parker finished slicing the meat, put a metal baking sheet into the oven, turned the oven on, and beat an egg in a bowl with a little water.

"Well, for one thing, spinning class is fast-paced," she said, finally answering his question from before. "And we listen to music. And there's sweating."

"You like to sweat?" His tone dripped with disbelief.

She looked up. "I like to sweat when it's appropriate and I'm dressed for it."

"Meaning, you like it when you're working out, but not so much when you're rolling out dough in a hot kitchen."

"Something like that." She set the rolling pin aside and stepped back. "There."

"And, you like the fast pace and the noise of the workout?" He pinched off a piece of the crust and held it up to her.

She frowned and he held it higher. She took it from his fingers and tasted it. It tasted like dough. She shrugged. "Yeah," she said, answering his question about her workout.

"And sweating during your workout makes you feel like you've done something. Accomplished something."

"Yeah, I guess so."

"Even though you haven't gone anywhere and all you've really done is sit and pedal and stare at some other girl's ass for an hour."

She frowned. "I've burned calories, worked off my stress, and gotten my heart rate up."

"I'm not saying that staring at a girl's ass for an hour is *bad*, I'm just clarifying," Parker said. He covered a wooden cutting board with parchment paper and then reached for the dough, carefully transferring it to the paper.

"I'm not staring at another girl's ass for an hour," Ava said, even though she knew he was just pushing her buttons. "I use the time to decompress. I think. I relax. I'm hardly aware of the other people."

"So what you like about it is that you can get away from your desk and think about something besides work."

She watched as he covered half the dough with meat, then cheese, then the vegetable from the skillet, then more cheese.

He held up a raw piece of the vegetable.

"What is that?"

"Fennel."

She took the piece and bit into it. It was crunchy and fresh tasting. And reminded her of black licorice. She wrinkled her nose.

He smiled slightly and crossed to the pan. He lifted a piece of the cooked fennel out and brought it to her. She took the bite, trying to actually think about what she was tasting. It was definitely better that way.

"Butter makes nearly everything better," he said, reading her expression.

He held up a bit of the meat next. It tasted a bit like fatty, spicy bologna. With pistachios in it. The texture was similar too. And again she wrinkled her nose.

Parker looked amused. "The cheese is fontina."

Ah. She'd had only a slight idea what fennel was, but cheese she knew. She took a pinch between her finger and thumb and tasted it as well. "That's my favorite part. If you're wondering."

He didn't confirm or deny that he'd been wondering.

"And I come up with some of my best ideas while spinning," she said.

He brushed the dough with the egg and then folded it over, crimping the edges. He brushed the whole thing with the rest of the egg and then salted and peppered it. He cut a few small slits in the top and then carried the dough pocket to the oven, sliding it in on top of the pan inside. He shut the door and turned to face her.

"So my assessment stands," he said.

"Which assessment?"

"That you really don't do anything for pure pleasure."

As tingles slid down her spine as his voice got *that tone* in it again on those last two words, a few ideas flashed through her mind. But they didn't involve bicycles. "I don't think that's totally accurate."

"Well, we already established that you don't eat for pleasure."

"Right."

"Walks in the park?" he asked.

She had to shake her head.

"Movies? Where you don't also have files and paperwork in your lap and you're not checking your email on your phone?"

Movies were just sitting... She shook her head.

"Bubble baths?"

She swallowed. That sexy tone was back as he said it. Almost as if he was imagining a bubble bath. With her in it. But again, she had to shake her head. Baths seemed so...long. It took a while to fill the tub up and then it was just sitting again...drove her crazy.

"Sex toys?" he asked, almost sounding a bit exasperated. "Do you at least have *orgasms* just...to have them?"

Ava felt her mouth drop open. Had he just said the word *orgasm* to her? And asked about her vibrator? But yes, he definitely had. The humming in her body, like echoes—or memories —of said vibrator, told her he had. But he didn't look surprised that he'd said it. Or apologetic. He was just watching her, almost as if challenging her.

"I really don't think my orgasms or vibrators are any of your business," she told him coolly.

But his shoulders relaxed slightly. "Vibrators. As in plural. Well, that's something."

"I'm not saying I have more than one!" she protested.

"But that means you do have at least one," he pointed out. "Thank God."

She started to argue that as well, but it was more a knee-jerk reaction because she did, in fact, have one. She had three, actually. She'd even brought one with her to Bliss.

But, if she was being honest—not that she was going to be

with Parker—she kind of used it more to get to sleep than for just the pleasure of it. Of course it *was* pleasurable and all of that. Who didn't enjoy a good orgasm? But it also helped her fall asleep more quickly. It was a lot like spinning, come to think of it. She fell asleep faster the nights she went to class too.

She frowned. She'd also happened to bring the vibrator that seemed to get the job done the fastest of the three.

Well, damn. She was multitasking even with her vibrator. And doing it as quickly as possible. That was probably a sign of something. Or...something.

"Which date is the sex date for you?" he asked.

Her eyes flew to his, and she realized she'd been a little lost in thought about vibrators. She felt her cheeks heat when she also realized that he knew that's what she'd been thinking about. Dammit. She did *not* blush. "Excuse me?"

"I'm about ninety-nine percent certain that you have a plan for dating," Parker told her. "You have a checklist of things you look for in a guy."

"My dad told you that," she interrupted. She did have a kind of checklist. It was simply a waste of time to date men who didn't have a few of the basic things that she was looking for. They had to be in a certain age range, for instance.

"He did," Parker agreed. "But I bet it goes beyond that. I bet you have a blueprint of how things should go. For instance, what point you should be to by date three. Which date you have to get to before the guy meets your family. Which date you have to get to before you sleep with him."

Well, that was ridiculous. She hadn't introduced a guy to her family in forever. Of course, her dad had usually known them already. Or of them. He'd known their fathers or grandfathers at least.

She frowned. She honestly couldn't remember the last time she'd introduced a guy to her mom. Why was that? Her mom and dad had never married. The story went that Rudy had seen

Jennifer at a big fundraiser and been immediately smitten. They'd had a brief, romantic affair, but even after she'd become pregnant with triplets, Rudy couldn't talk her into walking down the aisle.

Rudy had always adored Jennifer though. At least it had seemed so on the few occasions the girls saw them together. They'd lived with their mom and had seen their father very sporadically until they were about ten. He'd become a more regular fixture in their lives then, but the one who'd truly raised and parented them had definitely been Jennifer.

And Jennifer was still a big part of her daughters' lives. They didn't see each other as often as they'd like. Ava was a workaholic. So was Brynn. Though their work was incredibly different, with Ava running a huge company and interacting with people around the world every day, while Brynn preferred being stuck in her lab with only her test tubes for company. And Jennifer did a lot of charitable work that required evening and weekend fundraisers and events. But they talked regularly and had lunch at least once a month. But no, Ava hadn't introduced Jennifer to any boyfriends since, possibly, high school. But they were always guys Rudy would have known and approved of...

Ava quickly shut that down. She did *not* have Daddy issues. She didn't. Had she respected and admired her father? Yes. Had she tried to emulate him in business? Yes. But that just made sense. He'd been successful in a business and a company that she wanted to be successful in.

So why had she only dated guys Rudy would have approved of? Didn't girls go through a period where they rebelled and went for the bad boy? Or at least a guy who their fathers wouldn't approve of? Ava had never done that. Not once.

She looked at Parker. Rudy had loved Parker. But he was completely different than the men she'd been dating. The guys she'd been so sure Rudy would like. She lifted her chin, suddenly annoyed with Parker. And not because he was digging into her love and sex life. But because her father had loved him…and if *this* was the kind of guy her dad respected and liked, then she'd been missing the boat all along.

"Date six," she told him, to show him that he couldn't rattle her. That he had no upper hand here. "If they make it that far." Fine. So she had a blueprint. So what?

A tiny smile tugged at the corner of Parker's mouth. "How many do?"

"About twenty percent," she told him honestly. Not many. She went long periods without dating anyone, actually. And when she did, it was unusual for a guy to keep her attention for six dates. Some of them only made it past date three because she needed an escort to something.

Parker nodded as if not surprised.

"I suppose you would have bet on that too?" she asked. She didn't know everything her father had shared with Parker but she got the impression the diner owner knew more about her than she was comfortable with.

"I would have," he confirmed. "And I'm guessing a much smaller percent gets to date seven."

She narrowed her eyes. "What's that supposed to mean?"

"That I'm guessing you have a checklist for the bedroom as well."

Her mouth opened but nothing came out. Mostly because she couldn't tell if he meant that as an insult. Or a compliment. And she didn't want to accidentally admit that she did. Kind of. It wasn't a written checklist, of course. That would be crazy. But she *might* have a few things that she was looking for in that department as well.

Nothing wrong with having standards.

She did, however, accidentally say *that* out loud.

The laughter her response pulled from Parker surprised her. But also made her smile.

"Just tell me your standards include dirty talk and leaving the lights on," he said.

Leaving the lights on? Um, no. And she'd had some bad experiences with "dirty talk". "I actually prefer they just focus," she said. "No talking necessary if they know what they're doing."

Parker didn't look surprised. But he didn't stop smiling. "Well, Boss, that's one place we're going to have to disagree."

She cleared her throat and crossed her arms, even though she knew it was a hugely defensive move. "You're not a big talker outside of the bedroom. Are you telling me that's different inside?"

She did *not* want to know this. She really didn't. She didn't want to even think about Parker Blake in a bedroom.

Except that she already had. A few times.

But she hadn't thought about him *talking*. Right now, though, she could definitely imagine some gruff demands from him. And that had her clearing her throat again and shifting her weight.

His gaze seemed to be burning into hers when she finally got brave enough to meet them again, and she braced herself even before she knew for what.

"I would think a woman like you would appreciate the praise," he told her, his voice rougher than before. "You know, the *yeah, like that* and the *your mouth is perfect* and the *you feel fucking amazing* stuff."

Holy. Crap.

Ava felt her body erupt with hot shivers—that was the best way to describe them—as she stared at him. Or rather at his mouth. That had just said a bunch of stuff that no one had *ever* said to her. Inside the bedroom. Or out. Certainly not standing in a small-town diner's kitchen with fennel in between them.

"Praise?" she finally managed, her voice sounding bizarrely breathless. Or maybe not so bizarrely, considering she hadn't taken a breath in several seconds. "I don't need *praise*," she told him, trying to insert some offense into her tone. And failing. "For anything."

He nodded slowly. "Yeah, Ava. You do. It's why you only do things you know for sure you're good at. It's why the pies are making you nuts. It's why this whole pie shop is something you resent. You want to be back in New York doing what you know you're good at. What you knew your dad was proud of. He'll never see you here in Bliss, making pies, running the shop. And so it doesn't have any meaning for you."

Ava sucked in a deep, quick breath. How had they gotten here? How did he feel comfortable saying that stuff to her? How the *hell* did he know that?

Just then the timer on the oven went off, jerking her out of the stare down with Parker Blake. The guy who had so easily talked about orgasms with her and who knew things about her that made her feel even more itchy and restless than she'd felt before.

Parker didn't say anything—certainly didn't apologize—as he removed the mortadella and cheese pocket from the oven and set it on a cooling rack. She watched him retrieve dishes and silverware and plate a piece.

"Okay," he said, returning to the island. "Try this." He held up a forkful.

As if he hadn't just said all of those things. As if he hadn't just shot her awareness of him up to level *critical*.

"Why?"

"I'm going to show you the difference between food and *food*."

8

Ava blew out a breath. Her options here were: turn and stomp out, offended by the things he'd said, or stay and learn about food, and hope to hell that some of this rubbed off for the pie shop.

That was still her end goal. Making the pie shop profitable and stable was the whole reason she was doing this. So yeah, she had to stay. She was tough. She'd been in smaller rooms with far more offensive people in the course of her career. She could handle being in the kitchen—a room that, admittedly, made her more uncomfortable than even those tiny conference rooms—with a man who knew her on a level that probably only her sisters knew. Probably.

Feeling incredibly *aware*—the best word to describe how Parker affected her—of everything she was doing and everything *he* was doing, she leaned in and opened her mouth.

He slid the fork between her lips, and she closed around the tines. She took stock of everything—him pulling the fork back, the slick metal prongs sliding over her lips, his eyes on her mouth, how dark brown his eyes were...then the taste hit her. The combination of salt and spice. The buttery flakiness of the crust. The gooey cheese with the nutty flavor. She felt her eyes slide shut, and she sighed as she chewed. It was so good. Right up there with the soup. And the chicken salad. And...dammit.

She *did* like food. At least, she liked Parker Blake's food.

She opened her eyes as she swallowed. "Huh."

He cocked an eyebrow.

"It's good," she allowed. "Really good." She frowned at the fennel remnants still on the countertop. "It's good when it's like this."

He smiled. "I've found that a lot of things that aren't so palatable on their own can be downright amazing when combined with the right other ingredients. And even ingredients that are awesome on their own can be made better."

It was strange, but she thought maybe he was talking about more than food. She nodded. "It's the same in business," she said. "I have a lot of people on my team that are capable and creative and smart and reliable. But when I bring them together in one room and give them a project, the results can be absolutely brilliant. And I have a few that are hard to work with one-on-one, but who really contribute well in a group."

He seemed very pleased that she'd made the analogy. And maybe slightly surprised. "How's this compare to the soup earlier?"

She frowned. "How can you compare a meat pie thing with soup?"

"It's about flavor and texture, temperature, flavors on their own and in combination, your preferences. Once it's in your mouth, you can definitely compare."

She hadn't realized how sexy cooking could be. There was a lot of talk about mouths anyway. Which of course made her flash back to his *your mouth is perfect* thing from a little bit ago. She cleared her throat. And actually thought about his question. "I would still choose the soup. It was creamy and smoky. Then there was the spice at the end. It felt..." She trailed off, realizing what she was about to say was going to sound strange.

"It felt what?" he asked, leaning in slightly, clearly very interested.

"It felt better in my mouth." She almost winced. That definitely sounded weird. She shrugged. "I don't know how to explain it. I just liked the feel of the soup better." She had never thought about how food *felt*. She was aware of textures and such, she supposed. On a subconscious level. But she'd never tuned in and really thought about food having a feel.

Parker seemed to be having a hard time coming up with a response.

"I know that sounds weird," she finally said. "But that's—"

"Hang on." He turned and strode to the fridge, withdrew a covered container, and quickly put it in the microwave. "I want to see something," he told her as he hit buttons and started reheating whatever it was.

More food. Ava rolled her eyes behind his back. She had *never* given food this much thought. And she'd never seen someone as into it all as Parker was. She looked down at the mortadella and cheese pie thing. He was really good at it too. He was clearly into far more than burgers and fried chicken. Why didn't he put some of this on the menu? He said this was a burger town. Okay, fennel and dill pickles weren't exactly in the same class when it came to additions to meat and cheese. But maybe he just hadn't given them a chance to really try these other things.

The microwave beeped and Parker poured from the container into a bowl. His back was to her as he added some things to the bowl, then slid it into the oven, so Ava snuck another bite of the meat and cheese pie. Yeah, it was good. Really good.

Was he right that she just hadn't found food she really liked before and that was why she thought she didn't care about it? Or was it because she'd never tuned in and taken time with her food? She'd definitely been focused on it today. With Parker's questions and conversation. And his...*intensity.* It was really hard to not focus on him and what he was doing and talking about, frankly.

Did she do the same thing in other areas? She really felt like she focused at work. But she also always had a lot going on. She was a master multitasker. She had to be. And yes, even when she was with her sisters, she was doing other things.

With that, she realized she hadn't checked her phone once during her time in the kitchen with Parker. In fact, her phone was next door in the pie shop. Damn. She had never left her phone for this long. But she hadn't checked it during her time with him yesterday either.

Her thoughts were interrupted as Parker removed whatever he was making from the oven, then carried it over to her. Rather than handing it to her, however, he came to stand directly in front of her, dipped a spoon into the contents, pushing it through what appeared to be melted cheese—which she could honestly say she was a fan of—and held it up.

For a moment, the aroma of beef and onion touched her nose, but it was followed immediately by the scent of...Parker. Laundry detergent, and lemon, and man. How that scent beat all of the others out, she had no idea. It was a kitchen, after all. There was garlic and bacon and any number of other strong scents hanging in the air. But this close, with his brown eyes watching her intently, and the air around her heating from his body, all she could smell was him. It was probably exactly what he'd said—focusing on something allowed you to fully appreciate it.

"Ava." His voice was husky. "Take a bite."

She suddenly wanted to sink her teeth into his bottom lip and make *him* moan for a change.

She opened her mouth instead, and he slid the spoon past her lips. She tasted the broth, the onion and beef, the French bread and melted Swiss and provolone. She knew she was tasting French onion soup. Amazing French onion soup. But all of that registered at the back of her mind. What was at the forefront was the scuff along Parker's jaw and how she came to exactly the right height to brush her lips along that jaw and how his whiskers would feel against her cheek and how his skin would taste. Yeah, if he wanted her tuning in to sensations, this was working.

"How is it?" he asked gruffly, not moving back an inch, though he was quite firmly in her personal space.

She swallowed. "I don't know."

A slight line creased between his brows. "The soup? How does this one taste...and feel...compared to the other?" He used her own words and he clearly wasn't mocking her. He wanted to know. He understood her thing about how the soup felt.

But she honestly couldn't answer. She shook her head. "I don't know."

"How can you not know?"

"I'm...distracted. It's hard to taste and appreciate food when I'm not paying attention to it. Just like you said."

"You can't shut your mind off for even a few minutes?" he asked. But he didn't seem perturbed exactly. If she didn't know better, he almost said it with a touch of affection.

Again she shook her head and decided to be totally honest. "Not with you standing so close."

Heat and surprise flickered in his eyes. But he didn't say anything. He did, however, *do* something. He lifted a hand and put it against her cheek. Then ran his thumb along her bottom lip.

She sucked in a quick breath. She was used to numbers and schedules and tables and colored tabs. Parker was trying to get her to focus on feelings and sensations. Well, this was definitely helping.

"Yeah, there's no way for me to have any idea about soup right now," she said softly as his thumb rested just below her bottom lip.

"Damn," he breathed.

"You okay?"

"It's just that I wanted to keep cooking for you even before this," he said, gruffly.

"Before wh—" But she didn't have to wait to find out what he meant.

His lips touched hers, and all of the prickly, sharp snaps of energy that had been affecting her over the past couple of days cascaded over her at once, making her feel jumpy, itchy, and like she couldn't *stop*. She couldn't stop from going up on her tiptoes and running her hands up his arms to the back of his neck and opening her mouth. And then, once she'd pressed her body to his and he'd stroked his tongue along hers, all of that gathered into one hot flame that seemed to melt her from the inside out. She leaned into him, everything went soft and almost quiet. No longer jumpy, she wanted to stay completely still. Right against Parker. For a very long time.

The only thing on her mind right now was *Parker*. For a woman who multitasked in everything, who always had a million things going on, who had a hard time stopping her brain from constantly working, there was nothing on her mind right now but the man who was tasting her mouth as if *she* was a decadent combination of flavors he was hungry for.

It wasn't until a beeping suddenly started next to her ear that she jerked back.

It was his watch alarm. He reached up and shut it off but didn't take his other hand away from her face.

Their time was up.

"We didn't bake any pie," she said, her voice breathless. "Again."

"Nope."

He didn't look sorry. And she didn't feel sorry. And that was a problem. The pie was the goal. Or it was the basis of the goal. And this guy was supposed to be the answer to the struggles keeping her from that goal.

And he was distracting as hell.

She stepped back and he let her go, but he didn't move away.

"I'd better let you get back to the diner," she said.

He nodded. "Okay." No protest. No *just another minute*. No *it can wait*.

And she got that. Business couldn't wait. She'd never put business off for anyone other than her sisters. And even then, it didn't happen often. If Cori came to New York more than once a month or so, Ava would have probably said no to their outings once in a while.

But in that moment, she really wanted Parker to play hooky from work. With her. For her.

"Tomorrow," she said, forcing herself to think about pie—or the lack of it—instead of melding her mouth to his again. "I'm going to insist you do your job tomorrow and make pie with me."

It took him a second to respond, but finally he gave her a nod and said, "Whatever you want, Boss."

Then he turned on his heel and headed out to the front of the diner.

And she made her escape through the back door and into the pie shop.

But she couldn't escape all of the things that were rushing through her mind that she *wanted* from Parker. And none of them involved pie.

Dammit.

She stopped in the middle of the pie shop's kitchen and looked around.

Well, now what? If she could do anything good in this kitchen by herself, she'd already be doing it. She needed Parker for that.

She stomped over to the counter and grabbed her large mixing bowl. She heaved it at the wall. The plastic made a good cracking sound, but it bounced off, unharmed. Cori and Brynn had gotten her plastic mixing bowls and measuring cups because she'd found that throwing things helped her get rid of some of her frustration in the kitchen. And because she'd broken all the glass ones.

Glass shattering against a plaster wall really was far more satisfying than plastic. But the cleanup was more involved. And replacing the bowls and cups was gouging their tiny budget.

Thinking of their budget, and the fact that she had to worry about keeping the electricity on in the shop and buying glass mixing bowls, made her want to throw something else. She'd never had to worry about stuff like that before. She dealt with budgets, of course. But the numbers were generally in the seven-figure range. And there was always more of those numbers in the profit column than in the expense column. She had enough money in her personal account, of course, to keep the shop running for the rest of their twelve-month stint and then some. But her father's trust did say that she and Cori and Brynn couldn't use their personal money for the pie shop. It was supposed to be self-sustaining. But considering they'd inherited a business that had been essentially a place for her father to hang out with his buddies to drink coffee and gossip, they had some work to do.

She'd never in her life had to think about if she could pay a phone bill or go to the grocery store. Then again, she'd never paid a bill or gone to the grocery store before coming to Bliss. She had staff for both of those.

And for the record, she hated doing both.

Ava looked around, grabbed an apple and heaved it at the wall. It hit with a thud and split open, falling to the floor in pieces. Okay, that felt good. She picked up another and threw it as well.

Yep, she liked breaking things. She'd discovered that the first time she'd heaved a whole bowl full of beaten eggs against the wall. That was a startling side to her personality, but she found it strangely satisfying.

Too bad it made such a mess.

She turned back to the counter and took a deep breath. Okay. So Parker was going to be of no help today in *her* kitchen. Not that he'd been helpful in *his* kitchen. All she'd done was eat. And get distracted. And get kissed.

Her fingers went to her lips as she flashed back to that moment. Damn, the guy made great soup and was an amazing kisser. He'd provided two of the most basic human needs...food and human touch.

Neither of which she'd ever been all that into before.

Then her stomach growled. The traitor.

Blowing out a breath, she went to the fridge. But the yogurt and fruit she had in there didn't look appealing at all. Nothing like the mortadella and cheese creation next door. That was downright delicious. Then she noticed a plastic container behind her three yogurt cartons. She pulled it out and popped the lid. And just stared. It was a container of the chicken salad Parker had made yesterday. Which meant, at some point he'd come over and put it in here. For her.

Ava felt something flutter in her chest, and the melty feeling she'd experienced when Parker had kissed her ran through her again. It definitely wasn't the sharp, prickly stuff. This was the feeling she liked.

But she put the container back. She wasn't going to eat it for lunch today. She definitely wasn't going to eat yogurt. She had a better idea.

She slipped into Parker's kitchen a moment later. It was empty but she could hear voices out front. She searched for only a minute or so before finding a tray and a stack of paper napkins. She quickly cut the mortadella pie into small slices, eating two and putting the rest on the napkins arranged on the tray. Then she flipped her hair back, put on a big smile, and pushed through the swinging door. She crossed the diner before Parker even noticed her and was out on the sidewalk in front of the diner before he came after her.

David Dixon was just coming to the diner's door when Parker pushed it open.

"Hey, Parker," David greeted. "Hi, Ava."

"Hi, David," Ava said, ignoring Parker for the moment. "Would you like to try a sample today?" She handed him a napkin with a piece of the mortadella and cheese concoction on it.

"I...um..." David clearly didn't know what to do other than accept it. "Thanks."

"Try it," she said, giving him a bright smile.

He did. His eyes widened. "What is this?"

"Something new," she said. "Parker made it. We're were playing around in the kitchen with new recipes." Again, if David, or anyone else, took "playing around" as something other than cooking, that was fine with her.

David nodded. "It's good." He looked at Parker. "Really good."

Ava felt a surge of satisfaction as she looked up at Parker. And immediately sobered. He wasn't happy.

"Thanks," he said shortly.

"Fennel," Ava said, drawing David's attention from Parker's clear irritation.

"What?" David asked.

"There's fennel in it. Have you ever had fennel before?"

"Uh, I don't think so."

"I hadn't either, but I swear, if Parker puts his hands on something, I become a huge fan." And yes, she realized how that sounded.

David made a little choking sound, and one of Parker's eyebrows arched.

"But it's good, right?" she asked David.

"It really is. Good job, Parker." David slapped Parker on the shoulder as he stepped past him into the diner.

The door swung shut behind him and Ava found herself alone with Parker. Yes, they were on a public sidewalk in front of one of the most popular businesses in town, but they were alone for the moment, and a thought flashed through her mind that whenever he stood this close, she would feel alone with him, like she couldn't concentrate on anything else.

"What are you doing?" he asked, his voice low and definitely displeased.

She lifted her chin. "Showing people that maybe they don't always want burgers."

"Stop."

"But it could be so good," she said. "Maybe you just need to give them the chance to try something new."

"No."

She frowned. It wasn't like people *never* said no to her. Okay, people didn't say no to her very often, but there were times when people thought they had a better idea than hers. Temporarily. Still, those people at least offered an argument or an explanation. Not just a "no".

"Why not?"

She thought for a moment that he was just going to turn around and storm back into the diner. He definitely looked like that's what he *wanted* to do.

But instead, he took a deep breath and said, "Because sometimes change sucks, okay? Sometimes new isn't better. Sometimes you just need one fucking thing in your life to be the way it's always been in the midst of all the changes that you can't control."

"Ah." She felt...stunned. And like she really wanted to kiss him again. And maybe hug him too. That was the strangest feeling of all.

But, like Parker, instead of doing what she *wanted* to do, she said, "I see."

Something flickered in his eyes. It looked a little like what had been there just before he'd kissed her earlier. But this also included curiosity. And trepidation.

"Do you?" His voice was rough.

She nodded. "You haven't changed the menu in this diner in *fifteen years*. And, let me guess—you've touched up the paint and repaired the upholstery—but always so it still looks the same. You don't even change the prices—which is crazy. You don't have a staff. Because those people would come and go. Unlike you. In the midst of businesses starting up and closing, and people moving in and out, and people passing away, you can control this little corner and keep it the same for everyone. But while you make it out to be about them and because *they* don't like change, it's also about you. This is your haven where you always know what to expect and you never have to really adjust. Where *you* don't have to change."

Neither of them moved or spoke for several long seconds, but the molecules of air between them seemed to be bouncing and zinging back and forth.

"Exactly," he finally said.

She breathed out, relieved beyond reason by his admission. And warmed beyond reason about his adamant stance to keep things the same for the town, even if he was doing it for himself too. Still, there was something more there, something she sensed in him. He loved being creative in the kitchen. He loved surprising her with the food he'd fed her. He loved the off-menu food that he so clearly also liked to eat. "So you don't want *any* changes? At all? Are you sure?"

"Not here, Ava," he said, his voice sounding tight. "Okay? Just not here."

She knew what he meant. Not at the diner. She glanced at the pie shop next door, then back to him and nodded. "Okay. Not here."

He stared at her for another several ticks, and she thought that maybe he was considering kissing her. Her lips tingled with anticipation. But finally, he gave a single nod and then headed back into the diner.

"Is there even any vodka in this?"

Cori rounded her eyes but tipped the vodka bottle over Ava's martini glass.

"Don't look at me like that," Ava told her. "And don't pretend you weren't diluting it with chocolate syrup and salted caramel. That's all fine and good, but I want liquor in my martinis too."

"Wait, you taste the salted caramel?" Cori asked, clearly surprised.

"Yes." Then Ava realized what she'd just said and sighed.

They were in the kitchen at the house their father had left for them in Bliss. It was a big, old house, like most of the other big, old houses in town. She was used to the polished, steel and glass of Manhattan. She had floor-to-ceiling windows on two sides of the living room in the condo she owned. She had floor to ceiling windows on two sides of her office at Carmichael Enterprises. And through those windows she had amazing views. Of more steel and glass. But his old house, with its original woodwork and fifty-year-old light fixtures was growing on her.

"What's with you?" Brynn asked. "You usually just drink them down."

"Usually they're just chocolate," Ava said with a shrug. "I always taste the chocolate."

"Yeah. They're not always just chocolate," Cori told her.

"No?" Ava actually wasn't surprised to hear that. Or that she'd missed other flavors.

"I've added marshmallow," Cori said.

"You and your s'mores," Ava muttered.

"And peanut butter."

Ava took another drink of the martini in her hand. Yeah, she could absolutely taste the caramel. "Seriously?" she asked of the peanut butter. How had she missed that?

"Seriously. And cherry. Those were really good," Cori told her.

"You added *cherry* to a chocolate martini?" Damn, that sounded good. "And I didn't notice?"

"You're always very...focused," Brynn said, clearly trying to be diplomatic, as usual.

"Yes. With work and stuff," Ava said, drinking again.

"With everything. When you drink a martini you..." Cori shrugged, "...drink a martini. I know you like chocolate better than other kinds, but I don't think you're necessarily drinking to appreciate the taste of it."

Ava started to reply. But she took another drink instead, savoring the flavor of the caramel and chocolate together. Cori was right. Not that she didn't like the taste of chocolate martinis, but beyond that she didn't really think about it. "Dammit."

"Really, what is going on with you?" Brynn asked. "There's been less crashing and swearing in the pie shop kitchen the last couple of days. And I caught you sitting in your office last night, staring into space."

Cori's eyes widened again. She looked from Ava to Brynn and back. "You were daydreaming?"

"I've just been—" Ava blew out a breath. "Distracted."

"Is everything okay?" Brynn asked.

Ava debated lying. But she realized that she could maybe use some perspective from the two people who knew her best. "It's Parker."

Brynn and Cori exchanged a look.

"How is Parker distracting you?" Cori asked. She seemed amused.

Ava frowned. "He has me *tasting* things."

Brynn made a little choking sound.

"*Food*," Ava said. "And thinking about it. And enjoying it."

"The bastard," Cori said dryly.

She knew Cori and Evan had talked about her and Parker.

She wondered what Parker had said to Evan. Then reminded herself that they weren't twelve and in junior high school. She wasn't going to ask her sister to ask Parker's friend what Parker had said about her. Probably.

"We've spent four days together, surrounded by butter and sugar and we haven't even baked a pie yet!" She glanced at Brynn. "That's why there's less swearing and breaking things in our kitchen. I've been at Parker's in the afternoon. Supposedly getting baking lessons. Instead all I've gotten is fed and frustrated."

Cori shook her head. "Man, are you doing the food thing wrong. Frustrated is *not* how food makes *me* feel."

Actually, it wasn't how it was making Ava feel either. Unless it was *sexually* frustrated. There was definitely a little of that going on. But the food itself? And watching Parker make it? And watching Parker watch her eat it? That was hot and weirdly intimate and...the reason she was daydreaming.

That was why she was frustrated. Because she'd spent the last few days *not* working toward any of her goals.

"All I want him to do is teach me to bake a pie. Or bake it himself. That would be even better. That's it. I don't want to taste his sausage or his avocados."

Cori coughed as she swallowed down the wrong pipe. "Excuse me?"

"Not even a euphemism," Ava told her soberly. "Actual sausage—mortadella to be precise—and avocados."

Brynn and Cori didn't seem to know what to say to that.

"He's been cooking and I've been eating." And he'd been strangely insightful and she'd been, hell, also strangely insightful. "We've now spent all this time together...in a kitchen no less...and have yet to actually make a pie."

"Okay," Brynn said.

"Wow," Cori added.

"And he should *want* to bake pies. It's going to partly be his shop. He should *want* this," Ava insisted.

"Yeah," Cori said, though she seemed thoughtful.

"What?" Ava asked. "What have you and Evan figured out about all of this?" Because she knew that's what was coming.

"We've just talked about how weird it is that you haven't *made* him do the baking and that he hasn't insisted. Both of you can be really damned bossy and stubborn when you want something. It's almost like you're both enjoying the other stuff."

Ava frowned. The food was good. And having Parker's full attention had been really nice. He was an intense guy, and she liked that about him. He tried to come off as laid-back, but it didn't work. At least not with her. She didn't like being distracted, but she kind of liked that *he* seemed entirely focused on her when they were in that kitchen together. Well, her and food.

"Whatever," she said, trying to seem more put out than interested in all of that. "The guy is obsessed with food and is showing off."

"Yeah, but he never lets anyone in his kitchen," Cori said. "Evan made that really clear. If his mom's there helping out, she goes in and out with dishes, but no one helps him with the food."

"It's not as if I asked permission," Ava said with a shrug.

Brynn laughed. "I've seen him take a grilled cheese away from someone who was dipping it in ranch. Pretty sure if he didn't want you in his kitchen, he'd get you out."

Ava didn't like how her pulse raced with all of these bits of news. It didn't mean what her sisters seemed to think it meant. She and Parker had a common goal—making the pie shop successful.

Of course, they still hadn't baked a freaking pie.

"And no one eats back there. And Evan had never heard of chicken avocado salad. Also, I've had Parker's tomato soup. It does *not* have basil in it. So it's not like he cooks this way for other people all the time. Just you."

Those last two words caused Ava's heart to thump hard, and she grimaced. She didn't want heart-thumping. She wanted to complete her to-do list from Rudy. Period. She wanted to get back to New York. She wanted Cori stable. She wanted to get back to her regular life where she ate...well, whatever she'd been eating for twenty-nine years. She wanted to go back to dating guys who did absolutely nothing surprising. She wanted lawyers and CEOs and investment bankers. Not guys who came off as grumpy and nonchalant, but deep down had passion and creativity and gave up what they wanted to do in order to keep their diners a haven for people in the midst of a world that wouldn't stop changing and challenging them.

Ava rubbed two fingers against the center of her forehead. This was supposed to be a pretty basic recipe. Make pie + date a nice guy for six months = inherit Carmichael Enterprises. But, like every other recipe she'd tried in this town, it wasn't turning out the way she'd expected.

"The basil doesn't mean anything," she finally told Cori. "He puts a little more flare into the food he makes for me because he doesn't want me criticizing or complaining."

Sure, that made sense.

"I might think that was true for someone else," Cori said. "But Parker Blake doesn't really care about criticizing or complaining."

That was true. He didn't care about *her* complaining. A lot of the time it had seemed that Parker liked annoying her.

So why was he putting basil in *her* tomato soup?

I wanted to keep cooking for you even before this. Her body flushed as she remembered Parker's words from the other day. Just before he'd kissed her.

"What is *that* about?" Cori asked, her eyes narrowing as she took in Ava's blush.

Which deepened the heat in Ava's cheeks. "Nothing."

"Kissing Parker was nothing?" Cori asked.

Ava sat up quickly. "What?"

Cori smiled smugly. "You kissed Parker."

"Parker told Evan?"

"No. You just told me." She held her hand out toward Brynn, who laid a five-dollar bill in it with a sigh.

"You *guessed*?" Ava asked, watching her sisters.

"You've been acting strangely for the past four days. And you didn't even come into the shop yesterday or today," Brynn told her. "I thought you and Parker had gotten into a fight. Cori thought you'd kissed. I lost the bet."

Ava looked back and forth between them. "So me acting weird has to have something to do with Parker?" she asked. "Why didn't you guess it had something to do with Carmichael Enterprises or that I wasn't feeling well?" She wasn't sure she wanted the answer to this.

"Because you never act weird. Even if you're stressed with work or sick, you're still...you. Calm, cool, under control," Brynn said. "You know what to do in every situation. You never hide out."

"I wasn't hiding out!" Ava protested.

But it was clear from their expressions that neither of her sisters were buying that.

Because she had definitely been hiding out.

She didn't know what to do with Parker Blake. He was not just surprising her, but he was distracting her. And making her like it. She definitely didn't feel like she had any control in this whole *situation* with him. He was her employee and she should be able to insist that he come to the pie shop and make pies. That seemed clear and straightforward. But she was afraid he was going to make her come to him, and if she went over to see him, she'd end up even more infatuated—with his food, of course— and possibly begging him to kiss her again.

That was not okay.

She was also afraid that if he did decide to come over to the pie shop before she went to get him from the diner, that she'd end up even more infatuated—with *something*—and begging him to kiss her again.

Also not okay.

So she couldn't win. And she didn't like not winning. So she'd stayed home for the past two days. The intent had been to use the time to focus on business other than the freaking pies that were turning her life upside down. To get back in the saddle of being a kick-ass CEO. To remind herself that she did actually know what she was doing and was in control. At least when there weren't aprons and whisks involved.

Of course, that wasn't a long-term strategy. Especially since she'd found her mind wandering even in the midst of being a kick-ass CEO who knew what she was doing and was in control.

She had to go back to the pie shop tomorrow. She had to see Parker and insist that they actually make a damned pie. Which was why she was drinking now.

She drained her glass and handed it to Cori. "Can you make me one of those chocolate martinis with cherry?" she asked.

"Or I was going to try a new one," Cori said. "What about lime and pineapple?"

Go completely away from her chocolate martini? But the idea of combining lime and pineapple with her vodka was intriguing. "Sure." She couldn't wait to taste it.

Damn Parker Blake for making her think differently and even have *feelings* about things she'd never paid attention to before. He wasn't letting her stay in *her* comfort zone like he was doing for everyone else in Bliss. Did he know that?

But she had a suspicion that he did.

9

By 12:32 the next day, Parker was disgusted to find himself watching the front door for Ava.

By 12:44, Parker was frustrated to find that he was disappointed she hadn't come over yet. The last two days, he'd been disappointed to find out she wasn't even at the pie shop. But he knew she was next door today. He'd heard the crashing and swearing. It had been too damned quiet over there for two days.

By 12:55, the diner was cleared of customers and tubs of dirty dishes were stacked next to the dishwasher.

For the last two days, he'd had people out the door by one. Thanks to the help of Hank and Roger. Ava had hired them to come help clear tables, roll silverware and refill salt and pepper shakers. And it had actually been helpful. A little distracting, of course, but nothing like when Ava was waltzing around the diner in her apron, looking *cute*.

Of course, with their help, he was free from one to four. With nothing to do.

That wasn't entirely true. He had all the same stuff to do as always. He just hadn't wanted to do it. He'd wanted to make Ava lunch. And flirt with her. And kiss her some more.

But today the last customer paid their bill at five to one without a word from Parker. Whether it was that the new habit was catching on and people were believing the posted business hours—for the first time in fifteen years—or because they also knew Ava was next door today, and they were all in on some scheme to be sure he had time alone with her, he didn't know. Or care. They were gone.

By twelve fifty-six he was out his back door and stalking into the pie shop's kitchen.

"Well, son of a bitch!"

Parker found himself ducking as an egg went sailing past his ear and smashed into the wall to his left. He watched the shell drop to the floor and the yolk and egg white slide down the wall and hit the tile next to two other egg shells and three apples that were busted open.

His own irritation seemed to evaporate as he felt a smile stretch his mouth. He turned to face Ava. She was just watching him.

"What?" she asked.

"It's almost one."

She glanced at the clock. "Yes, it is."

"You didn't come over today." That was a stupid thing to say. It almost sounded like he'd *wanted* her to come over. And, clearly, he could get rid of his customers by one o'clock on his own. So what else would he want her to come over for?

"No, I didn't."

"Why not?"

"You work *here*," she said. "You're the employee *here*. So I think it just makes sense that you should come over *here* at one."

She might have a point there. But it only served to inch his frustration up another notch. She didn't want to come over to his kitchen? She didn't want to see what he'd concocted today? She wasn't curious or interested at all? She didn't want to talk to him while they cleaned up? She didn't want to maybe, possibly, kiss him again? She'd left the other day with the firm assertion that they were going to bake pie the next time they were together. As if the stuff they'd done together up to that point had been a waste. And now she was avoiding his kitchen completely?

"Fine," he finally said.

He wasn't going to tell her that he had a butternut squash soup ready to go. It had been between that and a split pea with rosemary, but she seemed to like the creamier soups better. Not that he would ever admit to her that he'd thought of all of that.

Though he supposed he could kiss her in this kitchen too.

He scowled. He did *not* like this. He was distracted. He was watching the clock. He was thinking about her and wondering why she hadn't been at the pie shop for two days and resisting asking about her because there was no reason to ask about her. She had Cori and Brynn and Evan and Noah to help with whatever she needed. She didn't need him.

And yet, he'd let the pasta for the macaroni salad boil over this morning and he'd undercooked the bacon. And he'd had to take the Philly cheesesteaks off the menu today because he'd forgotten to order hoagie buns. He was never distracted. Not when it came to food and cooking and his diner. These recipes and routines were so engrained he should have been able to do them half-asleep and one-handed. It was how he was able to manage the restaurant all on his own.

But Ava Carmichael was messing with him, and his menu, even if it was indirect, and he didn't like it.

Which meant today they were *baking pie*. They had to. It had been a week since she'd proposed her plan to have him helping out in the pie shop kitchen, and they hadn't made a single pie yet. They were going to focus today. They were going to talk about apples and cherries and nothing else. And they were going to fucking make pie.

Still, he couldn't help but ask, "What the hell are you doing over here?"

"It's a kitchen in a pie shop," she said. "What do you think I'm doing?"

"Showing me why you're always in *my* kitchen borrowing eggs."

"I'm baking," she said, gesturing toward the countertop beside her.

"And how's it going?" he asked dryly.

"The way it always goes, Parker," she said with a sigh.

Her tone wasn't pissy or frustrated. She sounded resigned.

He took in the details of her countertop. She'd clearly been working on pie filling. Apple, obviously. "You're not even making crust."

She glowered at him. "I'm not quite there yet."

"But you don't need eggs for apple pie *filling*."

"I know."

"So what did you take my eggs for?" He was down a dozen and had known immediately who had pilfered the carton when he'd seen it. And he'd smiled. She now had him smiling about stealing food from his kitchen.

She reached and plucked an egg from its cardboard cup and threw it at him. Not at the wall beside him. Directly at him. The egg hit him in the chest, the shell falling to the floor, the innards sliding over his black T-shirt before slipping to land at his feet.

"You're just throwing the eggs and breaking them?" he asked. He reached for a towel and wiped away some of the egg slime from his shirt.

"Yes."

"Why?"

She lifted a shoulder. "Turns out I like breaking things."

He tossed the towel back onto the counter. "You just discovered this?" he asked. He'd never admit that he was fighting a smile.

"Well, since moving to Bliss. Which is probably good. The lamp on my desk in New York cost six hundred dollars."

Parker rolled his eyes. Of course it did. "I think my egg budget is getting there."

She actually laughed and he let one corner of his mouth curl.

"So dramatic," she said.

"Where's this destructive streak come from?" he asked.

She lifted a shoulder. "It's pretty obvious. I've spent my whole life trying to put, and hold, things together. In business, with my sisters and dad, in my *life*. Being the one breaking things, doing it on purpose, knowing the reason things are coming apart and splattering all over, feels strangely great."

Parker felt the breath whoosh out of his chest. He'd been prepared for something sarcastic and sassy. He hadn't expected her to say something meaningful.

Ava Carmichael embodied sarcastic and sassy. He liked that about her. She was tough and competent and confident. Until it came to pie. Or at least that was what he'd thought. He'd even thought that the whole pie thing was good for her. Taking her down a bit, giving her some humility. But apparently there were other things that made her feel less than on-top-of-everything. And—son of a bitch—that made him want to build her up. She didn't have to be a champion pie baker or even a good cook. But she had to be okay with not being those things. She had to be able to walk into a kitchen and not feel inferior or hate everything from the ladles to the—he glanced at the mess on the floor —the eggs and apples.

There was also something strangely hot about her breaking things. That sounded crazy even in his head, but Ava was so put together. It seemed that she *couldn't* get messy. She was throwing eggs, and apples, at the wall, even at other people, and yet she stood before him in a skirt and blouse—and high heels, for fuck's sake—looking like she was ready to have tea with the queen.

"You even wear those damned heels to bake over here?" he asked, unable to ignore that.

She looked down. "Yes."

"That seems like overkill."

She met his eyes again. "I like overkill."

Ah. The other day on the sidewalk in front of the diner, he'd given her some insight into him and his reasons for not changing things up at the diner. Now she was giving him some peeks inside her. And he really fucking liked it.

He took a deep breath, already deciding he was going through with the very crazy, change-everything idea that had just occurred to him. He strode toward her and got into her personal space. Close enough that he could smell her. And she smelled like apples and cinnamon. She might not like sweets, but he definitely did.

She had to tip her head back to meet his gaze. But she did it.

"Those heels make you feel in charge and kick-ass, Boss?" he asked, looking down at her.

She was clearly surprised, but she didn't back up, and there wasn't a flicker of anything in her eyes but desire. "Yeah, they do."

He nodded. Then put his hands at her waist and lifted her onto the counter behind her. She gasped.

"Parker."

He didn't answer. His coasted one hand down the back of her bare calf to the heel of her shoe and then tugged. The pump slid from her foot, and he let it drop to the tile with a *thunk*.

"What are you doing?"

He could tell that she'd meant to sound demanding, but she was too breathless to pull that off.

"You don't have to be the boss in this kitchen anymore," he said, sliding her other shoe off as well. "I'm here now."

She wet her lips. "Oh, really."

"Yep." He straightened. "And I've decided that what you need is a really good kitchen experience."

Her pupils dilated, and he felt a surge of *hell yeah*.

"You think that if you seduce me in here, it will make me like cooking?"

He looked down at her and decided to be fully honest. "No. But it will make you feel other things besides angry and frustrated the second you walk into this room."

The look in her eyes softened. She was still, clearly, turned on, but she seemed touched by that too. "Why does that matter?"

He blew out a little breath. "I don't even know. But you not liking food and hating this kitchen bugs the hell out of me."

She bit her bottom lip, but it was in no way coy. She seemed almost conflicted. "I would really like to not hate this kitchen," she finally said softly. Almost sadly.

A protectiveness ripped through Parker. He couldn't have explained it for anything, but the idea that she wanted some good feelings from this place, a place that had meant so much to her father, a place that her father had given her in hopes that it would help her somehow, made Parker want to wrap her in his arms and tell her it was all going to be okay.

"Yeah?" he asked gruffly.

"This was my dad's," she said. "I don't want to feel my stomach knot when I walk in here because I'm falling short and don't get it." She dropped her eyes to his chin. "I've always gotten it. We were always on the same page with the business. And I was always good at everything he gave me to do and asked of me. Until now."

Dammit. Parker wanted to kiss her. He wanted to strip her naked. He wanted to cover her in cinnamon and sugar. But could he do that now? Now that she'd revealed some vulnerability? A soft side? Now that he knew that she needed something beyond learning to bake?

Hell yeah, he could. He cupped her face, bringing her eyes up to his. "Then this is perfect. What I want you to do in this kitchen right now is something I'm guessing you're really good at."

He wanted a smile. He wanted sass. He wanted confidence. Instead he got a blush.

"I'm not so sure about that."

"You're not so sure that you're really good at twisting me up and making me want you more than I've ever wanted someone?" he asked. "Let me assure you that you are. You *really* are."

She gave him a small smile that, if he didn't know better, was almost shy. "Even when I'm having sex, I'm thinking about a million other things," she confessed. "I don't even focus on that."

Oh, was that all? He took her mouth in a deep, soft, hot kiss, tasting her thoroughly, not letting her move her head, making her hold still to feel and taste him. He lifted his head and looked into her eyes long moments later. She had that faintly dazed look again, and he gave her a cocky smile. "You're going to focus on this," he told her firmly. "You're going to be all-in here, Ava, I promise you."

"Well, you've already got me smelling nutmeg and reading about apples," she said.

He realized if he'd been expecting something like "oh, Parker, you're amazing," he was stupid. He grinned and dropped his hands from her face. But he braced them on either side of her hips, caging her in. "You were smelling nutmeg?"

"I got all the spices out and was smelling them, trying to figure out if I could tell the difference between nutmeg and cinnamon."

"And?"

She shrugged. "Kind of."

He couldn't resist lifting a hand and tucking her hair behind her ear. It didn't matter if she could tell the difference between nutmeg and cinnamon. She'd tried. "And you were reading about apples?"

"There are so many," she groaned. "I read about apples for an hour last night. When I should have been doing other work."

She'd been thinking about him—or at least about baking and the cooking they'd done and the idea of tuning in and really tasting. She'd been focused on that. He felt victorious, he couldn't lie.

"Sorry." But he wasn't. At all. And he knew she knew that.

"And are you aware of the number of uses for that puff pastry stuff?" she asked. "It's crazy. I need to buy stock."

He laughed and cupped her cheek again, unable to help it. He ran his thumb over her jaw. "You're distracting the hell out of me too," he told her.

"I haven't taught you anything new about cooking or food," she said.

"But you've taught me some new things about *you*." He realized it was true even as he admitted it to her. She fascinated him.

Her lips parted and his gaze dropped to her mouth. Her breathing was coming a little faster now.

"Where are Brynn and Cori?" he asked.

"With Noah and Evan. Somewhere else. Not here. The front door is locked."

Anticipation tightened his body. "Ava," he said, his voice low. "Yeah?"

"We're not going to bake a pie today either."

She nodded. "I know."

So he kissed her. Or she kissed him. It was hard to really tell who started it this time. But they were both fully participating once their lips touched.

Ava's hands ran from his shoulders to the back of his head. His hands slid to her ass, pulling her closer. But not close enough. With a little groan of frustration, Ava grasped her skirt and she began bunching it up. Which caused her to wiggle against him, eliciting a groan of his own.

But a moment later, she pulled back. "Dammit."

She pushed him away, and Parker took a step back but opened his mouth to protest. Or beg.

But his words died on his tongue as she reached behind her and he heard the rasp of a zipper. She wiggled on the countertop again, this time pushing the skirt down rather than bunching it up.

A moment later, she sat on the counter in a white silk blouse and peach panties.

Parker blew out a quick breath. "Damn."

She was gorgeous. The pale peach panties matched her skin almost exactly. But it wasn't her delicious curves or her long silky hair that he wanted to wrap around his fist or the hard nipples pressing against her blouse as if begging him to touch. It was the way she was looking at him. Like this—this kitchen, *him*—was all there was in her world right now. And having Ava Carmichael's full focus was huge. He wasn't going to waste one second of it.

Her skirt dropped to the floor and Parker had to grin. That was one way to finally get flour on one of her skirts.

"What?" she asked.

Her smile was almost playful, and he absorbed that as he stepped forward. "I'm determined to get you messy, Boss," he told her. He was smiling, but he was dead serious.

She pulled in a shaky breath. "I think I can be okay with that."

"Oh, yes you will be."

He reached for the apple pie filling she'd made. He dipped two fingers into the glass bowl and lifted them to his mouth. He licked the tip of one finger, watching Ava's cheeks flush.

"It's not bad actually," he said.

"It's too runny." Yeah, her voice was definitely breathless.

"Ah, yes, well there's that." He held his fingers up, letting the too-runny filling drip. And land on the V of skin revealed by her blouse.

Her breath caught, and Parker watched the filling slide slowly toward her cleavage.

"It also needs a little more sweetness," he told her. He met her eyes. "Unbutton."

She did. He'd really thought she might resist. Or sass him a little, at least. But all she did was lift her hands and open the buttons down the front of her shirt.

Maybe she could read his surprise, because she smiled as she shrugged out of it. "Don't want to get it dirty," she said.

He gave a little growl and swiped the shirt from the counter where it pooled behind her. He dropped it on top of her skirt. "You're not leaving this kitchen without being a little rumpled... and a lot sticky."

He lowered his head and licked up the trail of pie filling on her chest.

Her fingers tangled in his hair, and she arched closer.

He wanted to rip the peach bra and panties from her body and take her just like this, spread out on the countertop of the kitchen she hated. He wanted her to walk into this room and smile. And if fucking her on the counter was the way to that, well, he was a giver like that.

But there was something about her not liking food, not appreciating the tastes and textures and aromas, that drove him crazy for some stupid reason. He hadn't fully analyzed it. He was vaguely aware that it had to do with how much he loved food and how he felt a connection with Ava he didn't feel with anyone else and how he wanted those things combined. But he didn't want to go into it any further than that. He did, however, have an idea about how to increase her appreciation for being in the kitchen and some of the food he loved.

He ran his tongue over her bottom lip and then pulled back. It took an extra couple of seconds for her eyes to open. He liked that. Probably too much.

"Close your eyes again," he told her.

She did, without question.

"Now open your mouth." He picked up the bottle of ground cinnamon and shook a little of it on her thigh. It was so light, she didn't even feel it, but when he wet the end of his finger and touched it to her leg, she wiggled. He lifted his finger to her mouth. "What is this?" he asked.

She frowned. "Cinnamon."

"Good."

Then he picked up a pinch of white sugar and sprinkled it over her bottom lip. Some of it fell against her chin and chest, sparkling against her skin. "How about this?"

She licked her lip, her eyes opening. "I'm practically naked here and we *are* going to cook?"

"We're going to *taste*," he corrected. "And yes, Ava, having you practically naked is going to be a huge part of that. Open your mouth."

Her eyes widened slightly at that. "You're going to make me like this food by seducing me with it?"

"Yes."

"That's pretty arrogant of you."

"Yes." He dragged an apple slice over the cinnamon on her leg.

And she opened her mouth. Her eyes stayed open though. Her lips parted and he slid the apple inside. With her eyes locked on his, she licked the apple first. Parker watched her, not reacting. He was going to make this sexy, hot, and something she would think of every time she smelled cinnamon from now on. But he was not going to rush it. Or let her rush it.

She bit into the apple and chewed, watching him.

"I want you to have a really positive association with ingredients that you're going to be spending a lot of time with," he said huskily, popping the rest of the apple into his mouth.

"Well, that's a lofty goal," she said. There was a haughty note in her voice, but there was definitely heat in her eyes.

"Well, Ava," he said, mimicking her tone. "I can promise you that having me suck cinnamon sugar off your nipples and lick melted butter and brown sugar from your belly button will make you feel differently about them."

He licked his finger and dragged it over her collarbone where some of the sugar clung. Then he lifted it to her mouth. Her hot, soft lips closed around the tip, and her tongue ran over the pad of his finger, sending bolts of heat through him.

Slow, he reminded himself. Slow and thorough.

"What about the apples?" she asked.

"Oh, you're going to *love* the apples."

She studied him with her bottom lip between her teeth as visions of apples and Ava danced through Parker's mind.

Finally, she said, "Can we use ginger too? Right now, I'm not a big fan."

His body tightened. He cleared his throat. "We are going to make you love ginger."

"Then let's get on with it." She reached behind her and unhooked her bra.

The most gorgeous breasts he'd ever seen were suddenly on display. Within touching distance. Within tasting distance.

"Ava—" He didn't know how to finish that statement. It wasn't even a statement. It was a...feeling. An out-loud feeling.

Ava reached for the cinnamon and as Parker watched, his body temperature climbing, she sprinkled the spice over her breasts.

He made a sound—part groan, part growl—and started to reach for her.

She put up a hand to stop him. "Hold on."

She then tried to kill him by licking a finger, wetting one nipple, then sprinkling sugar that clung to the hard tip.

"Okay, now you can—"

He didn't let her finish that thought. He leaned in, put one hand on the back of her neck, and one on her hip. She gave a little squeal as he pivoted her onto her back on the countertop. "Okay, Boss, how about you let me do some work for you now?" He lowered his head and kissed her.

Her foot kicked an apple to the floor and upset the bowl of melted butter. He smiled against her lips and used one hand to bend her knee so she wouldn't knock anything else over. This was no time for breaking things. "The only thing coming apart right now is going to be you."

She gave a little moan, and he nipped her bottom lip before moving down to her neck.

"Kissing you is as delicious as I thought it would be," he told her gruffly.

"The sugar helps," she said, breathlessly as he spread his palm over her stomach. The muscles quivered under his hand, and her chest rose and fell rapidly.

"You're way sweeter than sugar." He kissed along her collarbone. "I could eat you all day."

She gasped, and he kissed down her sternum. Her skin was silky and sweet with a hint of spice, but none of it had anything to do with the cinnamon or sugar.

She laughed breathlessly. "Sweet is definitely not an adjective many people use for me."

"That's because you don't let them see it," he said, moving a hand to cup her breast, running his thumb over the tip. "You think sweet is already taken."

"What do you mean?" she asked even as she arched into his touch.

"Cori gets to be the fun, free spirit who gets to play, and Brynn gets to be the sweet, bookworm who gets to experiment. You think that leaves perfectionistic, workaholic for you." He didn't know if the tension in her body was from what he was doing to her nipple or because of his words, but he circled the tip with the pad of his finger, rubbing the sugar granules against the sensitive skin. She gave a little whimper. "But I'm going to make you let go of that, Boss," he told her sincerely, watching her face as he played with her body. Her cheeks were flushed, her pupils wide, her lips parted with her fast breathing. "I'm going to show you how fun and freeing it can be to let go and get messy and that it doesn't have to be perfect to be...perfect."

"*You* like to have things just right," she said, her voice soft, her legs moving restlessly against the countertop.

"I do. Strange that you make me want to get a little messy too." And he didn't mean with the apple pie ingredients. And it definitely was strange. Very. He'd always thought he should be with someone sweet, who would go along with all of his planning and organizing, who was laid-back and would let him just do his thing. Instead, this woman, who hardly fell into line and was the opposite of easy-going, was making him want to throw out the plans and see what surprises would come up.

Ava pulled him down and kissed him. He didn't know what she was thinking or feeling exactly. Maybe she just felt like it was too difficult to make eye contact at a moment like this. But he kissed her with feeling. What that feeling was exactly was the question.

"No one else has ever said anything like that to me," she said softly as she let him up for air.

He knew she meant the other men she'd been with. "That's because you've been hanging out with assholes who hide their loser side in suits and ties," he told her, that affectionate feeling welling up again.

She gave him a small smile. "They like that I'm tough."

He bet they did. Because they liked the idea of getting close to someone powerful like Ava. He understood the appeal of thawing the ice queen. He'd had similar thoughts, frankly. But Ava's icy layer was thin, and there was a lot of warmth underneath. It didn't take much to break through the frosty outside. Because it was a cover. And he liked the idea that none of the New York jerks had ever found that out. "None of them ever met your sisters, did they?" he asked. He knew Cori was only in New York for a couple of days a month and that Brynn spent most of her time in her lab.

She seemed surprised that he'd figured that out. "No."

He liked that. He loved it in fact. "Then none of them have

really known you," he said. "Without knowing your sisters, they don't see all of you. You are, most definitely, kick-ass. But you're more than that." Did he know that because of something Rudy had told him? Or had Evan or Noah shared something that made him understand this about Ava?

But he realized that if Rudy hadn't really seen Ava with her sisters, then he hadn't *really* known her either.

He knew as soon as she asked, "Why do you think that?" how he knew what he did about Ava Carmichael.

"Because you still come to this pie shop every day and try to make pies from scratch," he said. "You hate this place. It makes you feel incompetent. It frustrates you. It confuses you because you thought you knew and understood your dad, and this place makes you question all of that. You found a loophole for making the pies that would meet that stipulation, and you could just leave it at that. But you come in here every day anyway, because the shop makes your sisters happy. And it's gotten Cori to settle down and Brynn to come out of her bubble. So you'll sacrifice feeling good, you'll put up with the frustration and confusion for yourself, because that's what you've always done. You don't get to have fun and softness and sweetness because you're making sure *they* have it. But it's not because you're kick-ass, Boss," he said huskily. "It's because you *are* soft and sweet."

He took a breath, his hand just resting on her breast now. It was an intimate position, but not as lust-filled as before. It still felt amazing in his hand, of course, but this was very different. She was mostly undressed, while he had all of his clothes on. His hands were on her body. And he was revealing the things he'd figured out about her. He would put good money down on the fact that this was something new for Ava.

She blinked rapidly and took a deep breath. Then she said, "For God's sake, kiss me."

10

S he pulled him down into a hot kiss again. This time it was hungry, her mouth opening under his almost immediately, her back arching and her hand moving to cover his. She pressed it more firmly against her breast and stroked her tongue against his.

Parker could hardly argue with a woman who so clearly knew what she wanted. At least in this moment. And the fact that what she wanted was *him*, got him fully on board instantly. He kissed her deeply as he plucked at her nipple, then slid his hand to her stomach as he lowered his head and licked, then sucked the cinnamon and sugar from her skin. She moaned, and he moved to the other nipple. She took his hand again and moved it down to the peach silk of her panties. She was hot and wet as his finger coasted over the fabric between her legs, and he had to suck in a deep breath as he returned his finger to press against her clit. She gasped his name and he circled, relishing the way her hips bucked up closer to his touch.

Parker had to grit his teeth and force himself to remove his hand.

"Parker," she protested.

"Patience, sweetheart," he said gruffly. He reached to swirl his finger through the melted butter spilled on the counter, then dipped it into the brown sugar. He lifted it to her mouth.

She sucked it from his finger, tightening his balls, then said, "I'd happily suck that off of your cock if you put your hand in my panties right now."

He coughed, then groaned. "This isn't a negotiation."

"Everything's a negotiation."

He shook his head, fighting for the firmness he needed—with both of them. "Sorry, Boss. You're in no position to give directions right now."

He loved the position she *was* in, however. Her hair spread out on the countertop, her body laid out for his enjoyment, her breasts thrust into the air, one knee bent and falling to the side.

"Well, I can—" She started to roll, presumably to sit up.

He put his hand on her stomach, holding her in place. "As much as I would love to feel your sassy mouth around my cock," he said roughly, "right now, I have some plans for this butter and sugar."

She pressed her lips together, clearly torn between wanting his hand in her panties and wanting to be in charge. So he took the decision away from her. He swiped up more butter and sugar and swirled them in her belly button as he'd promised. Then he trailed his finger down to the top edge of her panties. As he felt her body relax and give in, he realized that maybe taking decisions out of Ava's hands more often would be a good way to go. He lapped up the sugary mix from her belly button with long, slow licks of his tongue, then followed the sticky trail to her panties. He inched them over her hips and kept going, kissing down to her bare mound.

Without a word, she lifted her hips and he pulled the peach silk to her knees. And revealed the pinnacle of deliciousness. He looked up to find her watching him. He wanted to just lean in and devour her. But he had a bigger purpose here. He reached for an apple slice. Watching her back, he licked the wedge, then put it against her clit.

She gasped as he pressed gently, then circled. "Parker," came out on a soft breath.

He slid the apple lower, into the slick folds, rubbing against her most sensitive flesh.

She moaned, and her leg moved to the side, giving him more access. He slid lower, pressing against her wet center and she whimpered slightly. He made sure her eyes were locked on his when he lifted the apple to his mouth and licked the sweetness from it that was all her.

"Oh, my God, Parker," she moaned.

"I'm telling you, sweeter than sugar." He slid the apple against her again, this time lifting it to her mouth.

Her eyes went wide, but she opened her mouth without a verbal command. He ran the wedge along her lower lip before slipping it inside. "Suck," he said softly.

She did. Then she licked the slice before he took it and bit into it. He watched her run her tongue over her bottom lip.

"See what I mean?" he asked. He shifted to put his mouth against her nipple again, licking and sucking there as his hand ran over her stomach and down to cup her sweet heat. "You're fucking delicious, Ava. I could do this all day."

She slid her fingers in his hair, gripping tightly. "I've got nowhere to be," she panted.

That made him smile. Suddenly, he was all she wanted to do. That was a damned victory right there.

"Well, in that case, no sense rushing things." He kissed his way down her stomach again, gathering up bits of butter and sugar as he went.

"I didn't say that," she protested, wiggling on the counter.

"You did," he said, reaching for the ginger. "Having your undivided attention isn't something I take for granted." He wet his finger by dipping it between her legs and earning another soft moan. Then he shook the ground spice onto his finger. "And we haven't tried the ginger yet," he said, lifting his finger to her mouth.

She seemed to be trying to glare at him, but she parted her lips. He chuckled softly. "What kind of employee would I be if I ignored your requests?"

Her lips closed around his fingertip and she swirled her tongue over the pad, licking it completely clean and making Parker adjust himself behind his fly.

"Your employee evaluation could really go either way at this point," she told him.

"So bossy," he chided. Then he slipped a finger through her slick folds again and into her heat. She was tight and wet, and they both groaned as he filled her. He circled her clit with his thumb and put his mouth to her nipple again.

"That's better," she managed breathlessly.

"It's fucking perfect," he muttered against her breast. He sucked hard as he thrust deeper, curling his finger to find her G-spot.

She sighed his name, and Parker thought that was just about the best thing he'd ever heard. He added a second finger and picked up the pace, making sure her clit got the friction and pressure she needed.

He left her nipple and took her mouth in a hungry kiss as he felt her inner muscles begin rippling. "Fuck yes, Ava. Come for me, Boss."

"So bossy," she managed between gasps of air.

"Damn right," he growled.

"Parker!" she gasped, then she gripped his wrist, arched her back, and went over the edge, tightening around his fingers.

Suddenly, the tinkling of the bell over the front door drifted to them.

Their eyes met, his fingers still deep inside of her, her naked and spread out on the countertop. And they both grinned.

"Thought it was locked," he said, slipping his fingers free and helping her sit up.

"It was. But Cori and Brynn both have keys."

Her hair was mussed, her lips pink, her whole body flushed. And she looked so fucking gorgeous it hurt. He leaned in and kissed her quickly, then swung her to the floor. He grabbed her clothes and stuffed them into her arms. "Next door is still locked up." He nudged her toward the back door, then because he couldn't resist, he swatted her ass.

She gave him a surprised looked, followed by a grin. "I'm supposed to walk outside naked?"

"It's like a foot between our doorways," he said.

"So?"

"So, hurry."

He watched her go, inappropriately proud of the fact that this was surely the only walk of shame Ava Carmichael had ever taken.

He'd just turned back to the counter and grabbed a spoon when Cori came through the door from the front of the shop.

"Oh, Parker." She glanced around. "Hey."

"Hey." He pretended to stir the butter around in the bowl he'd just righted, hoping Cori wouldn't notice it was just butter. Or the fact that even looking at the butter was giving him an erection.

"What are you doing here?"

"Baking lesson," he said.

"Where's Ava?"

There was something in Cori's eyes that looked like mischief. But that was a pretty consistent look for her so Parker ignored it. "She popped next door to get something."

"I hope she's not looking for her bra over there. She'll never find it," Cori said.

Parker looked up to see Cori pointing at the countertop next to him. Where Ava's peach bra lay.

"Um, no, I think she knows where that is." What was he supposed to say?

Cori lifted an eyebrow and gave him a half smile. "This place looks like things got a little out of hand," she said, taking in the countertop covered with spilled sugar and butter and the apples and eggs on the floor.

He didn't even look around when he said, "Yeah. Sometimes things get messier than you expect when you start a project." He had definitely not expected all of this with Ava when he'd agreed to be her baking coach. They were absolutely making a mess. A surprising, hot, beautiful mess.

Cori nodded. "Yeah, sometimes they do." She paused, then added, "She's often on her own when it comes to cleanup after things...boil over."

"Not this time," he said firmly, meeting Cori's eyes directly. "She's not on her own now."

———

"Apple pie shots? Really?" Ava asked Cori as her sister positioned shot glasses on the tray, preparing to carry them into the dining room.

"It was Parker's idea," Cori said.

Ava sighed. Subtle, he was not.

"When he requested we have game night tonight," Cori added, with a knowing grin.

"*Parker* requested game night?"

"Yep."

"And you just jumped to accommodate," Ava said with a frown.

"Of course. I love game night. It's the perfect way for me and Evan to hang out without it being a 'date' and it's a great date for Brynn and Noah that they don't have to call a date."

Brynn and Noah spent so much time together—and with no

one else—they were basically going steady, but they refused to call any of their times together dating. Their father had included a dating stipulation for Brynn to date at least six different guys while in Bliss. Since the quiet introvert had never dated...ever... that was going to be as much a challenge as the conditions for Ava and Cori. And Brynn was stalling. With Noah's help. Ava was certain that the big ex-Marine would prefer Brynn not date at all. At least, not anyone but him. And it seemed that they thought as long as they didn't label what they were doing as dating, then it didn't count...and she didn't have to stop seeing him to move on to five more guys.

The stipulation in the will for Cori's love life was to not date at all. She and Evan were getting around that by not doing anything either of them had done in a relationship before. That meant they were taking this seriously, actually getting to know each other, and doing normal things like just hanging out, in contrast to the short-term flings they'd both had in the past.

So game night had become a thing. The six of them got together, played cards or board games, and hung out so that Cori and Brynn could date Evan and Noah without dating them.

Usually Ava enjoyed the game nights. Yes, she snuck off to the bathroom or to refill her drink more than anyone else so she could check her phone throughout the evening. But tonight felt different. She was back to jumpy and itchy and that was just thinking about Parker being there. And she hadn't checked her phone once. In fact, at the moment, she wasn't even sure where her phone was.

The bastard. She wasn't going to be able to sit across the table from him and not think about his mouth and hands and...the fact that he'd stayed completely dressed. He'd taken care of her, very well, on the *counter*, in the *kitchen*, and he hadn't even unbuttoned his shirt.

That made her feel very...defenseless. Or something. And that bugged her. Sex had never been one-sided like that. If anything, *she* had always felt in more in control. Men were easy. Show them breasts and they were putty.

Well, she'd shown Parker breasts. And more. And *she* had been putty. Mush. A melted pile of orgasmic goo.

And, perhaps even bigger than that, it had been intimate. Very, very intimate. Not that sex didn't have a level of intimacy always, of course. But...no, it didn't. Being naked with a person was one thing, but being *exposed* with a person was something else. And she'd never been exposed before. Not like that.

Worse—he'd surprised her. Again. She'd be a damned liar if she said, even to herself, that she hadn't imagined getting frisky with Parker. And because Parker was Parker, some of those fantasies had involved food. But she'd expected him to be demanding and gruff and bossy. And he'd been those things... while also being sweet.

What the hell was that?

She couldn't adequately prepare for spending time with him —and therefore get her defenses firmly in place—when he didn't act the way she expected him to.

He'd talked to her. The whole time. Not dirty stuff, but insightful, sweet stuff that made her feel seen, cared for, and wanted. In spite of the things he knew about her. She'd never felt that for sure. The men she dated saw exactly what she let them see—a cool, in control business woman who was *letting* them get close. Parker just...got close. She definitely hadn't pushed him away, but he certainly hadn't hesitated or even thought twice about getting right into her business. So to speak.

There was also no way she was going to be able to taste apples or cinnamon and not get all flushed and hot and wet. Maybe ever again.

And he knew it.

"I should work tonight," Ava said.

"You've been working for the past three days. Here. At home," Cori said, looking annoyed.

Technically she'd gone in to the pie shop in the morning three days ago, but she'd only been there for two hours and had come home. And not gone back.

"Yeah, I know," she said. "But I need to be here." She did. Here, she was still distracted and thinking of Parker far more than she wanted to be, but at least she could get *something* done. Because she could avoid the smell of cinnamon and nutmeg and ginger. And it wasn't a huge overreaction to tuck the canister of sugar behind the blender so she couldn't see it. She'd gone to the kitchen for coffee and water and lunch, but she'd carefully stayed away from the drawer with the apples and hadn't even touched the butter.

She knew it was all ridiculous but avoiding him was necessary.

Because the other morning, in those two hours in the pie shop, she'd made a good pie. From scratch. By herself.

It wasn't an amazing pie. It wasn't the best thing anyone had ever eaten. But it was good. It was by far the best one she'd made.

And it was because of Parker.

She'd found herself tasting as she went. Something she'd never done before. And as she tasted, she made adjustments so *she* liked it. She'd decreased the ginger, increased the cinnamon, and used honey crisp apples. She'd gone off-recipe. And it had worked. And that freaked her out. Because that wasn't how her life was supposed to work. Plans, schedules, routines and *recipes* were supposed to be dependable. Following them was supposed to ensure a good outcome. But that hadn't been working for her in Bliss. Or really since she'd gotten the phone call that her father had passed away in a tiny town in Kansas far from home. Far from her. That hadn't been expected either. And it had thrown the plan she *did* have into a tailspin. That hadn't stopped spinning yet.

And now she'd made a pie that was good, and she couldn't remember how much of which thing she'd put in because she'd just added until it tasted good and not having exact numbers was giving her heart palpitations.

As did the idea that she maybe *could* reproduce it just by taste. Because then she wouldn't need Parker anymore.

That was the thought that sent her from palpitations to thumping-blood-rushing-chest-aching.

So, she'd decided to pretend that pie had never happened. It hadn't really. It had been a fluke. Out of the millions of pies she'd tried, statistically she was bound to get one right eventually.

And all of that chest-hurting-heart-pounding stuff didn't matter anyway.

Parker lived in small-town Kansas, she lived in New York City. He made burgers for a living—even if he wanted to make more than that—and she made...money. Even if she wanted to make more than that.

"Ava?" Cori was waving her hand in front of her face.

"Sorry. What?"

"I asked how you thought you were going to avoid him in this tiny town, working next door, for the next eight months."

"I don't know."

"So you are trying to avoid Parker."

Ava looked at Cori's huge grin, realized what she'd just admitted, and blew out a breath. "Fine. Yes."

"Because you had a fight?"

"No."

"Because he made fun of your pie?"

"No."

"Because he kissed you and took your bra off and made you not care about pie?"

Ava had no idea why she ever even considered keeping a secret from either of her sisters. "I have never cared about pie." Until maybe the last few days. Well, *caring* about pie was stretching it, but she didn't *hate* pie now. As much.

"So he kissed you and took your bra off and made you not care about stockholder year-end dividends?" Cori teased.

"Well..." She sighed. "Yeah."

"Thank God," Cori said, picking up the tray. "That guy's getting extra shots."

"Cori," Ava said, before she could stop herself.

Cori turned back. "Yeah?"

"Parker and I are a bad idea." They were, at least, an inconvenient idea. Bliss and New York were very far apart. In many ways.

Cori tipped her head. "So you're not just having hot sex and baking lessons?"

Ava frowned as she thought about that question. And realized something. "We haven't technically had either of those things."

The other day had been hot, and she'd...appreciated...the orgasm. But it hadn't been sex. And they still hadn't baked a damned thing together. But he was under her skin, in her thoughts, messing with her plans. Or threatening her plans anyway.

Cori seemed unsure how to respond to that. "What have you had?" she asked, lowering the tray and looking almost concerned.

They'd had conversation. They'd had flirtation. They'd had insight and some confessions and food. They'd had lots of food. "I have no idea," she finally told Cori honestly.

Cori studied her from across the kitchen, her puzzled look fading to surprise and then to understanding. "Oh."

Ava didn't like the sound of that. "What's that mean?"

Cori wet her lips and then lifted a shoulder. "Let me just say that there was a while there when I didn't know what Evan and I had either. Because it was so different and so unexpected and so complicated."

Yeah, she *definitely* didn't like the sound of that. "I don't want different or unexpected or complicated," she said.

Cori nodded, seeming almost sympathetic. "Yeah, I know."

"So what do I do?"

"You mean to avoid all of that?"

"Yes."

Cori shook her head, a soft smile touching her lips. "I have absolutely no idea. I'm up to my eyeballs in different and unexpected."

"But you like it."

Cori's smile grew. "I love it."

Ava groaned. This was *not* helping.

"If you're not going to just enjoy it, I've only got one option for you," Cori said.

"What? I'll do anything."

Cori held up the tray. "Lots of shots."

————

"Of course he's falling for her," Noah said, pulling the cards out of the game box. "I think we were all already half in love just from what Rudy told us about them before they ever got to town."

Evan laughed. "Yeah, except I think Rudy thought we'd pair up differently. He thought Ava and I would be good for each other, and that Brynn could be the sweetness Parker needs, and that Cori could make you have some fun."

Noah looked up. "I'd say it's all working out pretty well as is."

Evan nodded. He was sitting back in his chair, his beer bottle cradled in one hand, the picture of nonchalance. But he was watching his friend carefully. "Me too. Obviously. Of course, there's the little issue of Brynn needing to date five more guys before this is all over."

Noah frowned. "Six guys. She's supposed to date six guys before it's over."

"Then you're sticking with the assertion that the time you spend together doesn't count as dating?" Evan asked. "You're not guy number one?"

Noah shook his head and started shuffling the cards. "We're not dating."

"Right. You just spend all your free time together, socialize together, don't socialize with anyone else, scowl at any guy who tries to talk to her for more than five minutes, and stare at her like a love-sick puppy dog whenever she's not looking. And sometimes when she is looking," Evan said.

Noah didn't actually refute any of that. He just said, "We're friends. I'm getting to know her so that I know which guys I should set her up with." But he didn't make eye contact as he said it. He was very busy shuffling the cards that said things like *a funeral* and *Denzel Washington* and *smelly*. And that basically didn't need shuffling.

"What about the love-sick puppy dog thing?" Evan asked, clearly not willing to let Noah just ignore that part.

"Every guy who meets her looks at her that way," Noah said, lifting a shoulder as if it was no big deal. "Every guy looks at Cori that way too, in case you haven't noticed."

"I've totally noticed," Evan said. "Which is why I make it crystal clear that she's taken. Kind of like what you're doing with Brynn."

"That's not what I'm doing."

But there wasn't a guy in Bliss who dared do more than smile at Brynn and hold doors for her and ask her how she was. Because Noah was big, and he was an ex-Marine, and he'd made it clear, albeit nonverbally, that Brynn was his. Even if he hadn't exactly *meant to.*

"You haven't set her up with one single date yet," Evan said. "How long does getting to know her take?"

"We don't all think we know everything important about someone after just a few days," Noah said, obviously referring to how quickly Evan and Cori had bonded.

Evan shrugged. "Well, it's only taken Parker about four months with Ava. How come you're still getting to know Brynn?"

"Parker knew a lot about Ava from Rudy," Noah pointed out.

"You didn't know a lot about Brynn from Rudy?" Evan asked.

Noah's frown darkened. "Rudy didn't know Brynn very well." The look on Noah's face was one of protectiveness and almost anger. Considering Noah had been as close to Rudy as Evan and Parker had, the anger was interesting.

Evan obviously read the situation. It was better not to provoke the big guy who made a living taking things apart with tools that Evan and Parker had never even heard of. "So you think Parker is pretty much screwed?" Evan asked. "I mean, the second I kissed Cori, I was a goner. I didn't know it, but there was no coming back from that."

"Yeah, I think he is," Noah said arranging the game cards for the third time.

"I wonder how long it will be before he realizes it," Evan said.

"Well, *you* needed us to tell you that your mini-panic attack and indecision about having sex with Cori was because you were in love with her," Noah reminded him.

Evan nodded. "So should we just *tell* him?"

"You mean before he asks us?" Noah asked.

"Yeah."

"I don't know. He's not very good about taking advice," Noah said.

"That's because I know better than either of you about most things," Parker said dryly, finally inputting into the conversation. He was seated across from Noah, even if it seemed that he wasn't even in the room. He had a beer in his hand too and was half listening to his two best friends run their mouths.

He was also half listening for Ava's voice and footsteps.

Which meant his friends were absolutely right. He was screwed. But he already knew it, so he was still ahead of these two.

Evan hadn't realized his feelings for Cori went beyond lust and friendship until Parker and Noah—and Hank—had helped him see it. And Noah was still sitting there holding bright red and green playing cards, getting ready for another game night, after stitching cushions and painting walls and arranging tartlet pans full of pie-scented wax crumbles on the tables at the pie shop, and thinking that he and Brynn were just friends. Noah hadn't even known what a tartlet was before Brynn had come to town. And none of the guys had heard of wax crumbles, scented or otherwise. Noah was in deep. But the guy was mentally tough. Clearly. His denial was almost as strong as his feelings for the sweet, nerdy triplet.

So yeah, Parker was aware of his feelings for Ava. He knew that things had gotten complicated. Somehow, in the midst of avocados and cinnamon, he'd developed feelings for her.

Actually, the feelings had probably started somewhere in the midst of her throwing him out of her kitchen on the very first day, and the way she'd stomped into his kitchen the next day *demanding* to know the difference between whisking and beating.

Okay, *actually*, it had probably started somewhere between Rudy telling him about Ava organizing Rudy's assistant's desk on her first Take Your Daughter to Work Day when she was twelve, and his story about Ava asking for a briefcase for her fourteenth birthday.

And it had gotten official when she told him she'd been taste-testing cinnamon and nutmeg and reading about apples. The colored tabs on her pie filling report hadn't hurt either.

The door to the kitchen swung open just then, and Cori emerged with a tray full of shot glasses.

Parker gave her a big grin as he saw the cinnamon sticks poking out of the glasses. Cori could plan a party in thirty seconds. She loved a theme, so when he'd suggested game night, said "What about Apples to Apples?" and requested apple pie shots as the drink, Cori had nearly swooned. She'd taken over organizing game nights ever since the first one, when Ava had rolled out beer and chips and dip with poker. It had been fine, of course, but Cori couldn't tolerate boring or "typical". Which meant even Apples to Apples was going to have a twist or two.

If nothing else, there was no way Ava was going to sit across from him and ignore him. If he had to make pie jokes and insert the word "apple" into every other sentence all night, he *was* going to have her attention.

Which was just one more indication that he'd gone around the bend. He was perfectly content without attention. He'd certainly never worked for a woman's attention before. He hadn't really had to, he supposed. But he'd also never met a woman who was as complex as Ava Carmichael.

He should really settle down with a Bliss girl. They were mostly sweet and uncomplicated, and at least eight out of ten of them could bake a fucking pie.

"Where's Brynn?" Noah asked.

Evan smirked, as though he'd just been waiting for Noah to ask.

"She's Skyping with Jeffrey," Cori said. Jeffrey was one of Brynn's lab assistants and was the guy keeping things going in her absence.

Noah frowned. "How long have they been on?"

Parker just shook his head. Noah was jealous of some scientist geek from New York who was talking about microbes with Brynn via Skype. Yeah, he was going to handle her dating experiment really well.

"About an hour?" Cori said. Then she got a sly look in her eye and added, "All I heard was giggling when I went by."

Noah got to his feet and started for the stairs. Cori burst into laughter as his foot hit the bottom step. "I'm kidding," she called after him. "Brynn doesn't giggle."

"Yeah, she does," Noah shot back and stomped up the stairs.

Evan, Parker, and Cori all shared wide-eyed looks.

"Damn," Cori said.

"What?" Evan asked, reaching out and pulling her into his lap. "You like guys who get all possessive and growly?"

She wrapped an arm around his neck. "Well, yeah. Duh. All girls like that. At least within reason."

"I can be possessive and growly," Evan told her, pinching her ass.

She kissed him and then said, "Can you get some tattoos too?"

Evan arched a brow. "You like Noah's tattoos?"

"Uh, I might be in love with you, Mr. Stone, but I'm not dead."

"Is that a yes?" he asked, getting a little growly even as they sat there.

"*All* girls like Noah's tattoos."

"Is that right?" Parker asked. Did that include Ava?

"Even Ava," Cori said with a nod, as if reading his mind.

Parker felt a little growly himself suddenly.

The kitchen door swung out again, and the hot, long-legged blonde who emerged this time was the one that *he'd* like to pinch on the ass.

11

A va was carrying a martini glass with a creamy brown liquid in it—a chocolate martini, Parker knew—and he got the message loud and clear. She wasn't drinking his fucking apple pie shots.

Yeah, well, that was too subtle anyway. If Noah could stomp up the stairs because Brynn was Skyping with some guy, then he could absolutely do what he was about to do.

He might end up carrying his balls home in a to-go bag, but it was worth the risk.

Because the thing was...he might owe her an apology.

Ava wasn't the type to run and hide, and the fact that he hadn't seen her in three days wasn't just making him itchy in a place he couldn't seem to scratch, but it worried him.

"Hey, Boss," he greeted, still sitting back in his chair, just watching her.

"Hi, Parker," she said. "Evan."

"Hey, Ava," Evan said. He cast a glance at Parker. "So, our theme tonight is apples, huh?"

Parker rolled his eyes. Yes, it had been his idea, and yeah, the theme was on the nose—at least for him and Ava—but Evan couldn't be content to just let it be. He had to point it out.

"I guess so." She sipped from her martini glass, making her point *subtly*. Okay, so she *didn't* feel more fond of apples now. That was...not okay.

Parker got to his feet. "Since Brynn and Noah aren't down here yet, can we talk for a second?" he asked Ava.

She met his gaze directly. He realized he should have expected nothing less. "I don't think we need to talk," she said.

"Then I'll talk."

"I'd rather just get going on the game. I have work to do tonight."

Her tone was *don't push me,* but now she wasn't meeting his eyes, and Parker simply couldn't not push. That was the problem. Now that he knew how she looked and sounded when she came, now that he couldn't look at a stick of butter without getting hard, now that he'd seen her pitch eggs against the wall because she'd discovered that she liked breaking things, he was, most definitely, going to push her.

He moved around the table. "Boss, I really hate to do this."

"Do what?"

He took her glass from her, tipped it back, swallowing the rest of the contents—and hopefully clearly making the point that he didn't really fucking care what she was drinking, it wasn't making this go away—and set the glass on the table. Then he bent, lifted her over his shoulder, and headed out of the dining room, through the living room, and into the room she'd commandeered for her office.

He was, however, impressed that she didn't even yell as he carried her through the house.

He kicked the door shut behind him, deposited her on the floor, and then, without stepping back even an inch, looked down at her.

"Parker, I—"

"I just want to say I'm sorry."

That clearly surprised her. She stopped, and a crease appeared between her eyebrows. "You're sorry? For what?"

"I wanted to make it so that you smile when you walked into the pie shop kitchen. If that's not what turned out, I'm sorry."

Her mouth fell open and she stared up at him.

He didn't resist the urge to tuck her hair behind her ear. "I realize it got a little intense and deep. It was supposed to be fun and silly and hot. I should stop trying to predict how things will go when we're together because it never turns out that way. But anyway, I hate that you've been avoiding the shop and me. I'm sorry."

She snapped her mouth shut, opened it again, then shut it again. She frowned. She took a deep breath. Then she blew the breath out and said, "Well, you're right that I've been avoiding the shop, but that's not why. I walk into the pie shop kitchen now, and my heart pounds and my nipples tingle and my panties get wet."

Her words took a bit to sink in. But when they did, he crowded close, his gaze burning into hers. "Is that right?"

"It is."

"And that's why you stayed home?"

She swallowed. "Yeah."

"You don't like tingling nipples?"

"Not when I'm supposed to be doing other things."

"You couldn't do other things?"

"I could. Technically. But...I didn't want to."

Damn. He blew out a breath.

"What?" she asked, studying his expression.

"I just know how much you like to do other things."

She shrugged. "Yeah. I do. Usually."

"So you hid out instead of coming over?" He moved a little closer. There wasn't much air between them anyway, but he *needed* to be in her personal space. Completely. "I'm very happy to help with tingling nipples. And wet panties."

Now she blew out the breath. "Yeah, I hid out."

"You don't seem like the type."

"I'm not."

He really liked that confession. His lifted a hand to her cheek. "I burned garlic bread today and left the cream out last night so it was ruined."

Her mouth lifted on one corner. "You don't seem the type."

"I'm not."

She shook her head, her tiny smile dying. "I don't like being discombobulated. At all. Not even a little."

"And you don't feel that here at the house?" Because he sure as hell was thinking about *her* everywhere he went.

"No. I mean, I was still a little distracted, but I didn't think of you every time I took a deep breath."

He really liked that every breath at the shop made her think of him. But he wasn't so sure he liked that she could get him out of her mind when he could still conjure the taste, smell, and feel of her even in the center of Main Street in the middle of the day.

"Huh." He started backing her up until her butt hit the edge of her desk. He cupped her face and then leaned in and kissed her. It started sweet and soft, but that only lasted a few seconds. They both opened their mouths at the same time, their tongues tangled, and like a spark to dry kindling, every molecule between them seemed to ignite.

But after a few seconds, she put her hands on his chest and pushed. "Whoa. I know what you're doing."

"Kissing you."

"And trying to make it so I think of you *here* too."

"Yep." Damn right, even.

"Parker," she said softly. "I...need...space. Breathing room. *Some* ability to do something productive over the next eight or whatever months." She looked almost pleading as she grabbed his forearm and squeezed. "I can't be mooning around and distracted and thinking about the cute boy next door to the point that I can't be...me."

Okay, whoa. If he'd been expecting her to get all snotty and frosty and haughty—and he had been—she'd just swiped the rug right out from under him. This kept happening. Every time he thought he knew her, thought he knew what to do, how to handle her, she did...this. She became real and vulnerable and...amazing.

"You don't think you can be you and have tingling nipples at the same time?" he asked, trying not to let on that he felt like there was a vise around his chest. He wanted her. So fucking badly. And it had nothing to do with the black three-inch heels she was wearing. Well, maybe it had a little to do with those. He knew those made her feel confident and kick-ass. He also knew she didn't sleep in them. Well, he was ninety-six percent sure that she didn't sleep in them. Which meant, she'd needed to feel kick-ass tonight, in her own house, playing board games with her friends.

Because of him.

Fuck.

"I'm definitely not used to having tingling nipples just because a guy smiles at me a certain way."

His entire body tightened with her admission this was all new for her. And the idea that he affected her like this. "I would give up my favorite kettle for a chance to bend you over this desk right now," he told her.

That startled a laugh out of her. "Wow, that's something."

"You have no idea." He took a breath. "But I hear you. I fucking love that I'm getting to you, because, Boss, you have absolutely gotten to me. But I hear you. So— " He went on as she started to respond. "Even though it might kill me, I'm not going to do anything with your nipples or panties. Right now. In here. But you have to pick a room in this house—I don't care if it's the laundry room or the basement storage closet or the attic—but I *am* going to kiss you again before I leave tonight."

She wet her lips, her cheeks slightly flushed. "And will my nipples and panties be involved?"

He put his forehead to hers, running his thumb over her lip. "If there's even a glimmer of goodness in your soul."

She huffed out a soft laugh. "That bad?"

"You want my fancy new cheese grater? It might be my most prized possession at the moment and I'll gladly give it up."

She tipped her head, kissed him quickly, and then stepped back. "Keep all your damned kitchen appliances away from me."

"Well, technically it's not an appliance…"

"How about you promise *not* to make me use any graters of any kind ever and I'll let you do whatever you want with my panties." She gave him the most adorable, and cheeky, smile he'd ever seen.

"Deal. Because what I want to do with your panties is very simple—rip them off of you."

She sucked in a quick breath. "Should I go change into my cheap white cotton ones?"

"Fuck no. You stay in those fancy, expensive, skimpy things that you have on now. Us small-town, blue-collar guys don't get to see a lot of expensive lingerie."

"Or rip them up?"

"Exactly. And I'm doing it with my bare hands. Very manly." He gave her a slow grin.

A little shiver made her wiggle.

"You okay?" he asked.

"We need to get out of this office right now if I have any hope of preserving the ability to work in here."

She stepped around him and started for the door. He took in the sight, especially appreciating the ass that was currently covered in the fancy, expensive, skimpy stuff he couldn't wait to get his hands on.

"Full panties or a thong?" he asked, noticing there wasn't even a hint of a panty line.

She stopped with her hand on the doorknob and turned back, an eyebrow up, "Get out of my office. Now."

He did. Chuckling—and giving that fine, panty-covered ass a swat as he went.

————

S he couldn't even concentrate on Apples to Apples, for fuck's sake.

Because she was human. And Parker Blake, underneath his grumpy, gruff, I'm-always-right exterior, was sweet, and charming, and got her. In a way that no one else did. And he was hot. He was very hot. With a mouth and hands that she couldn't stop thinking about. Even though she'd had barely enough of either.

Ava laid her cards down and studied the man across from her. He must have felt her eyes on him because he looked up and gave her a wink.

And her heart flipped over.

The men she dated weren't winkers. And her heart never...got involved.

She sighed internally. Crap. Her heart getting involved was so stupid. This was temporary. It wasn't even supposed to be real. It was *supposed* to be about pie.

But if it was about pie, it would be over. Because she'd figured that out. Kind of, anyway. The fact that she was keeping that information from everyone said a lot about her feelings for Parker that she didn't want said.

She watched as he laid his cards down as well, his long fingers and wide palms making her body heat, even from across the dining room table, playing a silly card game surrounded by other people, with people all around.

As Brynn, the judge for this round, deliberated about who

had made the best matchup, Parker drew the cinnamon stick from his shot glass and, as Ava watched, licked it from top to bottom.

She met his eyes and rolled hers. He grinned. She ran her finger around the edge of her glass, picking up the cinnamon and sugar that Cori had rimmed the shot glasses with. She slid her finger into her mouth and sucked.

He coughed and shifted on his chair and she felt victorious. The whole apple pie theme had been his idea. Turning it around on him was fun. She was grinning way too brightly for a game of Apples to Apples, but she didn't care. Because she also felt...lighthearted. That was a very unusual feeling for her. She didn't really flirt. She didn't have to. The men who she dated didn't go out with her because she was cute and flirtatious. And she definitely didn't tease about blow jobs. She also had never wanted to give a blow job as much as she wanted to give one to Parker.

And she was sure she'd never wanted to give a guy a blow job because he was the reason she'd discovered that she preferred Golden Delicious over all the other apples.

She also wanted his big hands all over her body. She wanted to find out where exactly his tan line from working shirtless ended. She wanted to find out what sound he would make when she wrapped her hand around his cock and stroked. She wanted to hear all the sweet, dirty things he would say as she kissed her way down his body and asked him which position he wanted to start in.

Now it was her turn to shift on the chair. Good grief. She had never sat across a table from a man and daydreamed about sex. Never. When she was at tables with men they were talking business, and nothing distracted her from that.

Except apples. And cinnamon. And the idea of Parker ripping her panties off in the mudroom at the back of the house. That was where she'd decided they'd go for the goodnight "kiss". She never went in there, for one thing, so that made it safer. And where better to get dirty with Parker than the mudroom?

She giggled and then froze almost instantly. She slowly looked up from her shot glass. Sure enough, everyone at the table was staring at her.

Ava never giggled. Well, maybe with her sisters after a couple of martinis. But she *rarely* giggled. And never in mixed company. Not to mention that, as far as they knew, she had no reason to be giggling anyway.

"You okay?" Cori asked.

Ava took a deep breath and then nodded. "Completely." And she was. She was distracted and horny. And not used to being either of those things. But she was very much okay.

As everyone went back to their cards, she shot a glance at Parker. He gave her a slow smile and mouthed, "Me too."

Her heart stuttered again and she felt warm. Not take-her-clothes-off hot, though that was just below the surface, but warm like she felt when she caught one of her sisters' eyes and they communicated with just a look. She liked Parker Blake. While she was increasingly glad that he was attracted to her, she was also glad he seemed to like her. She didn't really have many friends. People in her world were mostly business acquaintances. She had her sisters and that had always been enough.

Now, as she looked at Parker and Evan and Noah, she realized that they were her friends and that, somehow in a very short span of time, they'd come to matter to her. And vice versa.

Her gaze settled on Parker as he and Noah gave each other shit about their card matches. Ava had played her card without even looking at it. She had no idea what she was supposed to be matching it with or if *kitten* was even close to being appropriate. She also couldn't care less. She just liked being here with these people. That might have been the most unusual thing of all. She wasn't worried about the rules or if she was playing by them. And she didn't care about winning.

She propped her chin on her hand and studied Parker as he laughed with the others.

He'd understand how uncommon, and meaningful, it was that she just wanted to play the game with everyone and not worry about rules and winning. And he'd really like it. It might even get one of those hot growls he sometimes made when she'd said or done something that pleased him and turned him on at the same time. She'd have to be sure to tell him later in the mudroom. She did love those little growls.

Ava looked over at Cori and Brynn. Brynn's smile made Ava's grow. Brynn had definitely started coming out of her shell since they'd been in Bliss. The fact that Brynn was sitting here playing a card game instead of peering into a microscope or reading research papers in her room was as big a step as Ava playing along for fun without memorizing every rule printed on the game box. Her sisters would also get how big it was that she wasn't concentrating on the game.

They were the people in the world closest to her. They'd shared everything, always. But even though they definitely knew where she was coming from and accepted her, they didn't fully understand her need for rules and control. Though they were triplets, it was like they'd each taken a third of a whole personality, each different, but complementary to one another.

Cori was a free spirit through and through. Rules had never mattered much to her. Brynn was a scientist, which, on the surface, with the equations and precise titrations might seem to stem from a love for rules and numbers and the need to control. But science didn't really work that way. There were mutations. There seemed to be more questions than answers. For every rule, there seemed to be an exception. All of that would have made Ava crazy. Whereas Brynn saw it as a challenge. In some ways, when Ava watched Cori cook and listened to Brynn talk about her work, she saw many similarities in her sisters. They were both creating things, and their sense of reward came from people responding positively to those things. Ava, on the other hand, made it possible for people to create things that made people respond positively.

She looked at Parker again as an idea took seed. That was what she did—she saw potential in other people and businesses and provided them with the resources and opportunity to do what they wanted to do and what they were good at. Yes, her sisters and mom were her focus, always, but she did it for other people too. All the time.

When Cori rose to refill drinks and Noah leaned over to say something to Brynn, Ava took the chance to slip a piece of paper from the notepad Noah was using to keep score. She hesitated for just a second before quickly writing *mudroom*, then crumpled the note in her fist.

Evan said something to Parker about the mini-golf course Evan was putting in at the park with the trust Rudy had bestowed upon the town. Ava leaned back in her chair and tossed the note to the floor next to Parker's chair.

Without a hiccup in his reply to Evan, Parker shifted forward in his chair, leaning a forearm on the table and reaching for the wad of paper with the other.

She'd never passed notes to cute boys in class. She'd been far too busy taking notes on the class to really even notice the boys around her. Even in high school, she'd had her eye on the prize. She'd figured a relationship would eventually come along, fit right in, and seamlessly become a part of her plan.

She also, somehow, knew that Parker would really like knowing how off the rails she felt lately. He was a guy who appreciated a good plan, who valued routine and predictability. Yet, he would like knowing that he'd shaken hers up a bit. For a guy who didn't like change himself...

But she trailed off on that thought. Parker didn't change. That didn't mean he didn't want to. He would love to add to his menu. He'd love to experiment with new recipes and techniques. He'd probably love to buy some crazy, fancy appliances and tools. But the most elaborate thing in his kitchen was a cheese grater.

For him, the stability—for the town and for himself—was more important than his own wants. She knew a little about that. She loved her job, she was damned good at it, she wasn't really qualified to do anything else. But if it weren't for the stability she was providing for her sisters and mom, and even the employees that depended on Carmichael Enterprises, she wouldn't be working sixteen-hour days and that would mean more hours in her fuzzy slipper socks. Or bare feet. As much as it would shock Parker, she did enjoy kicking her heels off as much as she liked putting them on.

Then again...maybe that wouldn't surprise him.

It was a little disconcerting to think about Parker knowing her so well. They'd met not even quite four months ago. No matter what Rudy had told him about her ahead of time, how could she feel like Parker really got her? But as he finally opened the note under the edge of the table, read the single word, and nodded without looking at her, with a tiny smile pulling up the corner of his mouth, she loved the sense of connection she felt with him.

"One more round?" Noah asked, shuffling the cards together.

Cori and Evan and Brynn settled in, but Parker shifted forward on his chair. "Actually, I think I'm ready to head out."

Noah gave him a look. "Really, old man?"

"I have to feed everyone bacon before they bring their cars in to you," Parker said, shoving his chair back. "Bacon at six-thirty, car repairs at eight. You want to switch it up?"

Noah shook his head. "I don't want to deal with any of them before their bacon."

"Exactly." Parker stretched to his feet. "You're welcome."

"How about you guys?" Noah asked, already dealing cards to Cori, Evan, and Brynn.

Noah was stalling so he didn't have to leave Brynn, and everyone at the table—except maybe Noah and Brynn—knew it.

Cori grinned and picked her cards up. "I'm always in."

That was for sure.

Ava realized that Noah hadn't dealt her in. "I'm not playing?" she asked.

Noah didn't even look up at her. "Figured you needed to walk Parker out to his car. Or something."

She did. Through the mudroom. But they knew that? Then she sighed. Of course they did. Maybe this was why she didn't really have many friends. Having people observing and figuring things out about her was bewildering.

"Yeah, since you *will* be in to the pie shop tomorrow, I've got something else you should read up on tonight," Parker said to her. His emphasis on *will* did not go unnoticed.

She got up. "Fine." She added a sigh for everyone else's bene-fit. Judging by Parker's grin, he wasn't buying it.

Judging by Evan's, he wasn't either.

They started for the kitchen together, the fastest way to the mudroom.

"Hey, didn't you park out front?" Evan said to Parker.

"Evan?" Parker said without looking back, holding the swinging kitchen door for Ava.

"Yeah?"

"Shut up."

Ava stepped through the door before giggling again. So only Parker heard it. But he didn't even pretend to ignore it as he stepped in behind her, grasped her hips, and pulled her back against him. "Fuck, making you giggle and blush makes me want to hike up this skirt right here and now."

Her smile died as heat and desire washed over her. She grabbed his hand and started for the mudroom off the back of the house. "Hold that thought for ten seconds."

They practically tumbled into the mudroom and Ava slammed the door. She winced. That would alert everyone else in the house to what was going on. But who was she kidding?

They already knew. The room had a light, but she didn't hit the switch. There were windows along one side of the room, and the moonlight was enough to keep them from being totally blind. And there was something about fumbling around in the dark with Parker, trying to be quiet, feeling like they were sneaking—even if no one was fooled at all about what they were doing—that added to the sense of fun. She'd never made out with a guy when there were other people only a few rooms away. She'd never made out in a mudroom. Hell, she'd never been *in* a mudroom—or even heard of one—before coming to Bliss.

Parker's hands were already on her face, holding her still, so he could take her mouth. His kiss was immediately hot and deep and she gripped his biceps, arching closer.

She started walking backward toward the thick wooden table against one wall that would be the perfect height for her to sit on while he thrust. Her whole body clenched at the idea. She'd never had hot and steamy sex like that. One thousand thread count Egyptian cotton was more her usual than an old table in a room with "mud" in the name. But this felt good.

And when Parker slid one hand from her cheek all the way down her body to her ass and pulled her up against the hard length behind his fly, it felt better than good. It felt right.

"Where're you going?" he asked huskily, pulling his fingers through her hair, then wrapping the ends around his fist and tugging to tip her head back.

"Table." She took another step.

"And what do you want me to do with that table?" he asked, kissing her and running his tongue over her lower lip before lifting his head so she could answer.

"Put me on it."

"And then what?"

She drew a shuddery breath. "Touch me."

"I can touch you right here." He squeezed her ass, then ran

his hand up her side to her breast, thumbing the hardened tip of her nipple through her blouse.

"Touch me like you did at the pie shop," she told him. "And maybe get naked yourself."

He gave a low, deep laugh. "And then what, Boss?"

She slid her hands up to his face, staring up at him in the dim light. He wanted to play employee-boss right now? Fine. She'd never role-played either, but telling people what she wanted and expected of them was like breathing to her. "Get on your knees and make me come with your tongue this time."

His whole body went rigid against her, and she could feel the heat in his gaze even in the near-dark. "You gonna say please?"

"Nope. But I'll give you Christmas and New Year's off if you do a good job."

"From the pie shop or from fucking you?" His voice was low and Ava felt the rumble of it to her bones. That seemed to instantly liquefy.

She pulled in a breath, gripping him a little harder to keep from melting to the floor. "The pie shop."

"Good. Because buried deep between your legs is exactly where I'd like to end this year and start the next one."

He kissed her with enough heat Ava was pretty sure she was going to need to be poured out of the room in the end. His tongue stroked deep and hot, his hands were almost rough, in the most delicious way, as he pressed against her, his fingers squeezing, then flicking her nipple.

He had a good enough hold on her that Ava felt safe letting go of him to start working to open the buttons of her shirt. The blouse didn't fall away since his hand was still cupping one breast, but once it was unbuttoned, she unzipped her skirt and started to step out of her shoes.

"Keep 'em on," he said gruffly against her mouth.

"You made me take them off the other day," she reminded him breathlessly. Though once she lost the three inches, she was going to have to get up on the table to maintain the near-perfect alignment of their bodies.

"I needed you a little less kick-ass that day. But the next time I make you come, I want those damned things *on* your feet."

Hearing him say *make you come* got her about halfway there. They'd established that her shoes made her feel tough. "You want *me* to be in charge here?" she asked. "Because I can do that." But deep down—or not that deep down—she wanted *him* to take over. It was a very rare occasion when she didn't run the room. But when it came to kitchens, Parker was definitely in charge. And she wouldn't mind adding mudrooms to his resume.

"Nope. I want to show you that I can be in charge even when you have your I'm-better-than-you shoes on. And that you like it."

12

Thank God. But she couldn't resist saying, "Well, just so you know, I'm notoriously hard to impress."

Parker paused and she could almost see the smile he was fighting. "I'll bet you are, Boss." He shook his head. "Probably why you have seven vibrators, right?"

Her eyebrows shot up. "I wasn't talking about *that*." Though, she couldn't remember the last time she'd been *impressed* in the bedroom. "And I don't have seven!"

He chuckled. "Well, I think I'm going to need some time to prepare to *impress* you."

"No!" She grabbed the front of his shirt. "I was just teasing you."

"Oh, Boss, come on," he said, shaking his head and taking her wrist, removing her hand. "You and I both know you're not the teasing type."

No, she wasn't. But she decided to be honest. "But... I am. With you." She wanted to tease and laugh and flirt and goof around. It was the most bizarre thing she'd ever felt.

He tucked a hand in his front pocket. "Sweet of you to say, but don't worry, my ego can handle it."

"Handle what?"

"Being just another one of the guys who goes all gaga when you walk in the room."

"But I—" She paused. He went all gaga? Seriously? Parker Blake? She narrowed her eyes. "Oh, come on," she mimicked. "We both know you're not the gaga type."

"But..." he said, stepping closer again. "I am. With you."

She didn't think many guys had actually ever been *gaga* over her. Maybe over her limo. Or her regular table by the window at the top three restaurants in New York. But not really *her*. And she felt a warmth in her chest thinking that Parker might be even *a little* gaga. He'd never seen her limo, and she'd never pulled strings for a last minute reservation. And now she kind of wanted to wine and dine him in New York.

They were teasing. Kidding. Messing with each other. That had to be it. Not only was he *not* the gaga type—at all—but *surely* he wasn't leaving this room without touching her.

She whimpered softly at the possibility.

"But..." He leaned in, his lips nearly on hers. "Don't worry, Boss. I intend to get my mouth on every inch of you eventually. But I need a way of standing out from the crowd with you."

Another wave of heat hit her and she had to swallow before speaking. She didn't even bother assuring him that he was already as different from the guys in New York as anyone could be. Parker knew that. She knew that he knew that. She just asked, "What do you mean?"

"I'm guessing that not only do not many of those New York suits make you scream when you come, they also don't make you wait for... anything." He lowered his voice. "Or beg."

She blew out a breath. This guy was making her crazy. "I don't want to wait."

He kissed the tip of her nose. "Exactly."

Got it. He was going to be in charge. Completely. *Damn him.* She thought about making a quip about finding someone who wouldn't make her wait, but the truth was, there was no way that was going to happen. And she kind of thought he knew that too. And she was a little afraid of what he might do to punish her for teasing about *that*. "You want me to beg?" she asked.

"I really do."

"I can do that now."

She could almost feel the heat emanating from him. They both knew that she didn't tease, and she *never* begged.

"I intend to hear that, Boss," he said, the nickname now ironic. "But I'm going to let you use one of your plastic friends tonight, while you think about me, so that you have a really good comparison for when I get you all spread out and desperate."

Desperate. That word should *not* be hot. And she should be a lot more annoyed than she was right now.

"So you're really *not* going to put your hands up my skirt tonight?" she asked, propping her hands on her hips.

"Oh, I didn't say that." He knelt on one knee in front of her, his hands going to the back of her calves.

Ava's heart jumped into her throat, pounding hard, making it hard to breathe. She couldn't see him very well, but she could *feel* him. His hands skimmed up the back of her legs to her thighs and higher. He palmed her butt.

"Ah, thong," he said approvingly as he felt her bare cheeks. "Is there lace? Please tell me there's lace."

A second later, he felt for himself as he hooked his thumbs under the thin strip of lace and silk that crossed each hip.

"I fucking love lace," he muttered.

Then he jerked his hands apart, literally ripping that lace from her body.

Ava gasped, shocked and more turned on than she'd ever been.

Parker slid his hands back down her legs, stretched to his feet, tucked the ruined thong into his pocket, and said, "See you tomorrow," as he started for the back door.

She scrambled to pull her thoughts together through the lusty haze. "You're *leaving*?"

"Yeah. And you better not try to hide out here anymore. You need to work on the pies, at the pie shop, and if you don't show up I *will* come and get you."

She wasn't sure she would mind that.

"What... But..."

He pulled the door open and stepped on the top step, but he turned back, his hand around the edge of the door as if keeping himself in place. "I'll see you tomorrow," he said. It was more of a command than just a form of goodnight.

She took a deep breath and nodded. "Yeah."

He looked at her for a long moment, then he nodded. "Yeah."

"By the way," she said, before she could think better of it. "The other day when you thought you were seducing me with apple pie filling?"

She saw his hand tighten around the edge of the door, but he stayed where he was. "Yeah?"

"It didn't work."

"That's not how I remember it, Boss." His expression said clearly that he wasn't buying that for a second.

But she shook her head. "The pie filling didn't work. Because I was already seduced by then."

He white-knuckled the door again but showed amazing restraint by nodding and then shutting the door firmly between them.

But Ava was still smiling as she made her way back into the house. She really did like getting the last word.

———

P arker tossed an egg up and down in his hand, lost in thought.

He'd actually walked away from Ava. A turned-on, please-put-your-hand-up-my-skirt Ava.

What the *fuck*?

Butter popped and sizzled in the pan in front of him, and he absently cracked the egg into the skillet. It was a good thing he could make bacon and eggs in his sleep, because he had a feeling he wasn't going to be very on the ball this morning.

He picked up another egg, thinking about the night before. Daydreaming. For fuck's sake. He didn't do that. Not over women, for sure. Maybe he'd occasionally get sidetracked thinking through a new recipe. But women? Definitely not.

He also didn't walk away from a woman who was on the verge of begging him to make her come.

Except Ava.

And why the hell was that? Because he'd wanted to be sure she remembered that *he* had the upper hand whenever he wanted it? Or because he'd needed to remind himself? Or because he really wanted to stand out from the crowd of men who wanted to be close to her?

But no. It was none of that. It was the damned chicken salad.

Okay, the chicken salad hadn't specifically gone through his mind while he'd been kissing her, but *something* had stopped him from going further. And on the drive home with Ava's thong in his pocket and a raging hard-on, he'd figured out what.

He wanted Ava to love his burgers like everyone else did. But she'd never even tried one. He wanted everyone to be satisfied with the burgers exactly as they were. Exactly as they'd always been. And there was nothing wrong with being content with things that were just consistently damned good. But instead of the burgers, Ava had eaten his chicken salad. And she'd been wowed. And now he wanted to make her chicken salad, and other off-menu things, all the time.

He'd walked into that mudroom with clear expectations. So had she. They could have easily, happily, had quickie "burger" sex last night. But he couldn't help it—he'd wanted to give her...

chicken salad. Something unexpected. Something that would *affect* her. The woman barely gave food a thought, but she'd loved that chicken salad. That mattered to him. And if the food mattered, the sex definitely had to be amazing. Different. Special.

It was the perfect illustration of a battle he'd been waging within himself for a long time now. He wanted the diner, and his life, to stay the same. But he couldn't help trying new things in the kitchen and being tempted to take them out front. Of course, the temptation was as far as it went. So far. Until now. Until Ava. She was making him think about, and want, and try new things.

The diner—the decor, the smell, the burgers, the routine and consistency, the *sameness*—had saved him after his father had died. It had been comforting. It had made sense to him. He'd been able to carry on, and it had given him a sense of control while reeling from the realization that everything could be ripped away in an instant.

And, as he'd told Ava, he thought maybe the diner did that for other people too. It was a place that didn't change. That could bring back good memories with a simple bite. Where things were straightforward and made sense—because, dammit, ordering a jalapeno burger and actually eating the jalapenos *made sense*. And sometimes simple and easy were exactly what they all needed. Even if it was just for an hour in the middle of the day.

So why did he feel this nagging desire to change things up sometimes? Why couldn't he just be content? Grateful? *Blissful*, even, that when he came to work, he knew exactly what was going to happen and how to handle it? There were no surprises in his usual work day. Something he'd always really appreciated.

Until Ava Carmichael had come along.

She surprised him nearly every day. And he wasn't just getting used to it—he was enjoying it. He wanted more of it. And he wanted to surprise her too. He wanted to watch her eat his food and be wowed. And so much more. Apple pie shots, ripping her panties off, making her hot and needy in a mudroom...and then walking away from her to build the anticipation...those were all definitely new. Fun. Tempting.

Parker shoved a hand through his hair. So here he was, distracted, sexually frustrated, and with this battle raging between wanting everything simple and straightforward...and wanting new and wow and...Ava. Who was anything but simple.

Parker picked up another egg and, without thinking, heaved it at the wall behind him. It connected with a *splat*. He picked up a second one, chucking it in the same direction. The cracking sound was satisfying as was the sight of the thing exploding into pieces.

Of course, his thoughts went right back to Ava. But yeah, this felt good. He looked around. Bacon wouldn't break. Bananas would make more of a thud. But an avocado... He grabbed one of them from the bowl and sent it flying like he was on the pitcher's mound and had been given the signal for a fast ball.

It thudded against the wall, but broke open nicely, sending green globs flying. The eggs were best, but that wasn't bad.

But he needed more. More noise, more pieces, more *breaking*.

Knowing it was a dumb idea even as he did it, he reached for a glass measuring cup, wound up, and threw it as hard as he could.

He relished the sound and sight of it shattering against the wall.

He stood looking at the glittering glass pieces on the floor and felt a smile spread. That did feel good.

Then he frowned. Shit. Now he had to clean it up. Especially because Ava would have to walk right through that mess if she came in his back door and, with her heels, she could easily slip or turn her ankle on the bigger glass chunks.

Ava.

It always came back to her.

He was so fucked. Which, ironically, was the one thing he hadn't been.

And his ire was back. He started toward the broom in the corner by the back door when the smell of something burning hit him. He swung around, realizing he'd forgotten the fried eggs.

Son-of-a-bitch-fucking-dammit-shit. He stomped to the stove, grabbed the pan from the burner, tossed it to the back of the stove, then shoved his hand through his hair.

He was losing it. Completely. Because of the woman next door. Who wore ridiculous heels, didn't even like food, and couldn't bake a pie to save her life.

What the *hell* was he doing?

Pulling in a deep breath, he had only one idea about how to feel better. He managed to make a new plate of eggs and bacon and finally carried Hank's breakfast order out to him.

Hank was the first one in the diner this morning. And most mornings lately. For years, he'd come in around seven a.m., prior to meeting his buddies at seven thirty. But over the past couple of months Hank had started coming in right at six when Parker turned the sign on the front door to OPEN. Hank said that even though Parker's coffee always sucked, it sucked less first thing in the morning. But Parker knew the truth. Hank had started coming downtown early almost as soon as the Carmichael triplets had taken over the pie shop. Hank was keeping an eye on them.

And, even though the pie shop didn't open until eight—at which time Hank and his friends moved over there for their "coffee hour", which was really more like three hours—Hank planted himself in the first business to open on Main Street so he knew what people were saying and wondering about the girls. He'd corrected a lot of misinformation about the girls themselves, Rudy, and the will that had brought the girls to town. He'd also planted seeds about how hard Cori, Brynn, and Ava were working and what kind of people they were and how much he liked them. The older man had lived in Bliss all his life and was currently serving his sixth five-year term as the town's mayor.

Hank's opinion carried a lot of weight, and his endorsement of the triplets meant that the rest of the town would give them a chance.

Parker had known that and appreciated it on some level even before all of *this*. Whatever *this* was between him and Ava. Now, he felt even more grateful thinking about it. As if Hank was doing *Parker* a favor.

Wow. He was a mess.

He set Hank's plate down. "Sorry that took a little longer than it should have."

"No worries." Hank reached for the salt and pepper. "I lost part of a finger because of a woman once."

Parker cocked his head to the side. "What?"

Hank held up his left hand and wiggled his fingers. If you looked really closely you could see that his third finger was missing the very tip. "That's not really 'part of a finger'," Parker told him.

"Well, it's not part of a toe. Though I could have lost a couple of those too."

"What the hell were you doing?" Parker asked, intrigued in spite of himself.

"Changing her tire." Hank's mouth curved into a soft grin. He wasn't looking at Parker, but staring off into the distance, clearly remembering something fondly. "She was on the side of the road and I pulled over to help, of course. Got the thing jacked up and the flat off but then she started singing. Got caught up in her voice and the smile on her face and lost all train of thought—and the jack. Came crashing down and took the tip of my finger with it." The look on Hank's face was one of pure adoration.

"Who was the girl?"

"My wife," he said with a nod.

Parker realized he would have been disappointed if the woman in question had been a girl that got away. "What was she singing?"

"'Come Fly With Me.'"

"Sinatra. Nice."

"I was a goner for her from that moment on. Even bleeding profusely."

Parker laughed. Then sighed. "What made you think of that?"

"You're burning stuff in the kitchen. And throwing and breaking stuff," Hank told him. "You never do that."

"How do you know I didn't just drop something?"

Hank gave him a look that said *seriously?*

"Fine, but how do you know it's about a woman?"

"A sudden change in who a man is and how he acts? It's always a woman."

He'd give Hank the part about there being a change in how he acted, but who he was? Was that changing? Because of Ava?

But it only took a second for him to remember that he'd just thrown an avocado against his kitchen wall.

Parker thought for only a second about his next move. Hank's eyebrows went up as Parker set the bottle of hot sauce on the table.

"You need to have a seat?" He gestured with his fork at the booth across the table from where he was sitting.

Parker sighed. He didn't let people put ketchup on their eggs in here. Salsa was fine if he was serving them a Denver omelet. But hot sauce on fried eggs was borderline, and everyone knew its use depended on Parker's mood. Today he was hoping for some advice, so was going to let Hank defile the eggs right in front of him.

"Yeah, I think I do."

"Let's hear it." Hank scooped a bite of eggs doused in hot sauce into his mouth.

And Parker didn't even care. That was how messed up he was. He slid into the booth and rested his arms on the tabletop. "My dad had a really specific idea about the life he worked to give me."

Hank nodded. "I knew your dad. You and your mom were the most important things in the world to him."

"By the time we came here," Parker agreed. "It wasn't always like that. His work was his priority up until the last three years or so. And it killed him."

"You're afraid Ava will be like that?" Hank asked.

Parker gave a short laugh. Clearly it was quite obvious who the woman was. "Maybe not that she'll kill me." But he sobered quickly. "But that she'll make me start looking for *more*. For bigger and better, and I'll forget to appreciate the good stuff I've already got."

"You're scared of her," Hank observed.

"Yep," Parker said without hesitation. "And scared of what she makes me want. She stirs up all of this energy and a bunch of what-ifs in me. She gets me excited about things, gets me thinking about making changes to this life that I've built a very specific way for a very specific, *good* reason." He took a deep breath. "Hank," he said seriously. "She makes me want to close the diner early, take days off, stay up late, try new things."

"And you don't want those things?" Hank asked.

"I want to be content," Parker said honestly. "Why can't I just look at this great life that I've got, that my dad gave me, and be happy? Bliss, and my dad, saved my life. This diner saved me after Dad died. It's easy and laid-back and peaceful and stable, and it should be enough. Ava is the opposite of Bliss. She's always on the go, she's never content with the status quo, she stirs things up—stirs *me* up—rather than calming things down. How can I think being with her is better for me?"

Hank leaned in, pinning Parker with a serious look, and pointing his fork at Parker's nose. "Ava Carmichael is *not* the opposite of Bliss. She's hardworking, loves her family more than anything, and will do whatever it takes to make them secure and happy. She loves them enough to come to Bliss in the first place. She has all of that in common with most of this town. They live here because this place gives them what they need and what the people they love need." He looked thoughtful for a moment. Then he leaned back and set his fork down. "Hell, Parker, Ava is really just like your dad if you think about it."

Parker let that roll around in his head. Ava had come to Bliss because it was what her family needed. No, she hadn't thrown a dart at a map, and maybe she'd argued about it for a couple of hours, but in the end, her family needed to be in Bliss, and she was right there beside them, leaving her life behind, trying new things, dedicated to doing whatever it took to insure their stability and happiness.

Ava was just like his dad.

Parker felt his heart turn over in his chest.

"The main difference is that she got to Bliss earlier in her life than your dad did," Hank went on. "But that, of course, is nothing but a *good* thing."

Parker nodded, his thoughts spinning. His father had only lived in Bliss for three years. But he'd been so much happier in Bliss than he'd ever been anywhere else. Rudy had lived in Bliss for only five years, but he too, had found an unequalled happiness. Happiness that he'd wanted to pass on to his daughters.

Ava had *years* to be happy in Bliss. Parker's life here *was* good. Very good. Maybe being involved with her didn't mean *he* had to change. He could change *her* life. He could give her what his father had given him. What her father had wanted so much to give her. A home. A community. A family. A purpose. And really amazing chicken salad.

Hank sat back in the booth. "Help her find her Bliss, Parker, and I think you'll find yours."

Hank's words hit Parker directly in the chest, and he had to swallow hard as his whirling thoughts slammed to a stop.

This was all supposed to just be a way to get Ava through the stipulations of the will and back to New York. He sighed. That had lasted all of a day and a half.

13

Two hours later, Parker was in his kitchen, finally cleaning up the broken glass, eggs, and avocado. The breakfast rush had come in shortly after his conversation with Hank, and Parker had been, gratefully, busy nearly nonstop since.

Of course, his thoughts had still been on Ava, but he hadn't stomped over to the pie shop to check on her. Or to demand that she let him show her why Bliss was better than New York. Or to kiss her.

Nope, he hadn't done any of that. Yet.

As if on cue, he suddenly heard a loud crash against the wall that separated the pie shop from the diner.

This was a big one too. Without a second thought, he propped the broom against the wall and headed out his back door and through hers.

There was a glass pie pan lying in pieces in a mess of apples, crust and filling at the base of her favorite egg-throwing wall.

But what he was focused on mostly was the gorgeous blonde who was wearing a white and black striped skirt, black blouse, and bright red heels. She was sucking on the tip of one of her fingers.

"You okay?" he asked from the doorway. Because once he stepped fully into the kitchen, he was going to touch her and once he started touching her, he wasn't sure how that was going to end. Or if it would.

"I burned my finger." She held up the digit she'd had in her mouth.

He gripped the doorknob in his hand, memories from the night before flooding his head and mixing with a strange sense of protectiveness. Burns could be serious, of course, but the finger was only red. There was no blister or anything. She'd be fine.

But a second later, he made a decision. It felt like it was a lot more than just letting go of the doorknob and crossing the kitchen to where she stood, but he did those things with some kind of subconscious realization that once he did, everything was going to change.

He took her hand and pulled her to the sink. He started a stream of cold water and held her finger under it.

"You chucked the pie because you burned your finger or you burned your finger chucking the pie?" he asked, watching her finger instead of looking at her.

Their bodies were touching, he could smell her shampoo mixed with the scent of cinnamon, and even cradling her hand in his under a stream of cold water made him want her with an intensity that shocked him. Sexual desire, want, lust—none of those were new. But with Ava he felt like he was feeling them for the first time.

This had seemed so obvious to him when it was happening to Evan with Cori that Parker decided to be a grown-up and not deny or ignore the truth of what he knew was happening—he didn't just want to sleep with her or even date her. He was going to fall in love with her.

"No. I—" She glanced at the counter next to his right hip.

He followed her gaze and saw that she had a couple of file folders and papers laid out. "What's this?"

"Work." She lifted a shoulder. "I was on a conference call while I was baking this morning."

"And you got distracted?" he guessed. That was a lot of her issue with being unable to make a decent pie. She didn't pay attention to textures or timers when she was doing something else at the same time she was baking.

"There's a big merger that was supposed to go through last month and now it's stalled."

"You chucked the pie at the wall because you were pissed off about Carmichael business stuff?"

She hesitated. "I threw the pie at the wall because things aren't going my way this morning."

Parker shut off the water. He grabbed a towel but paused. Then he lifted her finger to his lips and placed a kiss on it. "Wait right here. I'll be back in a second," he said, wrapping the towel around her hand.

Her eyes were wide. "Um. Okay."

Parker blew out a breath. Then he pivoted and headed back to the diner. He strode through his kitchen, shutting off the oven and the stove burners under the pots on his way. He pushed the door open and stepped into the main part of the diner.

"Okay, everybody, closing time," he announced loudly.

Everyone in the diner seemed to freeze. Conversation stopped. There was no clinking of silverware. Nothing. They all turned to look at him. Parker put his hands on his hips and lifted an eyebrow. "What?" Though he knew very well *what*.

"Everything okay?" Al asked.

"Yep. Ava needs me today. So I'm shutting down. I'll be open for breakfast tomorrow morning."

If the first announcement had shocked people, the news that it was because of Ava sent a tremor of amazement through the room that was almost palpable.

But damned if everyone didn't start getting up and pulling their wallets out.

"Just put the money on the counter," he said, gesturing toward the counter where the register sat. "You all know what you owe."

As Ava had pointed out to Al, they'd all been eating here long enough and often enough to know what their bill would come to approximately. If they were off by a few dollars, he didn't care.

And if he made *that* admission out loud, he'd probably cause a rift in the space-time continuum or something. Because words like "approximately" weren't in his vocabulary, and he did care that things added up correctly. Literally and figuratively.

Until today. Now he just wanted to get back over to Ava.

"Hey, Hank?" he called. "Can you be the last out and lock up?"

"Yep," the older man replied. With a wink.

He was back in Ava's kitchen a minute later. "Okay, come on." He grabbed her purse, took her unburned hand and started for the parking lot behind their businesses.

———

A va didn't even try to figure out where they were going as Parker helped her up into his truck—his hands lingering at her waist—and then pointed the truck out of town. Nor did she ask. She didn't care. The guy had kissed her finger after she'd burned it. She'd go just about anywhere with him right now.

Hell, she'd thrown the pie at the wall to get his attention. In part anyway. She'd also tossed the damned thing because it had turned out great. Again. Better than the one before. She'd even baked it while on a conference call. Still, the pie had turned out.

She'd actually cried over that pie. A little.

It had been delicious. It was something she would be more than proud to serve, and she hadn't been able to help wondering what her dad would have thought of it.

And, without warning, tears had welled up.

She'd been relating to Rudy's challenge of making the "perfect" pie. He'd been trying to recreate a pie that he remembered from his childhood. With no recipe. She could imagine how hard and frustrating that had been when she was having trouble even coming up with something edible. Even *with* recipes.

And then suddenly, unexpectedly, she'd done it. She'd tossed the recipes and had found the right combination all on her own. She was astounded by how satisfying that was.

All her life she'd been following in Rudy's footsteps, sure of her course, because he'd mapped it out first. Then he'd made her leave everything that was familiar and had given her a to-do list to accomplish, without a plan for how to make any of it happen. Here she was, having to make up her own recipes and strategies.

But she was actually succeeding.

She was making something *she* liked. All on her own. She had Cori and Brynn's support and Parker's general tips. But she'd made the pie that morning with her own two hands.

She had no idea if Rudy would have loved her pie or if it was even close to being *the one* he'd been looking for. Really, she would never know that. And that thought was a little sad. Rudy's pie quest had died with him, and there was no way of knowing if that pie would ever exist again.

But maybe this was even better in a way. She'd had to create a pie that *she* liked. That *she* approved of. It was *her* pie. And she was proud of it. She didn't have to follow Rudy's paths to be happy and satisfied and proud of herself. She really could be successful with her own plans.

And then, staring down at that pie, right on top of the feeling of accomplishment, she'd realized she wasn't ready to fully own that pie and success. She liked the idea of her and Cori and Brynn working together to make this all happen and all of them falling just a bit short on their own. And she liked the idea of needing Parker's help.

So she'd thrown the pie against the wall before anyone else could discover that she'd figured it out. Which she'd known would get Parker over to her kitchen. That was multitasking at its finest.

She glanced at Parker. It was silly to get all swoony over him kissing her finger probably. It was actually probably just a good excuse to give herself for not putting up one iota of resistance when he'd said "come on." But she'd had very little coddling in her life and she liked it from the gruff diner owner who didn't coddle anyone.

But as she studied him, she realized that wasn't true either. He did coddle. The entire town, as a matter of fact. They got to eat Rueben sandwiches well past closing time. Of course, they couldn't substitute provolone for the Swiss, but they also didn't pay a nickel more than they had a decade ago for it.

He did coddle people. He just wasn't showy about it. So the finger kiss and running her hand under cold water were stupidly significant to her.

Ava had loved being seen as capable and independent and able to tackle any issue and handle any complication. She'd had to show her dad that she was the one that solved problems, not the one that needed to be looked after so that he would ultimately trust her at the head of the entire company. But from Parker, a little extra attention to her needs, was very, very nice.

Bottom line—she wanted to get this guy naked even more than she wanted the Ashton merger to go through, or the second quarter profit reports in her inbox, or to go over the spreadsheets showing amazing growth in their west coast branch. And she *loved* mergers and profit reports and spreadsheets showing growth. But there would be more reports. There were other mergers, other companies, other deals. There was only one guy who made her feel the way she was feeling right now, and even studying the way his hands curled around the steering wheel, the way his thigh muscles bunched under the soft denim of his jeans as he pressed the gas pedal, the way he tensed his jaw as if keeping from saying—or doing—something at the moment, all made her stomach fluttery, and her body feel warm, and her panties damp.

Her phone pinged, interrupting her thoughts. She glanced down. The text was from Cori.

You're taking the day off?

Ava glanced at Parker. She didn't know what exactly he had planned or how long it would take, but she was sure he had his watch alarm set. *Just a long lunch,* she replied to her sister.

Are you with Parker?

Yes.

Well, whatever you're doing, he's not planning on recovering quickly ;)

What are you talking about?

He closed the diner for the day.

Ava stared at Cori's response. That wasn't right. He'd been open when she'd gone to the pie shop that morning. *Are you sure?*

Hank just put a sign on the door.

Ava looked over at Parker. "You closed the diner for the day?"

Parker rolled his eyes. "It's been like fifteen minutes and everyone already knows?"

"It's true?"

He focused on the road but lifted a shoulder. "Yeah."

"You're just not going to go back? What about when people show up for lunch and dinner?"

"Pretty sure no one's showing up for lunch or dinner," he said dryly.

Ava pivoted on her seat to face him more fully. "Why?" And why was her heart pounding like it was?

"Because when I threw them all out, I told them it was because you needed me."

Ava felt her mouth part in a surprised O. And her body heat. "I...need you?"

Now he did glance over at her, the corner of his mouth curling up. "You sure do, Boss."

Yeah, she sure did.

Her heart skipped and her stomach flipped. "And the whole town knows you did this for me?"

He sighed. "Apparently."

Ava sat back in her seat, chewing her bottom lip, as emotions swirled through her. First and foremost was anticipation. Whatever he had planned, she wanted in. She knew what she *hoped* he'd had planned. And she was suddenly thinking that she might like to know what it was like to make out in a pickup for the first time in her life.

Or maybe that wasn't so sudden.

Parker had closed the diner. For her. He grumped about the food because the food was very personal to him. But he also let people linger in his diner nearly thirteen hours a day. Because they were personal to him. The diner was about his dad, on one level. On another, it was all about him. Because fulfilling the needs of the town fulfilled *him*.

And now he'd closed it all down for her.

"The town will think there's something going on between us," she finally said.

That was part of *her* plan, but now she needed to know how Parker felt about it.

He looked over as he turned off the highway onto a dirt road. "Yeah, they will."

The look in his eyes made her heart thump. "You're okay with that?"

"I am," he said with a short nod. "You?"

She nodded. "Yeah."

"I figure this can count as your six months of monogamy. I fit all the criteria."

Ava decided she shouldn't be surprised that he was thinking along the same lines. He was a smart guy. A goal-driven guy. He wanted Ava to meet all the conditions of the will for a number of reasons.

But this didn't feel like just a means to an end.

"You do," she agreed.

"And we've already spent some time together," he went on, his eyes on the road again. "We maybe wouldn't have to do the whole six months. We could count some of the time before now."

Yeah. Exactly. But Ava said, "Or we could start counting now. I mean, just to be *sure*." Six more months with him instead of two? That seemed like one of her more brilliant ideas.

His hands tightened on the steering wheel and he swallowed before answering, "Yeah, we could do that."

Ava felt a little flutter of what might have been giddiness. She'd never actually felt giddy before so she couldn't be sure, but this had to be it.

They were quiet for a minute. Ava watched the fields passing the window, marveling at how far she could see out here. She'd barely noticed the drive into Bliss from the Kansas City airport. Her attention had been riveted on her laptop. As usual. And her three months so far had been spent in the town. She hadn't really experienced the countryside. She wasn't sure what struck her most—the lack of buildings, the lack of traffic and people, or the lack of noise.

"Wow, it's *really* different from New York here," she commented. She turned from the window as he chuckled. She smiled. "I know. That's dumb to say. I mean, in my head, I *knew* it would be different. I even knew the ways it would be different. But it just hit me."

"I remember driving to Bliss for the first time. I was so pissed. I was convinced that I'd die without having pizza available twenty-four seven."

She frowned. "You remember coming to Bliss? You knew what pizza was? Weren't you a *baby*?"

He laughed. "Nope. I moved here when I was fourteen."

Her eyes widened. "Really? You're not actually from here?"

His smile got smaller but also softer. "Oh, I'm from here."

There was emotion—love—in his voice. "I just didn't come home until I was older."

There was something about how he said it that made her throat tighten. She loved New York. That was where she'd grown up. She appreciated everything that made New York City New York City. But she didn't feel *that*, everything that was on Parker's face now, about the city.

"How did that all happen?" she asked, suddenly wanting to know all about him.

He blew out a breath. "I was a spoiled brat rich kid hanging out with other spoiled brat rich kids. Thinking nothing could touch us. Bored because everything was being handed to us."

"You were a rich kid?" Ava asked, completely surprised.

"Well, not Carmichael rich," he said with a little smile. "But yeah. We had money. My dad was an investment guy and did really well. I spent fourteen years in Chicago."

"I had no idea you grew up in a city."

He shook his head quickly. "I didn't grow up until I came to Bliss."

Ava felt herself smile. He was so in love with this town. It made her like it even more. But in that moment, it occurred to her that she liked it a lot anyway. Somehow, in a short time, Bliss had grown on her. It was a bump in her road, or so she'd thought, but there was something about a place that ran according to its own rules and everyone was accepted for who they were and where everyone had a place, no matter how quirky.

Life was pretty simple here. Everyone got up in the morning, did something that contributed to the lives around them, gathered for a meal, and went to bed happy, safe, and content. She supposed the same things happened in New York, just on a bigger level. People went to work to produce products or offer services that other people needed. But it was harder to see there.

Here, Noah opened his garage, people brought their cars and trucks in, and he fixed them. Parker opened his diner, people came in to eat, and he made them food. Evan opened his office, people came in to trademark their homemade jam and to transfer the ownership of their farm to their kids, and Evan reassured them that he'd take care of them. Teachers went to the school and taught the kids of the town. Farmers planted their crops and took care of their animals. Ed, the electrician, fixed people's wiring. Nancy, the bank president, gave people loans so they could add on to their house, and Josh, the local builder, built that extra room for them.

It was so much easier to see how lives intersected and interacted here.

It had definitely grown on her. Especially considering that she very rarely got to see the impact of her work directly on the lives it affected.

Unlike the pie shop.

She sighed. She sucked at making pies, but she understood the interaction that her father had enjoyed. Even more, seeing it on Parker's side of the wall. Okay, so Rudy hadn't been *entirely* off base in having her come here.

"So how did you end up in Bliss from Chicago?"

Parker turned the truck onto a narrower dirt road. "Dad threw a dart at the middle of a map of the US," he said.

Her eyes widened. "Seriously? He literally threw a dart at a map? The dart hit Bliss and so you up and moved here?"

"Kind of. I was getting into some stuff that concerned him and he determined we had to make a change. He thought the Midwest was a good bet but didn't know anyone or any place in particular. So he put a map up on the wall, closed his eyes, and left it up to Fate. As soon as he saw the name Bliss, he knew this was the place."

Ava turned the rest of the way on the seat and tucked her leg underneath her. *This* was fascinating stuff. She'd never trusted Fate for a damned thing. She worked for everything. With a carefully laid-out plan and lots of research.

The Fate idea kind of sounded nice. Letting it go. Trusting it would work out instead of sweating it.

"What were you getting into?" she asked, trying to picture Parker as a spoiled rich kid with an attitude.

It wasn't that hard to imagine, actually. She grinned. Sure, he wore denim like he'd been born in it, and he nearly always paired that denim with a cotton T-shirt—she'd seen him in a button-down shirt exactly twice in almost four months—but she could definitely picture him challenging authority with an I'm-better-than-you attitude. Maybe not so much in a prep school uniform with khakis and a tie, but she had no trouble visualizing a young Parker with a smirk, thinking he was above the law. It was interesting, really. He liked order and routine, but it wasn't hard to believe that, while rules mattered, he would think *his* rules were the ones that counted. He exuded confidence and if he thought he knew better about how people should eat grilled cheese sandwiches, then she was sure he thought he knew better about bigger things too.

"My group of friends decided to make some money," he said. "They started...acquiring objects and then reselling them."

"Acquiring?" she repeated, noting the slight pause before the word. "You mean stealing?"

He nodded. "From their parents."

She felt her eyebrows rise. "A bunch of fourteen-year-olds stole from their rich parents and resold the stuff?"

"Pretty much. Though there was a fifteen and a sixteen-year-old too."

She shook her head. "Wow. What kind of stuff?"

"Jewelry. Small art pieces. Antique dishes and vases and stuff." Parker shrugged. "Had to be small so they wouldn't be noticed."

"And what did they need this money for?" she asked.

"We didn't need it for anything. We were bored. And thought rules didn't apply to us."

"Because the rules were different for you than for the rest of society," Ava said. "I know what that's like."

He glanced over. "Yeah. And I think we wanted to see what would happen. How long could we get away with stuff and what would happen when we got caught. But then things started getting bigger. A couple of the guys broke into a neighbor's house and I knew things were getting out of control."

"How did you get caught?"

"My dad found me going through my mom's jewelry. I was trying to find her grandmother's wedding ring."

Ava winced.

"Yeah," he said with a nod. "It had gone from little stuff our parents didn't really care about, to bigger stuff and then on to meaningful stuff. Things that couldn't be easily replaced. But that night—" Parker paused. "I think I wanted to get caught. I was getting nervous. Some of the buyers weren't exactly nice people. And we were kids."

"And you wanted to know what he would do," Ava guessed.

He nodded. "I wanted to see if he'd sweep it under the rug, or yell, or punish me, or what." Parker took a breath. "He'd never done any of that. He wasn't around much, for one thing. He worked all the time. When he was around, his head was somewhere else. Always thinking about—worrying about—work."

"You were trying to get his attention?" Ava asked, feeling a knot in her stomach. She knew exactly what it was like to never really mentally leave her work. And how it felt to look around and realize she'd missed stuff in the process. And how it felt to regret that.

"Not at first," Parker said. "But I think it was bugging me how easy it all was. I did want his attention that night. I wanted to show him that things weren't perfect, things weren't just going along easily in spite of him not being there."

He was frowning and the knot in Ava's stomach tightened. "You wanted to punish him," she said.

Parker pulled to a stop and shifted the truck into park. She barely noticed anything around her. She was completely focused on the man beside her. It seemed he was one of the few things that could capture her full attention.

He turned slightly, resting his arm on the top of the steering wheel. "Yeah," he finally said. "I guess so. He was living in this world where his work took all of him, and he just assumed—and hoped, I learned later—that the money, the nice things, made me and my mom's life easy and so everything was fine."

"And when he found out what was going on?" Ava asked.

"I'll never forget it," Parker said, his voice a little gravelly now. "He asked what I was doing and I told him. I mean, I just confessed the whole thing. It just poured out of me. I remember feeling relieved. And then he stared at me for a long time, ran his hand through his hair, and then went to his desk. He pulled the map out, stuck it on the wall, and threw the dart. He quit his job the next day, and we were driving into a Bliss a week later."

Ava swallowed hard as jealousy wrapped around the knot of what felt like regret in her gut. "Wow. I mean, that was…"

"Everything," Parker filled in. "It was everything. He stepped up. Immediately. And he left it all behind to come here and make a life here that was about family and community and straightforward hard work that paid off in fewer dollars but a million other ways."

She pressed her lips together and nodded. She understood all of that. A few months ago, she wouldn't have. She would have been amazed to think of a man doing what Parker's dad had done. But now…it was the perfect expression of love and fatherhood.

"Your dad did the same thing," Parker said, his voice quieter. "He didn't do it soon enough, he didn't do it in the right way, maybe. But he got you here. He gave you a chance at a life you never would have imagined if not for something major making him look at things and realize it wasn't going the way he wanted it to."

She swallowed hard again, her throat tightening. She understood, cerebrally, that Rudy had been trying to give his daughters something good, something he'd found in Bliss, when he'd mandated they come to this town for a year. But she hadn't really believed it would happen. Until Cori had fallen for Evan. Until Ava saw Brynn with Noah. Until she'd walked into the pie shop one morning and smiled at the bright colors and the curtains covered in pictures of fruit, and the scent of coffee and spices that hadn't been there before she and her sisters had taken over.

The pie shop had been just one more thing Ava had to handle, that she had to make work for her sisters' sakes. But slowly, she'd started to like it. She'd started to feel proud of the things she and Cori and Brynn had done together. And lately, with Parker, she felt something happening to *her*. She didn't really worry about herself. She was in control of the things that happened to and around her. Usually. With Parker and the pie shop though, she'd come up against the first things that seemed to be happening in spite of her. When she'd wanted the pies to turn out, they hadn't. Now that she didn't want them to be perfect, yet, they were turning out great. And she had realized that she had no control over Parker and the things he made her feel.

And the lack of control made her a little nervous. But it also felt kind of good. New. Exciting.

"He changed the rules on me," she finally said. "I always knew exactly what he was expecting, what he wanted to see with the company, what I needed to do, how he would react to things. I made running that company like he did, my entire focus. And then suddenly...this." She sighed. "He dies of cancer before I even knew he was sick. Then I find out that he's put together this trust and I have to live in this tiny town in Kansas that I've never heard of. I find out that he was running a barely-making-it pie shop simply because he liked pie. He wants *me* to make pie. I mean, it's all crazy."

He'd left her completely recipe-less.

Parker nodded. "He changed the rules on purpose."

Yeah, she knew that. And she suspected that Rudy had known how good it would feel to succeed without following a recipe. By finding her way on her own.

"I figured out pretty young that Dad wanted us to go into business with him," she said, her voice sounding raspy. "It wasn't until I was older that I realized it was because he didn't know how else to relate to us. It was all he could imagine having in common with us. He'd never been around kids, had no idea what to do with girls, not to mention three of us at once, and especially girls who were being raised by a woman who was socially conscious and was the one person he could never negotiate or bully into doing what he wanted—marrying him." She smiled, thinking of her mom. "So he exposed us to his business because it was really the only thing he had. It wasn't like he could take us to ball games or teach us to play violin or talk to us about his fascination with American history. He didn't have any other interests. He didn't know what else to do with us. For a while it was really frustrating, for everyone, because Cori and Brynn had no interest in any of it. But then I figured out that as long as *I* was interested, then Cori and Brynn could do their things in relative peace. It kept Cori from trying to make him happy and getting her heart broken when it didn't work, or he didn't get her. It kept him from trying to pull Brynn out of her shell, which just exasperated them both."

"Basically, as long as *you* were interested in the business and could talk to him about it, he left Cori and Brynn alone?" Parker asked.

She nodded. "Cori didn't get hurt and Brynn didn't get pushed."

"So you pretended to be interested and got in too deep to get out?"

"No. No, nothing like that." She shook her head. "I really was interested. I loved the numbers. I loved dressing up. I loved the intense meetings, the negotiating, the victories. I figured out that people would underestimate me—because I was young and a woman—and I loved showing them what I knew and proving them wrong. I know everyone thinks I work too hard and too much and I'm super stressed out but the truth is, this fits me. I don't think the job made me this way, I think the way I am makes me really good at the job. And it's not bad for me. My blood pressure is below average, all of my other numbers are great. I get checkups every six months, I exercise to work off the stress, I sleep really well. I recognize it's not for everyone, but it works for me. I'm not fun and sweet, but that's because *that* stresses me out."

He laughed. "You are fun and sweet, Boss."

That made her stomach flip. "But not like Cori and Brynn," she said with a smile. "And that's okay. Honestly. Being fun and spontaneous and creative like Cori gives me heartburn. I can't abandon schedules and I *need* a plan. I can't just be sweet like Brynn because I can't let stuff roll off. When people are being assholes, I call them on being assholes. Letting it go makes my stomach hurt and makes me want to yell at *other* people when it's not their fault. Lots of people aren't good with confrontation. I, on the other hand, excel at it."

"So, *not* being fun and sweet is better for you?" Parker asked.

"Exactly."

He seemed to think about that, but after a moment he nodded. "I get it."

"You do, don't you?" she asked with a smile. He did because he was the same way.

"I can have fun, but only if there's a plan in place. I'll go to a barbecue if I know what time it starts and what I'm supposed to bring. Pop-up parties aren't really my thing."

"Because you already have a plan and don't want to just drop it at the last minute, right?" she guessed.

"Exactly." He smiled at her. "What's with these people who only plan for an hour or two at a time?"

"Right?"

They laughed. "And yeah, I'm not so good at sweet either."

She felt everything in her soften at that. Soften. Not something she was used to feeling, but with Parker it seemed to be happening with some frequency. Interesting that a by-the-book grump would be the one to soften her up. "I think you're better at it than you think."

"Well, you let me do dirty things with butter," he said. "That definitely helps my mood when I'm around you."

The air in the truck heated but she laughed, feeling happiness soaking in clear to her bones. She loved that they could be matter-of-fact about everything—the things they were good at, the things they sucked at, their pasts, and their attraction. "I will definitely let you do dirty things with butter whenever you want."

"You mean, if it's on your schedule for the day." He gave her a wink.

Nope, pretty much any time.

"You can put it on *your* schedule," she said. "As long as our calendars on our phones are synched, we'll be fine."

He kept his eyes on hers as he reached for his phone. He swiped a couple of times, then typed. A second later, her phone pinged with a notification.

It was a calendar reminder that said simply *Get naked.*

14

Well, it was on the schedule. She didn't have a choice. Ava started unbuttoning.

Parker gave a choked laugh. "Right here, right now? I never would have taken you for the type to jump when a guy says jump."

His eyes were hot as she parted the shirt and let it fall to the seat around her hips. "I think it's cute that you think you're telling me to jump," she said. "It's me who's telling *you* to tell me to jump. Because it's hot." She reached for the zipper on her skirt. "And I really want to jump, Parker."

He ran a hand over his face. "I can't believe I'm about to say this, but—not like this, Boss."

"See?" she said. "There you go thinking you're in charge again."

She leaned over until their mouths were centimeters apart. She put a hand on his thigh, then ran it up under the edge of his shirt to the hot, firm abs underneath. The muscles tensed and Parker let out a long breath. "Ava—"

She did like it when he called her Boss, but something about the way he said her name made her pelvic muscles clench. "You did say you wanted to show me something."

He looked over her shoulder but his gaze returned quickly to her mouth. "I did. My house."

She froze. All that had really registered was that they were out in the country far from town. Alone. But they were at his house? She had no idea where she'd thought they were or where he was taking her. She'd had no idea where he lived either.

She pivoted quickly, her hand slipping from his shirt. She stared out her window.

The house looked like everything she would have ever expected a farmhouse to look like. It was two stories, painted a light blue with white trim, and had a huge porch that sat up five steps from the ground and ran the entire length of the front of the house. There were flowers in beds on either side of the walk that led to the porch steps, and there were white wicker chairs with a table between them arranged to one side.

There were two huge trees—she had no idea what kind beyond big and tall—lending shade to the front yard. One even had a tire swing hanging in it. She'd seen tire swings in movies and read about them in books as a kid, she supposed, but she didn't realize that people really had them.

Her eyes wandered past the house to a big building on the east, then to the barn behind it, and to the fields beyond that.

"Oh my God, you actually have haystacks," she said, stupidly. She didn't know what she'd expected. She realized that she'd never pictured Parker's house. Because the diner felt like his home. It was where he was for fourteen hours a day, every day, for one thing. And because it just fit him.

Thinking of him reclining on a sofa in front of the TV didn't seem right somehow.

She had, maybe, pictured him in one other room than the kitchen at the diner. And the kitchen at the pie shop. But she hadn't gotten beyond the tangled sheets and clothes strewn across the floor to think about the details of Parker's bedroom.

He chuckled. "A friend rents the fields from me. So those are technically his haystacks. And the horses are his too. I don't have time for crops and livestock like that."

"So why did you buy a farm?" she asked.

"This is where I grew up," he told her. "My mom moved to town to be closer to her friends and so she'd have less upkeep after my dad passed away, and I took the house."

"I don't know why it didn't occur to me that you might be bringing me to your house," she said.

"Because things have been business before this," he said. "About the pie shop."

Yeah, that made sense. They'd essentially had a business arrangement going. That didn't require them to be in one another's homes. Though he'd been in hers. Still, not like this. Not just the two of them. Not without some other excuse like game night.

"It hasn't felt like it's been about the pie shop," she admitted. She didn't know if telling him that was a good idea. It felt like she was giving him something without knowing what he was offering in return. She never did that. She always knew what the other side was willing to give up before she put her cards on the table.

But again, this didn't feel like business.

"Ava."

She looked up at him.

"This is definitely not about the pie shop."

Her heart thudded against her chest. She wet her lips. "Good."

Then he got out of the truck.

While she sat on the passenger seat in a bra and skirt. Okay, so...

But a second later he was at her door, pulling it open, and scooping her up into his arms. He swung her out of the truck, kicked the door shut, and headed for the porch.

This was looking promising. She looped an arm around his neck and snuggled close. She'd never been literally carried to bed, but she wasn't complaining a bit.

"You realize that you're only fueling my fantasies about being waited on hand and foot."

He snorted. "You work too fucking hard, and love it, to ever let someone wait on you hand and foot."

"Well, I'm not minding this."

"This is only because the shoes you're wearing are ridiculous. Especially for walking around on a farm."

"Yeah, kind of. But they're also strategic."

"Oh?"

"I get more done when the person I'm talking to is distracted."

"The men, you mean."

"Women too."

"You think they all want to do to you what I want to do to you when you wear them?"

She grinned. "Maybe not. But they are either wondering where I got them or jealous because they can't afford them."

He shook his head. "You're a brat."

"Yep. But you like my shoes."

"I do."

"In fact, when we were in the mudroom, you said the next time you make me come, you want these on my feet."

She felt his fingers curl into her thigh where he held her. "I did say that."

"So I'm hoping that you don't want me to take them off when we get inside."

He cleared his throat. "No. I think you can leave them on."

"Thank goodness."

He gave a little groan. "I had plans," he told her. "I wasn't going to get you naked right away. I wasn't going to do the boring bedroom thing with you. I was going to make this different. Because I want to do more, something new, something better.

And I feel like I can do that with you. I feel like you'll *make* me do more and better. And I actually want that. Even though it scares the hell out of me."

He reached for the front door, shifting her weight so he could let them in the house—the house that was apparently unlocked in the middle of the day—but Ava stopped him with a hand on his face. "Parker."

He focused on her. "Yeah?"

"What's going on? I don't understand the more and better stuff. I'm not worried about this being anything short of amazing."

Heat and affection flickered in his eyes, but he sighed. And swung her feet to the floor of the porch. Her back was against the front door and he braced a hand on the wood beside her.

"I've been very happy with the status quo," he said. "I've been perfectly fine keeping things as is. In fact, I've worked at it. And that applies to relationships too. When I go out, it's for a late beer or maybe a movie and then we go to her place or here and have sex. It's the same, no matter who the woman is."

"And you wanted this to be different?" She felt a ripple of what felt a lot like desire mixed with that thing she'd labeled as giddiness before. "Why?"

He studied her, his eyes roaming over her face. "I've never had a really good reason to change things, to do more. Until now."

Her stomach flipped. She was that reason? Wow. She stepped close. "I don't know what exactly you think I'm expecting in the bedroom," she said, trying to keep her tone light. "But I was ready to do anything you wanted the other night in the mudroom, and all you did was kiss me and talk dirty. I'd say if you have a big soft bed and some more of that dirty talk, you've got nothing to worry about."

He groaned and chuckled at once. "You think I'm worried about making you come? Because that's so not going to be a problem, Boss. I'm going to make your toes curl and your heart pound and your pussy weep for joy."

She sucked in a quick breath. The dirty talk just seemed to come out of nowhere. Almost casually. Except for the heat in his eyes. But that all meant that this was just Parker. These views on sex were just natural for him. And the confidence? Yeah, that was hot. And completely a part of who he was. "Then what are you worried about?"

"The after," he said honestly. He lifted a hand to her face. "Doing things right after."

Her eyes widened. She'd never had many expectations about after. She didn't need roses and wine and diamonds and promises. Hell, she didn't really want that stuff. She could get her own wine and diamonds, promises didn't matter if they weren't written down and notarized. And sex was sex. Typically, she was rolling over to check her email as soon as possible. The guys who didn't want to stay over were her favorite. The ones who did were out after coffee and that was okay too.

Which meant, she didn't have expectations for after because she didn't really *want* an after with those men.

But she realized, looking up into Parker's face, that had now changed.

"I've never really had an after," she finally said. "So, I'm not going to know if you're doing it right or not."

He studied her eyes, considering that. He took a deep breath. Finally, he said, "I think it's safe to say that part of the after will involve food."

The smile that stretched her lips felt incredibly good. "Man, I hope so. I've been having lots of dirty thoughts about the things you can do with avocados."

His eyes locked on hers, he reached past her and pushed the door open. "So we're going to stumble through this after stuff together? Maybe make a mess?"

It was a big deal for either of them to get into something

messy on purpose. They were both used to being in charge in their world and were the ones to clean things up. But when Parker was doing dishes and Ava was making deals, the cleanup was always for someone else. They both kept their worlds very carefully put together and organized so that they *could* effectively clean up for others.

This was different. This was personal. And was going to affect the two of them most of all.

She nodded. "Let's make a mess, Parker. On purpose. Everything thrown in."

There was a long pause, full of tension and anticipation.

Then, he said firmly, "Get in the house, Ava."

"So bossy."

"You ain't seen nothin' yet."

———

Ava only made it to the bottom step before Parker couldn't take it anymore. He grabbed her wrist, twirled her, bent over and hoisted her over his shoulder. Then he headed up the stairs with her giggling.

Ava Carmichael giggling was like an aphrodisiac. He had to get her naked now. Right now. Except for the shoes. He hadn't been kidding about those.

A minute later, he dumped her on his bed and reached for her skirt as she undid her bra. There wasn't a hesitation, she didn't even look around. She was fully focused on him and *that* was an aphrodisiac too. Being the center of Ava's attention meant a lot. He knew for a fact her phone was still out in the truck. He'd left in on the seat on purpose when he'd hauled her into his arms. But she hadn't hesitated. Hadn't looked for it. And that had been hotter than anything else she could have done.

He slipped her skirt down her legs and dropped it to the floor on top of the bra she'd already tossed. They both reached for her panties at the same time.

With a sexy smile, she held her hands up, letting him do the honors. He nearly ripped the lace from her body. Again. These could join the ripped thong that he had in his bedside table. But he managed to get them off in one piece and threw them to the floor as well.

He sucked in a deep breath, just taking in the sight of her on his bed, completely naked. And he suddenly had a deep fondness for afternoon sex where the sun was streaming through his bedroom window, letting him see every damned inch. He would be closing the diner at one o'clock sharp for the next few months, for sure.

She was gorgeous. But he knew, as he drank in the curve of her neck, the swell of her breasts, the dip of her waist, the smooth length of her thighs, and the sweet V between her legs, that she had been more exposed than this with him before. She'd let him see her failure, her sadness about her father, her insecurity, and her frustrations. He knew she didn't let people see those things about her. Only her sisters, probably. And being one of her inner circle mattered to him. It fucking mattered a lot.

"Damn, Ava." He felt humble. He'd never felt that before with a naked woman.

Her legs shifted on his sheets. "That's not bossy," she said.

His eyes went to hers. He cocked an eyebrow. "You like it when I'm bossy." It wasn't a question.

"People don't get bossy with me very often," she said.

"It's the shoes," he told her, picking up one by the heel and spreading her leg to the side, his cock aching at the sight.

"They keep people in line?" she asked, her lips lifting in a small smile that Parker felt clear to his gut.

"I'm sure of it."

"They don't work with you."

"No, they don't. They make me want to boss you around and

watch you do every fucking thing I tell you to do and make you beg while you're wearing them. They make me harder than I've ever been." That was all true. So, so true.

"They make you want to take my power?" Her tone was light. He didn't think she really thought that.

But he had to answer her seriously, and honestly. "They make me want to show you that you can be soft and vulnerable and trusting and still feel strong and respected, and that you don't need these shoes to get me firmly wrapped around your finger and ready to beg you right back."

She just blinked at him. And Parker felt his mouth curving in a cocky smile. He really did love surprising this woman.

"So...does that mean you're *not* going to be bossy in the bedroom?" she finally asked.

He ran his hand up her leg from her heel to mid-thigh. "Ava?"

"Yes, Parker?"

"Slide up the bed and grab onto my headboard."

Her eyes widened for just an instant. But low and firm seemed to do it for her. She quickly wiggled up the bed, her gorgeous breasts bouncing as she did.

He stripped his shirt off and unbuttoned his pants, easing the zipper down to relieve some of the pressure against his granite hard cock, but he didn't push them off yet.

Ava gripped his headboard, her hard nipples begging him for attention. Her cheeks were flushed, her breathing fast.

"Don't move your hands," he told her.

"Okay."

"I mean it." He put a knee on the mattress and grabbed both of her shoes. He slid her legs apart, crawling up between them as she opened for him.

She let out a shuddery breath, and he saw her grip the wooden slats in his headboard tighter. Parker moved his body over hers, dragging his chest against her stomach, then her pink-tipped breasts. She shivered as he abraded the stiff points. His tongue tingled with the anticipation of taking one in his mouth, but first, he had to kiss her.

His cock pressed against the sweet heat between her legs as he lowered his head. Just before their lips touched, he said, "Things might get kind of dirty for the next little while, Boss. And you are absolutely going to feel out of control. But you keep your hands up there and let me do all the work, and I promise that you're going to be just fine with letting me be in charge."

She shivered again and he realized she really liked the nickname. And the fact that right here, right now, like this, it wasn't true.

"But I won't be able to do anything that way." She arched up against him.

He lifted his head and looked down at her. "Oh, if I want my cock in your mouth, I'll put it there."

She sucked in a quick breath and her eyes darkened. A thought occurred to him.

"Please tell me you've had and done a lot of oral."

She wet her lips. "It...takes a long time."

Which was a no, not really. And Parker wanted to simultaneously beat the crap out of and buy a drink for every man she'd ever been with. Because those jackasses had failed her. But it was going to make Parker a freaking hero.

"Well, if you've got emails to return, they're going to have to wait. A while."

She nodded. "I'm okay with that."

"And *that* makes me want to reward you."

"Yes. Okay. Definitely."

He gave her a slow grin. "Your safe word is spreadsheets."

Her mouth curled. "But spreadsheets are a turn-on for me."

He chuckled softly. "Okay, apple pie."

"That will wo—"

He took her mouth in a hot kiss before she even finished her answer. He took his time tasting her, stroking his tongue over her tongue, nipping her lip. His hand skimmed down her side, over the swell of her breast, her ribcage, her waist, to her hip. He squeezed, pressing into her with the erection that was begging to be freed. But he had to cover all the bases here, and if he got undressed, it would be over in a minute.

He kissed his way down her neck, moving a hand to palm her breast. He thumbed her nipple, then rolled it between his thumb and finger. She arched closer and moaned his name, but her hands stayed on the headboard.

His mouth fastened on to her nipple, licking then sucking hard. Her hips bucked against his and he could feel the heat through his clothes. He moved a hand between them, cupping her where she was aching, and she half sighed, half moaned as he pressed the heel of his hand against her clit.

"Please," she said softly.

"My name, Boss," he chided, before biting gently on her nipple and making her gasp. "When you beg, use my name."

"Please, Parker."

"That's better." But he held his hand still, sucking and teasing her other nipple.

"*Parker.*"

He moved his hand away from her clit. "Don't get impatient now. This is all going according to plan."

She squeezed her thighs around his waist. "Let's renegotiate."

He couldn't help but laugh. "No way. I've got you right where I want you."

Then he pressed against her clit again, slipping a finger into her heat at the same time.

She moaned and her inner muscles gripped him.

"Say 'okay, Parker, whatever you want,'" he told her huskily. He had no idea how he was going to hold on here, but he was going to drag this out, make her wait and beg and fucking *submit* for as long as he could stand it.

She hesitated. Even in the throes of passion, it was hard for her to verbalize acquiescence.

He circled her clit with this thumb and sucked on her nipple again. "Say it," he commanded gruffly against the stiff tip. He slipped another finger into her. "Say it, Ava."

"Okay, Parker." She was breathless and panting. "Whatever you want."

"Damn right," he muttered. Then he slid down her body, widened her legs, and put his mouth against her pussy.

She was hot and wet, and the sound she made when he tongued her clit went straight to his cock. He had to reach down and grip hard to keep from coming right then.

Fuck. This woman was everything.

"You thought you weren't sweet?" he asked her. "You have no idea how fucking good you taste."

He was never going to get over any of this. She still held the headboard and that sent a shaft of satisfaction through him. He pumped his fingers deeper and faster, flicking his tongue over her clit.

"Oh, yes, like that." She lifted her hips, trying to get closer.

Parker lifted his head, needing to see her face. He replaced his tongue with his other hand, rubbing the sweet nub as he continued to move his fingers in and out in a steady rhythm. "My name, Boss," he reminded her with a growl. "And if you say it nicely, I'll make you come."

"Parker," she gasped obediently, right on the edge. "Oh my God. So good. You're so good."

Yep, that was pretty nice. He curled his finger and put his mouth to her clit again, and she came with another gasped, "*Parker*," her muscles grabbing his fingers. He pulled away and pushed himself off the end of the bed, quickly shedding his jeans and boxers.

Her gaze wandered over him, her breathing ragged. Her eyes on his now bare cock made him ache, and he took his length in his hand, squeezing and stroking as Ava lifted her head to watch. He crawled up the bed, taking her chin and devouring her mouth, making sure she tasted herself on his tongue and lips.

"Sweetest thing I've ever eaten," he said against her lips.

She moaned and Parker pushed up to kneel next to her. He was suddenly overcome by the reality of tasting her. It seemed tasting was a consistent theme with them, and he needed it to be complete. He took his cock in hand, giving it another much needed hard stroke.

"Open up, Boss," he said gruffly.

Her eyes widened as he turned her face toward him with his other hand. Her lips parted and he leaned in, rubbing the tip of his cock over her bottom lip. Her tongue flicked over the top, and he had to brace himself with a hand on the wall above the headboard.

He pressed forward and Ava took him in. He kept a hand around his shaft, controlling how far he slid in. He gritted his teeth, fighting the urge to thrust.

Ava moaned, the vibration zinging along his length. His breath hissed out. This was the perfect example of how it seemed he was in charge, but she had him knotted up and on his knees. Literally. Figuratively.

He pressed in and pulled out a few times, the hot suction of her mouth exquisite torture. "Suck on me, Ava," he demanded roughly.

She complied and then knocked the air of his lungs by looking up at him.

Her fingers were still wrapped around the slats on his headboard, her breasts bouncing as he slid in and out of her mouth, and she pressed her legs together as if she was aching. And still she had all the power here. He wanted to give her anything she wanted. He wanted to *be* what she needed. What would most make her feel like she'd finally found how to be happy and fulfilled.

He couldn't wait any longer. He pulled from her mouth and he reached into his bedside table drawer. He tossed her thong out of the way and grabbed a condom, quickly sheathing himself. He took her hands from the headboard. He rolled to his back, taking her with him. "Ride me, Boss."

She didn't argue, didn't hesitate. She straddled him, reaching behind her to position him, then eased back. She was slick and hot and he slid home slow and easy, in spite of how tight she was.

Ava braced her hands on his ribs and her head dropped back as she took him. They paused when he was as deep as he could go. He gripped her hips and let her adjust to his length and girth.

"Damn," she finally breathed. "This is even better than your chicken salad."

Caught off guard, Parker laughed. Then he squeezed her hips and thrust upward. "You're not moving. Need you to move."

She swiveled her hips.

"More," he said through gritted teeth.

She lifted slightly, then sank back down.

"*More*, Boss." He worked not to grip her hips too hard. "That all you got?" She was teasing him. And while he appreciated the idea of Ava being playful, he was about to lose his mind.

"I guess so," she finally answered.

"Bullshit." He thrust up, grinding her hips down on his. "Fuck me, Boss. Now."

She swallowed. Then she started moving. Really moving. She lifted and lowered her sweet, tight body on his, making Parker have to work to not flip her over and pound.

"Parker." Her voice was soft.

He lifted his hands, brushing her hair back from her face. "Gotta feel you come again, Ava."

"I'm close. Help me."

Gladly. "Lean back. Play with your nipples."

She obeyed and he moved his thumb to her clit, watching her

fingers tug on the dusky, pink tips, her expression filled with passion and pleasure.

"I've never come twice in a row," she told him, raggedly.

"Of course not. It takes longer to get there twice, right?" He sounded like he was in the middle of a five-mile run.

"It does. And at the moment I can barely think at all, not to mention remember the password to my email."

"Highest compliment," he said, sincerely.

"I love that you know that."

"I love that you admitted it."

"This is going to go to your head, isn't it?"

"Already has," he told her honestly. "As is the fact that you're about to beg me to fuck you hard. In exactly those words." He pressed against her clit and reached to tug on a nipple at the same time.

She gasped, but then managed, "I've never said *fuck me* to anyone." She was trying to use her haughty tone but considering she was straddling him with his cock buried deep, her hair wild around her shoulders, her lips swollen from his kisses, it wasn't entirely convincing.

He knew he was about to get everything he wanted. Still, he lifted his hand to her hair, gathered it back and wrapped it around his fist. He tipped her head back. "Beg me, Ava."

She gave a little moan and then gave in. "Fuck me, Parker. Hard. *Please*."

With a grown, he flipped her and thrust deep. "Dig those heels into my ass and hang on, Boss."

Ava's long legs wrapped around his waist and he felt her shoes against his butt. He thrust again and again, picking up speed, until he was pounding into her, relishing her *oh Gods, oh yeses* and *oh Parkers*.

He felt his orgasm building and he reached between them for her clit, swirling his thumb through the slickness, and she shouted his name just as her muscles squeezed and she shot over the summit. He was right behind her, his orgasm thundering through him.

He held himself still over her, letting the waves of satisfaction roll over him long after she'd melted into the mattress, her arms flopping out to the side and her eyes sliding shut. After his breathing slowed, he flopped to his back beside her.

"Holy shit, Boss. It's official—cooking really is the only thing you're not good at."

She laughed, also clearly trying to catch her breath. "Until you got involved, I never really appreciated food or sex."

"That's so, so sad," he said, but he absolutely felt like beating his chest.

She rolled to her side, and he ran his hand up and down her back while she splayed her hand on his stomach. "Parker, I have to tell you something I've never said to another guy."

He tensed but what went through his mind was *fuck yes.* He covered her hand with his. "Okay."

"I don't know where my phone is. And I don't care."

His fingers tightened on hers. Not what he'd been expecting —and that was a *good* thing because what he'd been expecting was ridiculous—but it was monumental. "Love that," he said honestly. "Not worried about your sisters?"

She toed her shoes off, the *thunk*s against his bedroom floor making him smile. Then she turned her hand over and laced her fingers with his. "They've got Evan and Noah."

Parker looped an arm under her and pulled her close. That was big too. She was letting it all go. Which reminded him of why he'd brought her out here in the first place. But she was relaxed right now. Warm and soft—and *naked*—against him. No way was he disturbing any of this.

15

Ava awoke a half hour later, plastered again Parker's body, feeling like she was curled around a furnace.

She took a deep, contented breath. And marveled at that word —*contented*—and the feeling. She hadn't taken a nap since she'd had the flu six years ago. She rubbed her cheek against his chest. She was napping in the middle of the day and her phone was not just out of arm's reach, it wasn't even in the same building. And she didn't care.

She lay still for a few minutes, just absorbing the feel of Parker beside her. But slowly, as she came further awake, she started thinking. This was nice. She and Parker were taking the day off. Together. This was epic in many ways. Neither of them had much downtime. And that he'd chosen to spend his with her was really nice.

But she could check a couple of things on her email if he was going to sleep a little longer.

Ava looked up at Parker. He was dead asleep, and she loved the idea that he was also content like this. She doubted very much that he took regular afternoon naps. She wanted to kiss him. Her gaze focused on his mouth and she felt warmth wash through her. But not lusty warmth—though his mouth certainly contributed to her physical pleasure with the things it could do and say—but more of a warmth that just felt...good. She loved when his mouth smiled. The things he said that were sarcastic and funny. And sweet. She loved when he got passionate about cooking and food. He had a way of making being fanatical about cheese seem manly and perfectly reasonable.

She grinned and started to wiggle out from under his arm. She was going to let him sleep. For now. But she wasn't much for just lying around. She'd check in on a few things and then when he woke up, she'd be all his. A pleasant little shiver went through her. *All his.* She could definitely get used to that.

Ava pulled on Parker's shirt and her panties and tiptoed down the stairs, realizing she'd left her phone in his truck. He lived far enough out here that she could probably run out to the truck naked, but she wasn't a country girl. At all. She had no idea what else could happen to her when she was naked outside. There were bugs, she was certain. That would be a lot of exposed skin for them to feast on. And she supposed it was possible there were wild animals. She wasn't sure what kind of animals were native to the plains of Kansas—she made a note to look that up once she was safely back inside—but it was possible there were bears or wolves or something, she supposed.

Ava got to the front door before she realized she'd left her shoes upstairs. She peered through the window in the front door, eyeing the wooden porch and the paved path leading away from the steps and the swath of dirt between the end of the path and the truck. The last time she'd been barefoot outdoors, she'd been on the deck of a yacht. She glanced around and noted a pair of dirty, scuffed tan boots that would go past her ankles. They had a thick rubber sole and looked entirely practical for the farm. Which made her grimace slightly. Farm footwear was not going to be her favorite thing. But as she bent to pull them on, Parker's scent wafted up from the shirt and she smiled. She could maybe put up with some ugly, practical boots once in a while if it meant hanging out here with Parker.

The boots were huge on her, but she laced them tightly enough that she could pick her foot up without the boot slipping off her foot entirely. She shuffled across the porch, down the steps and to the end of the paved path. But as she stepped off onto the dirt, a rooster crowed. She froze, one boot on the path, one on the dirt. She looked around furtively. That sound came from a male chicken. And that was the sum total of her knowledge about roosters. Fuck. She took a deep breath. Okay, roosters were common barnyard animals. And barnyard animals were generally mild-tempered and kept inside pens. At least according to the children's books she'd read about farms. Surely publishers wouldn't allow authors to lie to children, right? But then, there were all those books about Santa Claus and the Easter Bunny. Yeah, they would totally lie.

She eyed the truck door, then glanced back at the house. How much did she need her phone? The rooster crowed again and, with her heart thundering in her ears, and gigantic, thousand-pound boots on her feet, she scooted to the truck door, ripped it open, grabbed her phone and was back on the porch within seconds.

Once inside, she leaned against the front door, breathing hard. Damn, doing stairs with weights on her feet as fast as she could while adrenaline pumped had the potential to be a great workout.

She took the boots off and worked to steady her breathing and slow her heart rate as she typed *do roosters attack people* into the search bar in her phone. The first thing to pop up was *How to Deal With Aggressive Roosters*. Uh-huh. Ava read it quickly, frowning harder as she delved into the article. When she got to the part that said, "they can even put out a child's eye", she'd read enough. Adults most definitely lied to children.

She climbed the stairs to Parker's bedroom, thinking about the suggestions in the article for dealing with aggressive roosters. They included things like giving them treats, picking them up, or rolling them over with your foot when they attacked. It was all about showing them you were not the enemy but were higher up the food chain than they were. Ava sniffed. She definitely understood that part of it. Sometimes you had to demonstrate your dominance.

But she didn't want to get that close to a rooster. Or maybe any other barnyard animal. If all the children's books were lies, then she knew even less about farm life than she'd expected. Which would make dating Parker more difficult. Even temporarily. She had to keep reminding herself that this was not a permanent change in her life. It didn't matter if she figured out how to deal with farm life.

But...she felt like it did. Because it didn't *have* to be temporary. She had a private jet. It wasn't like she could never see him again once she went back to New York.

Or she wouldn't have to go back to New York...

Cori wasn't leaving Bliss. And Ava had been running Carmichael Enterprises from here for four months now, and it was working pretty well. A monthly trip to New York could be enough.

She shook her head as she climbed back up onto the bed next to a still sleeping Parker. Those kinds of thoughts were crazy. What she should be focusing on was that six months was plenty of time to be maimed by an aggressive rooster. But then she looked over at Parker. Really looked at him. And...yeah, her private jet was nice. She'd have no problem traveling between New York and Bliss.

Ava felt a wave of contentment wash over her again as she propped pillows behind her against the headboard. She liked his bed. It was big and comfortable, and he'd probably had it for at least ten years. She also liked his house. It was an old farmhouse that had maybe been repainted here and there but hadn't really been changed in years. If ever. It was very Parker in that way. She was still surprised when she thought about his childhood in Chicago, but the man he was now, was the guy he was going to be in ten years, fifty years, eighty years. And there was something so comforting, and appealing, about that.

And this house. It was the kind of house that had squeaky steps that you learned to avoid out of habit, and trees in the yard that grew along with the people in the house. His closet was no way big enough for her clothes, or even her shoes, but...they'd deal with that, if needed. She wasn't ready to downsize her shoe collection—she was falling for him, not going crazy—but if there wasn't room here, she could turn her bedroom at the house in town into a huge closet.

And she was very much getting ahead of herself here.

Still, she pulled the very-farm-cliché patchwork quilt over her legs and started flipping through the internet on her phone, reading articles about living on a farm.

———

"You went and got your phone?"

Twenty minutes later, Ava was reading about canning. Something she could still not picture her father doing. Ever. She looked over at Parker. He was watching her with sleepy eyes and a grim set to his mouth.

"Just until you woke up," she said. She set the phone on the bedside table. She was *not* going to be canning. But the farm-life rabbit hole she'd gone down had taken her there. Reading the article about aggressive roosters had led her to alpacas—which, besides having fleece that was amazingly useful, could also be used to guard smaller animals, something Ava begrudgingly found fascinating—which led her to goats—some of the animals an alpaca could protect, which led her to vegetables—she didn't remember how exactly—which led her to canning. And she'd kept reading because of Rudy.

Ava slid down until she was lying on her side next to Parker. He looped an arm around her, and she was more than happy to press up against his naked form.

"Thought you were going to nap with me," he said.

"I did for a little bit. I'm not much of a napper."

"Me either." He frowned. "Guess I was hoping you'd relax out here with me though."

"I'm relaxed."

"You're on your phone."

It was too soon to tell him that she'd been reading about farm life. It was too soon to tell him that she could fly back and forth from Bliss rather than going back to New York full-time. It was too soon to even be thinking all of that.

"My phone doesn't automatically mean I'm not relaxed," she said with a smile. In fact, usually *not* being on her phone made her *more* tense than being on it. She liked to be connected. She'd actually intended to check her email, but she'd gotten caught up in the idea of watching alpacas take care of goats. And now that she was up against Parker, she didn't care what was in her email. Or about alpacas. Though she did have some lingering anxiety about that rooster.

"I like you in my shirt."

"I like you out of your shirt."

He gave her a grin and ran his hand up and down her back. "We're to the after part, Boss."

Parker's deep voice rumbled through her and she shivered with pleasure. Then his words sank in. The after part. The part they wanted to be different. The part she didn't have a plan for.

Ava pushed up onto her elbow. Parker's gaze dropped to her bare legs and where his shirt had pulled up to nearly expose her butt, and she felt heat shoot through her. Yeah, maybe they could just keep sleeping together. The plan there seemed pretty clear—

let him take the lead, lie back, and enjoy. It was true that she typically took charge of most situations, but she was also really good at recognizing other people's talents and giving them the opportunity to show them off.

But she pulled the comforter up over her ass. It might be too soon to talk about how she was going to get along on the farm, but it was never too soon to have a plan. They were both expert organizers. They could make this work. "So, we should talk about this. Right? Probably?"

"Talk about what?"

"This next part. Make a plan for what we're going to do."

Parker looked at her for a long moment. He ran his hand over her hair, down her back to her butt. Then he gave her a swat and pulled his arm from under her as he swung his legs over the edge of the mattress. "I don't think so."

"What?" She sat up, pulling the comforter with her.

"Thing is," Parker said, reaching for another shirt draped over the end of the bed and pulling it over his head. "Nothing has gone according to plan between us so far." He looked over his shoulder and gave her a sexy grin. "And it's all turned out pretty damned good as far as I'm concerned." He stretched to his feet, pulling on his boxers and jeans. "So I think we should forget about plans, Boss."

She watched him dress, thinking how intimate it seemed. And how dressed really seemed the opposite of how she'd like to keep him. And *they* were going to forget about plans?

But, she couldn't deny he had a point. Things really did seem to be going well. And the plan had been to bake pie together. Something they still hadn't done. "So what now then?" she asked.

"Now it's lunchtime."

He started for the stairs, but he paused in the doorway and looked back at her. "And don't bother putting your skirt back on."

That sounded promising. So Ava followed him, barefoot, to

the kitchen. Then through the kitchen to the laundry room. "Um."

But a moment later, he thrust a pair of jeans and socks at her. "My mom's a little bigger than you. Taller for sure. But these will work for now. Though we'll have to get you some of your own, I suppose."

Ava stared down at the jeans. "I'm going to wear those?"

"Can't have you traipsing around outside in those heels," he said.

"I'm going to be traipsing around outside?"

"That's where the food is."

She took the clothes as she stared up into his face. He looked so excited. "Why does your mom have clothes here?"

"She helps out with the garden and animals."

Animals. Plural. She'd been right to start reading, it seemed. But unless he had alpacas, she really only knew about aggressive roosters. "What kind of animals?"

"Chickens. Ducks. Goats. Rabbits. Dogs. Cats."

"You *do* have goats?" she asked.

He lifted an eyebrow. "I do. For milk. And fun. My mom loves them."

She'd read about the advantages to goat's milk over cow's milk. And no way was she going to tell him that. "Not cows?"

"Cows are a lot bigger and take more work," he said.

Then a horrible thought occurred to her. "Do you...eat the chickens?" she asked. She was definitely not ready to watch someone take a chicken from living on his farm to roasted on his table.

He looked amused. "Sometimes. Mostly I use them for eggs."

"Are we...going to eat one now?" she asked.

He looked at her with a very cute, very puzzled look. "No. I think we'll stick with meat I've already got. If that's okay?"

"Totally fine," she said breathing out. She knew that she wasn't really cut out for farm life. She'd bookmarked a blog called *City Girl Goes Rural* and another called simply *The Farm Wife*, but she'd been hesitant to read. For one, that was assuming *a lot*. For another, she wasn't sure she wanted to read a whole article that would basically prove she had no business building up daydreams around pickup trucks and chicken coops. Parker owned a diner. She barely understood *that* and knew there were messy, gross parts to that business. She was sure that the diner had nothing on some of the things that happened on the farm.

"Then what are we going outside for?" she asked. Eggs, possibly. She liked eggs.

"I'll show you."

She took a deep breath, then stepped into the jeans. They were too long and a couple sizes big around the middle. She hooked a thumb through one of the belt loops to keep them up. She looked up at Parker. "I don't think these are going to work."

"I don't think I can take you out there without pants on," he told her, his eyes wandering over her.

"Because of bugs?" she asked. Then she dropped her voice, "Or attack animals?"

Both his eyebrows rose. "Because I'll want to fuck you on one of my work tables."

"Oh." She thought about that and wet her lips. "Would that be so bad?"

"How do you feel about splinters in your ass?"

She didn't relish the idea, but she was distracted by another thought. "So there aren't any animals out there that would attack?"

He blinked. "Well..."

"There are?" she asked, her voice rising.

"None that would attack you for walking across the yard," he said. "And the dogs would definitely raise hell if something came that close to the yard anyway."

"Something like what?" she asked, aware her eyes were huge and round. "Are there bears out here?"

"Bears? What? No," he said with a shake of his head. "There are no bears here."

"Then what?"

"Maybe a coyote." Parker lifted a shoulder. "Possibly a mountain lion, but not likely."

"What about roosters?"

Parker blinked at her again. "What about roosters?"

"Are your roosters aggressive?"

"I've only got one and...no. What are you talking about?"

"Roosters can be aggressive," she said, pulling the jeans up slightly.

"Yes. They can. But why are *you* worried about that?"

"I thought *you* were worried about it."

"Why would *I* be worried about that?" Parker asked, looking more and more confused.

"I thought that was why you didn't want me going out without pants. Before you mentioned the work table thing."

He ran a hand through his hair. "I'm not worried about you being attacked when you go out there, Ava."

"Okay, good. So I don't have to wear pants."

He sighed. "You're not worried about the splinters then?"

"Maybe *your* ass could be the one on the table," she said with a little grin.

He stepped forward. "You want to ride me on my work table, Boss? I'd put up with some splinters for that."

"And it will be easier if I don't have pants on." She let go of the jeans and they slipped down. She pushed them off and stepped out of them.

Parker shook his head. "Can't argue with that. But—" he added as she started to step around him. "You have to wear something on your feet. And not your heels."

"I don't have anything else."

"My mom has boots here."

Ava looked to where Parker was pointing. It was a pair of

work boots, a lot like the ones she'd slipped on to go out to the truck, but smaller. She bent and began pulling them on.

"Just like that?" Parker asked.

She looked up. "Yeah. Why?"

"You're just agreeing to put work boots on instead of heels?"

Crap. She couldn't let on that she'd spent her time reading about farms and that she understood and accepted that boots were far more practical than heels out here. Or that she was worried she was going to have to roll a rooster over with her foot if he got feisty. She pulled the boots on and straightened. "You really think I'm going to fight you about not getting my nine hundred dollar Louis Vuitton pumps covered in goat poop?"

He looked skeptical for a second, but finally said, "I guess I figured you'd go barefoot and I would have to carry you out there."

"Hmm..." She eyed his biceps. "Now that you mention it..." She moved as if to toe off one of the boots.

"Well, too bad, you look completely adorable and totally fuckable in only my shirt and a pair a boots."

He grabbed her hand and pulled her toward the back door that opened off the laundry room as she was still processing looking adorable and fuckable. In a T-shirt and work boots. If that was the case, she'd been spending way too much time and money on Armani and Prada.

Or maybe not. The last thing she wanted the men around her conference tables thinking of her was "adorable". With "fuckable" a close second.

"But I swear," Parker said, as they hit the paved path that led away from the house at the back. "I'm going to get you into blue jeans again sometime, Boss. Worn-out blue jeans. Maybe with a ripped knee and some dirt streaked across the ass."

"Yeah? What's that about?" They walked side by side across the yard toward one of the structures she'd noticed when they'd pulled in. It wasn't a barn, at least not a traditional one, but it was huge with a high, pitched roof. The roof and the walls looked translucent. She could make out forms inside the building, but not what they were exactly.

"Honestly?" he finally asked of her question. "I guess it's about seeing you a little more a part of my world."

She tripped. She hadn't been expecting that kind of answer. She tugged him to a stop. "Seeing me dressed in work boots and jeans makes it more believable that I could fit in here?"

He shrugged. "Not really. Obviously, it's not about what you're wearing. But yeah, I guess there's a part of me that thinks if you can strut around, as confident and kick-ass in work boots and jeans as you do in heels and skirts, then that means you've really acclimated. "

"You want me acclimated here?" she asked, her voice softer. Maybe it wasn't so crazy that she'd been reading about farm life.

He lifted a hand and tucked her hair behind her ear. "I guess the idea of you sticking around, being comfortable here, is nice."

She thought about that. And the fact that he would look incredibly hot in a tux, and that she would love to see him wearing one confidently at a party or dinner in New York with her. Yeah, she liked the idea of them fitting into each other's lives too. A lot.

"I think Armani makes jeans," she said lightly, trying not to let on how much she suddenly wanted to wear blue jeans.

He shook his head, but he was smiling. "Levis. That you buy downtown."

She sighed. "So bossy."

His eyes heated slightly. "Don't forget it." Then he started for the big translucent building again. "And since you're wearing my shirt and my mom's boots, I don't have to worry about how dirty I get you."

She tripped along beside him, not used to the weight of the boots, even though they fit much better than his had. "Like you've ever cared about that."

He just laughed. When they arrived at the door to the building, he pulled it open and ushered her in. But she didn't get very far inside the door before he had his hands on her hips and her body up against his again. That seemed to be a move he really liked. And it was true that they fit together perfectly this way.

But Ava's mind was only partially on the feel of the hot, hard man behind her. The rest of it was busy being amazed at what she was looking at.

It was a greenhouse. Clearly. The building was filled with long wooden tables covered in pots and boxes that held a variety of plants. Ava wasn't sure she'd ever realized how many shades of green actually existed in plant leaves, stems, and vines. More plants hung from wooden arches, some in pots, some just meandering freely. There were even some trees. Trees. Indoors. They were small, but still. The air smelled like soil and sunshine. Ava was sure she'd never thought about how sunshine smelled. Or maybe she'd never really smelled it. But this scent was fresh and earthy and somehow clean even as it was coming from dirt. Amazing.

"Wow, Parker, this is all yours?"

He pressed into her, and she felt the hard ridge of his erection against her butt. "Every inch."

She laughed at the juvenile quip but couldn't resist wiggling against him. "I meant the plants. This is what you do during the hours you close the diner?"

"Yeah."

"Wow."

He kissed the side of her neck, running his lips up and down and making sparks shoot to her nipples. They hardened against the soft cotton of his shirt and she moaned. His fingers curled into her hips. "Let me give you a tour."

He ran his hands over the dip of her waist to her ribs. "Along the sides are the garden plants that like more sun." He moved one hand over her belly, then up between her breasts.

"The middle has less sun and is where the plants like lettuce and spinach are. Toward the back on the left," he went on, cupping her left breast, "are a couple of dwarf orange trees. And on the right—" He moved to cup that breast as well, "—is a strawberry patch." He tugged on her nipple, and his voice dropped low as he said, "You have to be gentle when plucking those."

Ava was panting but enjoying the "tour" immensely.

"On the shelves are herbs. And over there, on that mound—" He slid his hands down and into her panties.

Ava gasped and clutched his wrist. "*Parker*."

"—is the corn, squash, and beans." He slid the pad of his finger over her clit. "Those three grow well together." He circled and pressed. "The corn stalks in the middle give support to the bean plants." He slid his finger lower and into her to his middle knuckle. "And the squash leaves give shade that prevent weeds."

Ava didn't care at all about beans or squash, but she loved having Parker's hands on her. And strangely, garden words like *stalks* and *mounds* made her even hornier. Okay, maybe that made sense, even if these were mounds of dirt.

"So do you want your front or back dirty?" he asked.

"Either. Both. Just please tell me you're talking about sex dirty and not dirt dirty," she answered, breathlessly as his fingers moved over her clit.

"You didn't mind food dirty," he said gruffly against her ear. "And good potting soil is essentially the start to food."

He had a point. He'd also slipped his two middle fingers into her, so she was pretty much ready to agree to anything.

"Hey, yeah. You have strawberries in here." Her eyes slid closed and her head fell back against his chest as he continued to play between her legs. "We could have gone strawberry picking that very first day after all."

"Yeah." He pumped his fingers deeper.

"But you didn't want me *here*. In your greenhouse then," she said as that realization dawned even as he walked her forward to the wooden table in front of her.

There were no pots on the very end, but potting soil was scattered over the surface along with a variety of green and brown leaves.

"This is like letting someone into my kitchen," Parker admitted.

Ava knew he meant the kitchen at the diner, not in his house. And she got the message loud and clear. This—and his kitchen—were more intimate than even his bedroom. And that was as much a turn-on as his mouth against the back of her neck and the one hand teasing her nipple while the other worked his finger magic between her legs.

So when Parker leaned his chest into her back, bending her forward to the table, Ava went willingly. In spite of the dirt. Hell, maybe because of it. When he slid the shirt she wore up over her ass, she pulled it up further, over her breasts. She felt the mix of softness and grit underneath her, abrading her nipples and shooting surprising jolts of pleasure through her body.

"God, *yes,* Ava," Parker muttered. He stripped the shirt off of her entirely, pulled her panties to her ankles, and gripped her hips. "And I thought fucking you in heels was hotter than hell." He lifted one of her thighs, setting her foot—in the work boot—on the table's lower shelf. "Brace your hands," he almost growled.

Ava straightened her elbows as she heard his zipper, the sound of his jeans rustling and then a condom wrapper tearing. "Parker," she said softly, the need in her voice clear.

He reached past her and knocked a glass jar to its side. Clear liquid ran over the table. He swirled his hand through what she assumed was water and the dirt, then lifted his hands to her breasts.

She gasped as he painted the cool mud over her breasts and nipples, then down her stomach to her hips. Then he thrust. He sank into her easily and they both groaned, and he paused. But only for a moment. He pulled out and sank deep gain, slowly, but Ava moved along with him the next time, craving the friction and fullness. She pressed against the tabletop, the mud slick under her left hand, the rough wood under her right hand keeping her from slipping completely. Parker's thrusts quickly picked up tempo.

"Ava...*fuck*. Touch yourself. You gotta come, Boss."

"You," she panted, her clit aching.

"Dirty hands," he muttered, squeezing her hips and thrusting deeper.

She reached between her legs with her clean hand, needing pressure against that aching spot as he filled her over and over.

He tugged a nipple as he bit down gently on the spot where her neck met her shoulder and she shot into orbit. He gripped her harder and thrust faster when he heard his name bouncing off the walls of his greenhouse. He shouted her name only a few moments later.

He pulled out almost immediately and turned her quickly to face him. He took in the sight of her, covered in streaks of mud from his hands. His mud. Then he bracketed her face with his still muddy hands and pulled her in for a hot, deep, sweet kiss.

When he finally let her go, she smiled up at him, her heart feeling strangely full. "So gardening, huh?" she asked.

He laughed and pulled her in to kiss the top of her head. "Yeah. Gardening."

16

Parker grabbed paper towels and wiped his hands and Ava's cheeks, then disposed of them and the condom in a nearby bucket. He pulled his pants up before going to one knee. He placed kisses up her thigh as he pulled her panties up and then grabbed the T-shirt. He also pulled that over her head and kissed her again, hard on the mouth, before saying, "Now, about lunch."

They held hands—of all the sappy, weird things she'd never done with a guy before—as they wandered the greenhouse gathering spinach, tomatoes, and peppers.

"Salad?" she asked.

"Frittata."

He led her out the back of the greenhouse, but she pulled to a stop outside the door. "Frittatas need eggs."

"Very good, Boss."

"And you don't buy eggs from the store."

"For the diner, I do," he said. "The girls can't quite keep up with that demand. But no, not for out here."

"So we're going to *get* the eggs. From your chickens?" This had to be the most bizarre date of her life.

"We are." He lifted an eyebrow. "You have a chicken phobia?"

ERIN NICHOLAS

"I didn't think I did," she muttered.

"I'll do the hard work," he said with a wink.

"Which is?"

He thought about it. "There's not really anything hard about it."

"Uh-huh." But she let him tug her across the yard to the wooden structure that she would have identified as the chicken coop even without being told. Since there were actual chickens surrounding it. There was an enclosed box that actually looked like a little house. It was even painted in the same light blue as his house. A wooden ramp led from the front door of the little house to a "yard" in front of it. It was mostly dirt with some sparse grass covering it. There were four chickens pecking at the ground. And one rooster. Ava's steps stuttered, but the entire thing, yard and house, was surrounded with a high wire fence and topped with a pitched roof.

"My mom built the coop," Parker said as they neared the door that would lead into the yard. He chuckled. "She thinks it's cute. I don't think the chickens care."

The light blue walls, white trim, and, now that she was close enough to study it and not stare at the rooster, the white shutters on either side of the tiny windows, were all pretty cute.

But it was still a chicken coop.

Parker opened the large door that led into the enclosure, but Ava hung back. He looked at her. "You okay?"

She was frowning at the rooster. Who was now looking directly at her. "You can go in without me, right?"

"I could. But what would be the fun in that?" He tugged on her hand and Ava, never one to back down from a challenge, stepped through the door.

But she kept her eye on the male with feathers.

Parker strode confidently toward the coop. "Let's see what we've got this afternoon."

She watched him walk through the chickens who just scattered as he passed. She followed carefully. He rounded the one side of the coop and lifted a wooden hatch.

"Come here." He motioned her forward.

Ava stepped toward him, but a chicken got in her way and she bumped it with her foot. The chicken squawked and flapped her wings and Ava let out a little scream. And the rooster started for her.

Roosters didn't like it when their hens got riled up.

Ava sucked in a quick breath and lifted her foot, prepared to roll him over. She had no idea how that was actually going to work, but she was grateful for the boots now. But the bit she'd read about showing him who was in charge flashed through her mind. At the last minute she frowned and bent, scooping him up in her arms and tucking him against her side snugly. He squawked and tried to flap his wings, but she just kept him tucked in tight and ignored him as she walked toward where Parker was standing with his eyes wide and his mouth open.

"What did you want to show me?" she asked as she joined Parker at the side of the coop.

His eyes were on the rooster that had settled down surprisingly quickly. Though she wasn't sure why she was surprised. She had no idea what to think or expect in any rooster situation.

"What the *hell* are you doing?" he asked.

She noted that he was holding an egg in each hand. She peered into the side of the coop he'd opened. There was a line of boxes, each with what looked like straw at the bottom. Two were empty, one had a chicken sitting in it, and two others had eggs cradled in the straw.

"This is where they lay the eggs?"

"Nesting boxes," Parker said absently. "What are you doing with my rooster?"

Ava glanced down at the bird under her arm. "Showing him who's boss."

Parker looked from the rooster up at her. "How did you know how to do that?"

"I read about it."

"You read about roosters?" He seemed completely baffled by that. "Why? When?"

"While you napped," she said. "After I heard him crowing when I went out to get my phone from the truck."

"You looked up how to boss a rooster around?"

She shrugged. "Pretty much."

There was a pause, then Parker burst into laughter. Then he reached for her, on the rooster-less side, and pulled her into a half hug.

"What?" she asked against his chest, not really able to hug him back.

"Just...thank you for always being you," he said. "You are exactly who you seem to be. Even in the middle of a farm for the first time in your life, wearing work boots and very little else." His hand skimmed down her back to her butt. "You look at a situation and just do what needs to be done." He kissed the top of her head. "Thank you for kicking ass, all the fucking time."

She felt her heart expand and had a hard time taking a deep breath for a second. She gave the rooster a little squeeze, suddenly glad that he'd gone on the attack. Crazy as that was.

"Also, thanks for making egg gathering incredibly sexy," Parker said, letting her go.

She sniffed a little, composing herself as he stepped away. The sniff brought in the smell of the coop even stronger and she grimaced. "Sexy, huh?"

"I'd put you up against this coop and gladly show you, but I do think Ras would have a problem with that." Parker reached for the other eggs in the nesting boxes, then shut the hatch.

"Ras?" Ava asked.

He pointed at the rooster. "Rasputin."

Her eyebrows shot up. "This rooster is named *Rasputin*?"

"My mom named him."

"So, he's evil." She looked down at him. He was, actually, just sitting on her hip as if perfectly fine being there.

"My mom might have had a run-in with him." Parker seemed to be mulling that over. "I never really asked her why she named him that."

"She never mentioned that he was an attack rooster?"

Parker chuckled. "She's kind of like you. She just takes care of stuff. She wouldn't have mentioned that." He looked back at the coop. "She built this herself. Just did it. Didn't ask for input, or permission, just did it. One day I came home and the frame was up."

Ava liked his mom already. "And that was fine with you?"

He shrugged. "Her taking care of the chickens a lot of the time helps me out. It's time I don't have to spend cleaning or repairing the coop. I throw some seed out and gather eggs two or three times a day. It's pretty low-key."

"I'm glad someone's helping you with stuff," Ava said. "You work hard." He really did.

"Well, thanks." Parker seemed pleased with her comment. "But this is my day off. And I don't want to spend any more of it in a chicken coop. And I don't want to spend much more of it with you in clothes."

It was just that easy for him to get her body humming.

She looked down at the rooster. She'd read about how to pick him up, but the article hadn't talked about putting him back down. She supposed she'd just set him on the ground and hope to get out of the pen before he decided she'd wounded his male ego.

But when she set him down, he just wandered off, pecking randomly at the ground.

"All males are just putty in your hands, huh?" Parker asked, holding the door open for her. He had the five eggs in the pocket he'd created by holding up the bottom of his shirt. That exposed a strip of skin over hard abs, and Ava was shocked to find herself wanting to lick him right there. Right now. In a chicken coop.

Instead, she stepped through the door and started for the house. She really needed to *not* be smelling barnyard before she licked anything.

Parker showed her how to wash the eggs in the utility sink in the corner of the laundry room, then he stored them in the fridge, threw her over his shoulder, and took her upstairs to the shower. Where they had hot, slippery sex before washing each other from head to toe.

By the time they made it back downstairs to the kitchen, Ava was hungry, but incredibly relaxed and...happy. It was a simple word that people used all the time without thinking, but today it had a new meaning for her. She was as out of her element as she'd ever been, spending time in kitchens, and greenhouses, and chicken coops with a man who rattled her, who didn't care that she was a CEO worth billions, who liked her in work boots as much or more than he did in heels. And she was *happy*.

"You want to help me in the kitchen?" Parker asked. He was shirtless but had a clean pair of jeans sitting low on his hips.

Ava took a seat on one of the high stools across the counter that separated his enormous kitchen from the living room that was filled with casual furniture. He had two sofas, a recliner, and a rocking chair in the corner, along with a huge coffee table that she could imagine covered with snacks, mugs and bottles, while a game played on the big screen TV suspended over the stone hearth fireplace.

"I can honestly tell you that I would *love* to sit right here and just *watch* you cook for me," she said.

He gave her a grin. "Good thing cooking is my third favorite thing to do with you."

"I have a really good idea about number one," she said. Her body was still tingling from the things he'd done to it in the shower. She never would have guessed a guy like Parker would have a mesh body puff. And she would have never guessed the things he could do with it. She shifted on the stool and cleared her throat, watching Parker bend to retrieve ingredients from the fridge. Hot, naked skin, and hard, bunching muscles, and denim that molded deliciously to his body, and she couldn't remember what she'd been about to ask him.

"Number one has several subsets," he said, straightening with his arms full of food and crossing to the center island. "But yeah, it's probably pretty obvious."

"So what's number two?" she asked.

He looked up from positioning the vegetables on the cutting board. "Talking."

For some reason that made her throat tighten. "Oh."

He gave her a nod. "Yeah. *Oh.*" He grabbed a knife and chopped the top of the pepper off. "I'm as surprised as you."

She laughed. "We probably shouldn't be. We have a lot in common."

He smiled, continuing to chop. "Take away your private jet and we're practically the same person."

She chuckled. Absently, she picked up the pencil lying by a notebook and stack of junk mail. She knew that he knew they did have a lot in common. They were both hyper-organized, liked to get their way, and ran their businesses with a firm but purposeful plan. They also had a similar sense of humor and just seemed to get one another.

But he also wanted her to be more a part of his world. That still made her heart flip. And it made her think about him in *her* world too. "You know, speaking of that private jet," she said, fiddling with the pencil. "I was thinking...what would you think about going to New York with me?"

She heard the chopping stop and she glanced up.

Parker had a hand braced on the island and was studying her. "Parker?"

"What would we do?"

She couldn't help it—she blushed. Because she had an amazing, six-nozzle shower in her apartment and she'd already had some thoughts about that shower and this man.

His grin was slow and made deep-down-oh-yeah muscles clench. "Besides that, Boss. Because yeah...we're going to do that no matter where we are."

Now he was reading her mind. Or her expressions, at least. She blew out a breath. "Dinner, a show, sightseeing, whatever you want. I just thought—" It had sounded so effortless and sweet from him, but she had never, ever said something romantic or sentimental to a man before.

"You just thought what?" he prompted.

His voice was low and even from across the few feet and two countertops that separated them, she felt like he was touching her.

"You want to see me in blue jeans again. I want to see you in a shirt and tie."

"Ah," he said, nodding slowly. "You want to see me in your world."

She started to answer, then pressed her lips together and thought about her words. She decided to go ahead though. "I want to see how we can maybe...be together...in both worlds."

He took a long breath and Ava braced for him to say, *I want nothing to do with your world* or *we're not together*. But that wasn't what he said.

"Dammit, woman, I need food at some point today."

She frowned. "I don't mean we should go to New York *today*. And there's food there. Lots of it. Great food, as a matter of fact. Some of the best in the world."

"And I look forward to trying a bunch of it," he said. "But if you keep saying things like that, I'm never going to get around to eating today. At least not *food*."

"I don't—" But then she *did* understand. Her wanting him to come to New York, into her world turned him on. She felt her body heat. She loved that she'd had that effect. "Okay, you finish cooking and then we can talk about New York."

"Naked," Parker said.

"What?"

"We can talk about New York while we're naked." He started cracking eggs and whisking.

"Okay." She smiled. "We can talk about New York while we're naked."

He continued with the meal preparation, and Ava found herself watching his hands and his shoulders and arm muscles bunching as he mixed and diced and sautéed. And thinking that they didn't really need food *that* much.

To distract herself, she decided to make a to-do list. One of her favorite things in the world. She borrowed the notebook in Parker's stack of stuff on the counter and started writing. She should call her assistant so Maggie could get them show tickets and a dinner reservation and get the jet ready. It would be so much fun to take Parker out and spoil him a little. He worked hard with not much time off. He not only cooked for the entire town for more than twelve hours a day, but he also took care of chickens and a whole greenhouse and...goats. She hadn't even met the goats yet. Ava added "research goats" to her list. Then she turned the page. Maybe Maggie could pull together a quick meeting on the Ashton merger. It would be easier to go over the glitches in person. She'd just finished her notation on some things she wanted to check in the file, when she noticed a list and some notes on the next page. She assumed it was Parker's list.

Chicken, sweet onions, apples. Try sweet and savory crust. Cinnamon? Thyme? Sugar? Light. More sweet.

She studied it. It was kind of a grocery list. But not really.

Chicken and apples? She flipped the page.

Pork and peaches. Tenderloin? Increase sugar. Less lime. Try lemon.

The next page had a list that included beef and cherries.

"Fruit and meat pies?"

He glanced over from the stove. "What?"

She held up the notebook. "Are these new recipe ideas?"

He opened his mouth, then shook his head and turned to remove the cast-iron skillet from the oven. He set it on top of the stove and then tossed the oven mitt to the side. "That's nothing," he finally said.

"Really? Because they look like the starts to recipes," Ava said.

"Just some things that were going through my mind." He leaned against the counter, bracing his hands beside his hips.

But Ava focused. "So they are recipes."

"Kind of."

"For the pie shop?" she asked. She looked down. "Because this is *really* amazing."

He didn't say anything and when she glanced up again, he was frowning. "I don't know that they're amazing."

"They are," she said, her enthusiasm growing as she thought about it. "I mean, you're taking the classic pies that we serve—apple, cherry, and peach—from sweet to savory. This is a really great idea for expanding the menu. Still pie, still our classics, but something new. These could be lunch additions. And they wouldn't compete with the diner." Ava was vaguely aware that she was talking faster as she went along, but she felt her excitement building and couldn't stop. "You can keep the diner menu as is, all the comforting, familiar stuff everyone wants most of the time. But when someone is in an adventurous mood, ready to try something new, they can just come next door." She set the notebook down and scooted forward on her stool. "It's a chance for you to keep giving everyone what they need from the diner, but give in to some of that creativity that you can't show off there. This would be good for *you* too." She grinned at him. "This is a great way to start showing them more of what you can do. The diner can be tried and true, the pie shop can be new and creative."

Parker was just watching her with a mix of wonder and trepidation. "I was just messing around one night," he said, gesturing toward the notebook. "I don't have any plans to do elaborate, creative things at the pie shop."

He might not have *plans*, but he had *thoughts* along those lines.

She nodded. "But you *could*," she said. "I know you think this is a sandwich and burger town, but *you're* not just a sandwich and burger chef. It's okay for *you* to have something else besides the diner."

"I love the diner."

"I know. Everyone knows," she assured him. "And making pork and peach pies next door to the diner doesn't mean that anyone will doubt that."

He took a deep breath. "I don't know."

She gave him a smile. God, the way he treated *her* was addictive, but the way he treated the town and his father's legacy was equally so. Even as it was incredibly frustrating. "Okay, so let's start smaller. You *have* had thoughts about the food at the pie shop?"

"Of course."

"I mean beyond how sucky *my* pie has been." She grinned. "You've thought of adding to the menu?"

"Yes."

"So how do you think you should start? Cori will be adding the specialty pies—the s'mores and stuff—what do you want to add?"

He shrugged. "Just simple stuff. Blueberry, strawberry."

She nodded. "Makes sense. Most people would expect a pie shop to have those, so that probably wouldn't rock Bliss's foundation too much, right?" She resisted an eye roll. He was so careful with them. And she understood. Mostly. His business model had worked for a long time. Messing with it was risky. And he liked what he was doing too. But she knew he was capable of so much more.

"They might even survive adding chocolate silk," he said dryly.

Ava gasped and put a hand to her chest. "Are you *sure*?"

Parker sighed and turned to plate the frittata. "I'm not being ridiculous. People here like the things they like."

"Of course they do," Ava agreed. "Because what they have and like is so good." She meant that. And not just at the diner. "But that doesn't mean they can't like other things." She looked down at the plate he set in front of her. It looked and smelled delicious. "Parker, this is about you too. So you make a new pie that they don't like. Big deal. You try something else. I get that people come to the diner expecting certain things and you want to give that to them, but they don't really expect anything specific from the pie shop." She took a bite of the frittata, briefly registered that it was amazing, and went on. "That's one bonus of having the pie shop in such a state of change. They don't have set expectations yet. They know things there are going to be different. And they weren't that devoted to it in the first place. This is your chance to stretch your chef wings. Let them see what you can do. Maybe pork and peach won't be a big hit. It may never replace the jalapeno burger, but at least *you* have a chance to try it."

Parker took a bite, chewed, and swallowed. "Maybe."

Maybe. She could totally work with maybe. She took another bite of the frittata, thought about what she wanted to say, swallowed, and took a breath. "You know, I understand wanting to follow in your father's footsteps." She looked up when he didn't respond. He was just chewing and watching her. She laid her fork down. "My *whole* life, as long as I've been old enough to understand even the smallest bit of what he did for a living, I was all about doing what he did. It was the only way to be close to him and to really spend time with him. And he was successful. So I just focused on doing things his way. But..." She pulled in a long breath. "Then I come here, and I find out that he wasn't truly happy until he left there. He had to leave behind everything we did together, everything he taught me, everything I was working for, to really find what he wanted." Her throat was tight and she had to work to swallow.

Parker set his plate to the side and braced his hands on the counter again. "Rudy..." He stopped and frowned. "That wasn't about you, Ava. He didn't leave *you.*"

She lifted a shoulder. "Maybe not. Maybe it wasn't *directly* about me." She knew he hadn't left because of her, but he had still left, and found happiness, away from her. But she was starting to understand that Bliss, and the people here, kind of did that to a person. She didn't think Rudy was looking for happiness when he'd come here, but it had found him. And she was glad. "But the point is," she went on with Parker. "I get what it's like to want to do things his way because of whatever you saw in him, in what he was doing. But maybe that's not all he wanted for you. Just like the company wasn't all Rudy wanted for me."

Parker shook his head. "This is exactly what my dad wanted. It was what he brought us here for. What he built for us."

"But he didn't have five years of sitting around in the pie shop with Hank and Walter and Ben and Roger," she said dryly. "Maybe he would have figured out that this isn't perfect for you."

Parker didn't agree. But he didn't argue either.

She pushed her plate to the side and grabbed the notebook and pencil again. "So maybe we start with offering one of the savory pies once a week or something."

"Huge waste of good food if they don't come in," he commented, picking his plate up again. Well, that wasn't a no.

"So you make one. And if it doesn't sell, we'll just have it for dinner." She lifted a shoulder. "It all sounds amazing to me."

"Yeah?"

She looked up. "Of course." She frowned. "But you have to give *them* a chance to come around, you know. You can't just make it once and decide it's a failure."

"If you eat it, I'll keep making it," he said.

That made her smile. "You will always have at least one huge fan of your off-the-menu offerings," she told him.

He gave her a look. "I'll show you off-the-menu."

Her pulse stuttered, but she laughed and held up her hand. "Hang on, we're planning here."

"*We* are planning here?" he asked.

"Yes." She gave him a smile. "You're about to tell me about all of the other pie ideas you have." She pointed at the notebook. "I know these aren't all of them."

"How do you know?"

"Because I know you." And it hit her that she really did. At least a lot better than she had a few weeks ago. A lot better than she'd ever expected to know him. "I know that you can't *not* think about this stuff."

He took a long time to answer. Finally, he said, "And since you can't *not* plan and scheme, I will tell you that I can make almost anything into a pie."

She lifted her eyebrows. "Yeah? I mean, I was thinking something like pot pies. And hey, pizza is called pizza *pie*, right? We could do a whole line of gourmet pizzas." She bent her head again. "You could turn traditional sandwiches into pies. You could do a Reuben. Oh, maybe a meatball. And that mortadella and cheese thing you made me. They could be just individual pies. Like the size of pot pies. But pot pies seem kind of boring, right? Do you have pot pie on the diner menu? It wouldn't be direct competition, just another option. I guess we should stay away from the sandwiches that you already do. But we could start just a lunch thing with them. At first."

"Ava."

She looked up. "Yeah?"

"Stop."

"I..." She frowned. "What?"

"Take a deep breath," he said. "And think about what you're saying. You're getting carried away."

She did as he asked and breathed deeply. Then she said, in her very best negotiator voice, "This is why it's great you have a few months before the shop is officially yours. We can iron all of this out before I..." She trailed off. Something she'd never done in her negotiator voice before.

"Before you leave," he filled in after a beat.

Yeah, she was leaving. In eight months. To go back to New York. All of this planning...she wouldn't see it actually in place and working if they didn't do it now. And she wouldn't be here to eat leftover pork and peach pie. Unless he started making it now.

But this is what she did. She put plans into place. She gave people resources to make things happen. And she did it all from afar. Where she only saw the results on the bottom of a spreadsheet. And that was good enough. Carmichael Enterprises would be backing the pie shop. She could still track if things were working or not.

But that felt very empty suddenly.

"I really want to help make this happen," she told him, meeting his gaze. "I'd love to see all of this in place before...then. And I think it's very possible."

He pulled a deep breath in through his nose. A number of emotions crossed his face.

Then he pushed away from the counter and started across the kitchen. He got to the doorway of the laundry room and looked back. "You coming?"

"Where are we going?" But she was already off the stool.

"Outside."

"Why?" But she rounded the edge of the island.

"Because you're making me want to throw eggs against the wall. And I've got a better idea. The reason I brought you out here in the first place."

"The sex and the greenhouse wasn't the reason?" she asked, following him through the laundry room to the back door.

He waited for her to slip the boots on again, then held the

door open for her and stepped out after her. "No. The greenhouse was definitely not the reason."

Right. Because that was very personal for him and he hadn't intended to share that with her. She felt a rush knowing that he had anyway. "What about the sex?" she asked.

"I knew the sex would happen," he admitted as he headed across the yard. "But that wasn't the main reason."

Huh. The possibility of sex with him had been a huge reason she'd gotten in his truck. She hurried to keep up with his long strides.

He strode past the greenhouse to a cluster of bushes and trees about twenty yards behind it. He stopped next to a tree that now lay on its side. He bent and picked up a pair of plastic goggles and four work gloves from the ground. He handed her the goggles and one pair of gloves. "Here."

She took them both, with no idea what was going on. "Uh, Parker..."

"Put them on." He pulled gloves on as well, settled another pair of goggles on his face, and picked up a chainsaw.

A chainsaw.

She'd only seen them in movies. And because of those movies, she was suddenly slightly concerned. "Uh, Parker..." she started again.

"You like to break things? You're going to love this. You get to destroy an entire log, but in the end, it's actually productive."

"Productive?" She was already pulling her gloves on.

"Very. You get the tree out of the way and you get firewood out of the deal too." He knelt to the ground and started the chainsaw.

As the saw started with a grinding growl, Ava put her goggles on. She couldn't believe it, but she was excited about this.

Parker showed her how to use the saw and soon she was holding the thing herself, cutting through the log, and feeling like a badass. And he was right, it was better than breaking eggs. It was loud, it took some real muscle, it was dirty, and the wood pieces flying around gave her a rush. Reducing a big tree trunk that was in the way to small logs and scraps that could be tossed aside was highly satisfying. She thought she might even have a blister from it. She got blisters occasionally from new shoes, but this was totally different. Totally better.

She cut through the last of the log and shut off the saw. She pushed her goggles to the top of her head. "What else can I cut up?"

He laughed and shook his head. "You liked it."

"I did." She looked around. "Do you ever have to blow stuff up?"

He took his gloves off, holding them in one hand while tucking the other in his back pocket. He looked so sexy out here on the farm, in his blue jeans and work boots, dirt streaked across his cheek, and that look of amused what-am-I-going-to-do-with-you on his face. "I've never blown something up and can't think of a reason I would need to. But maybe you could hammer something sometime."

No explosives. Well, okay. She set the chainsaw on the ground. "So now what?"

"Now I'm ready to talk about a reasonable starting point."

"For more sawing?"

"For the pie shop."

Okay. Reasonable. She could be reasonable. What was a reasonable starting point that would get them to individual mortadella and cheese pot pies for lunch on Tuesdays at the pie shop by the end of the just-under-seven months she had left here?

"How about we start with adding blueberry and strawberry?" She pulled her gloves off. "Made with berries from *your* strawberry patch. That's a great advertising angle."

He frowned. "I don't want an angle."

"We have to let them know that we've added strawberry pie," Ava said. "And it's *really* great that you can do it with fresh berries even when they're out of season. Maybe there's someone who only likes strawberry pie and so has never come into the shop before. We have to *tell* them about the changes before we can expect them to come give them a try."

"So we're going to hang flyers up around town?" he asked, the note of skepticism hard to miss.

She thought about that. Bliss had a small weekly newspaper and a website, but actually, putting signs up might work best of all. That was how people found lost dogs, sold bicycles, and advertised yard sales after all.

"Yes," she decided. "We put up big red, strawberry shaped signs all over, advertising the strawberry pie." She glanced toward the greenhouse. Would he let her take pictures of it? It was one of his personal havens but would be such a great advertising tool. "Oh! I know! You add a limited time strawberry salad at the diner. Have you had it before? It's spinach and candied pecans and feta and strawberries. Balsamic dressing. It's amazing." She wished for that notebook on his counter. "You add it for one week, also with spinach and strawberries from your greenhouse. It comes free with every entrée. Then with their bill, we give them a little flyer about the strawberry pie next door."

Parker sighed. "No."

She looked at him. "No?"

"No."

She stood a little straighter. "You give them the salad automatically. For free. Then you don't have to worry about them ordering it—or not. Everyone will take at least one bite. And then they'll realize how amazing it is and will keep going."

"No."

"Parker—"

"I don't have time to pick a bunch of spinach and strawberries and make extra salads with everything, even for a week."

"Oh." She nodded. "Of course not. I'll do that part." Yes, that was good. She could do that part. He didn't have the time, but she did. And if she could finally get an apple pie to turn out, she could surely put together a salad that didn't require cooking. She frowned slightly. At least, she didn't think it would require cooking. She needed to make a note about learning to make candied pecans. Or where to buy them. Parker would probably balk at that, but sometimes it was easier to get forgiveness than permission.

She made a mental note to add *research how to know when strawberries are ripe* and *how to pick strawberries* on her list.

"What?" she asked, when she noticed him watching her with a weird expression.

"*You're* going to pick spinach and strawberries and make salads at the diner?"

"Yes. If that's what you need to get this going. I can do that. You'll have to make the pie though."

He looked like he wanted to say something, but he just shook his head.

"You'll consider it if I can get the stuff picked and salads made?" she asked.

"Tell you what," he said, leaning to take the gloves from her. He tossed them to the ground with his gloves and the goggles. "I will let you give out samples of the strawberries—berries cut up in little plastic cups—in front of the diner and talk about the pie. *If*," he added as she opened her mouth, "you wear your short red skirt and red heels with a black blouse and stand right in front of my window where I can see you the entire time."

He wanted her to dress up like a strawberry? "Should I get a green hat to go with the outfit?" she asked.

"As long as that sweet ass," he said, pointing at her butt, "is in full view while I work."

"You want to use my sweet ass to sell your pie, Mr. Blake?" she asked. But she couldn't deny the little thrill that went through her. He wasn't doing it exactly as she'd suggested, but he was entertaining thoughts of making changes and doing more at the pie shop. This was awesome.

"No," he said. "But it will make me less grumpy about the whole thing."

She smiled up at him. "Well, in that case, I'll do whatever I can."

"To sell pie."

"To make you happy."

He made a little growling noise at that and muttered something that sounded like "who needs food?". He scooped her up in his arms and carried her back to the house and up to his bedroom. Where he proceeded to make her forget all about strawberries and chainsaws and to-do lists for the rest of the night.

17

Being swept off his feet wasn't bad. It wasn't bad at all. In fact, it was something he could get used to.

Parker leaned back into the buttery-soft leather of his seat and stretched his legs out. As if there weren't enough nice things about traveling in a limo, the extra space for his legs was definitely a plus.

And this wasn't some rented limo, this was Ava's personal car. She used it to travel from her incredible apartment that occupied the entire top floor of her building and overlooked the city to her equally incredible office on Madison Avenue so that she could work while her driver navigated the city traffic. It was practical. Parker had to give her that. But it was also very classy and luxurious too. And he didn't mind that as much as he would have expected.

But, while he'd been impressed with her condo—and the six spray nozzles in her humongous shower...and how much fun those were when they were in there together—and he had enjoyed the Broadway show and he was a little fascinated with the lights and noise and bustle of the city, none of that had made the biggest impression on him.

What he knew he'd remember most from this trip was the way Ava had slipped her hand into his as they walked down the sidewalk, the way she'd leaned into him when he'd draped his arm over the back of her seat during the show, the way she'd turned and whispered in his ear, the way he'd caught her eye across the lobby when she emerged from the ladies' room and that split second when they'd communicated silently and met at the base of the stairs leading back to their box seats.

Yes, what he would remember most was the way she was letting him *date* her.

Sure, it was her apartment, her boxed seats, her jet and limo. But those weren't the important things here. It was how she was letting him close. How she was so...soft with him.

He knew that she didn't hold hands with the men she typically went out with. She didn't share private looks across the room with them. She didn't allow them to play with her hair during a show. She didn't lean over as the lights in the theater were going down and say that she loved her date's tie...and that she hoped he'd blindfold her with it later. And she didn't introduce her dates to other people as her boyfriends.

Somehow Parker knew that all of this was new.

And he felt like a fucking king.

Ava Carmichael was possibly the most high-maintenance woman he'd ever spent time with and yet, he didn't need to plan the perfect night out, buy the perfect gift, say the perfect thing. He just had to adore her and want to be here with her more than he wanted to be anywhere else. And though it was kick-ass CEO and billionaire heiress Ava Carmichael, things had never been simpler.

As the car wound its way through New York City traffic on the way from the theater to the restaurant, Parker wasn't looking at the incredible interior of the limo or at the big buildings and bright lights of New York City passing his window. His eyes were on the woman beside him.

"Hey," he said softly.

She looked over at him and smiled.

"Come here."

Her smile grew, but she shook her head. "You can't mess me up. We have dinner."

He gave a low laugh. "I'm not going to mess you up. Yet. Come here." She slid closer and he put his arm around her, tucking her up against his side. "Just want you against me right now."

Her hand rested on his thigh and she looked up at him. "Oh, yeah?"

He put his nose against her hair. "Yeah. I know when we walk into that restaurant you're going to be kick-ass and in charge. I want you soft for just a few more minutes."

"And you think you make me soft?"

"I do."

She laughed lightly. "I guess you do."

He reached to her face and tipped her chin up. "I didn't mean that sexually. Though I do make you soft that way." He leaned in and kissed her. Then, resting his forehead against hers, he said, "But I mean in other ways. You don't have to put on your kickass-in-charge side with me."

She sighed against his lips. "Because you know it's all an act."

He laughed at that. "It's definitely not an act. You're soft with me because I know the ways you're kick-ass that have nothing to do with business deals and power suits and high heels."

She looked surprised, and he turned in the seat so he could look at her more directly. For some reason, at this moment, in this place, he needed to tell her this.

"I know the *real* kick-ass stuff, Ava," he said, possibly more earnestly than he needed to. But...he needed to. They'd been playing in New York for the past two days and it had been fun and sexy and light and flirtatious and all of the things he'd wanted for her from them *dating*. They'd done it all right. Back in Bliss they'd gotten to know one another. They'd flirted and laughed and argued and talked about the things that were important to them. They'd spent time together because they wanted to. And then they'd rocked each other's world in bed and decided to take a weekend getaway. Dating. Just like it was supposed to be done. Then in New York there had been sex and showers and the theater and dinner and more sex and then more sex again and then more sex again. And another show. And now dinner.

It had all gone perfectly. And not at all according to any plan. And it was all really good.

And now, suddenly, in the middle of New York City, without a pie or a rooster or a spreadsheet anywhere near them, he felt *earnest.*

He swallowed. "I know how you love your sisters and will do anything for them. How you keep trying to find a way to make something work even when it seems impossible—maybe *because* it seems impossible. How your beautiful brain never stops working. How you throw eggs against the wall just because you like to break stuff." He shook his head. "How you'll march in and pick up a fucking rooster. How you'll barely hesitate to grab a chainsaw and then want more stuff to cut up and pound on and blow up. And," his voice got rough, "how you are actually incapable of really napping, but how you like to hold hands and snuggle. And how you don't really care about food but you let Cori and me feed you because you know how much we love it."

If he wasn't mistaken, Ava had tears in her eyes. "Wow."

He nodded. Earnestly. "Ditto, Boss."

She wet her lips. Then she took a deep breath and, looking a little earnest herself, said, "I made a good apple pie."

He lifted an eyebrow. "What?"

She nodded. "Four times now actually."

"You...made a *good* pie?" That was definitely not what he'd been expecting her to say.

"I couldn't believe it either. It was just like everything

suddenly clicked. After I started tasting it as I went and adjusted it to how *I* liked it, it started to work. And..."

She bit her bottom lip, and Parker had to just make himself wait for her to go on. He had to hear this.

"It was as if, after we started hanging out, I stopped worrying about it so much. I stopped thinking I had to get it perfect, because I knew I had you as a backup, and I knew that you would fix it if needed, and I knew...it didn't matter. Me being perfect and getting it exactly right didn't matter. And then, it just worked."

He wasn't sure what to say to that. But his heart was pounding. "Why haven't I tried any of these pies?" was all he could come up with.

She smiled, almost sheepishly, and he wanted to start kissing her and not stop until sometime the next day.

"I got rid of the evidence," she said.

"What? Why?"

"If I could do the pies, then you wouldn't have to coach me anymore. And I wanted to keep having that time."

"We have *never* actually baked a pie together, Boss," he reminded her, his chest feeling tight.

She gave him a grin. "I know. That's maybe the best part." Her voice got soft. "I've learned a lot even though we never actually did what we'd planned to do."

Well, he couldn't argue with that. Nothing that had happened between them was anything he'd planned.

He lifted a hand to the back of her neck, pulling her close. "Kick-ass," he said gruffly. He kissed her, this time taking a few minutes to really taste her. But he pulled back before he wanted to, not wanting to mess her up. Yet. "Tell me we can make this work," he said, finally having to say what he'd been thinking about since they'd first boarded the jet in Kansas. "Tell me you can travel back and forth. That you don't have to be in New York that much. That you can work from Bliss for the most part."

Her eyes widened and she took a deep breath, but as Parker

steeled himself for her to tell him all the reasons that was crazy and would never work, she said, "We can make this work. I can travel back and forth. I don't have to be in New York that much. I can work from Bliss for the most part."

"Really?"

She nodded. "I've been thinking and...I can simplify."

Parker felt that word, one of his favorites, rock through him.

But Ava kept going. "I do way more than I really need to as CEO. I've loved having my hands in everything, but now there are some other things that need more of my attention." She gave him a little smile that made him want to crow like Ras did when the sun came up in the morning.

"Everyone here in New York is actually doing a great job," she said before taking a deep breath. "And one of the things I'm really good at is seeing other people's potential and truly, there are some people in our organization that I should give more responsibility."

"So you're going to let go of some things. And simplify."

She nodded.

He squeezed her neck and dragged in a breath, relief and happiness coursing through him. "If you don't want to be messed up, you better slide over."

"We're here," she told him as the car pulled up at the curb in front of a high-rise building with a black awning with gold lettering. A literal red carpet stretched from the glass doors to the curb, and a man in a tuxedo came to stand by the door to help them out. "And you should know that there are a number of very important people inside. People who, once I go through those doors, will want to talk with me. People I should talk to and reassure that me being in Bliss these past few months doesn't change anything. People who are dying to know what's going on with Carmichael since my dad's passing and who have heard only gossip and snippets of the stipulations of the will."

"So, you're going to be busy for the next couple of hours," he said, resigning himself to the fact.

"I am," she said with a nod. "Busy eating the frittata my very hot boyfriend is going to make for me back at my apartment."

Parker stared at her. "You don't want to go in?"

She glanced at the building and then back at him. "I really don't."

He let out a breath he didn't realize he'd been holding. "You sure? Why not?"

"Because I can't reassure them that nothing has changed," she said, putting her hand against his face. "Everything has changed."

Parker took her hand, turned his face and kissed the palm, then said, "You're going to get messed up before you make me slave away in your kitchen."

She settled back in her seat with a satisfied smile on her face. "I can absolutely live with that. Making you my slave in the bedroom sounds more fun anyway."

However, by the time they made it to her bedroom, she had already gotten messed up in the back seat of her limo. And in the elevator to the penthouse suite.

————

*I*s everything ready?

Ava glanced at Parker as she sent the text to her sister, but he was reclining in his seat on the jet, absorbed in a book. She wondered when he'd last had a chance to just sit and read.

Yep! Cori responded.

Everything is cleaned up?

Not a speck of sawdust or paint anywhere. Relax.

She couldn't. She was way too excited. She'd been planning this surprise for Parker for about a week, but nothing had been *done* until they'd lifted off for New York. She was paying an exorbitant price and had needed to pull contractors in from Great

Bend because no one local could get the supplies and do the work fast enough, but it was worth it.

Cori and Evan had helped her put it all together, and Cori had been texting her updates throughout the process, but Ava had been nervous about it right up until Parker had asked if she could work from Bliss and travel back and forth rather than returning to New York full-time. That was the moment she'd realized that he really was feeling everything she was and that this was definitely the right move.

And you baked the pie?

Yes. The entire place smells like apple pie now.

Ava had made a pie—one of the really good ones—before she'd left and frozen it so that Cori could bake it for tonight. Ava wiggled in her seat. This was going to be so great. Cori had sent her a few photos, but she couldn't wait to see the whole thing in person. And see Parker's reaction.

It was Sunday night and the diner had been closed since Friday. Parker needed to do prep for the Monday breakfast crowd and she'd offered to help. It was the perfect excuse to get him down to the diner as soon as they got to Bliss. She had debated about having Evan, Cori, Brynn, and Noah there. She thought there was a very good chance she and Parker would want to celebrate privately with some apple pie filling...and no clothes. But in the end, she'd decided to have all of their friends there. Cori was, of course, a big part of the new endeavor, and Evan had been the one to draw the paperwork up. And just as they'd done when the girls had first cleaned and redecorated the pie shop, Brynn and Noah had pitched in with paintbrushes and hammers and nails over the past two days. So it was fitting they all be there when she revealed the big surprise to Parker.

They'd just have to take the pie filling back to his house afterward.

And you'll have the shots ready? Ava asked Cori.

Of course.

Instead of champagne to toast with, Ava had decided that apple pie shots were more fitting.

And the aprons are there?

Cori sent her a GIF of Krysten Ritter rolling her eyes, but added *Yes, they're all here. Everything is good.*

Ava grinned. She'd ordered aprons especially with Parker in mind. He seemed to love her in aprons. And in blue jeans. So she'd found a woman who made aprons out of old jeans. They were waist aprons, had an apple on one pocket and a cherry on the other, and a red ruffle at the bottom. She couldn't wait for him to see them. He might even want her to take one home and wear it, and only it, for him privately.

"What are you grinning about?"

She looked over to find him smiling at her, with a look in his eyes that made her toes curl. She'd never had a man in love with her before, so she couldn't be *sure* that's how he was looking at her now, but if that wasn't what he was feeling, it was something very close. She felt her stomach flip and was incredibly happy that she'd paid to use the private airstrip outside of Great Bend to land this time.

"Just happy to be almost home," she said, lifting a shoulder.

His expression changed slightly and it was her heart that flipped this time. He looked...pleased. And intense. Intensely pleased.

"You just called Bliss home," he said.

She had. "I know."

"I like that."

"Me too."

Finally, nearly two hours later, they drove into Bliss.

"You're still going in to do prep for tomorrow, right?" she asked. She was nearly bouncing in her seat and she had to work to keep the excitement out of her voice.

"Yeah, guess I better," he said, turning his truck down Main. "Rather do it now than get up early tomorrow."

She laughed. "You already get up at a God-awful time of day."

He gave her a grin. "Yeah, well, you better get used to it."

"Me? No way. I'm a nine a.m. girl at best. No heels until after the sun comes up for sure."

"Yeah, you're definitely going to be wearing your heels before the sun's up once in a while," he told her.

"Come on. *I'm* not the farmer here." She was, actually, willing to get closer to Parker's chickens and pick some of his spinach, but she was waiting to tell him that as a part of the surprise too.

"Well, I didn't say you'd have to get out of bed with them on."

Ah, now she understood. She grinned and nodded. "Right. I guess early morning meetings *can* sometimes be productive."

"I definitely have some motions I'd like you to consider."

She laughed as they pulled up at the stoplight just a block from the diner. "I think we can come to a consensus on most points."

But Parker's attention was no longer on their banter. He was peering through the windshield and frowning. "Why are all the lights on at the diner?"

It was clearly a rhetorical question. He didn't expect her to know.

When the light turned green, he drove through and pulled up in front of the diner rather than parking in back like he usually did. He shut the truck off and got out, still frowning. "It looks like Evan's in there. And Noah."

Through the big front window, it was easy to see their friends standing in the middle of the diner talking. Dammit. Ava should have texted Cori to let her know how close they were. But it wasn't as if they'd planned to hide and jump out yelling *surprise*.

She felt the butterflies in her stomach swooping in bigger, faster circles. This was a big deal for her. Would he understand what the gesture fully meant? She had always had everything in her life organized in very particular way. Each part of her life went under its own colored, labeled tab. Or even more accurately, the parts of her life each had its own box. The pie shop was one of those boxes. It was almost perfectly square-shaped, in fact. And while it had been overwhelming over the past few months, everything she'd needed to handle had been contained within those four walls.

Until she'd started going outside of that box and into Parker's. The diner was no more familiar or comfortable for her than the pie shop had been, and yet, she'd been drawn over there, first by needs like butter and eggs, and then out of necessity for a baking coach. And then by desires. For Parker's off-menu food. And for him.

The boxes around the parts of her life had started opening up and combining. And at first, that had freaked her out and caused her to hide out at home. But now...she wanted it all in one big box.

She really hoped he would see that.

Parker strode through the door and into the diner with Ava on his heels.

"What are you guys—" But he didn't finish his sentence as he turned slightly to his left.

Ava stopped short too, seeing it all for the first time in person.

She'd wanted to knock the entire wall down between the diner and the pie shop, but Cori had suggested this as a unique, fun design instead. And it was really...unique.

Where there had been a solid wall between the two restaurants, there was now a wide doorway that led from the diner into the pie shop. On either side of the door was a window, and above the door it read *Blissfully Baked* in the same script font used on the front of the shop. Where the rest of the diner's interior was painted white, the wall around the doorway was the exact shade of light green as the outside of the shop. The door and windows were bordered in white, complete with pink shutters, and there was even a pink and green striped awning over the door, making the whole thing a miniature version of the actual front of the pie shop.

"We need to see the other side too." She started for the doorway. Evan handed her the papers he'd drawn up as she passed. Then she realized Parker wasn't following her. She went back to grab Parker's hand and pull him into the pie shop with her.

On the pie shop side, the doorway mimicked the front of the diner, including the bright blue color of the siding and the yellow trim and CAFÉ stenciled in block letters in the window on the right.

Wow, this was amazing. She turned to look up at Parker with a huge grin.

That died almost immediately.

He didn't just look surprised. He looked like someone had just slapped him across the face.

Evan stepped forward. Seeming cautious. "Hey, buddy?"

Parker said nothing.

Noah joined Evan on the other side of the doorway from Parker. "Deep breath, man. It's all good, right? Big surprise, but kinda cool."

It sounded like he was trying to convince Parker. Ava frowned and stepped in front of him. "Hey." She waited until Parker looked at her. "What's going on? Say something."

"Okay," he said slowly. He focused on her fully, his gaze intense. "What the *fuck* did you do?"

18

A va felt her eyes widen, but she took a deep breath and gave him a smile. It was all just sinking in for him. It would be fine. "This is my way of making sure you have everything you want," she told him.

He took a deep breath. He swallowed. He clenched his jaw. Then he scowled. "When did I ever give you the impression that I *wanted* a hole in my wall?"

Okay, so that wasn't exactly the reaction she'd expected, but this was a big surprise. He just needed a little time to get used to it.

"You're going to be a partner in the pie shop. This way you can be in two places at once," she said. "It will be so much easier to go back and forth and take care of things on both sides."

"So basically," he said, crossing his arms. "You've now doubled my work, rearranged my diner, and made it impossible for me to say no because it's already done."

She blinked at him. "Well...no." None of that was what she'd intended.

"The pie shop is now connected to the diner, Ava," he said, his exasperation clear. "That means people will be expecting pie.

The pie that I've adamantly refused to serve in the diner. And there is now more space to clean. More supplies to buy. More tables which means more people at once. That all means more work."

She felt her own frown start. He didn't have to do all the work by himself. That was also part of her plan. As she and Hank and Roger and Cori and Evan and Brynn and Noah had all proved over the last few weeks, other people could pitch in and help him out.

"You don't have to do it *all*."

"But I *want to*," he said. He blew out a breath and dropped his arms. "This is *my* diner. I run it the way I want to, by myself, the way it's always been. The way I *like it*."

She counted to ten before she responded. "But you were excited about being a partner in the pie shop. How did you think you were going to do that exactly?" she asked.

"By letting Cori take the lead in the kitchen and helping her however I could on the side."

"But *you* have ideas for the pie shop too," Ava insisted. "Why not do both?"

"Because I'm already doing what I want to do!" He looked completely frustrated as he shoved a hand through his hair. "That diner has been the way it is for *fifteen years*. And I like it that way. I...*need* it to be that way."

Her heart was pounding and she was trying like hell to understand. But frankly, people didn't say no to her when she was trying to give them things. Honestly, more often than not, the meetings she had were with people *wanting* her to give them things. "Here." She shoved the papers she held at him. Maybe this would help show him what she'd intended.

"What's this?"

"The deed to the building. I assumed the loan from the bank and, thanks to Evan, those documents turn the whole thing over to you. You now own every part of the diner, just like we'd discussed, *and* you own the pie shop too."

He looked at the cover page but didn't bother to flip through the pages.

"Cori is completely fine with it," Ava added, glancing at her sister. Cori gave her a wide-eyed look. Ava just shrugged. "You'll still be partners in the business itself but you're the owner of the physical building."

"You weren't supposed to use your personal funds for the pie shop," he said, scowling at the page.

"I didn't," she said, shaking her head. "I reinvested the pie shop's profit into this."

He turned his scowl on her. "You *what?*"

She frowned back at him. "I did what any smart business person does. I took our profits and reinvested them in an idea that will make us even more money."

"You have to have that profit to fulfill the stipulations of the will!" Parker exclaimed. "You just got back to a positive balance."

"Yes, because everyone heard that you were getting involved," she said. "And using it now, when we still have six months left, to make this very positive change, was a smart decision."

He pulled a deep breath in through his nose. "So you really did put a hole in the wall of *my* diner and turned the building *I* own into one big restaurant without asking me about it first."

Ava put a hand on her hip, frustration and disappointment and yes, hurt, welling up. "Actually, I turned the building *I* own into two restaurants that are now connected," she said coolly. "And now I'm *giving* it to you."

Now he did look up. "Well, I don't want this."

"You don't want it to be even easier to manage both businesses and to make even more food for more people?" she asked.

He handed the papers back to her. "No." He turned and started for the kitchen.

Ava simply stared, perplexed, watching him go. Then realized what he was about to walk into. "Parker! Hey, we need to talk about this!" She ran after him, but he hit the door to the diner's kitchen before she could get to him.

He stopped so suddenly on the other side, she nearly plowed into him. She took a deep breath and slipped around him, holding her hands up.

"Okay, just, hang on," she told him before he could speak. "Don't freak out."

But he wasn't saying anything even though his mouth was hanging open.

Shit, shit, shit. "Parker, I—"

"*Dammit, Ava!*" He finally erupted. He looked down at her, his eyes stormy.

So, in spite of the brand new, shiny silver industrial oven that could bake multiple pies at once, and the additional prep space and the new bigger fridge, he wasn't thrilled with the hole in the wall between their kitchens either.

Yes, this was a big hole. Bigger than the one in the front. In fact, this one had more or less made the back rooms of the two businesses into one big kitchen. But it was a very *nice* big kitchen. And if he opened the new fridge, he'd see it was fully stocked with butter and eggs. Because she'd thought that would be kind of funny and sentimental and sweet. She'd taken down her egg-throwing wall to put all of this in, because she didn't need that egg-throwing wall anymore. She wasn't frustrated with her lack of ability in the kitchen anymore. And she now had access to a wood pile and chainsaw for when she did need to work off some steam.

But it didn't look like Parker would find that quite as meaningful as she'd intended it at the moment.

Still, she had to *try* to make him understand what she'd done. Or rather, *why* she'd done what she'd done.

"I want to combine our lives, Parker," she said, keeping her voice calm. "That's what I'm trying to show you here."

"There is no way you had enough profit to afford all of this," he said, his voice dangerously low.

"Okay, I might have gone to the bank for a *small* loan."

"Dammit, Ava!" he exploded. "You had just gotten Rudy's loan paid off and started making money! Now you're right back where you started!"

"I believe in this, Parker," she insisted. "I know what I'm doing. And not only is this a good business decision, it's good for *us*. Personally. I want to spend most of my time in Bliss and I want to be a part of your world and I want you to be a part of mine. All of it. All the time."

"You want to be a part of my world when it's the way *you* think it should be."

Whoa. She frowned. "What's that supposed to mean?"

"You want to be a part of my world if it's bigger and better and under your influence. You couldn't be happy with just my simple diner that's always the same." He was scowling at the new oven. "I don't know why I ever thought you could maybe be satisfied with burgers. It's always going to have to be chicken salad with you."

"What? No." Did she want to encourage him and give him opportunities and support him? Yes. But the way he said "influence" it sounded like he thought she wanted to take over.

"You do realize that I call you Boss sarcastically, right?" he asked, focusing on her directly again.

She felt her mouth fall open and her eyes started to sting. She blinked and drew herself up tall. "Actually, I thought you called me Boss affectionately." She was glad her voice didn't wobble. Her throat definitely felt tight.

"Well, you're *not* the CEO of this diner," he said, his scowl deep. "This wasn't your decision to make."

Ouch.

Okay, so, she wasn't used to asking for, or waiting for, permission. She was not usually the one pitching ideas and getting approval. She was the one giving the thumbs-up or down. So no, she hadn't thought to run this past him. The idea had come to her and she'd made a phone call. Putting things into motion was easy for her, and she never really gave much thought to the fact that wasn't true for everyone. But she had contacts and connections everywhere for just about everything. If she didn't know someone directly, she definitely knew someone who knew someone. She'd come up with an idea, something she thought was really creative and meaningful, and then she'd just...done it.

"I'm not trying to be the CEO of the diner," she told him. "I don't want to change it. I just want *you* to be happy. To have everything you want."

"But you *did* change the diner! My dad's diner. I messed up his life in Chicago, Ava. I was the reason he came to Bliss. And I've been determined to *not* mess things up here."

She sucked in a breath. This was not going even remotely the way she'd intended it to go. She didn't want him to see this as a mess. "Parker, I know what it's like to try to follow your dad in his business. But I've also realized that what he really gave me was not a business, but an opportunity. A chance to find my own way rather than just following his path. That's what you have here from your dad too."

"I like my path. I have exactly the life I've always wanted to have," he said, suddenly sounding tired. "And yes, I wanted you to be a part of that. But I was hoping that what I already had was enough for you."

"So you're fine having me in your world, in your greenhouse, in your chicken coop, in your bed, as long as *I'm* the only thing changing," she said, tears pricking the backs of her eyes again.

"I thought you were happy about the changes you've made."

"I *am*. But I thought...we would make changes together," she said. She blew out a frustrated breath. "You're so talented and you *love* food and you love creating new things. You don't want other people to love it as much as you do?"

"I thought *you* loved it as much as I do," he said flatly.

She frowned. "I do."

"That's enough for me."

"Cooking for *me* is enough for you?" she asked, disbelievingly.

"Cooking for you. Picking strawberries with you. Cleaning up the diner with you. Gathering eggs with you. Making love to you. That's enough for me. And I thought you were starting to feel the same way. I thought you were starting to feel at home. To feel something for Bliss that you couldn't get in New York."

She swallowed hard. "I do feel something for Bliss I can't get in New York."

"But it's not enough."

Ava felt her breath catch in her chest. It *was* enough. It was.

Wasn't it? She thought about the cooking and the strawberries and the kitchen and waking up next to him. Was that enough? Then she looked around. *This*, this new stuff, the new pie ideas, the possibilities, were all amazing too. "I know this is bigger than you've ever imagined. But you still have everything you've always had. Nothing's gone away."

He took a deep breath. "The one thing you knew, the most important thing, was that I didn't want the diner to change." His voice was low, but not sexy low. It was super-pissed low. "And you knew why."

"But I—"

"The other thing you knew, was that I believed our trip to New York was about us. Personally. Our relationship. The next step."

"It was, I—"

"But the entire time we were gone, you were thinking about business and orchestrating all of *this*. Behind my back."

His voice was rising, and Ava felt her defenses growing.

"As a surprise! Because I wanted to do something appropriately big and wonderful for this *next step*. Because New York *was* about us! It was what convinced me that I can be in two places, doing *all* the things I need, and want, to do. And it was what made me realize you can do the same. This is practical, but it's also *symbolic,* dammit!"

He actually rolled his eyes at that, and Ava drew her spine ramrod straight. He was *rolling his eyes about her*? About her symbolic, sweet, I-want-to-share-everything gesture? "This *is* the next step, Parker. Sharing our lives. I have *never* done something like this for someone other than my mom and sisters. I did this because you're important to me!" She was almost shouting now too.

"You should have fucking asked me."

"Then it wouldn't have been a *fucking* grand gesture!"

He just stared at her. She wasn't sure where that had come from either. She didn't make grand gestures. Even with her mom and sisters. She usually just put money into their accounts. That was as grand as it got. But Parker had her thinking about...more. How much she wanted to *do* something that would make him happy. It had been *fun* thinking up ways to demonstrate to him how she felt about him. No, she hadn't literally knocked down the walls herself, but she *had* put thought and a personal touch on all of this. That's why there were denim aprons with ruffles and apple pie shots on the center island of Parker's kitchen. Strangely, it was those little details that were also pretty grand in her book. It had all taken a lot more thought and heart than she really ever gave to anything else.

"I don't need grand gestures, Ava," Parker finally said, sounding tired. "I need to come to work, like I've always done, and live my life...like I've always done."

Her throat was tight and she had to clear it before she asked, "And where am I in that plan?"

He sighed. "An hour ago? I would have said in bed next to me and in the kitchen next door to me. Now..."

He didn't know. He didn't say it out loud, but she knew that's what he was thinking.

Ava felt a chill sweep over her. "Life changes when you have a relationship, Parker," she said, her voice softer now. "At least a real one where you want that person involved in the things you care about."

He nodded. "Yeah, I guess it does."

Ava felt tears welling up. "Especially when it's with someone really different from you. Who has different ideas and wants to be a part of things—even the things you've always had to yourself."

He nodded again. "I guess so."

She waited for him to say more. Then hoped he wouldn't if it was something like "I can't do this. You've messed up my kitchen, my diner, my *life*."

She could pay to have everything put back the way it had been. Maybe she even *should*. But other than that, she didn't know what to do here. And she knew, somehow, that wouldn't actually fix this.

Because he wasn't really mad about the hole in his wall. Okay, he definitely was. But it was more because she was insinuating herself into his life, and he was losing a bit of his control of the life that he'd so carefully constructed and protected. He was fine with having her at the farm when she was picking up chickens and having sex with him in his greenhouse. But he had really liked when her phone had been out in his truck and not in her hand. He hadn't even wanted her to pick his spinach and straw-berries for salads. And now she'd opened up the wall between the pie shop and the diner when he'd been very comfortable with that wall being there. That wall between his domain and the place she and her sisters were changing and expanding.

Feeling her frustration building and her reasonableness decreasing, she took a deep breath. She didn't yell in business meetings. She didn't get her feelings hurt. She was always in control. And she was absolutely going to treat this like a business meeting.

Because she had no idea how to handle a relationship with emotions like this.

This was one more situation where she was way out of her comfort zone.

"I think we both need some time to think about everything," she said, lifting her chin and putting her CEO face on.

Parker nodded. "Yeah, you're probably right."

"I'll..." She looked around. He'd brought her here. She didn't have a car. And he still needed to prep for tomorrow.

"I've got it," he said, as if he'd read her mind.

"I can stay and help."

"No." He said it firmly. "I've got it."

Right. He probably wanted to be alone. She knew she did. But it was also because of her that he'd been gone for the past three days. "Cori and Brynn will stay." She knew they'd do it for her.

"Ava." Parker pushed a hand through his hair again and sighed. "I've been prepping this diner alone for thirteen years."

Right. And he obviously preferred it that way.

She turned and headed for the front of the diner. But as she passed the island, she not only grabbed the aprons, she took the tray of shots with her as well.

And she was *not* sharing.

———

"Dude."

"I know."

"It was bad."

"I *know*."

Evan and Noah had been leaning against the back of the building when Parker had pulled into the diner's back parking lot this morning at five. And they'd been sitting at his counter ever since. Parker had been expecting them. He was just grateful they hadn't come to his house and demanded he talk to them about it all last night. He'd scrubbed and diced and shredded for almost an hour. Then he'd headed straight home to his pile of wood to chop. And as he'd destroyed the logs with the chainsaw, he'd thought of her the entire time.

Parker threw the towel he was holding into the bin of dirty dishes and wished it was something that would make a louder, more satisfying, noise. Or break something when he threw it. Ava really had a point there. Breaking things on purpose—instead of inadvertently as he had last night—was pretty cathartic. Until he stopped and thought about how there were things in life, a lot of things, that couldn't be put back together once they were in pieces.

And as he picked up the tub, he realized that he was screwed if dirty plates and cups made him think of Ava. She had become a part of everything about the diner, even before there was a gaping hole in the wall, and there was no way for him to avoid thoughts of her. He was surrounded by dirty dishes almost constantly.

"So we're not going to talk about this today either?" Evan asked.

Parker turned toward the kitchen with Evan and Noah's breakfast dishes.

They'd been quiet while he'd cooked and they'd eaten. But he'd known it was too much to hope that pancakes and sausage would keep them from lecturing him about everything. They'd just been careful to get breakfast first.

He glanced at the hole in the wall...okay it was a *doorway*... between the diner and the pie shop. The girls weren't in yet, but he could already imagine how it would look and sound and smell once they were there.

Good. Bright. Cheery.

Those were three of the words that came to mind. He sighed. He could pretend that the increased noise level or the traffic back and forth between the two shops would be annoying. But the truth was, the opening into the pie shop would do nothing but make the diner brighter and smell like pie.

"No, we're not going to talk about it," he finally answered Evan.

"You overreacted," Evan told him.

Parker swung back. "Really? *I* overreacted? She knocked *two* holes in the wall of *my* diner."

Evan and Noah just looked back at him with expressions that said, *you're a dumbass.*

"She did," he said. "Without asking me. Without even hinting at the idea. Without even thinking for a second about how I would feel about it."

"Seriously?" Noah asked. "She didn't hint at it? *You* didn't hint at it?"

"At knocking walls down?" Parker asked.

"At combining the things that matter to you both."

Parker stared at his friend. In part because Noah never raised his voice. And in part because Parker suddenly couldn't take a deep breath. Nor did he have any idea what to say to that.

"How about in all the times she was over here and you were talking about the future of the pie shop and you were acting like you *liked* having her here? How about in all of the times *you* were over *there*, involved, helping, giving her the thing you complain the most about not having enough of—your time? You really think none of those were hints that you might be on board with combining your lives?"

Parker swallowed hard. "That pie shop is not her life."

"You sure about that?" Noah asked.

He wasn't sure about anything.

"Maybe she can't make pie, but that pie shop has everything she cares about in it," Noah said. "Her sisters' happiness." He held up a finger. "A happier idea of her dad." He added a second finger. Then a third. "A challenge that she's had to actually put her hands in to figure it out." He put up a fourth finger. "And a guy who doesn't want her money or her power, but who got involved with her life because of *her*."

Parker felt his throat tighten. Noah was a pretty insightful guy. He was more of an observer than a participant in most situations. But Parker had to assume a lot of this had also come from Brynn.

"I never once said that I wanted to combine the two businesses into one building," Parker said. But his protest didn't ring true even to his own ears. No, he'd never *said* that. But he'd also never said that he wanted to make her chicken salad for the rest of their lives...and he did.

"How about when you took her to your house and showed her the greenhouse and introduced her to your chickens?" Evan asked, a hint of you're-a-dumbass even sneaking into his tone of voice.

Parker narrowed his eyes. "What about that?"

"You don't take women home like that," Evan said, lifting his orange juice glass that Parker now regretted refilling for him.

"Like that?" Parker repeated. "What's that mean?"

"You take them home, fuck them, and send them on their way," Noah said bluntly. "You don't show them around, you don't cook for them—hell, you make a point of taking them home late enough and waking them up early enough that there are no meals expected—and you definitely don't take them into that greenhouse. *I* only got to go in there because I helped you build the damned thing."

"You think it means something that I took her to the greenhouse?" Parker asked, trying very hard to make it sound like that was a completely stupid assumption.

But it wasn't. It did mean something. It meant even more that she'd been impressed by it and had let him get her dirty—in every way—in there. After seeing her dressed up and totally at ease in her private jet and limo in New York City, it was even more obvious that Ava's time out on the farm with him had meant something to her too.

"I do. And even more, Ava does," Noah said.

Parker frowned at him. "How do you know that?"

"She told Brynn."

"And Cori," Evan added.

Parker sighed and set the bin of dishes to the side. "Good God, being involved with sisters is a pain in the ass."

Evan and Noah didn't disagree.

The door to the diner suddenly banged open and a loud, deep voice declared, "Holy shit! That looks amazing!"

It was Hank, leading Walter, Ben, and Roger into the diner for breakfast. They were always first in and didn't leave until the pie shop opened.

Parker sighed. The entryway—which was exactly what it was —to the pie shop did look nice. And for the four most regular customers of both businesses, it was probably a dream come true.

The men settled into their usual booth and Parker approached with coffee cups. The pie shop had far better coffee and everyone knew it, but these guys insisted on drinking his crappy stuff with their eggs and bacon anyway.

It wasn't until Parker reached for the first coffee cup that he noticed the pie sitting in the middle of the table. It had one piece missing.

"You brought a pie in here?" Parker asked, his chest so tight he was having trouble pulling air in.

"I brought *the* pie in here," Hank said, looking over the menu despite the fact that he could very recite it word for word and that he had had the same thing every Monday morning. He pretended to consider something new every week, but it never happened. Parker appreciated that about him. He already had the bacon ready to go.

"*The* pie?" Parker repeated. "What's that mean?"

Hank lowered the menu and met his eyes. "That pie is the pie Ava made for you last night. It is officially her favorite pie. A pie she figured out all on her own. And one of the best damned pies I've ever eaten."

Parker suddenly wanted a bite of that pie more than he

wanted all of these people to get the hell out of his diner. And he wanted that *very fucking much.*

"Why's it in here?" he asked, trying to sound pissed off. He thought he sounded more in pain than anything.

"Because I intend to eat it with my breakfast," Hank said.

Parker narrowed his eyes. "I see."

"The same breakfast I've had every single Monday morning for the past thirteen years," Hank added.

Parker couldn't look away from the older man. "The breakfast that has, apparently, been missing an apple pie chaser?"

Hank shook his head. "This breakfast hasn't been missing anything. It's great as is. And even with a piece of pie after it, it will still be great. And taste exactly the way it always has."

Parker swallowed hard. "What's your point, Hank?"

"That adding pie is only going to make this breakfast bigger and sweeter. It's not going to change that omelet and toast. Everything I love about that omelet will be the same." Hank gave him a look. "You get what I'm saying?"

Parker gave a bark of laughter. "You're not subtle, Hank."

"So, you understand that adding that girl to your life doesn't change all the stuff you love about it? It just makes it bigger and sweeter?" Hank asked.

Parker felt the vise around his chest ease a little with Hank's words, but he said, "And louder and busier and messier."

Hank chuckled and lifted his coffee cup.

"It's funny?" Parker asked.

"Hell yeah, it's funny," Hank said, looking around the table. "That woman's not only bossing you around in your own diner and tying you up in knots, but now she's literally knocking down the walls around you."

Parker felt the air whoosh out of his lungs. Damn. Talk about symbolic stuff. He glanced over at Evan and Noah, who had swiveled on their stools to face Hank and the guys.

"I don't—" Parker cleared his throat. "I don't actually care that she knocked a hole in the wall," he admitted. If he couldn't say it to these guys, who could he say it to? Because he wasn't even being honest with himself.

"So what's the problem?" Walter asked.

"Is it how she's doing it?" Roger asked. "Just barging in and doing it without tiptoeing around your feelings?"

Parker gave him a look. "Clearly the tiptoeing around feelings isn't a widespread problem here."

Roger laughed. "Those of us who like ketchup on our steak tiptoe."

"Those of you who like ketchup on your steak are screwed up," Parker said. "And that isn't about my feelings."

"What's it about then?" Roger wanted to know.

"It's about continuing to be served in here," Parker told him flatly. "You follow the rules, or you don't get my steak."

Hank nodded. "Ava doesn't really follow rules either though, does she?"

No, she freaking didn't. Like the rule of no one else in his kitchen. And no one else doing anything in the diner. And of eating only off the menu. And of following recipes...

Which was where his rules about rules got him into trouble. He knew better than anyone that recipes were best when regarded as nothing more than a starting point. Ava had seen recipes as rules and she'd really tried. It wasn't until she'd tossed those out that good things had happened between her and the pies.

"What's your point?" Parker finally asked Hank.

"That she didn't just knock one of your walls down," Hank said, meeting his eyes. "She knocked one of *hers* down too."

Parker felt like Hank had turned on a light in a dim room for him. What had been *almost* clear, was now suddenly bright and obvious.

Ava's grand gesture, as she'd called it, had been symbolic of combining their lives. But it was about more than her wanting to be a part of his life, even with changes. She was letting him into *her* life too. He wasn't the only one that had walls up carefully protecting his territory and controlling his environment.

"Rudy would get such a kick out of Ava finally getting pie inside this diner," Walter said with a soft laugh.

"But I don't think he'd be *surprised* that she accomplished something he couldn't," Evan said from behind Parker. "She's something and I'm sure Rudy knew that."

Everyone nodded at that as Parker's gut knotted into a ball of need and regret and affection all at once.

She'd done so much in a short time. She'd helped remodel the pie shop. She'd created the perfect apple pie recipe. She'd faced so many things outside of her comfort zone—from learning to whisk to handling a rooster. She'd changed her whole attitude toward her position at Carmichael. Hell, she'd moved to a place and taken on a job that was as foreign to her as she could probably get.

What had Parker done that was new or challenging or different?

He'd closed the diner a couple of days and made chicken salad.

Parker ran a hand through his hair, suddenly feeling like a jackass. Okay, he'd felt like a jackass last night too, but he'd ignored it. He wasn't ignoring it now.

He couldn't help but think of the way Rudy had come to town in a flashy Cadillac, how he'd thrown himself into life in Bliss, and had opened a pie shop next door to the diner, in part to show Parker that he wasn't completely in control.

His daughter had come into Parker's life a lot like Rudy had. She'd arrived in a limo rather than a Cadillac, but she'd become a regular part of his life when he wasn't looking. And she'd definitely showed him that he wasn't completely in control. And now he couldn't imagine a day in the diner without her. Or a day anywhere without her.

"Yeah, the smell of pie coming in from next door can't make anything *worse*," Ben said.

Parker cleared his throat. "You're absolutely right. I love the smell of apple pie too." It was something he could no longer smell without getting turned on, as a matter of fact. Which could be a problem if he was going to be smelling it all day long.

Or he could just pull Ava into the storeroom once or twice a day...

He drew himself up straight and took a deep breath. "I need to go."

"Go?" Walter asked. "But you haven't made breakfast yet."

Parker shrugged. "I need to make some changes."

Noah grinned at the older men. "Evan and I were smart enough to eat *before* we enlightened him."

Parker returned the coffeepot to the burner and untied his apron, tossing it on the counter as his thoughts spun.

"You're *leaving*?" Evan asked.

Parker nodded, distracted with the plan he was formulating. It was his turn for a grand gesture. And he knew just the one.

"What about the breakfast crowd?" Evan glanced around. "They'll be here any minute."

Parker shrugged.

"Do you want us to close up for you?" Noah asked.

"You can't close up again," Walter said. "You've been closed for the past three days."

"I've had cereal at home three mornings in a row," Ben added.

"Help yourself to the kitchen," Parker said. "Everything's in there." He wondered if he could convince Larry Miller to open the hardware store for him this early. He wasn't sure he had all the supplies he would need to pull off what he was envisioning.

"You're letting us into *this* kitchen?" Walter said.

Parker barely heard him. He shrugged. "Sure."

"And what do we do once we're in there?" Ben asked.

"Make breakfast," Parker said. "There's a stove, pans, what else do you need?"

"You," Ben said, as if it was obvious.

"Yeah, well, you're on your own today," Parker said.

"Uh, Parker?" Noah asked.

He looked concerned when Parker focused on him. "Yeah?"

"You're inviting people in to cook their own breakfasts in your kitchen?"

"Yeah."

"They're going to mess it up," Noah pointed out.

"And probably put things back in the wrong places," Evan said. "Maybe break dishes," he added quickly as if it had just occurred to him.

"Yeah, well..." Parker shrugged. "I've got something more important to do."

"More important than this diner?" Noah asked, but he was already smiling.

Parker grinned back at him. "Yep. Something more important than this diner."

"Well, holy shit," Noah muttered.

"But we don't know your recipes," Walter said.

Parker looked around, but he found himself meeting Hank's eyes. Hank gave him a little nod. Parker smiled. "Well, Walter, sometimes the best things happen when you don't follow a recipe." Parker felt the adrenaline, determination, and *rightness* of what he was going to do flood through him.

But just as he was stepping through the swinging door, Roger called, "Does this mean we can start putting ketchup on our steak?"

"Fuck no," Parker told him firmly, not even looking back. "Don't even think about it."

19

"You have to come down to the diner."

Ava frowned at the apple sitting next to her cup of tea. She was trying to deal with the fact that she was never going to eat another apple again—and the fact that she really wanted to cover this one in brown sugar, cinnamon, and butter.

"I'm in the middle of something." Like examining everything she'd ever thought about apples. And herself.

She'd never given apples much thought before coming to Bliss. But had she been asked what she thought of them, she would have said they were a little sweet and pretty satisfying, if maybe a little...unexciting.

And now she was realizing how many parallels there were between apples and her life. Previously, she'd thought they were both fine. Now though, because of Parker, she realized she'd been missing sweetness and spice that could make both apples and her life so much *more* satisfying. In fact, she couldn't help but think—

"Ava!" Cori snapped in her ear.

It yanked Ava back to the moment. It was really early in the morning to be having such deep thoughts about fruit. Or really anything.

"You have to get down here."

Ava sighed. "I was planning on working at home today."

"Well, you can't," Cori said. "I'll see you in ten minutes."

Then she hung up.

Ava stared at the phone. The last person to hang up on her had been the senior vice president in charge of marketing for the manufacturing branch of Carmichael Enterprises in London. He no longer worked for the company.

Ava started to dial Cori's number, but before she pressed the button, she sighed. Her sisters had, so far, stayed out of everything with Parker. They'd given her space last night. They hadn't told her that she'd messed up. They hadn't told her that she owed Parker an apology. They hadn't pointed out that she couldn't just ignore him—or her feelings for him—for the next seven months and one week that she had to live and work in Bliss. They also hadn't pointed out that she still needed to date *someone* and that it would be even more miserable when she was completely in love with Parker.

She blew out a breath. Okay, they were going to force her to face him. They were going to insist she apologize. They were going to urge her to tell him how she felt about him and that she'd knocked the wall down because she was in love with him.

A shiver went through her—part trepidation, but also part eagerness. She did want to tell him. He might not think that was a good reason to put holes in his stuff. But she needed to try to convince him that she could make it right. She could put the wall back up. She could cool it. She could stay on her own side and let him have his space.

Probably.

Fifteen minutes later, she walked into the pie shop. She'd made it to the diner, but walking in there directly seemed risky. Parker might be standing behind the front counter and she wasn't sure how she'd react. She never walked into rooms without knowing exactly how the people inside would see her and react to her. But this time...there was no way to know. And that made her jumpy.

But, of course, the second she was inside the pie shop, she was essentially inside the diner because of the wide-open doorway she'd put in.

"Ava!"

It wasn't Parker who was behind the front counter of the diner, however. It was Evan. With a notepad in hand as if he was taking orders.

The diner was packed. In fact, people were spilling over into the pie shop, eating eggs and bacon at the little round wooden tables. But then, there were people in the diner eating pie, she noted as she stepped through the doorway between the two restaurants. And was that a burger in Jeffery Jorgenson's hands? At nine a.m.? Burgers before eleven were unheard of in Parker's diner.

She started for the counter and Evan.

"Ava!" someone else called.

She could do nothing but give a little wave as Doris Christiansen lifted her forkful of apple pie—from a table on the far side of the diner—and said, "This is delicious!"

Then she noticed Hank and the guys sitting in the booth closest to the pie shop. They all lifted their coffee cups in salute and she saw they were cups from the pie shop. She assumed they were also filled with pie shop coffee rather than Parker's.

"What in the hell is going on here?" she asked as she made it to the counter. It seemed that every rule had been abandoned. "Where's Parker?"

Evan frowned as he turned and handed a slip of paper through the window to the kitchen. "I'm not sure. Larry Miller said he opened up early and that Parker bought a bunch of stuff from him. But no one knows for sure where he went from there."

"Larry owns the hardware store, right?" Ava asked.

"Yep."

She sighed. "He probably went to get stuff to patch up the huge holes I made in his wall."

Evan looked over at her but didn't say anything. "Cori was hoping you could help out. We're swamped."

"*We're* swamped?" Ava asked. "You and Cori are running the diner?"

"Do you want fries with that Reuben or what?"

Ava turned to find Brynn poking her head through the window from the kitchen.

"Fuck if I know," Evan told her.

"Well, Cori needs to know," Brynn said. She noticed Ava. "Oh, good you're here. Where does Parker keep the butter?"

Ava shook her head. "Um...in the fridge."

"There's none in there," Brynn said.

Ava flushed. She'd taken the last of his butter last week, but she'd assumed he would notice and restock. Of course, he'd been closed since then because she'd whisked him off to New York. "Go check the pie shop."

Brynn started to turn away, and Ava added, "And of course it's fries with the Reuben. It's always fries." Then she frowned. "Why are people eating Reubens at nine in the morning anyway?"

Brynn shrugged. "It's anarchy."

That seemed about right.

"Who's cooking?" Ava asked.

"Cori and Noah," Brynn said. "I'm helping some."

Well, Cori was an excellent cook. "Does she know how Parker makes everything?" Ava asked.

"I'm pretty sure we're doing Cori versions of things today," Brynn said with a grin.

Which meant they'd be delicious. But they wouldn't be the way Parker liked them. And for some reason, that bugged her. She headed through the swinging door.

If the front had seemed crazy, the kitchen was downright chaotic. Food and supplies were spread out over every surface, cupboard doors were hanging open, every burner held a pot or pan, and Cori and Noah were rushing around, nearly bumping into one another at every turn.

"Hey."

No one even looked at her.

Ava planted her hands on her hips. "Hey!"

They all stopped what they were doing and turned. Cori held a bunch of carrots in her two hands. Noah was holding a frying pan. Brynn had a stick of butter in her hand.

"Are you guys okay?" Ava asked.

"We're going nuts!" Cori exclaimed. "I have no idea how Parker does this every day all by himself."

"Well, when someone wants something on his menu, he doesn't have to stop and look up the recipe," she said, pointing to the two cookbooks open on the center island. "And he doesn't let people order Reubens before eleven and when they order the breakfast special number one, they get eggs, bacon, toast, and hash browns with no substitutions, and if they want pie they have to go next door so they're not taking up a booth someone else needs." Okay, so as she said it, she realized that his rules for the diner weren't just about control, but that there were some practical reasons for them too.

Cori nodded. "Yeah, okay. Well, none of that really helps us right now. Everyone's here and even if we wanted to stick with the breakfast specials, I don't know what every one of those are, and since we already made a couple of Reubens, we can't start telling people no now."

Ava thought about that. Maybe Cori couldn't tell them no, but she certainly could. "What can you make easily and quickly without a recipe?"

"Pancakes, scrambled eggs, bacon and fruit salad," Cori said.

"Then start making that." Ava turned on her heel and headed

for the front of the diner. She stopped in the middle of the room, put her fingers to her lips and gave a shrill whistle. Everyone stopped what they were doing and turned.

"Good morning, everyone," she said. "I'm so happy you're all here. But you're making us crazy. So, just to get everyone on the same page, here is the menu for the rest of the day. Breakfast is pancakes, scrambled eggs, bacon, and fruit salad. No substitutions." There was a low murmur in the room, but she held her hand up and it stopped. "Lunch will be..." She glanced toward the window to the kitchen. Cori shrugged. "Lunch will be Reubens." Hell, they'd already been making those.

"Just Reubens?" someone asked.

Ava put her hand on her hip. "Yes. Just Reubens. And they will come with fries. And only fries. And for dinner..." She looked over at Cori, but her sister just shrugged again. "For dinner, we will be serving pork and peach pie over at the pie shop."

The rumbling in the room started again and Ava crossed her arms and waited. It quieted quickly.

"The pork and peach is a new pie from the line of savory pies we'll be introducing at Blissfully Baked. There will be a new one each week on Mondays for the rest of this month. We hope you'll stop over and tell us what you think."

She was prepared to make those pies. She didn't have a recipe and they were maybe going to suck. But she was going to try. She'd sampled more than just cinnamon, nutmeg, and ginger when she'd been taste-testing the spices. She could probably make a filling that was edible if she tasted it as she went along.

But she was definitely stealing pastry dough from Parker's kitchen for the crusts.

She went back into the kitchen. "Okay, now what else can I do?"

Cori grinned at her. "You can go find Parker, tell him you love him, and then go...pick some peaches."

"And that's *not* a euphemism," Brynn said. "You don't have time for a euphemism."

There was a choking noise, and Ava looked over to find Noah running a hand over his face. She wished she had time to get into whatever *that* was. But her heart was pounding, thinking of going after Parker.

"Well, I think I might know where he is," she said of Parker. "If I don't have to go looking all over town for him, we might just have time for a *quick* euphemism."

She had no idea why she was feeling optimistic about their reunion. Except that she really did love him, and she thought he loved her, and she wanted him and...she always got what she wanted. Maybe not things that she couldn't *buy*, up 'til now, but this was as good a time as any to make that change too and go after something *she* had to work for.

"Peaches," Cori said. "Lots and lots of peaches."

And then Ava realized what she'd done. "Oh, *crap*," she groaned. "There are no peaches in season right now either, are there?"

"I can make a run to the grocery stores around," Noah said. "After this rush is over, I'll go get whatever I can."

"Really?"

He gave her a grin. "We'll figure it out. If nothing else, there are canned peaches."

She laughed at that. "But you don't have to work today?"

Noah shrugged. "Everyone knows that Parker walked out today. They'll know to find me and Evan here if they need us."

And for just a second, Ava felt tears pricking at her eyes. She'd never had people like this in her life. Everyone she knew came to work and put in extra time for the money, to kiss up to the boss, or for the chance at a partnership or promotion. None of them did it out of simple friendship. "Thanks, Noah."

"Of course."

And it really was that simple for the people here. Of course they would show up to help a friend. Of course they would stick with the crazy rules of the local diner so that it could keep operating. Of course they would show up to try the new pie at the pie shop.

She sniffed and nodded. "Okay, I'll go find Parker."

She was lost in thought as she made her way back through the pie shop toward the front door, and she was startled to feel a hand wrap around her wrist as she passed one of the tables. She stopped and looked at who was holding her. "Oh, hey, Hank."

He was eating a burger. In the pie shop. Parker would hate that.

"Hi, honey." He pulled her closer. "I'm going to need you to sit down for a minute."

"I can't right now. I really need to go find Parker."

"This is about Parker."

She glanced at the door, then back at the older man. "Okay, maybe for just a second."

"Do you know Barbara Spencer?" Hank asked as she slid into the chair across from him.

Ava shook her head. "I don't think so."

Hank pointed at a table in the diner. An older woman sat, eating pancakes and nursing a cup of tea while she looked at her phone.

"Oh, I recognize her. She works at the post office, right?" Ava asked.

Hank nodded. "And she's an excellent cook."

"Okay."

"Do you know why she eats pancakes in here every Monday?"

"I don't."

"Because she used to bring her granddaughter, Hannah, in for breakfast every Monday before school. Hannah just left for college this past fall. But Barbara still comes in for those pancakes. And she told me Hannah goes and has pancakes every Monday at a diner near campus. They text or talk on the phone while they eat. It makes them feel close even though Hannah is far away."

Ava blinked, her throat a little tight. "That's really nice."

Hank nodded. Then he pointed at another table. Ava turned to look.

"Those four guys in the corner booth?"

"Yeah?"

"They all went to high school together. They don't see each other much anymore, but Tyler is home visiting. So they all came to the diner catch up. They're sitting in the booth where they probably ate a hundred burgers together over the years growing up."

Ava nodded, starting to understand where Hank was going with this. "People come in here to eat, but also because they have happy memories here."

"Yep. But then there's Tom Conner," Hank said. "He and his wife will be in for an early lunch later on, like every Monday and Thursday. And the Perkins family. They have five little kids and they come in for dinner on Wednesdays after the kids are done with their different practices and rehearsals because it's usually late and their mom doesn't feel like cooking. And there's Jason Harper. He's a Big Brother to Hunter. They come in on Saturdays and Jason helps with homework and they talk about their weeks. So, see," Hank said. "They don't come in to relive memories. They're making them now."

Ava took a deep breath. "And having things be consistent and like they've always been is important to them."

"It is." Hank leaned in and covered her hand. "Parker is giving people around here a lot more than just good food."

She pressed her lips together. "I shouldn't have changed things up in here. This diner staying the same is important for everyone."

Hank shook his head. "That's not what I said."

"That's not what you meant?"

"Honey, Parker gets to help give people all these memories."

"Right."

"And that's really good for *him* too."

"I agree."

"But why should he be the only one?"

Ava felt her heart trip. "You mean me?"

Hank laughed. "Yes, Ava, you've already made this place a lot more memorable, and I think that *you* deserve to have a place that makes you feel the way this diner makes all of us, including Parker, feel."

"Like home," she said softly. "That's how this place makes him feel."

Hank nodded. "It's how it feels for a lot of us."

"I think it already feels that way to me too," she said, realizing it as she said it.

Hank squeezed her hand. "There you go."

On impulse, Ava leaned across the table and kissed the older man's cheek. "Thanks for making this place feel that way for my dad."

Hank was smiling but blinking rapidly when she sat back.

———

Parker's truck was in front of his house.

Ava parked Elvira, the Caddy Rudy had left her and her sisters, next to it. She took a deep breath and got out. Smoothing her hands down the thighs of her jeans, she looked around. She figured he was either in the greenhouse or cutting wood. She didn't know what he'd gotten at the hardware store—and even knowing that wouldn't have guaranteed she'd know what he was doing with any of it—but she assumed it was outside stuff. So she started across the grass. She didn't hear the chainsaw so she headed for the greenhouse first.

There was fresh soil on the floor next to the table where she and Parker had gotten dirty the other day and a new plant in a pot on the top of the table. But no Parker. She checked the wood pile, where there were new cut logs, and even the chicken coop, but there was no Parker.

That left the house. She picked up her pace as she realized that he might be in the shower after working outside. She wasn't sure she'd surprise him in there, considering she wasn't sure about their current status, but she could absolutely be waiting in the bedroom when he came out.

But as soon as she entered the house she heard the pounding —very loud pounding—coming from the second floor.

She took the steps two at a time and followed the noise to Parker's bedroom. More specifically to the closet in Parker's bedroom. Ava rounded the corner and...*whoa*.

The sight that met her surprised her and instantly made tingles erupt all over her body.

Parker was standing in his closet, shirtless, his blue jeans riding low on his hips, his feet braced, causing the denim to pull tight across his ass. He had his arms raised as he lifted a sledge-hammer. His skin was slick with sweat, his muscles bunching and rippling. She watched as he swung the hammer against the wall, enlarging the hole already there, the impact seemingly causing his entire body to tighten.

In response to the *what-the-hell* and the *I-want-all-of-that-right-now* that went coursing through her body, all she could do was make a strange little squeaking sound she'd never made before in her life.

Parker heard it and pivoted to face her. There was a beat where they just stared at each other. Then he pushed the plastic goggles he wore to the top of his head, lowered the hammer, and said, "Hey, Boss."

And just like that, tears filled her eyes. Yeah, he definitely called her that with affection. And it made her feel insanely hopeful. And like she was looking at something she *needed* more than she could even understand. She hugged her arms to her stomach.

She thought briefly about replying with a simple "hey" herself. Then thought about confessing that she'd messed with his menu today. Then about begging him to help her make peach and pork pies. But instead she said, "Parker, do you know what I'm really, really good at?"

"Everything."

She smiled at that response but shook her head. "I'm really, really good at recognizing people's potential, and giving them the opportunity to do great things."

He sighed. "Ava—"

"I might have been wrong to knock the wall down between the diner and pie shop without talking to you," she said quickly. "But I wasn't wrong about *you*." She took a step forward. "You have to know why I did it, Parker."

"I do know."

"I wanted—" She stopped. "You do?"

"I do."

She narrowed her eyes. "Why?"

He laughed at that and a twist of heat went through her belly. "Because you wanted to combine the things that are important to both of us. Mesh them together somehow. Make our worlds work together." He paused. "Because you can't stand being apart from me for even a few minutes now."

She knew he was teasing, trying to lighten the moment with that last sentence. But she nodded solemnly. "Yes. All of that. I love watching you work, working with you, helping you."

"I love that too," he said, still smiling, but his voice gruffer.

"And so, when I was trying to think of a way to show you that, and to make things better for you, I went with what I know. I'm not fun and creative like Cori. I'm not brilliant like Brynn. I'm not sweet and patient like my mother. I can't fix your car, or manage your legal affairs like Noah and Evan, and I can't bake and cook like you. But I can get things done. I can call exactly the right people for the job. And I can throw money—lots of money —at things. So that's what I went with. But—" she said quickly when he took a breath to respond, "you have to understand that it's just how I support the people I love. I don't know any other way."

He blew out a big breath and leaned to prop the sledge-hammer against the wall. He turned to face her, tucking his hands into his back pockets.

She was momentarily distracted by the way the position showed off the wide expanse of his chest.

"Do you know what I'm doing here?" he asked, gesturing at the hole in the wall behind him.

She made herself focus. "No."

"I'm knocking this wall down."

"Okay."

"I'm knocking a wall down," he said again, slower, as if waiting for her to catch up. "In a house that has been exactly the way it is now for as long as I've lived in it."

Oh. She felt her eyes widen. "You're changing something."

"Right. I'm making a bigger closet."

"Too many jeans?"

He gave her a half smile. "To make room for all of your shoes."

She blinked at him. She looked at the wall. Then back to him. "You're knocking a wall down to make more room for *me*?"

"You have a shit-ton of shoes, right?"

"I do."

"Well, if we're going to meld our lives together—at the diner and pie shop and here—we're going to need more room. For all of it."

"Parker, I...don't know what to say." That was amazing. It was a grand gesture. A grand, grand gesture. The grandest anyone had ever made for her. Ever.

"I wasn't mad about the wall at the diner," he said after a long moment.

"You definitely seemed mad about the wall at the diner."

"I thought I was, but it wasn't that. I was hurt. I wanted what I already had, what I was already doing, to be enough for you. I wanted you to be content and happy with what was already here. With a simple, straightforward setup."

She felt tears stinging and pressed her lips together, nodding. "I know," she finally answered. "But I didn't change it because I *wasn't* content or happy." She took a deep breath. "I changed it because that's all I know—knew—how to do."

"Ava—"

But she cut him off once more. "That diner is hugely important to this town. The food you make there is important to this town. And to you. But you're also washing dishes, and dicing onions, and ordering supplies, and going to the store for more butter all the time."

He lifted one brow in a very sexy, very knowing, somewhat amused, and completely resigned way. "So much butter," he said with a nod.

She felt her lungs expand as she took a big breath, not realizing she hadn't been breathing for a few seconds, or maybe minutes, there. She took another step forward, into the closet. "You want to do more. Maybe not nationally-distributed-specialty-pie more, but more than washing things and dicing things. You're happy when you're taking care of the people here, and the way that you take care of them is by making them food... and giving them a place where that food becomes a part of other things. And I think you do, actually, want to make them dessert and good coffee after all. So what I need to give you is a way to do more of what you love for the people you love. And...I can't actually do that with money, it turns out."

He stepped forward, now only a few inches in front of her. She wanted to run her hands all over his hot, slick skin, but she tucked her hands into her back pockets too and just stood, looking up at him.

"You've found something you couldn't buy, huh?" he asked.

"Yep." She gave him a smile. "It's something that has to be *done*."

"So you can hire someone to do it."

She shook her head. "Interestingly, I don't think anyone else can do it as well as I can."

He wet his lips and she could have sworn that he was fighting the urge to touch her too. "What's going on in that beautiful, crazy head, Boss?" he asked, his voice rough.

"*I* am going to take over all of those things that you don't need to be doing so that you can make your magic in the diner's kitchen...*and* the pie shop kitchen."

Now both of his eyebrows went up and she realized that she truly had surprised him. "Things like what?"

"Like everything but the cooking and baking. Though you'll have to share the baking with Cori."

"So *you're* going to wait on customers, bus tables, and do dishes?" Parker asked, clearly skeptical.

"And run the register."

He straightened as he clearly realized that she wasn't kidding. "You're not running the register."

"I'm very good at taking other people's money, Parker."

He ran his hand along his jaw, watching her. "I like doing things a certain way."

"I know. But my way is even better in most cases."

He opened his mouth. Then shut it again. Then opened it again.

"And I might hire Hank and Roger to help with the lunch rush," she said.

He narrowed his eyes.

"And I'm going to do some of the farm chores too."

"You like my rooster that much?" he finally asked.

She grinned and nodded. "Rudy was right. I didn't understand how satisfying it can be to actually have my hands on things. To directly affect what's going on. I'm so used to just sitting in an office and making decisions based on reports and papers and emails from other people. Now I can be *in* it."

"You're not going to be the CEO anymore?"

"Oh, I am. But...like I said before, I'm simplifying. I'm going to promote some people. I'll make once a month trips to New York, more as needed, I'll have Skype, conference calls. I can be bossy even over a long distance."

He finally reached out, put his hand on the back of her head, and threaded his fingers into her hair. "You actually want to do this, don't you?"

She met his gaze. "I really do. Parker, taking care of the people I love, making sure they have what they need, that's what makes me happy. And now I've realized I can do more than just writing checks and making bank transfers."

He took a deep breath. "The people you love? That's the second time you've said that."

"Yes. The people I love."

He pulled her closer, until she was nearly standing on his toes. "I love you too, Ava."

She was so incredibly glad she'd put her heels on when she'd left the house to head to the diner. She was at exactly the right height to wrap her arms around his neck and press against him. "I'm sorry I changed your diner."

But he shook his head slowly. "It didn't change. Not really. Not the heart of it. It just got bigger. And better. Like everything else in my life since you came along."

She sniffed. "Your greenhouse didn't get bigger."

"It's going to. I need to add on so I have room for all these salad things you're thinking about. And my crop already got bigger. I planted two avocado trees today."

Her eyes widened. "You did?"

"Of course. You love avocados."

"I do." She nodded, her heart flipping in her chest. That was the most romantic thing anyone had ever done for her. Well, maybe second to knocking out a wall in his closet to make room for her shoes. "I really do."

"And I've decided my flock of chickens will need to get bigger too. I'll need more eggs if I'm cooking for two."

She couldn't resist any longer. She put her mouth to his, kissing him with all of the love and hope and happiness buzzing through her. When she finally let him go, he cupped her face in both hands.

"So my answer is yes, I *will* be your boss, Boss."

She lifted a brow.

He shrugged. "You're going to be working for me. The tables, the dishes, the register..."

"*With* you." She pointed at him. "Kitchen." Then at herself. "Everything else."

"Partner in Blissfully Baked with Cori," he said, pointing at himself. "Full owner of the diner." He pointed at himself again. "Owner of the avocados." He pointed at his chest again. "Girl who's picking up after me and cleaning up my messes." He pointed at her.

She tipped her head, narrowed her eyes, then stepped back, pulling her phone from her back pocket. She turned away, pretending to scroll through her address book.

"Who are you calling?" he asked.

She could hear the amusement in his voice. "Evan. My lawyer."

"Ah, rethinking the partnership between me and Cori?"

She turned back, putting her phone to her ear. "Thinking I might just buy the whole thing."

"You're just going to keep that deed for the building?"

"I mean the whole town of Bliss."

There was a beat as he absorbed that, then he threw his head back and laughed. She put her phone down, grinning at the sight before her. The hottest, sweetest, grumpiest guy she'd ever dated. The man she was madly in love with.

He focused on her again. "Okay, get in bed."

"I'd love to, but we have to get back to the diner. Things are a little crazy there."

He nodded. "I'm sure. Get in my bed. Now."

"I need to tell you about the peaches." But she was already backing toward the bed.

He paused slightly at that, but then shook his head. "Peaches later. Bed now."

"And the lunch menu today."

"And I clearly have to prove who the boss is here."

She grinned. "How about we take turns?"

He had his jeans unbuttoned and unzipped. "Being the boss in bed? You can absolutely tell me what you want me to do to you once you're naked."

She actually meant taking turns in everything, but they could go through this "meeting" one point at a time. She pulled her T-shirt off as the backs of her knees hit the mattress. "How about we negotiate a few terms?"

He reached out and pulled one of her bra straps down, exposing her breast and rubbing his thumb over her nipple. She bit back a moan.

"Negotiate. As in, you give me something and I give you something?"

"Yeah, kind of like that." She pushed his jeans down his legs and ran her hand up the length of his erection. "I think this merger is going to be wildly successful."

He dragged in a quick breath, then pushed her back onto the bed, moving over her. "I actually prefer the term *acquisition*," he told her.

"Oh really, because the synonym is *possession*?" Strangely, she didn't mind that from Parker at all.

Heat flared in his eyes, but just before he kissed her, he said, "Another synonym is *prize*."

She melted a little at that and kissed him deeply.

Another word for acquisition was also *gain*. And that one felt most appropriate of all.

NEXT FROM BLISS

Next from Bliss, Kansas and the Billionaires in Blue Jeans!

Cashmere and Camo
Billionaires in Blue Jeans, book three

A friends to lovers romance...and then some.

Run a pie shop with her sisters for a year. Date for the first time at age twenty-nine. Don't be terrified.

Well, she's got the first thing under control at least. Mostly.

But this is exactly what a best friend is for. Advice, pep talks, matchmaking, sex education...

So what if her best friend is a guy? A very hot, tattooed, ex-Marine, mechanic guy? He's definitely well-versed in everything she needs to know. And she trusts him. Who better to teach her the man-woman stuff she's been missing out on?

But there could be one tiny problem. The only person causing her any butterflies...and dirty dreams...is her matchmaker himself.

Enjoy this excerpt from Cashmere and Camo!

"So, that's Brynn Carmichael," Mitch said to Noah as Brynn rounded the corner at the end of the block.

Noah gritted his teeth. He turned back into the shop and to the car he'd been working on.

Cars. Those he understood. Those he could fix.

God, he loved cars.

Everything else in life less so.

He picked up a wrench and leaned in over the engine. He'd known Mitch Anderson all his life. He wasn't worried about hurting the guy's feelings or offending him by getting back to work in the midst of a conversation.

A conversation he did *not* want to have.

"Mom said that things have been interesting since the Carmichael girls came to town," Mitch commented, moving to lean against the front of the car.

Noah didn't respond.

"Now I can see why. Have there been a lot of injuries?"

Noah frowned. "Injuries?"

"From all the men in town tripping over their tongues?"

Noah rolled his eyes. Mitch was a dumbass. A handsome, successful dumbass who had made Brynn blush. Noah gripped the wrench. "Everyone's been very nice to them."

"I'm sure," Mitch mused.

Noah tried to focus on the hoses he was supposed to be replacing. It didn't work. "Of course, Cori's been involved with Evan from day one and Parker and Ava have been together for about three months now," Noah said. "So it's not like guys have been lining up or fighting over them." Mitch made a *huh* sound and Noah glanced up. "What?"

"Just that Evan and Parker are with Cori and Ava." He looked over. "No one's with Brynn." He paused. "Right?"

Noah clenched his jaw and straightened away from the car. He wiped his hands on a rag. No, technically no one was *with* Brynn. Except that *he* was with Brynn nearly every spare hour either of them had. They both worked a lot. Brynn spent her days at the pie shop and then at least an hour each evening on the phone or computer with people running her lab back in New York in her absence. Brynn also had her sisters and he had his mom and dad and Maggie, his buddy Jared's mom, to take care of. So they both had other things and people taking up their time, of course. But yeah, they seemed to spend a lot of time together too.

"She's not dating anyone," he finally said in answer to Mitch. That much was true. What he and Brynn were doing wasn't dating. Because dating came with the expectation of things possibly progressing and becoming more over time. He and Brynn were exactly where and what they needed to be to each other. That wasn't going to change. She was here because her father had mandated it. And it was temporary. Thank God. Noah was looking out for her as her father had asked him to. But he could only handle it if he knew there was an end point. If he knew there was a *goal*.

Mitch hadn't replied to the news of Brynn's single status.

"You want to ask her out for real, don't you?" Noah asked.

"For real?"

"You were just testing the waters with the invite to your back porch." Noah didn't phrase it as a question.

Mitch didn't deny that. He nodded. "Yeah, I think I want to ask her out for real."

Noah sighed. Dammit. He had to get used to this. She *had to* date six men. It was in the will. If she didn't, she and her sisters didn't inherit Rudy's company, and his fortune. The money was important to Brynn because of the life-saving research she and her team were doing and it allowed her sisters to do what was important to them as well. She would do her part For sure.

And her time was running out. In three days, it would be exactly six months since the girls had arrived in Bliss. The pie shop was now fully renovated and open and doing fairly well. He didn't know the specifics of their finances, but business had definitely picked up. Her sisters had met their relationship conditions. So Brynn's dating mandate was all that was really left.

And Noah fucking hated even the thought of it.

He hated that she'd smiled at Mitch with that sweet, almost surprised smile. As if she was trying to figure out if he was really flirting with her or not.

He wanted her sweet smiles. But it was that surprised part that jabbed him in the heart and made him tamp down the urge to punch Mitch right in his pretty face. Brynn should *not* be surprised when a man paid her attention. At least attention that had nothing to do with her being one of the foremost pharmaceutical researchers in the country. He was sure there were brilliant, geeky scientist guys all over the place that were impressed with and intimidated by Brynn.

But Mitch wasn't appreciating her brain. He was looking at her as the beautiful, subtly-sexy-without-even-knowing-it woman who blended into the background until you got a good look at her. Then you couldn't look away.

She'd been sitting on his truck, in his shop, hiding out in the shadows, literally. And Noah fucking hated that. Even while he loved it.

He felt divided in two. He loved that Brynn felt safe and comfortable with him. They didn't talk much. They didn't really *do* anything a lot of the time. They'd painted and redecorated the pie shop. And she sat on the hood of the truck and read while he worked. But he loved that she felt like she could just *be* with him. He wanted to keep her all to himself.

But he also hated that even here in his garage—maybe especially here—she was hiding out from the world. How could she figure out that she was special and amazing and that people wanted to get to know her and be close to her if she was never *with* people?

"There are some rules that you should be aware of before you ask her out," Noah finally said.

Mitch turned to face him, looking amused. "Okay, like what?"

Noah sighed. He didn't love the idea of spilling the details of Rudy's will, but Bliss was a small town. Dating here was different. It was harder to date casually than it probably was in the bigger cities. Like New York. Or Kansas City, where Mitch had been living. Here everyone knew everyone else, knew their pasts, knew their relationship history, and paid attention to current relationships. It was also harder to date multiple people. The guys Brynn would be going out with knew one another. And their mothers were going to be upset if they only dated her once or twice and then she "moved on" to another guy. Everyone needed to understand what was really going on and not assume that this city girl was coming to sweet little Bliss to break as many hearts as she could.

That was one reason he'd held off for six months on insisting she get out there and date. He wanted the town to get to know her a little first.

And, of course, because it had taken about two hours for him to realize that he didn't want her dating anyone. Ever.

"It was important to Brynn's dad that she meet and date a variety of guys. She's..." He sighed. This was coming out wrong. "Brynn's quiet. She's sweet. She's happiest with her nose in a book or calculating chemical formulas in her lab," he said, starting again. "She's not a social butterfly, she's not a flirt, she doesn't date much at all."

"She inexperienced," Mitch filled in.

Noah had to nod. "Yeah. She's just had a lot of more important things to think about than relationships."

Mitch nodded.

"So when her dad decided she should live in Bliss for a year with her sisters and run his pie shop, he also made it clear that it was important to him that she go out and have some fun, but also get to know different types of guys. So she could maybe figure out what her type is."

Mitch nodded again. "That's pretty much what dating is, right? Looking for the perfect fit amongst all the options."

Noah had to admit he was surprised by Mitch's perceptiveness. "Yeah, I guess so. It's just that with Brynn it's actually spelled out that she has to date six different guys. And she's only in town for six more months."

"So nothing serious or long term. Just fun," Mitch said.

Noah nodded.

"Well, that takes a lot of pressure off," Mitch decided. "It'll be more fun if it's just about showing her a good time and knowing that no one's thinking marriage, right?"

"I guess." Noah supposed that was true. If the guys all knew that it was more of a project to introduce Brynn to the world of dating and that it was casual and short term and just for fun, then no one would get their hearts broken. And no one would be buying diamond rings. Noah felt like scowling even thinking about that. He knew, firsthand, how easy it was to fall for Brynn.

Even with the "casual and fun" rule firmly established, he couldn't guarantee that Brynn wouldn't be proposed to. Six times.

So far the guys in Bliss had been staying away from her. Evan and Parker maintained it was because Noah had made it clear that she was his. But she wasn't. They might think so, but he was simply her friend. Her guardian, maybe. He'd promised Rudy he'd look out for her and from day one he'd been determined to send her back to New York happier, more confident, and with her inheritance firmly intact. So he'd taken six months to help her adjust to small town life, get her pie shop going, and get to know her so he could more effectively set her up with the right guys.

Not because he was a selfish, possessive asshole who had taken about one day to realize that he didn't want to share her.

He just needed to establish with all of the single guys in Bliss between ages twenty-five and thirty-five—that seemed like a good age range for the twenty-nine-year-old Brynn—that they were just a part of a larger project to show Brynn how fun dating could be. To help her practice for when she went back to New York and had to pick the nice guys out from the dickheads.

He could do that. He knew all the guys in town. He could easily spread the word that each date was a *one time* thing and that it better be fun for her and they'd better all be gentlemen.

Meaning no diamond rings.

And no sex.

He felt his chest tighten at that thought. Yeah, he could definitely spread that around.

He frowned at Mitch. "If you're going to ask her out, it's only one time and it's just for a fun, casual date."

Mitch didn't say anything.

"You *are* going to ask her out, right?" Noah asked. He supposed he couldn't scare all of the other guys off. But he could make sure they knew he was watching their every fucking move.

"Yeah, I am. Eventually."

Noah felt his frown deepen. "Eventually?"

"Yeah, definitely. Eventually."

"What's that mean?" Noah asked.

Mitch pushed away from the car, gave Noah a grin, and clapped him on the shoulder. "Just thinking—five other guys need to ask her out too, right?"

"Right."

"Well, with a woman like Brynn, you don't really want to be the first, knowing she's got to date these other guys. You kind of want to be number six, you know?"

Mitch started for the door. Noah scowled after him. "You want to be number six?"

"The last guy? The one who can stick around? The one who doesn't have to give her up to someone else? Um, yeah." Then he gave Noah a little wave and disappeared through the doorway.

Cashmere and Camo

ABOUT THE AUTHOR

Erin Nicholas is the New York Times and USA Today bestselling author of over thirty sexy contemporary romances. Her stories have been described as toe-curling, enchanting, steamy and fun. She loves to write about reluctant heroes, imperfect heroines and happily ever afters. She lives in the Midwest with her husband who only wants to read the sex scenes in her books, her kids who will never read the sex scenes in her books, and family and friends who say they're shocked by the sex scenes in her books (yeah, right!).

Never miss any news from Erin!
Sign up for her newsletter today!
Find ALL of her books right here!
www.erinnicholas.com

And find **Erin** at
www.ErinNicholas.com,
on Twitter and on Facebook

Join her SUPER FAN page on Facebookfor insider peeks, exclusive giveaways, chats and more!

———

MORE FROM ERIN NICHOLAS

More sexy, contemporary romance...

Now Available at all book retailers

Billionaires in Blue Jeans

Diamonds and Dirt Roads

High Heels and Haystacks

Cashmere and Camo

If you love the Billionaires in Blue Jeans,

you'll love

Sapphire Falls

Welcome to Sapphire Falls

Getting Out of Hand

Getting Worked Up

Getting Dirty

Naughty and Nice in Sapphire Falls

Getting In the Spirit, Christmas novella

Getting In the Mood, Valentine's Day novella

Getting to the Church On Time, wedding novella

Ferris Wheels & Fireflies in Sapphire Falls

Getting It All

Getting Lucky

Getting Over It

Getting to Her

Getting His Way

Ever After in Sapphire Falls

After All

After You

After Tonight

Lots more from Sapphire Falls at

www.SapphireFalls.net

Made in the USA
Monee, IL
04 January 2021

56346756R00194